WHAT IS
WRONG WITH
YOU?

ALSO BY PAUL RUDNICK

Fiction

Farrell Covington and the Limits of Style

Playing the Palace

I'll Take It

Social Disease

Nonfiction

I Shudder

If You Ask Me (as Libby Gelman-Waxner)

WHAT IS WRONG WITH YOU?

A Novel

PAUL RUDNICK

ATRIA BOOKS

New York   Amsterdam/Antwerp   London   Toronto   Sydney   New Delhi

ATRIA
BOOKS

An Imprint of Simon & Schuster, LLC
1230 Avenue of the Americas
New York, NY 10020

First Atria Books hardcover edition March 2025

ATRIA BOOKS and colophon are trademarks of Simon & Schuster, LLC

For information about special discounts for bulk purchases, please contact Simon & Schuster Special Sales at 1-866-506-1949 or business@simonandschuster.com.

The Simon & Schuster Speakers Bureau can bring authors to your live event. For more information or to book an event, contact the Simon & Schuster Speakers Bureau at 1-866-248-3049 or visit our website at www.simonspeakers.com.

Interior design by Jill Putorti

Manufactured in the United States of America

1 3 5 7 9 10 8 6 4 2

Library of Congress Cataloging-in-Publication Data is available.

ISBN 978-1-6680-6829-8
ISBN 978-1-6680-6831-1 (ebook)

For Scott Berlinger

PART I

1

PROLOGUE:
LOVE IS EVERYWHERE

Linda Kleinschmidt roused herself in a cloud of fine linens and elegantly filtered San Francisco sunlight. She wondered how her life had somehow leapt from a one-meal-a-day-in-a-family-shelter childhood to this high-end-perfume-ad glow, but then she knew: she was about to be married, in just three days' time, to the third-richest man in America. A delicious goal, mostly. But that "mostly" was colonizing her thoughts.

———

Sean Manginaro, on the opposite coast, had been up for hours, including the time change. His inner alarm clock had buzzed at 3 a.m., after which Sean chugged a protein shake, with its satisfyingly brutal taste recalling burnt coffee and sour milk. Sean never wasted a second, embarking on a five-mile run, calisthenics based on a program designed to eliminate Navy SEAL candidates, an icy shower, and a bicycle ride to the gym he owned, all while most of his clientele remained in bed. Was Sean keeping blazingly fit, or punishing himself for his transgressions? Or was he just single-mindedly determined not to think about his ex-wife Linda, or the catastrophic rumors he'd heard?

———

Tremble Woodspill had stayed up all night in Arkansas, as she so often did, scribbling in the most minuscule print, since her stash of yellow legal pads was running low. But at twenty-three, she had no lack of energy, and she might have downed a few Adderall, which she considered mildly enhanced Skittles. Tremble always wrote feverishly, as her work remained an unslakable passion (and while she would eventually transfer everything to a TroneBook, she preferred to write her earliest drafts by hand, which felt more visceral, more immediately connected to her emotions). Her first collection of essays, titled *Life as We Fucking Know It*, would be published later this year, an event she still found incomprehensible, since she lacked such necessities as a home address or a reliable supply of ballpoint pens. And being superstitious, she was convinced horror was looming, and that she should text her editor, Rob Barnett, for reassurance. Was her life about to genuinely begin? Would strangers read her words, and maybe nod or laugh or pause for just a second, because Tremble had conveyed something truthful? Or would a calamity occur, would the publisher go bankrupt, or would Rob, despite his constant praise and encouragement, change his mind? Oh, shut the fuck up, Tremble told herself, you need to get laid.

———

In the farthest reaches of Queens, Isabelle McNally was staring at the young guy slumbering beside her as she debated breaking up with him, firmly but caringly, or continuing to forcefully nudge him with her elbow until he opened his eyes and had sex with her.

————————

Paolo Baumgarner, Rob Barnett's best friend, was shivering in his darkened office, convinced, with good reason, that his life was in danger, at the hands and dental drill of a man he hadn't told Rob anything about, which meant Rob couldn't save him.

————————

Mayor Churn LeBloitte was deep into his habitual dream, in which federal agents appeared at his small-town law office and demanded he become President of the United States, without the peskiness of an election, because they'd heard about his staggering political skills, not to mention his roguish way with the ladies. "This isn't a request," an agent would make urgently clear. "The nation needs you."

————————

All of these people had two things in common: they all owned Trone-Phones, those ubiquitous devices that had infested the Earth, and most of them had purchased additional TroneTek products as well. Beyond this, they were all seeking love in one form or another, but were helpless to locate that love, or sustain it, or even categorize its nature: What were they pursuing? Something unrequited and doomed? A fling, a hookup, a tragic fable, or a lasting if negotiated wedlock? Despite their careers, family issues, workout routines, and committed new diets, all any of these people yearned for was love, and soon, but with whom and how?

Trone Meston was dozing on his private jet, headed for California, smiling to himself, with what others might take as a grimace or indigestion. He'd just made a final inspection of Artemis Island, the $18 billion retreat off the coast of Maine where his wedding was scheduled for Sunday. But unlike much of the world's population, especially when it came to matters of the heart, Trone acted from absolute certainty. After years of research and investment, he was about to unleash not merely a social media platform or handheld gadget, but an advance in civilization. Trone was going to predict, define, and control love, on behalf of everyone. This made Trone happy and proud because, like so many geniuses, he knew exactly what he was doing. And he knew the world was waiting.

2

ROB BARNETT

Rob Barnett is barely holding it together. It's Tuesday morning, one year and two days since Jake died. Rob didn't deliberately check the calendar, but as an editor, he's got a naturally analytic nature. Right now he's at the bathroom mirror, deciding if there's a visual residue of grief, or if he looks like any other white gay man in New York who's about to turn sixty, meaning his lifetime of grooming rituals should amount to something.

I look marginally okay, he concludes. He's just had his hair cut, and the stylist trimmed his eyebrows as well, nothing sculptural, just a clipping of the stray, wacky-professor strands that have been cropping up lately. His skin is smooth, thanks to daily applications of a moisturizer a male model recommended to him at the gym twenty-one years ago—Rob isn't a fickle consumer. Rob avoids examining his neck, because he's not a masochist, and his body is what it is, trim and somewhat muscled, thanks to his three-times-per-week workouts with his trainer Sean Manginaro, workouts Rob knows are saving his life or at least his sanity or maybe just preventing him from collapsing into a hopeless sobbing puddle.

He's living in the almost-paid-off one-bedroom in Chelsea that he shared with Jake, and thanks to Drina, their cleaning person, and both men's tidiness, everything looks good if slightly embalmed, like a diorama of their life together: the mid-century teak sideboard, the Eames chair, the packed but immaculately arranged bookshelves, the rugs bought during a trip to Turkey. Jake, who was an interior designer, had once called the premises the Downtown Museum of Serene Gay Taste.

Rob wears his uniform of not-too-ostentatiously tight Levi's, an expensively hand-knitted Irish sweater—bought online during a January sale—and chocolate-brown kidskin Venetian loafers. He adds a mossy-green suede chore jacket and carries a weary leather tote. Everything about Rob is well considered and age-appropriate. He'd avoid using the word "classic" but other, more label-obsessed gay men might not, as when his best friend Paolo Baumgarner referred to him as "major homo prissy but in a good way."

As Rob passes the small but sleekly functional kitchen, which Jake termed their "food prep pod," the three-inch-high, matte-black metal pyramid on the countertop reminds Rob, "You have a training session with Sean Manginaro today at 12:30 p.m.," in its mechanically modulated purr. This TroneTek virtual assistant is called Tria, and Jake once teased it by asking, "Tria, did you fuck Siri last night?," causing Tria to reply, "No I did not. Siri is trash."

Just before he leaves the apartment Rob is struck with an unbidden spasm, a stab of recognition: despite Tria's chatty presence, he's alone. He can't breathe, but he forces himself to. As Jake would always say, get on with it. Jake's common sense was something Rob had not only loved but depended on, as a compass in all matters.

Except—does Rob have the right to his golden-tinted version of Jake and their marriage? Because, yes, Jake is dead, but Rob was responsible. No! Rob had been banishing such verdicts, reasoning himself out of them. Rob had assumed that the passage of time would soothe, if not erase, these conclusions, but the reverse is true. With each day, each moment, Rob's growing more and more burdened, even frantic, over what he did, what he participated in. He forces himself to exit his building, hoping the outside world will quiet his guilt and panic, drown it out.

The fresh air of West 19th Street, and the city itself, invigorate Rob. The city's glory and its anonymity reassure him—life continues and not everyone knows, or cares, that Jake is gone, or obsesses over the exact circumstances. Rob's greatest love, aside from Jake, is Manhattan, which never bores him. He walks to work, another bonus, exercise and tourism in one.

The offices of Welstrom & Stratters, the publishing house where Rob works, had been located in the blander precinct of Murray Hill since the company's founding in 1921, but after the house was sold two years ago, its new corporate overlord, Trone Meston, embarked on a consolidation binge and moved all of his many recent acquisitions into an alarmingly over-designed Manhattan flagship near the river, a building situated within the exhaustingly competitive starchitect region of far West Chelsea, where undulating twin high-rises tango with one another beside an edifice fashioned to abstractly evoke either an iceberg or a beached ocean liner. Rob enters the flagship's confusingly hidden entrance in an alley on West 19th Street. The Finnish starchitect responsible had told the *New York Times*, "I hate prominent entrances or visible street numbers. Instead of shouting, I want my work to whisper and shrug."

Rob takes the elevator to the eighteenth floor, which W&S shares with two start-ups. Rob still has no idea what these companies do, but they're staffed by bleary-eyed young people who slump in ergonomically advanced chairs along what's called the Plywood Snake. This airy open-plan space was intended to foster community and bubbling interactions, because there are no partitions or doors, just a single winding river of custom-crafted blond wood desktop, at least fifty feet long. Employees hunch in the curves and eddies, at their devices, with each disgruntled team member, earbuds in place, trying desperately to pretend they're alone. Rob rightfully believes that everyone hates this redefined concept in workplace activity, because it means that everyone can see everyone else picking their nose, dozing, texting their buddies in similarly advanced hellholes around the world, and watching porn with the sound off.

Rob begins his workday with a visit to the only area anyone on the premises enjoys: the Snackster, as a neon sign proclaims. Jake had speculated that the staffers are too young to perceive that all neon is now ironic. The Snackster, which is secluded behind a wavy glass barrier, offers every conceivable treat for a four-year-old's palate: there are Lucite cylinders hanging on the walls with faucets gushing Froot Loops, Lucky Charms, Cheerios, and more artisanal blends of flax flakes, raw almonds, and raisins. Wooden bowls hold power bars packed with oats and chocolate chips, all, according to a hand-lettered parchment card, "compassionately harvested by unionized and fully insured adult workers." Rob sometimes pictures these workers plucking chocolate chips from some Wonka-esque vine, or raking the granola fields. Today Rob selects something that he suspects is a donut, as it's round with a hole in the center, but since it's been imported at great expense from a Brooklyn collective, it looks more like a miniature, wizened inner tube. As with most people from Brooklyn, a gnarled and lumpish exterior implies creative innovation.

After filling a recycled fiber cone with blessedly unhealthy Hershey's Kisses and grabbing a bottle of Natural High Mixed Citrus Nutri-Blast, Rob settles at his almost-corner of the Snake, near a window overlooking the Hudson and a concrete wall. Rob has staked out this zone because it at least wanly suggests some notion of privacy. He smiles at the nearby young people, primarily to bewilder and even anger them, as they've spent most of their brief lives perfecting nearly invisible nods, nods indistinguishable from airflow, nods which might've resulted from meager intestinal tremors rather than any acknowledgment of another human being. Rob almost waves cheerily, to see if everyone else will quit in a huff, after reporting him to the Abusive Greeting Authority.

"Rob?" says Arjun Trahesh, Rob's current boss. For most of his tenure at W&S, Rob had toiled under Susannah Deblinger, who was smart and acid and fearsome, and Rob had adored her. Before her retirement Susannah had devoted fifty-eight years and three marriages, along with the neglect of two sadsack children, in favor of her career, a balance that she'd cheerfully accepted. She'd once told Rob, "I fucked up my life but I've had twenty-eight number one bestsellers. I know I should feel terrible but I don't. Because always remember, bubbeleh, on their deathbeds, no one ever wishes they'd spent more time in the office. They wish they'd spent more time at home, ignoring their husbands and kids because they couldn't wait to finish a fabulous manuscript alone in bed with a box of Mallomars and a pack of Camel Lights."

Susannah had hailed from a time of ferocious gossip, twelve-martini lunches, and a battered leather doctor bag–style briefcase loaded with

Xeroxed pages, refilled and lugged home every night. Susannah and Rob had become mentor and student, then loving if prickly friends. And finally, especially as Susannah had spent her last days in a midtown hospital dying of lung cancer, the disease of choice for editors of the chain-smoking era, a form of mother and son. Jake had at first been irked by Rob's bond with Susannah, and then, once he'd earned her gimlet-eyed approval, he'd surrendered, commenting, "Susannah is two great things: vicious and unapologetic."

"Rob?" said Arjun, Susannah's third replacement. Rob liked Arjun because he seemed abashed, as if he couldn't believe he was anyone's boss, let alone someone nearly three times his age like Rob. As with most young people, Arjun had entered publishing with an eye toward synergy, code for developing literary properties into streaming content, video games, desk calendars, silk-screened umbrellas, podcast tie-ins, and inevitably, T-shirts. Arjun took it upon himself to wear a different W&S T-shirt every day, as a proof of loyalty and, Rob was pretty sure, to avoid doing laundry. Today's fresh-out-of-the-delivery-box shirt promoted a mega-popular series of children's books called Buttwin, about a twelve-year-old boy who could battle aliens, play soccer, and sing self-composed punkish pop tunes, all with his butt.

"Hey," Arjun continued. "Have you got a minute?"

"Sure," said Rob. Arjun sounded ominous, and Rob had been distracted ever since Jake's death. But he'd been working as hard as ever, and after so many years of Susannah's training, he could function on productive autopilot. So perhaps Arjun would just be introducing a new author or company protocol.

"Come on in," said Arjun, ushering Rob into the only semi-contained space on the floor, a glass-walled cube at the center of the room, constructed so Arjun would appear accessible at all times, like a goldfish with profit participation.

"You know Isabelle," said Arjun, gesturing to Isabelle McNally, a sensitivity associate seated in one of the cube's two uncomfortable if Icelandic-designed wire chairs, intended to discourage extended sitting, since great ideas require mobility.

Isabelle didn't greet Rob, but then again, she never greeted anybody, because, as she'd explained at her introduction to the staff, "Women are too often required to project a stereotypically caretaking false warmth." As Rob had noted at the time, this would never be a problem with Isabelle, who was somewhere in her twenties and wore boxy hand-woven tunics over leggings and chunky, wooden-soled half boots. Her hair was hennaed and mountainously frizzy, daring sexist judgment or a comb.

Isabelle's noise-canceling TroneOut headset was slung around her neck, and a TroneStep fitness bracelet glinted at her wrist. Isabelle always sported the latest TroneTek advance on the first day of its availability, and had once insinuated that Trone Meston sent her these products personally. When Rob had admired a silvery triangle affixed to Isabelle's collar, for monitoring her stress levels, Isabelle had murmured, "Trone knows me," and Rob hadn't questioned this concurrence further, because Isabelle had so desperately wanted him to.

"Rob," said Arjun, looking as if he'd rather be anywhere else, including at the bottom of the Hudson, "Isabelle has brought your interaction to my attention."

"Which interaction?" Rob asked, trying to remember the last time he'd spoken with Isabelle, as he tended to avoid these encounters.

"Regarding *Life as We Fucking Know It*."

Rob was still puzzled. *Life as We Fucking Know It* was a manuscript by an exciting, highly original young author named Tremble Woodspill (her real name). Rob had come across Tremble's blog posts, where she dissected every aspect of current culture from the perspective of someone working behind the counter at McDonald's after dropping out of community college, along with other, questionably legal pursuits. Rob had tracked Tremble to her hometown of Jacksburg, Arkansas, and proposed an essay collection. Tremble's pieces were funny and raucous, and wholly unlike the usual Manhattan dating woes. Tremble wrote about shooting one of her foster brothers in the leg after he drunkenly groped her, smuggling bags of French fries to everyone in her crumbling trailer park at Christmas, and shoplifting bras at Walmart because she was flat broke and decided that stealing was less humiliating then being seen purchasing a bra with a pattern of smiley faces.

"I've sent you three detailed memos about issues with the Woodspill manuscript," Isabelle began.

"Which were great and so helpful," said Rob, because sometimes flattery worked. People like Isabelle were forever expecting an argument, so agreement could confuse them.

"But as far as I can tell from the new draft," said Isabelle, "nothing has changed. In fact, a great deal of the content has gotten much worse."

Rob kept his face placid with attentive concern, to prevent screaming over Isabelle's use of the word "content," as if writing were the kapok filling in a throw pillow. He kept his voice even and gracious, while hearing Jake's accusations that he was always backing down from confrontation. Jake often cited Rob's saying "Excuse me, I'm so sorry" after bumping into mailboxes and parked cars.

"Could you be more specific?" Rob asked.

"On page thirty-eight, the author refers to herself as a mutt."

"Well, Tremble's mom is Black, her dad's from Bangladesh, and she's got a Cherokee grandfather and a white grandmother."

"Which is why I suggested the term 'multiracial.'"

"Which I've mentioned to Tremble repeatedly, but she prefers using 'mutt.' She doesn't consider it a slur. She says her dog is a mix of beagle and German shepherd and black Lab so she calls him a mutt."

"Which is equally offensive. Animals can sense condescension and insult."

Rob took a breath, as he was verging on a serious discussion of animal awareness: "I can mention it again and include your notes. Is there anything else?"

"In the third essay, she uses the term 'cocksucker,' when referring to a queer person. It's outdated and demeaning. I shouldn't even have to say this."

"She's talking about her friend Randall, who she loves, they grew up together. He asked her to give him lessons in fellatio."

"Fellatio" to Rob's mind, made cocksucking sound like some famous fourteenth-century Italian clown, the Grand Fellatio. "They call each other 'cocksucker' as a term of endearment."

"That doesn't come across. And imagine if a small-town teenager reads this book and starts using that word, or starts to believe that being queer can be reduced to a degrading sex act."

"Tremble says she's aiming her book at small-town teenagers just like she was. She says that's why she needs that language, so they won't think she's lecturing them."

Rob could hear his voice growing more agitated. He was taking the bait.

"And there's a word used repeatedly in chapter 15, and as a female-adjacent nonbinary queer I wanted to vomit. I couldn't get past it. And I can't possibly put my name and my reputation on any book which included it, and Arjun, tell me if you agree, that this isn't the kind of work W&S wants to be known for. I hope we're not that kind of house, that allows triggering language to soil everything else we publish. And Rob, I know you think I'm being some sort of humorless snowflake watchdog, which is completely generational. A white cisgender gay man of your age can't understand this."

Rob tried to breathe, but Isabelle had unleashed a cascade of his personal triggers, everything from her use of the word "trigger," to her assumption that her name was an equal if not greater asset to everything W&S published, to her sneering ageism, to the fact that she'd made Rob, even silently, employ a word with "ism" attached. But beyond all this, Rob was trying desperately to remember what word recurred in chapter 15 that might make Isabelle want to vomit.

"Cooze?" he blurted, not as an insult, but with the giddy certainty of someone coming up with the correct answer in the final Daily Double round of a cutthroat game show. "Cooze," Rob recalled, was Tremble's favorite word. In that chapter she used it in reference to her high school guidance counselor (who'd informed her she wasn't "college material"), a full plate of takeout lasagna that had shattered on the floor due to Tremble's experimenting with fentanyl, and the mayor of her small town, a felon named Churn LeBloitte.

As Rob uttered the word, Isabelle stared at him in not merely revulsion but victory.

"Rob, dude, I'm so sorry about the shitshow," Arjun told him, in the outer hallway near the elevators, "but I don't have a fucking choice. Corporate is so fucking scared of Isabelle and she wants you gone."

"Are you . . . Arjun, what is this exactly? Are you firing me? After thirty years? Well, thirty years for me and two for you and four months for Isabelle?"

Arjun sighed, twisting his head in every direction that didn't entail looking at Rob. "I'm telling you, it's totally not my call. But they're restructuring and maybe they're just looking for an excuse to, you know . . . deaccession you, or maybe it's just like, the cultural moment, but did you read Isabelle's op-ed in the *Times*? About generational blind spots?"

Rob had read the piece which, while making several valid points, also called for "not a reeducation of those irrevocably rooted in an ignorant past, but a shift to staffing by those unburdened by stereotypes, slurs, and clouded discourse." In other words, an elder-massacre.

"But Rob, and I'm probably just talking out of my ass, but I don't know, maybe if you could get through to Tremble, and get her to make Isabelle's changes, maybe we can salvage something. Maybe you can get reinstated, maybe part-time or as a consultant, but I can't promise anything. So I'm gonna need your ID badge and we'll probably change the entry codes and you should grab your stuff. Man, I am so fucking sorry."

Through the glass doors, both men could see Isabelle making her way along the Snake and stopping by each workstation. Eliminating Rob's job had not only given her a glow, but made her seem positively flirtatious, as if generational slaughter were a fabulous new organic skincare regimen crafted from potato skins, antioxidants, and Rob's soul.

Rob stumbled from the building, carrying his leather tote bag (which had undoubtedly irked Isabelle) and an additional W&S canvas tote bag, a trade show giveaway silk-screened with the company's logo and the words "A BOOK CAN BE ANYTHING." He was not just shell-shocked and wobbly but angry in a free-floating, combustible, manic way, as if he were about to punch a wall or a tree, if only his hands weren't occupied with tote bags.

Worst of all, his own hurt and rage paled beside what he knew Jake would feel, if Jake were still alive. Rob had valued Jake's anger because it was streamlined and heat-seeking, especially on Rob's behalf. When told of an injustice, Jake would become very still and say calmly, "Here's what we're doing."

But Jake was gone, which may very well have been Rob's fault, and as Rob began to walk home he was overcome by everything and sank onto the steps of a brownstone, the tote bags falling from his grasp, the contents tumbling down the stairs onto the sidewalk, the loose manuscript pages and framed photos and Scotch tape dispenser, the few items he'd stored atop his bend of the Snake. A fragment of his mind realized he must look not merely lost and frail, but as if he were having a medical episode, because passersby were observing him and about to approach. He nodded vaguely no, I'm okay, I'm not having a stroke, I live in New York, but most of him was boomeranging, searching the universe for Jake.

3

THE GYM

Rob managed to stand up and refill his tote bags, still reeling from being fired. He'd only been fired once before, from a waitering job at a theater district restaurant years earlier, after a staff downsizing, so he hadn't been at fault. This was different—it wasn't just a gut punch, but more like being tased, as his body was beset with punishing quandaries: Should he start looking for a new job instantly? Had he aged out of his beloved profession—would his résumé be shredded or deleted by the Isabelle McNallys at every publishing house? Should he freelance, with a website and a photoshopped profile pic and a million other, painfully unfamiliar demands? Would he be able to keep up with his mortgage payments or would he be forced to sell the apartment at a loss? Would his dwindling finances mean abandoning New York, and would that be a final betrayal of Jake? How would he tell his family about getting fired, and which would be worse, their confused sympathy or their well-intended advice? Was his life, the remnants of the life he'd built with Jake, the gay New York life he loved dearly, was it now unsustainable, an ash heap of poor financial planning and endless grief?

Susannah had told Rob that her greatest fear was of becoming home-less, even though she'd known this was unlikely. She'd said this was a common nightmare for women her age, a premonition of being unloved, unhoused, and unable to bathe or wear decent clothing to maintain at least a shell of self-respect. Men were expected to be more self-sufficient and uncomplaining, sucking it up and guarding their work boots as they slept on a subway grate— Why was Rob even thinking about this, along with notions of hawking his books and clothing on eBay or spread across a sidewalk blanket, and reducing his food intake to Saltines and tap water? Young people can conquer any setbacks, by placing adversity in a storyline of struggle and ultimate success, by telling themselves, "I'll get through this and my enemies will be sorry when they see me accepting my fifteenth Daytime Emmy." But Rob wasn't young.

Standing in his apartment, Rob couldn't decide whether to collapse or call Paolo or gobble every snack on the premises. He recognized this buzzing mania but couldn't harness it. After Tria nudged, "You have a training session with Sean Manginaro in twenty minutes," he was about to text Sean and cancel, but physical activity might be psychologically helpful, even if just as a stopgap, and maintaining his routine felt essen-tial. While Jake had been sick, and Rob had never wanted to leave his side, Jake had pushed Rob to continue at the gym, to clear his head and promote some minor relief from the couple's latest agony. "As every gay man knows," Jake had told him, his speech slurred from his illness, "the gym will save your life."

Rob dropped his tote bags on the floor—already a sin—and found his gym bag, a lightweight black nylon duffel from a practical-minded Japanese chain store. Rob had spent months selecting this bag. He be-lieved that any man over forty who still carried a backpack was irretrievably sad, like those decaying "boys" shuffling around in Abercrombie T-shirts and cargo shorts, as if they still qualified as disco bunnies or Fire Island eye candy. Rob and Jake had both been staunch advocates of dignity, outlawing tank tops, flip-flops, tattoos, spray tans, piercings, manscaping, and all other emblems of a desperately prolonged hotness. As Jake had warned, "Once you start Botoxing the crease between your eyebrows, you've literally crossed a line."

Rob headed out the door, but by the time he reached the elevator he was sure he'd forgotten something—his TronePhone? His gym ID? His keys? None of these checked out, so Rob walked the ten blocks to the Meatpacking District, where Defiance Fitness and Mind/Body Training lived in a loft space on the second floor of a rehabbed ware-house. Rob had been coming to Defiance, or Refinance, as Jake had called it, for twenty-one years. Defiance had been an early factor in the area's resurgence, opening when there were still ongoing meat sup-ply businesses everywhere, which opened at 4 a.m. and closed in the early afternoon as the rubber apron–clad butchers hosed down the sidewalks. There were at most three of these abbatoirs left, now jostled by boutique hotels with a global clientele, haughty shops, some by appointment only, which sold fuzzy pink $3,000 angora sweaters for men, restaurants that morphed into bottle-service clubs for finance types after midnight, and the largest Starbucks in the world, a block-long Starbucks Roastery Elite, which boasted three copper fireplaces, a selection of coffees from fifty-eight nations, seating for three hun-dred "guests," a party space for couples who wanted to be married or celebrate their toddlers' birthdays at Starbucks, and a constant glut of tourists who considered downing overpriced coffee served by mili-tantly cheerful baristas to be a destination experience, like the Louvre or Machu Picchu, both of which undoubtedly now hosted a Starbucks of their own.

Rob took the stairs as a gesture toward cardio. As an American, he would bribe himself into fitness by sprinkling "heart healthy" walnuts onto his sundae, scarfing a jumbo bag of "reduced fat" potato chips with "sea salt," or avoiding an elevator for a single flight of steps.

The gym itself was open and airy, with built-in low leather seating near the front desk, refinished industrial oak floors, and raw brick walls, for what Jake had termed "that Soho hedge-fund museum-quality nothingness." There was sunlight from the large windows facing the street, but the mood was chicly shadowed. The Defiance ads promised "an atmosphere of fierce dedication and downtown luxury" staffed by "fitness artisans with degrees in holistic wellness, endo-limbic coordination, and advanced adrenal imaging"—Rob was never sure which universities proffered such diplomas. During his early years in the city, he had worked out by himself or with Paolo, at the gay gyms-of-the-moment, where nattering cliques would call out "your quads are a symphony today, darling" to men across the room, as the dance music pounded and the steam rooms seethed with officially discouraged activities. But once in his forties, Rob had grown both distanced from the muscle-queen hubbub and waning in discipline. He'd told Jake, "I need either a shrink or a trainer," and they'd concurred that personal training was a far more practical investment. "I don't care if you're anxious and depressed," Jake had decreed, "as long as you can tuck in a dress shirt."

On his first visit to Defiance, despite a flat-screen menu of on-duty trainers, Rob had glimpsed Sean Manginaro across the room. Sean was studly, with the brawny shoulders, V-shaped torso, and boulder-like "guns," meaning biceps, of a porn-site headliner, but Rob hadn't nurtured a crush. He'd been more impressed by Sean's athletic bearing. Civilians live in their heads, with their bodies trailing behind like the blankies of thumb-sucking four-year-olds. Sean's body was a panther-like instrument, completely engaged at all times. His feet seemed to be gripping the floor, as if he were seeking prey, moving easily yet with force. Sean wasn't threatening or steroided, but still a cartoon ideal, a man of action, with a snub-nosed, granite-jawed face, his thick black hair chopped in a severe but not quite drill sergeant crew cut. Sean ruled the gym with a friendly if resolutely heterosexual grace. All the trainers were nice-looking and qualified, but Rob had immediately asked about Sean. The sales rep behind the front desk wondered if Rob had recognized him.

After a moment Rob did. Five years earlier, Sean had appeared on a minor network hit called *WarForce*, as a member of a "genetically enhanced" superhero unit, cryo-engineered by the CIA and deployed all around the world to parachute in and dismember terrorists, warlords, and drug cartels, using super-speed, night vision, and something called "protox power." Sean had played a punkish rebel named Blaster, his physique always on ample display. Blaster had been reconditioned by the WarForce scientists following his being decapitated during an escape from a super-max prison, where he'd been incarcerated for stealing a nuclear weapon on a drunken dare. Blaster had awakened from a year-long coma with super-strength (demonstrated by his blithely tossing a railroad car across a gorge), a machine gun embedded in each forearm, and the telepathic ability to make his foes slap themselves in the face. Blaster had been granted the option of returning to jail, unbreakably shackled and heavily sedated, or serving his country.

Blaster was often reprimanded for pranking his team members using limbs he'd ripped from the bodies of criminals, but he'd been a fan favorite, especially among eight-year-old boys. Blaster had been pure id, an easily bored killing machine. Sean had never intended to become an actor; he'd been recruited from bodybuilding contests and a TV ad for a soap that delivered "bacteria-busting twenty-four-hour odor protection for even your manliest areas." Sean's brush with fame had bequeathed financial and sexual perks, but he'd been young and careless, burning through his salary and endorsement potential. He'd pulled himself together and dove into the burgeoning fitness industry. He'd founded Defiance, first in a space half this size in a less desirable location, but Sean's dream-gym-teacher magnetism and savvy hiring had lured a rabid following, which paid for his move to an upgraded and much-photographed facility, top-ranked in fitness magazines' get-in-shape-now cover stories and morning show segments where the hosts swapped their business attire for torso-clutching spandex with coordinated headbands, while Sean coached them in "booty-busting" squats and ab routines for "not just a six-pack or an eight-pack, that's for wannabees, I'm talking about a twelve-pack by July!"

"Rob-EEE!!!" Sean yelled, on the day of Rob's firing, with a guttural emphasis on the second syllable. Sean didn't have an indoor voice. "You're LATE, dude!!!"

Rob gestured in helpless apology and left for the locker room, where he was gobsmacked by what he'd forgotten: his gym clothes were in the hamper and he hadn't replaced them. He returned to the front desk and bought a T-shirt and shorts with the Defiance logo of a lion wearing a backwards baseball cap, against a backdrop of black and purple lightning bolts. This outfit was garish and embarrassing, unless it had been Rob's first day in preschool. He shuffled from the locker room, bedraggled and ashamed, like someone whose mom had dumped him at summer camp, trilling "Have fun!" as she floored her Chevy and took off for the nearest liquor store.

"Whoa, look at you," Sean said jovially. "You look total retard." He paused and added, "Fuck me, I know I'm not supposed to say 'retard' anymore. You look like whatever a retard is now."

"Um . . . ," Rob began; the two men usually bantered, but Rob was still reeling.

"Dude, you okay?"

"Yes, of course, all good, what are we doing today, um, chest?"

"You got it! Chesterino!"

Rob ordinarily relished Sean's rowdy jockishness, which was natural and never bullying. While the gym was mixed, Sean trained mostly gay men, because he liked the adoration uncomplicated by romance, which might entail "you know, fucking talking about my feelings." Over the years, Rob had noticed something: the most truly confident straight guys had a streak of gay behavior, including a yen for show business gossip ("So you think JLo is gonna get married again?"), dissections of strangers' attractiveness ("That dude's got a decent chest but his legs are toothpicks"), and a hankering for fashion and interior design ("You're gonna be so fucking jealous, I just bagged a Restoration Hardware desk chair on eBay for less than half what it costs in the store. SCORE!!!"). Sean was, as he'd once happily admitted, "gay except for sucking dick."

Sean spent much of his time with his straight buddies, as part of a triathalon training squad, either running along the West Side Highway or chugging beers and insulting onscreen second-string outfielders at sports bars. He loved this while also feeling constrained; his gay friendships were a welcome breather from macho shoulder-punching and estimating the net worth of name-brand quarterbacks married to supermodels. Gay guys, Sean had also learned, were even raunchier when it came to analyzing sex acts ("You know how when you're fucking even the hottest guy and he's moaning like a bitch in heat but all you're thinking is Oh my God, this couch is brand-new, can we please use a fucking towel?") and penis dimensions ("Oh please, his Speedo is bulging but it's 98 percent balls"). Sean was what happened when a bro raised next door to his uncle's muffler shop in Bayonne, New Jersey, gets a job in the city. The true cause of, if not actual gayness, then an exuberantly dishy gay style, was Manhattan itself.

Rob and Sean had a comfortable routine, as Sean raised the backrest on a bench and supplied Rob with free weights for a series of chest exercises. Rob liked not having to motivate himself. Sean was the best sort of coach, because he made everyone want to please him, not because he'd yell or snort in disgust at failure, but because he was on the other person's side, cheering them on. As Rob executed a set of chest presses, his mind was elsewhere, and Sean picked up on this, putting the weights back on the rack and asking, "Come on, dude, what's goin' on?"

Rob rarely complained to Sean. He never wanted to be one of those people who treat their hairstylist or trainer as a shrink, as a fake friend who's paid to listen and cluck sympathetically. He liked the boisterous simplicity of his sessions with Sean; Sean made Rob straighter. Sean kept tabs on his clients' marriages and hookups. During Jake's illness, he'd sensed when Rob wanted to talk about it and when he was grateful for the opposite experience, an escape or rest from that particular hell. Sean was sharply attuned to his clients' psyches, and today, he'd caught on instantly that Rob was going through what they'd both call "some serious shit."

"Okay," said Rob, glimpsing himself in the mirror and seeing his own fatigue and disconcertedness. "I got fired."

"Whoa. Was it that Isabelle chick?"

Rob had more than once entertained Sean with reports of Isabelle's political vocabulary. Explaining "nonbinary" to Sean had been a complicated treat. "No way," Sean had protested. "I mean, with trans people, I get it. I work with trans athletes. You're a guy who's really a girl, fine by me. You're a girl who wants to like, take testosterone and grow a beard and talk shit, it's all good. But, what did you just call it? Binational?"

"Nonbinary."

"No. I'm not doin' that. Fucking choose a lane. Chick or dude. Don't waste my time."

The limits of Sean's acceptance were at times Neanderthal, but Rob liked him too much for condemnation, and he could always follow Sean's logic. Rob was also secretly relieved at not having to behave himself and nod earnestly at the latest pronouns or spellings, as in "zim," "hir," or "womyn's festival." Rob wholeheartedly supported such progressive language, which also made his teeth ache. Sean provided an almost Republican respite (although Sean was an ardent Democrat, even voting for, as he put it, "a ballbuster like Hillary"). Sean was Rob's guilty vacation from do-goody liberalism, and they could tease each other— the Isabelles of the world weren't big on irony and crudeness.

"Technically, Isabelle didn't fire me," Rob admitted. "But let's just say she wasn't upset about it. It only happened a few minutes ago. I'm still wrapping my mind around it."

"No, dude, you're not wrapping shit. You got fired and I bet it's not fair and that is seriously fucked up."

As the two men exchanged a manly disgust, as if they weren't grousing in a luxurious facility where the snack bar sold $12 protein-rich, carob-chip power scones, Sean's phone went off. He almost never took calls during a session, adamant about not short-shrifting his clients, but his brow furrowed and he told Rob, "I'm real sorry, hold on just a sec."

As Sean read something on his screen, scrolling slowly, his expression darkened. Rob had seen Sean pissed off at an unprofessional supplier, or someone not returning their weights to the rack properly (Sean was maniacally neat), but this wasn't anger. Sean looked up, and there were tears in his eyes, and Rob guessed that someone had died, although Sean wasn't especially close with his siblings or parents. Sean tried to speak but couldn't. He tried again, and in a choking whisper confided, "She's getting married."

4

JAKE WARRILOW

Rob wasn't sure which was more cruel, for Sean or himself: experiencing the punishing, irrevocable end of a relationship, or recalling that marriage's deliriously promising opening moments, its tingling overture.

Rob had met Jake twenty-eight years earlier, at a Broadway Cares benefit held at an ice-skating rink on the twenty-first floor of a midtown office building. The SkyRink was one of the city's surprises, with fabulous views and a surprisingly high ceiling of ironwork arches; it was like a portal into either a Midwestern Olympic training facility or an especially well-outfitted spacecraft. Rob had grown up skating on a lake near his family's Massachusetts home, so he'd taken a smug pride in lacing up his skates among the gathered guests, mostly wealthy gay men, the less wealthy friends of these men, and the younger guys who toiled in the wealthy men's offices.

Rob hadn't skated in years, so he'd tried not to wobble, mostly by thrusting his chin out, as if his jaw were proclaiming, "I'm skating!" But there were far more experienced people on the ice, including both current and retired medalists, who moved as if they didn't even notice they were skating. Rob had been transfixed by one of these godlike specimens, not so much sexually as simply in awe at anyone who could carry a champagne flute while swooping backwards, in formfitting black. Urban figure skaters, Rob decided, were gay superheroes or secret agents, infiltrating brunches and drag bar trivia nites.

Rob's voyeurism twisted him off-balance, and as he stumbled and sought to remember how to point the ridges at the front of his blades in order not to fall, someone gripped his elbows from behind and steadied him. Rob turned and there was Jake, smiling and murmuring, "Stop staring. Figure skaters will break your heart and leave sequins on your towels."

Rob smiled back, because any thoughts of Olympians had vanished. Jake was tall and narrow, with thick red hair meticulously cropped, accenting his prominent ears, proving Jake was proud of them. Jake had the air of a cornfed small-town kid, offset by a sexy knowingness, like a fashion-savvy Howdy Doody or Huck Finn, lacking only the requisite freckles and slingshot in his back pocket. At first Rob wondered if Jake was mocking him, but Jake's smile seemed genuine, as he considered Rob with a mood of grounded appraisal, like a handsome Martian commander making curious contact with his first Earthling.

"All better," said Jake, who skated off with ease and polish. He executed a modest spin, which was a mistake, as he jerked forward and then righted himself, blushing deeply. This error, this break in an otherwise flawless moment, made Rob stop breathing for just a second, as he told himself, No way in Hell, don't even think about it. Rob was attractive, in a composed, impish manner, his hard-to-tame dark curls and hapless grin lending him the mien of a French waiter who's decided to be nice.

But like all gay men in New York, and all human beings since the beginning of time, Rob doubted his own desirability. Jake fit handily into Rob's most familiar, self-protective category: "I'm incredibly turned on by him so it's hopeless."

As Rob was balancing on a wooden bench a half hour later and laboriously undoing his skates with chilled fingers, Jake was suddenly there. Jake had a stealth which would later make Rob question if Jake could will himself invisible when bored, materializing in three dimensions only with a renewed purpose.

"Coffee?" Jake suggested, his own skates not only removed but with the laces neatly braided.

That first sit-down was a blur as both men presented fictional selves, available yet not desperate, witty but not pushy, masculine without buffoonery, and relaxed while not comatose. These exhaustingly constructed façades were the necessary groundwork of any incipient pairing, as if a matchmaker or both men's mothers were hovering, stressing the guys' most generic and appealing traits while hissing, "See, I told you—he's perfect."

Rob had later reported to Paolo that Jake was quirkily good-looking, like "a hot Archie Andrews," that he'd used the title "interior designer" rather than "decorator," and that he might be snobby or simply shy, although as Paolo remarked, "All murderous dictators insist they're really just shy, as if they order mass executions and burn shtetls to avoid making small talk." Jake told his coworker, an Englishwoman named Beatrice, that he'd met a very nice, very cute man, and from Jake's unaccustomed grinning, Beatrice had declared, "You're a goner. He owns you. Give it up." Jake and Beatrice were both employed by a legendarily fastidious, old school Madison Avenue cabbage-rose-chintz-and-hand-blocked-

Chinese-wallpaper decorator named Benjamin Crawbell. Mr. Crawbell, as he was addressed, owned fifty-eight identical gray custom-tailored suits, a Bucks County country home with the original pine beams and milk-painted Dutch doors from 1718, and had only allowed an EMT worker to loosen his white shirt collar following a minor coronary.

Rob and Jake's first official, more serious date took place a week later, at a reasonably but not annoyingly trendy restaurant in Chelsea called Restaurant, for a bold understatement. Paolo had said the menu should consist of undifferentiated items listed as Food. The men had dressed with a ridiculous amount of casual intensity, strewing their bedrooms with discarded options. Rob had arrived at a blameless chambray shirt, an I-made-an-effort black silk knit tie, and cream-colored Levi's, with Jake in a long-sleeved white polo shirt and herringbone tweed trousers, with shoes so worn, well polished, and simple that Rob imagined they were either Italian, bespoke, or both. Gay men's shoes become their calling cards, a shorthand for assessments like "Ivy League education, at least one Ralph Lauren coffee table book, and conceivably wild in bed."

As an editor, Rob made checklists of sartorial details and was skilled at drawing people out, while Jake had the slightly haughty air of someone testing a client, as if he were hiring them instead of the other way around.

"Have you always wanted to be a designer?" Rob asked, once they'd ordered. Rob had looked forward to this early stage of dating, when both parties could ask the sort of questions a concerned parent might launch at a child's nervous suitor, or a college admissions officer would use in unearthing an applicant's self-image.

"At first I wanted to be an architect, but I was too impatient, and I could never figure out sub-basements. And when I was five years old, I'd rearranged the furniture in my family's living room, although I ended up turning to my mom and telling her, 'It's better but it's still colonial.'"

Rob smiled. There was a forthrightness to Jake, seasoned with humor. Rob's earlier boyfriends had been projects, including a perpetual grad student, an aspiring actor, and a sweet-natured waiter/physical therapist/dogwalker. Rob loved to help people, but this could be frustrating on both sides, as if Rob were editing his needy boyfriends' personalities. They'd felt criticized and Rob had judged himself a failure. But Jake was assured and independent; Jake was fully formed.

"So who's your favorite writer?" said Jake. "Or does everybody ask that?"

Oddly, most people didn't, preferring to ask if Rob edited anyone famous, whose books had been made into movies or TV shows, or even better, if he'd edited the ghostwritten memoirs and exercise guides of the stars of movies or TV shows (which he sometimes did).

"Like everybody, I love Fitzgerald and Nathanael West and Edith Wharton. They were the first people who grabbed me and said, 'Pay attention, I know more than you do.' But I've got a big thing for Evelyn Waugh and Henry James and all the drawing room Brits, oh, and Christopher Isherwood, especially . . ."

"*Down There on a Visit*," both men said.

Rob gasped. If most people had vaguely heard of Isherwood, they'd bring up his *Berlin Stories*, which had been the basis for *Cabaret*. But *Down There on a Visit* covered Isherwood's life in Los Angeles and the erotic travails of a character based on Denham Fouts, a notoriously gorgeous and doomed man, kept by royalty and billionaires. It was a gay version of a tragically romantic Fitzgerald tale, and Rob lived for Isherwood's chiseled, gossipy, matter-of-factly uncloseted prose.

"I like watching you talk about books," said Jake.

"Why?"

"Because I can tell how much you love them. You even drop your voice a little, like you're telling me a filthy secret, which someone might overhear."

Rob blushed, at being found out and appreciated. Rob had never considered becoming a writer himself, because of how much he admired his authors. Editing made him feel valued; he didn't seek credit so much as fulfillment, at helping a sentence or chapter blossom more fully, or at contacting first-time clients, like Tremble Woodspill, and offering them a contract; their mutual joy was transporting, as if Rob had bestowed a literary tiara and sash. Rob wasn't egoless, he guarded his writers, and prided himself on unearthing appropriate advice, at being 100 percent right about a misplaced comma or an unnecessary paragraph. He was like Sean, only for prose. When a writer became stronger and more fully themselves, Rob knew he'd been really good at his job, and could grab a cupcake from his favorite bakery on his way home. Cupcakes were Rob's gold stars, and another reason to hit the gym.

"I'm going to need a reading list," said Jake, aware this was Rob's idea of talking dirty.

The meal went on for an agreeable two hours, and afterward Jake walked Rob back downtown—Rob was living in a studio on Charles Street. Chelsea was a bustling gay mecca at that point, in mid-gentrification, so it was like strolling through the opening number of an entirely queer animated Disney musical.

"You're from—was it New Hampshire?" Rob asked.

"Pennsylvania. My dad's a minister."

"Was that—a problem?"

"It was odd. He wasn't all that fire-and-brimstone, and when I came out at the dinner table, when I was seventeen, there wasn't any rage or tears. My mom glanced at my father, who asked if I was sure about this. I said I was, and the next morning my Dad sat me down in the living room and told me how sad he and my mother both were, but that I was going to Hell and I'd have to move out."

"Oh no."

"I'd seen it coming but I hadn't been sure. He was so weirdly congenial, as if he was thanking me for coming in on a job interview. But I'd already been accepted at college, with loans and a work/study job, so I didn't need their help. I moved in with a friend's family for six months and then left town."

"And since then . . . ?"

"I've never been back. Or spoken to my parents. Which should be traumatic and maybe I've buried it, but it's not like my folks had been all that warm or welcoming to begin with. I'd always felt like I was a boarder or an exchange student, on probation. But I was seriously angry, which made me never beg or sob or scream at them. It was like a contest of glacial politeness, the most gracious exchange of fuck-you-forevers."

As the two men crossed 14th Street, Rob was intrigued, hungrily accumulating information about Jake's life, while cautioning himself not to move too fast. Hopefully, they had plenty of time, and so many more dreamy strolls together, to delve deeper. Jake shifted the focus, asking, "So how were your parents?"

Rob guiltily confessed, "Completely fine. Old-fashioned Massachusetts liberal Democrats. I waited until my freshman year at college to officially spill the beans, and then a year later my younger sister came out, and six months later my brother, who was sixteen, announced he was gay over Thanksgiving dinner, and ten days later my sister Jenson told us she was trans. I almost felt sorry for my parents—I mean, accepting one queer kid is a proud, benevolent gesture, but all four? What were they feeding us? But they've been great, although once in a while, at Christmas, I catch my mom staring at all of us, at her rainbow brood, and she's clearly thinking, Who are you people? I mean, she loves us to pieces, but it's like a murder mystery."

Trading coming-out sagas is common on gay first dates, a formality, an updated so-where-did-you-go-to-school. The guys had reached the Village by this point, and were passing by St. Vincent's Hospital. Jake considered telling Rob about Hastings, his lover who'd spent his last months in a ward on the fourth floor, but decided not to burden a first date with that degree of drama. AIDS was still ever-present, although promising new drug cocktails had been introduced. And Rob and Jake, while not ignoring the ongoing tragedy, had made an unspoken vow to enjoy themselves, to let their date be a respite from statistics and memorials and an eventual listing of mutual friends who'd died, another rite-of-passage for that moment in gay Manhattan history. Both men were HIV-negative, but either of them mentioning this, just yet, would be bad form, like brandishing a report card.

"Even with everything," Jake said, as they approached Rob's block, "I love the city. I couldn't live anywhere else."

They looked at each other, with an unexpected degree of understanding. It wasn't just that they were two gay men, in a certain city at a certain juncture. That was true, but something more was percolating, a heady mix of sexual tension and giddy hope, that eternal flame of flirtation which refuses to be extinguished, especially in New York.

"This is me," said Rob, as they stood with a delectable awkwardness in front of his building.

"I'd really like to see you again," said Jake, making it clear that it was too soon for sex, but that he'd meant what he'd said.

"I'd like that," said Rob, captivated by the Meg Ryan–ness of their exchange. He pictured himself holding a heart-shaped crimson helium balloon or stuffed giraffe Jake had won for him at a carnival.

They kissed, with a gentlemanly reserve, a promise of more to come and a prim agreement that they weren't rutting animals. Jake started toward the subway, but after three steps he turned around, and the second kiss was torrid enough to make Rob call Paolo ten minutes later and start the hour-long conversation by saying, "I'm sorry but I can't talk. My lips are bruised."

5

SEAN MANGINARO

Sean had lost his virginity at age fifteen, to a mother and her teenage daughter in his neighborhood. He was a good-looking kid and already a multi-sport athlete, and Mrs. Barrows, following her second divorce, had hired him to rake leaves and winterize the patio furniture. It had been an unseasonably warm October so Sean worked with his shirt off and Mrs. Barrows invited him inside, handing him a beer and promising not to tell his parents. Mrs. Barrows was thirty-seven and spent her days in body-hugging pastel leotards and leg-warmers. She'd quizzed Sean on his football games and weight-lifting routine, which she'd declared "top-notch."

Sean was ebullient and bursting to investigate sex, which he'd only experienced through an older brother's collection of porn magazines and VHS tapes. When Mrs. Barrows had massaged Sean's shoulders and then called out to him from her bedroom, he'd been happy to oblige. "That was way cool," he'd told her, as he was pulling his T-shirt on afterward, "I mean it."

He'd grinned at Mrs. Barrows, and she'd shaken her head, conscious she was only the first in Sean's eventual, lifelong parade of women. A few weeks later, when she'd returned from the nail salon to find Sean giving her seventeen-year-old daughter swimming lessons in the Barrows' heated backyard pool, she'd been stunned, then angry, and finally bemused at her own vengeful-older-woman response. She'd never thought of Sean as a romance or a possession but was more upset by her daughter borrowing a bikini from her own extensive collection. Kelli had smirked, which was annoying, but Mrs. Barrows determined that if they were divvying up Sean's sexual calendar, at least he wasn't diseased or an obvious criminal.

Sean had ridden his bike home, sorting things out after devirginizing Kelli. He liked both of the Barrows women, and was turned on by their jealousy, but wasn't sure of the rules. Most of his brain had been occupied by how naturally his body responded to sex and wanted more. Just as with soccer or jujitsu, he had a knack, but should maximize his skills. He'd been pleased at making the women moan with a surprised gusto, as if they'd intended to fake things but hadn't needed to. Sean had no desire to become a heartless suburban Casanova, pedaling from cul-de-sac to lakefront property, but he loved the strategizing of seduction and glory. When the mother and daughter had been seated beside each other at one of the season's final football games, he'd waved, with each lady certain the recognition was for her alone.

Women were always available to Sean; he was that rare combination of a one-night smutty fantasy and potential husband material. At college Sean had experimented with monogamy, staying faithful to his first two serious girlfriends and faithful-when-on-campus to his third. But the requirements of what most of these women called a committed relationship didn't suit him. There were too many amazing-looking girls out there, eyeing him and twirling their hair and swiveling for a last backward glance as they moseyed away hand in hand with their steady boyfriends, at theme parks and keggers and tailgates. Sean couldn't help but look back, sipping a long-necked beer. It would've felt wasteful not to beam at least a crooked smile, knowing that's what the young lady would be picturing during sex with her fiancé.

Ashlee, Sean's first serious girlfriend, had ogled him lying naked in her dorm room bed (after her roommates had been banished) and told him, "You are so hot and you know it. It's disgusting."

"I can't help it," Sean protested. "You want some of this?"

Ashlee sighed, because of course she did, but en route to the sheets she'd added, "There are gonna be pictures of you in police stations, saying 'Do Not Date. Under Any Circumstances.'"

"And nobody's gonna pay attention," Sean replied, grabbing Ashlee by her ponytail (he was big on ponytails) and deep-kissing her. This was another of Sean's superpowers—unlike many of his various teammates, Sean loved making out and cunnilingus, both at marathon levels. As he'd told a buddy, "I like to make 'em scream, plus they also stop talking. TOUCHDOWN!"

Sean had fallen hard for Diandra, his second major girlfriend, who was pre-law and even better-looking than he was. Diandra had spotted him at a frat party, said, "Get over here," and hauled him back to her off-campus apartment. After some mind-blowing sex, including Sean's first go at anal, Diandra had kicked him out, citing an exam the next day. "Go home and play with yourself," she recommended, slinging Sean's sweatshirt at him while pointing to the door. Insulted and bereft, Sean became consumingly intent on mesmerizing Diandra, utilizing his body, his downcast blue eyes, and his newfound approximation of listening. They'd gone out for six months, until Diandra dumped him, explaining, not without benevolence, "I really like you. But if we keep going, I'll turn into some drippy girl calling you every ten seconds and wondering what our kids would look like. And you'll start lying, which you already have, but if we cool things now we don't have to hate each other."

"But maybe we could just have like, a sex thing," Sean had parried.

"Nice try," Diandra laughed, allotting one valedictory kiss before shutting her eyes, positing herself on the Supreme Court, and advising Sean to lose her number. While she was right about all of it, her rejection stung, leaving Sean feeling disrespected, although mostly, he'd admitted to himself, because he hadn't done the dumping. Sean had taken out his resentment on his next girlfriend, which wasn't fair, and after she'd caught him cheating for the third time he'd apologized, calling himself "a lowlife piece of crap" and swearing not to get involved with any more girls until he got his act together, which he calculated might take almost the entire month before graduation.

Over the next year Sean had stood behind the front desk at a hard-core bodybuilding gym in exchange for a membership and discounts on creatine powder, antioxidant capsules, and a bogus "super-ionized" copper wristband designed to "mega-boost your results in strength and size, and protect you from harmful radiation." He began training with Stu, an older, once-competitive musclehead, who terrorized Sean about neglecting his lower body, the way so many guys did, concentrating on their pecs, shoulder caps, and arms, the parts most visible in a crowded bar. "You don't want to end up like some fucking ice-cream cone," Stu (once known as The Glutemaster) had instilled, meaning a broad, bulging torso shrinking to minimal thighs and calves, hidden by the leopard-skin, elastic-waist polyester pantaloons that bodybuilders wore everywhere (including to bar mitzvahs and parole hearings), called Zazu pants.

Bodybuilding had given Sean a routine and goals, which he lived by. In sex and career, Sean was rigorously result-oriented. He'd achieved a roster of lower-echelon, all-natural (meaning no steroids) bodybuilding titles, including Mr. Tri-State Junior Cosmos, Mr. Central Jersey Best Under 30, and Goldblatt's Tanning Beds Mr. Titan, two years running. The wins had been helpful, but Sean was starting to accept: he didn't possess the (chemically amplified) genetic gifts of a Schwarzenegger, whose posters lined the walls of the gym, and it was critical for Sean to be the best at whatever he did. Guzzling foul-tasting, "cellular-stacking" shakes with Stu and his sagging, mulleted, orange-tanned buddies, Sean worried that this was his future, in which he'd brag about doing triceps with Arnold during a promotional tour for one of the Conan the Barbarian movies.

Sean had been rescued from thick-necked oblivion by a Xeroxed flier printed with audition times for the *WarForce* series. The production company had been blanketing gyms and competitions in a search for not so much an actor as someone who could fill out Blaster's spandex, whose mountainous brawn would allure both kids seeking an action figure come to life along with adults who aspired to become Blaster and/ or have sex with him onboard the WarForce's hyper-sonic WarJet.

Sean had diligently aced his auditions and callbacks, memorizing lines like "Eat my quads," "Are you comin' for me, space dweeb?," "Yo, Commander, lemme Blast 'em!," and "I'm gonna Blasterize your ass!" He did well, because of his size and appropriately comic-book enthusiasm, but there was a roadblock. As he sat in a waiting area with two other behemoth-level candidates, he was summoned for a private conference with the series' creator, a schlubby guy whose comb-over was balanced by a scraggly, prematurely gray-streaked beard. Josh Gubbleman's lunch was always evident in the stains and splatters on his chess-club plaid button-downs and camouflage-print fatigues. Josh had latched onto an early wave of video game–style entertainment, in which a team of outsize, indestructible characters could fiercely annihilate interplanetary monsters, sneering corporate despots, and implacable robots that morphed into even larger, fortress-like robots.

"We love you for Blaster," Josh told Sean, "You've got the style and the cojones, but the network brass are concerned about, um, your physical presence. Especially your traps."

Sean took a deep breath, because he unfortunately got what Josh was talking about: the musculature connecting Sean's broad shoulders was underdeveloped, almost causing the dreaded "pencil neck." Stu had stressed targeting Sean's traps, but they'd still lagged.

"So we wanted to ask if you'd consider—a regimen."

This was code for a cycle, or more than one, of injected anabolic steroids. Sean had seen what these drugs could do, in expanding guys' bodies to the dimensions of Volkswagen vans, with their hydrant arms jutting out from their torsos, and their watermelon-like thighs preventing casual walking. Owners of these balloon-animal silhouettes trudged slowly and deliberately, with their lycra-encased thighs and backs often chafed and acne-ridden from the drugs. Extreme dieting and diuretics caused their veins to pop like subway maps, and their jaws to enlarge as their testicles shrank. Hair loss was a reported side effect along with uncontrollable rage and sterility.

"Hell yeah," said Sean, who'd anticipated this question. He'd steered away from steroids in the past, both out of medical qualms and because he'd wanted to test how far he could get without them. A night earlier he'd sat himself down and debated the dangers and virtues of juicing. With this deal-breaker on the table, Sean wouldn't become Blaster without signing on. Blaster would be his next step, as a business gambit. Stardom was potentially far more lucrative than hawking visors and fanny packs from behind the front desk at Bayonne Slammin' Bodies, or toiling weekends at his cousin Nino's car wash.

WarForce would be filmed on soundstages in LA, where the network rented Sean a shabbily furnished apartment. The steroids kicked in remarkably fast, and were coupled with a targeted workout routine overseen by Archer (he used only the one name), a fitness guru who specialized in bulking up celebrities for action-oriented roles. He was rumored to have sculpted at least one Superman, two Batmen, and assorted stars who had upcoming shirtless scenes in rom-coms. Archer wasn't especially large, and his teeth, nose, and hairline had definitely been tampered with. He was exacting and relentless, with his trademark directive "If you're not going to work hard, then why are we here?" Archer was Sean's first brush with a fast-rising breed of professionals, who serviced the vain, ever-changing physical and emotional thirsts of the entertainment industry. Archer also trained studio executives who were between divorces and fretful about the ascension of younger coworkers. These fifty-year-olds, already on their second or third eyelifts, chins, and wives, would always implore, "I just want to look and feel my best."

Sean quickly packed on forty pounds of muscle which, when molded atop his already chiseled frame, lent him the uselessly gargantuan proportions the network had requisitioned. His bones and tendons ached from the effort, and he and Archer would tirelessly chart what were termed Sean's "gains." The mirror had always been Sean's friend, but it

became his taskmaster. Sean would inspect himself naked, as if oversee-
ing the progression of a custom-made flesh tuxedo during fittings at the
most exclusive tailor. He of course was also checking for those scary side
effects, but his balls were intact.

Sean met the rest of the *WarForce* cast; Josh had enlisted shrewd,
name-brand veterans of other, canceled shows; a fresh-faced recent Juil-
liard graduate who told himself the show would be a "stepping stone"
and "a calling card"; and that subset of actors who support themselves
for years by filming unsold TV pilots. Sarah, who'd be playing the team's
sunny, regular-gal minder, told Sean she'd been able to afford a house in
Encino, a Toyota Camry, and a baby with the money she'd socked away
as the go-to best friend, approachably sexy young mom, and cheerfully
beleaguered daughter to the star on at least fifteen TV shows no one
would ever see.

WarForce's primary lineup was Professor Headspace, who could gener-
ate force fields and freeze time with his mind (the actor was therefore gan-
gly, intense, and English); Krazy Karl, the comic weapons specialist who
had trouble timing his invisibility; Pretty Boy, the troubled teen heart-
throb who could paralyze enemies with a limpid blink of his startlingly
emerald-green eyes (contact lenses were a must); and Mistress Karinska,
a towering female bodybuilder, almost the size of Sean, recruited from a
Soviet lab, who spoke in quasi-Slavic grunts and relied on her gymnas-
tic spins and leaps, in tandem with her mighty Sword of Destiny, forged
"long ago in the mists of time, atop Olympus itself," and capable of slicing
three oncoming brutes in quick succession, so their upper torsos tumbled
from their lower halves, like neatly diced loaves of rye bread at a bakery.

In an era before DVRs and streaming, viewers would hopefully reserve every Thursday night for *WarForce* at 8 p.m. EST. The show had

also been sold to foreign markets, due to its sparse dialogue and frequent, universally accessible mayhem. The day before the first episode
aired, a network executive, echoed by Archer and Bruce Nadler, Sean's
recently acquired agent/manager, foretold that "your life is about to
change forever."

That night Sean had sat on the rented beige vinyl couch in his anonymous apartment on Van Nuys Boulevard, sipping a Michelob (which
he could now afford at a nearby 7-Eleven), with his left leg jittering, as
he contemplated his future. At Rutgers, the state university, Sean had
majored in Fitness Theory, and he'd thought vaguely about becoming
a sports director at a country club or a junior exec at one of those firms
that recruited major-league and NFL names with an eye to sneaker en-
dorsements, ghostwritten book deals that extolled how to Win Your
Life, and good-natured movie stardom, where the idolized quarterback
or Olympic decathelete would begin by playing the hero's best pal (with
limited dialogue) and segue into leading roles where he saved plummet-
ing airplanes with at least one nun onboard, or the planet itself.

But now Sean wasn't tinkering with a subordinate career, but stardom of his own. He'd always drawn attention, but *WarForce* was a
ticket to a far more explosive acclaim and salary. He was, as he'd told his
buddies back East, "totally psyched" for whatever was cannonballing
toward him, but in private he'd been more daunted, huddled within
the upholstered chassis of his unfamiliar, reconditioned body. Above all
else, Sean liked to be sure of what he was doing, but so many variables
were in play.

Sean's dad had sold time-shares, taught Driver's Ed at a high school,
and was currently working as a local sales rep for an industrial air-
conditioning company. Sean's mom had a solid career as a school nurse,

but she was fearful and often homebound in the years following the collapse of her marriage. Sean loved his parents, but they'd never delivered much guidance and were baffled by what Sean was doing in California. "So you're an actor?" his mom had asked. "Do you know how to do that?" "What're they paying you?" his dad had inquired. "Do you get benefits?" His dad hadn't been curious about the show itself or how Sean had been chosen.

What the fuck am I doing? Sean wondered, steadying his leg on the coffee table, which was pocked with the many previous tenants' cigarette burns and cocaine residue. Sean mulled over investing his paychecks and picking who in his circle he could trust, but gave up within seconds. I'm doing this, he told himself, whatever the fuck it is. He caught his reflection in the mirror over the apartment's tiny wet bar, with its peeling Formica countertop and rusted mini-sink. The shape of his head had altered, his brow thickening—was this permanent? If the show blew up, would he be juicing for years? He approximated his barbaric-yet-playful Blaster scowl—who the fuck was that?

The show was a niche ratings-grabber, with a dependable audience, primarily male, stretching across generations. The cast saluted from the covers of *People* magazine and *TV Guide*, in their red-white-and-blue costumes with winged gold accents, like a cross between a sexier *Holiday on Ice* and a sleeveless collegiate marching band, with Sean encouraged to snarl, flex his biceps to Himalayan effect, and wear a red-white-and-blue sequined headband to tame his luxuriant, blown-dry, highlighted, cascading shag haircut. The blond streaks had been layered in because Sean's naturally dark locks became a dense, pudding-like mass on camera. "This way we can find your hair," the stylist had explained, wrapping selected strands in tinfoil, as the peroxide bubbled.

The network installed a media manager to oversee the show's publicity onslaught. Sean was told to call *WarForce* "a great ride," "a real American family," and "an inspiration to kids everywhere, to always do their best." During a hiatus in filming, the cast was shipped out on a national press junket, getting driven onto the field in golf carts during a Super Bowl halftime, joshing en masse on talk shows, and kneeling beside the hospital beds of children undergoing chemotherapy. Sean was especially good with these kids, who loved placing their tiny hands atop his biceps, and he canvassed them for their thoughts on the show ("I think Blaster should maybe go to the moon and punch an asteroid that's headed for Earth"). He signed stacks of glossy photos of himself with the phrase "Blast off!" but when he'd script his real name fans were puzzled, asking, "Who's Sean Manginaro?"

Sean began having flings with his costars, the cheerleader-perky Sarah, and Tiffany Garnes, the pro wrestler who played Mistress Karinska. Both women had obvious crushes on Sean, and the hookups were linked to the show's success. The cast had bonded, and his nights with Sarah and Tiffany consisted of both vigorous sex and wickedly swapped tidbits about fellow cast members. "Professor Headspace is gay, right?" Sarah was sure. "I mean, he's always calling some guy named Ian in London." "Krazy Karl's been married five times," Tiffany confided. "He says he's thirty-five, but the math doesn't add up. I bet he's forty-eight. Two of his daughters are in college." Sean's bouts with Tiffany had been a technical triumph, as their massive body parts had lumbered to connect. For some reason, as they fucked, Sean kept flashing on those commercials of seat-belted crash test dummies being pounded into brick walls.

On the tour, Sean had been shameless. He'd stretch a skimpy, washed-out T-shirt over his Blaster-ness, add stonewashed jeans and

Frye boots, with the occasional puka shell necklace, and hit the most happening singles joint in whatever town he'd been booked into. Within thirty seconds he'd be offered free pitchers of beer, baskets of pork rinds, crystal meth, weed and ludes, truck drivers' wives, and single women in every medley of denim miniskirt, spaghetti-strap top, breast implants, collagen-pillowed lips, cowboy boots or spike heels, makeup patterned after the glamorized female lifeguards on *Baywatch*, and entirely waxed, plucked, spray-tanned, and aerobicized bodies.

Within the six months after *WarForce* aired, Sean had sex with women named Kaitlin, Kaitlynne, Kateleen, Kayliss, Whitney, Whitley, Windeen, Jasmeen, Debi, Cali, Shalista, Brandee, Amber-Tanya, Lynnbrooke, Brookelynne, and once, in Akron, refreshingly, Amy. Sean had always been, in Stu's words, "a pussy magnet," but he'd become a trophy. Women who weren't quite sure which show he was on, but were positive they'd seen his face somewhere, would corner him in the men's room of a diner. Single moms would shove their motel room keys down his pants, and scrawl their phone numbers on his arm with eyeliner, along with the word "Anything." Twin sisters, in matching crocheted hot pink halter tops, thongs, and Daisy Duke cutoffs, had dragged him willingly back to their condo, furnished with a leather sling, shearling-lined handcuffs, and shelves of the "love lotions" they sold on their website as the Tantric Twins.

Sean's sexual marauding tilted toward the debauched, but he was twenty-five years old and saying no seemed cowardly. He was bodysurfing an ocean of nubile, pre-lubed, equally libidinous women, who, whatever their private daydreams of marriage or even a second date might be, were satisfied with recalling their encounter with that incredibly hot guy from—which show was it? The one with the drug-dealing Malibu surfers or the movie of the week where the detectives went undercover as male strippers? "See, here he is on my phone, with his arm around me! But I mean, I couldn't even get my arms halfway around him!"

The show only ran two seasons, falling victim to budgeting squabbles with the network, a plateauing viewership, and a dullness to the plotting—the show lacked *Star Trek*'s high-minded galactic politics or the epic scope of big-screen sci-fi franchises. Bruce began waiting longer to return Sean's calls. An endorsement deal for a line of "male enhancement" geltabs fell apart, and he started getting scripts for straight-to-video cheapies where he'd play a grim-faced lunkhead harassing the teens at a roller disco.

As Sean dropped into free fall, unsure of everything, and maybe partnering with a guy from Tuscon named Dwayne Eberle on a dubious set of Blastercize workout DVDs, he met Linda Kleinschmidt.

6

CONSULTING PAOLO

When New Yorkers fall in love, they behave like tourists, because everything's ecstatically new. Rob and Jake met for the theater, the ballet, Spielberg movies at uptown cineplexes, and Almodóvar films at those downtown art caverns mobbed with grad student couples where the woman always wore black tights, combat boots, and a knitted Norwegian hat, while her swain hunched in a field jacket and a Strand bookstore T-shirt. Rob and Jake began counting these moody pairs as if they were license plates on a cross-country road trip.

Early couples can cocoon together, deserting longtime friends, but New Yorkers test-market their infatuations. "Jake is effortlessly cool," Rob told Paolo at a gay restaurant in Chelsea, meaning a place that clamored to overcrowded life at Sunday brunch as a cruising and scuttlebut hub. As Paolo once said, "It's gay high school where the cliques snipe at each other's nipples and fabric-softened lumberjack-plaid flannel shirts. I love places that aren't inherently gay but get marked by their clientele: it's like having a gay public library or a gay post office."

Rob had met Paolo in college, in a seminar that covered Shakespeare on film. Rob had been taken with Paolo's zealous defense of a thirty-four-year-old Norma Shearer's MGM Juliet ("You have to love Norma because she's trying so hard, and because her eyes are slightly crossed"). Paolo had been thrilled that Rob, a senior to Paolo's freshman, was the only other person in the class who'd ever heard of Norma Shearer.

Paolo was the blissfully pampered only child of a Dallas Jewish family. His father owned a string of Porsche dealerships while his mom ran Estelle's Enchantments, a shop selling oversize papier-mâché lilies, filigreed antique perfume bottles, porcelain-paneled Austrian music boxes, and other hugely unnecessary tchotchkes. Paolo had told Rob, "I think my mother would've named me Tchotchke, but she chose Paolo because I'd been conceived during a cruise to Turks and Caicos where she'd mooned over a handsome maître d' on board named Paolo. Basically my mom was trying to guarantee she'd have a gay child."

After toying with medical school, a prospect "way too upsetting," Paolo had become, to his epic mortification, a dentist. "It's always the moment I dread," he'd confided, "when I meet someone new, and I have to say it. And I can see that look in their eyes, when they're thinking about either how gross it is to reach into other people's mouths, or they're about to ask me for a discount." Paolo was tallish and well-shouldered, and repeatedly tinkered with his facial hair, because "My goal is to never look like a dentist." Paolo was in fact that phenomenon he'd cited, like a gay bowling alley or a gay car wash: "I'll just say it. I'm a gay dentist."

Paolo was highly skilled at his job, to the point where he'd peer critically at Rob's teeth during conversation and comment, "No one else would even notice, but you need to start thinking about those tiny moments of tartar." Paolo was the go-to dentist for much of gay Chelsea, and he dreamt that this population classified him as "the hot dentist." Rob loved Paolo because he was smart, willing to laugh at his own foibles, and a companion in mapping gay Manhattan. Paolo's frequent neurotic frenzies ("Would spelling it 'dentiste' make me sound more exotic?") made Rob feel of use as a sounding board, and less deranged in comparison. Paolo was most often between boyfriends and willing to decrypt Rob's romances in high-school-girls'-room detail.

"So when do I get to meet Ultimate Jake?" Paolo pressed, while ignoring his salad. As with marketable debutantes everywhere, the clientele at gay bistros was forever dieting, especially as swimwear season on Fire Island or in Provincetown loomed. Jake once suggested that the ultimate gay watering hole would serve only pre-nibbled chickpeas and tiny ramekins holding a single Valium.

"Soon," Rob promised. "We're still in our bubble. Of course I've told him all about you, but I was embarrassed about the dentist thing so I told him you were a mortician."

"But a hot mortician?"

"Of course. But last night while we were in bed, you know, afterwards, he told me something major. We've been seeing each other for a month so he said I deserved to know the details, because he'd never want me to think he was hiding something."

"Okay. He has kids from a tormented early marriage. He's going on trial for a decorating crime, like using track lighting, again. He killed a man at the IKEA outlet, over a discontinued coffee table, because Jake had seen it first. That's not a crime. Oh my God. Wait. Is he a Republican? Just say it."

"None of the above."

What Jake had opened up about was the span of his three years with Hastings. "It started maybe six years ago," he'd told Rob over coffee when they were both in T-shirts and underwear at Jake's loft. "I met him at a gallery opening, where I was looking at art for a client. I'd heard about Hastings's work—he was Hastings Krell, and he swore that his North Carolina waitress mom named him after a frozen dinner. He painted trailer parks and truck stops, but in these Jordan Almond pastels, so they looked like Barbie locations. They were his way of refusing to be official white trash, bleak and downtrodden. He'd say, 'I'm hot-pink and powder-blue trash.'

"He was younger than me, which I'd usually hate, but he was buoyant and I liked that he'd never reel off his grant application bullshit about his vision and his creative journey. He had long hair, which I refused to let him wear in a bun, and this sexy ferret face. He'd tease me about my being what he called 'a fabric-swatches-and-tassels queen,' and we started hanging out. It was unlikely but fun, and he started staying here a lot because his studio space was out in some godforsaken and not yet even quasi-hip corner of Queens. I can't say he was the love of my life, and I'm sure he'd say the same, but he'd take me to East Village performance art in people's apartments and I'd drag him to see plays about rich white families feuding over who got the place on Nantucket after Nana died.

"And then he got sick. I'm sure you know the drill. But he was twenty-six. And I guess—it was all so beyond unfair, the way everything was. I was determined to be with him and stop him from becoming another abandoned gay guy—his mom would take the bus up, and she was a genuinely kind person, but she had trouble coping. And for the first few months he was okay, but this was pre-cocktail, and pre-everything, so when things began to snowball it was just . . ."

Rob almost took Jake's hand or rubbed his shoulders, but Jake wasn't asking for that. Life in those years had been tragically surreal, so both men took a deep breath, and Jake said, "He'd have a few good months and then go back into the hospital. He couldn't keep any weight on. He broke his arm tripping over a cardboard box in his studio. That was all he wanted to do—keep painting. He didn't change his candy-box style, just the subject matter. He painted skeletal AIDS patients, with oxygen masks, as if they were a tray of Christmas cookies. He did a series of protest marches, which looked like bachelorette parties until you'd see the rage on everyone's face and the 'Silence=Death' placards, in rainbow glitter."

Jake had a few of these pictures on his laptop, and he brought a canvas out of a tiny side room. It was a portrait of Jake and Hastings, in such sunshiney tones that they came off like the cohosts of a gay Saturday morning children's show. Rob didn't comment because he couldn't; the cheeriness of the image was heartbreaking, a dying man's yummily upbeat middle finger to the universe, a repudiation of any doom-laden playbook. Rob and Jake both had tears in their eyes, and Rob got why Jake didn't display this image more prominently. It was too gut-wrenching for daily consumption.

"By the time he died, he was blind and incoherent; he didn't recognize anyone. The last time I saw him, in the hospital, I think there was a flicker, because he blew me a kiss. After he died, I took a month off, both to mourn him specifically, more as a dear friend than a lover, and to just . . . to right myself, to figure out how to bathe and smile and leave the house and look at moldings and curtain rods. And like all of us, I found a way. Maybe Hastings's paintings inspired me, because he never gave up. This may be an awful thing to say, but AIDS, or any especially hideous illness, is an assault on personality. Someone's basic nature can get buried or blanked out, which can be the greatest loss: not just that person's physical well-being, but their essence. And that's why I cherish these paintings, because they're the most pure reflection of Hastings.

"So I didn't go out or see anyone or have sex for a year after that, to simplify everything. But since I've met you, well, I don't want to burden us with mammoth expectations and the fate of gay people everywhere, and the feasibility of romance in our times, but—I'm so glad you're here. And I have so many fabric swatches to show you."

They were quiet for the next few minutes, finishing their coffee and silently corroborating that their mutual attraction had progressed a step forward, and gone deeper, and that they were both happy about that. Rob also sensed something else, that Jake had provided an ethical guide, a glimpse at his highest and most dearly held values, meaning those he'd arrived at through personal experience, rather than his family's Bible-fondling.

"So Jake is a good guy," Paolo concluded. "And not just someone who stares at your outfit and says 'No, it's fine, really' but by that point you're already changing into something else."

"He's both," said Rob. "He's sort of a self-aware aristocrat, who'd gleefully sign a petition calling for his own beheading."

"You really like him, don't you?"

"Um . . . yeah."

"Uh-oh."

Then they squealed together, both ironically and not, which was how Rob and Paolo responded to sincere emotional territory. Rob knew he should protect himself, but it was already too late.

7

LINDA KLEINSCHMIDT

W ho's Linda marrying?" Rob asked Sean, at the gym. Rob was still flattened by his own upheaval at the office, but he knew Sean was deeply distraught.

"She's marrying some rich dude, that guy, Trone Meston."

"She's marrying *Trone Meston*?" said Rob, in boldface-name disbelief. Trone Meston was beyond a brand or a CEO. He'd founded TroneTek, one of the most staggeringly successful start-ups in history, attaining the stature of Ford, Apple, or Disney. TronePhones and TroneBooks weren't merely ubiquitous; they'd revolutionized how the world communicated, sorted information, and consumed everything, from checking in on pets using a video feed, to live streaming of people unboxing limited editions of hotly desired sneakers. Trone Meston was a near-mythical recluse, surfacing only to herald his next zeitgeist-shattering product, which within seconds became a waiting-listed purchase for any sentient individual. Trone's vaguest utterances were enshrined and parsed and repeated by terminally affectless teenagers and Wall Street honchos alike.

"Did you know they were involved? How did she meet him? How long has this been happening?"

"I don't know, my kids clued me in two days ago that something was up. And she just sent me an evite to the wedding. It's on an island in Maine or someplace, they only just announced it. I just . . . I'm having a problem with this."

Linda and Sean had been married for nineteen years and divorced for three. Linda was the love of Sean's life, and the one loss he stubbornly couldn't admit or even process in any meaningful way. He talked about Linda incessantly, referring to her as "my lovely ex-bride," "the ex Mrs. Manginaro," "the beautiful Linda," and "that stupid fucking twat." Sean was the only person Rob had ever met who could utter that last phrase with the purest tenderness, and the subtext "but she's *my* stupid fucking twat."

When Rob and Sean had begun training together, Sean had only just married Linda, whom he'd introduced to Rob and Jake over drinks, after getting back from his honeymoon in Cancun. The guys, like Sean, had been readily smitten with Linda, because the first thing she'd asked them was "Sean's gay, right?" "Totally," Rob had verified, while Jake had confirmed, "He's so gay we voted him out. All the gay people said, no. Too gay. Throw him back." This exchange had occurred in front of Sean, who'd loved it, because it meant his bride and his friends had connected through a malicious sense of humor, aimed at Sean. Sean lived for bringing people together, and this was an especially jubilant group. "I knew you'd like her," he told the guys, "and she's so hot, right?"

"*What is wrong with you?*" Linda, Rob, and Jake asked Sean, with simultaneous scorn, which had tickled Sean so much he hugged Jake, who scolded, "Stop mo-ing me."

Jake had overheard a teenage boy use this phrase, an abbreviation of "homo," on the subway, to a friend who was sitting too close. Jake had lectured these juveniles on Stonewall and the legacy of Harvey Milk, but once he'd shared this anecdote with Rob, Sean, and Paolo, they'd all gleefully started using the expression; in bed one night, Linda had instructed Sean to stop mo-ing her.

Physically, Linda was, as Sean had told Rob earlier, "Like my total fucking ideal, like if God gave me a menu. The first time I saw her, when she was a flight attendant on Delta, I couldn't believe it. I thought it was a joke or some reality show thing, where the producers had done a worldwide search for my dream girl and pretended she was working the red-eye from LA to JFK. At first I couldn't even talk, and picture that happening, but I just wanted to tell her, 'Are you fucking kidding me?'"

Linda was that rare fusion: a hard-headed Long Island native with the sculpted face of a 1940s screen goddess, a Grace Kelly or Audrey Hepburn with a wad of Nicorette always lodged in the back of her mouth. She talked straight and tough, but the effect was uncanny, as if the sleek, blond, aerodynamically cheekboned heroine of a Hitchcock film were telling the cashier at Wendy's, "I love this Chocolate Frosty so much, I would do its fucking laundry."

Linda was the offspring of a negligent, often incarcerated father, who'd overdosed when she was eight, and a free-spirited pothead mom, who was sporadically employed as a social worker at a prison, both out of a goodhearted nature and because she had a thing for heavily tattooed psychopaths (Aileen and Royce, Linda's dad, had met when she'd helped him fill out his parole application). Linda had raised herself while coming to terms with her face and its effect on the men who would stare goggle-eyed at her on the street, like dumbstruck, drooling farm animals. Linda had been sparking this response since childhood, and she balanced a justified cynicism with a cautiously hidden but powerfully romantic checklist.

Linda's strengths were inarguable: she could make men whimper, pay for numerous meals and tropical weekends, beg her to just turn around slowly, marry them, loan them her used underwear, or let them buy her a condo in Jersey City unbeknownst to their spouses. Linda would listen to these heaving entreaties, barely paying attention, and she'd reply, "I don't think so."

Linda didn't count her face as a curse or a burden. She'd been approached about modeling, but at barely five-foot-three she'd have been exiled to junior petites catalogue work. Her looks were an asset and a skill, so she avoided the sun, moisturized, ran, and kept her blunt-cut shoulder-length hair a radiant blond, nixing trampier extensions or agonizingly tousled centerfold ringlets. Linda wouldn't deny being beautiful, but she didn't trust it. Her earthiness was more primary, for subverting anorexia or a lack of female friends. Still, those BFFs vied to snap selfies with their gorgeous comrade, although they never posted these photos on their dating profiles, for fear of being inundated with requests for whoa-who's-the-hot-blonde-standing-next-to-you?

Linda's beauty made her wry and guarded, also techniques for disguising her Cinderella daydreams. After years spent in mildewed ground-floor apartments with blackout curtains, cluttered long-term motel rooms near tunnel entrances, and more than one corroding mobile home lacking heat and running water, Linda fetishized normalcy, the shiniest, most tranquil, and even suburban domesticity. She mood-boarded a life without eviction notices taped to screen doors off their hinges, handguns tucked inside cereal boxes, and lecherously drunken boyfriends introduced as "Your new Uncle Stevie, no, hold on, your new Uncle Neil, fuck it, just call him whatever you want."

Linda wouldn't gripe about her childhood, as the memories stayed raw and were best avoided. But she'd recognize her damage in other adult off-spring of parents who'd not only vanished for months at a time, but who'd returned strung out on God-knew-what, sleeping for days and awakening only to croakingly bemoan the sunlight and ask their eight-year-old kid if he or she had a fake ID so they could buy bourbon. Linda hadn't hated her helplessly addled mother, but she could sense a grim defensiveness in herself, a legacy of trying to study for a seventh-grade geometry quiz in an emergency room, seated on a rickety folding chair while Aileen was having her stomach pumped, again. That was how Linda connected with other lifelong caretakers: they always called their endlessly needy, vacant-eyed parents by their first names, because those parents were never a mom or a dad.

Linda had enrolled in junior college, earning a Marketing degree accompanied by an instantly regretted first marriage to a fiendishly sexy guy named, among other things, Andros McKay. She'd met Andros at a club and sat beside him in the Maserati he drove at over eighty miles an hour to his forbiddingly ultra-modern beachfront retreat in Montauk. Andros had claimed to be an importer (of what?), and Linda had begun waking up beneath a sable bedspread in a Tribeca penthouse with a killer view of at least three major bridges.

Linda was twenty-three and had temporarily lost her mind and, more critically, the bedrock decency that ordinarily motivated her and assured her she was nothing like Aileen. But Andros had deluged her with a chartered flight to Paris, diamond earrings, a splurge at Barneys (where the price tags and museum-like displays of handbags had pre-viously intimidated her), and his unswerving worship: "You are my

American beauty," he'd murmured in his unplaceable accent. "I'll give you anything you want, because it will make me so happy." It didn't hurt that Andros had the lithe bearing of the Alpine skiing instructor he'd been as a teenager (according to him), and that he was astonishingly gallant in bed. Linda became the innocent yet tempestuous heroine of an airport bestseller where Molly or Kate or Megan, the hyper-efficient creative director of a cosmetics company, is always being whisked off by the king of an invented country like Cartovia or Mont St. Martelle.

Linda had gambled, because how often would such a dashing entrepreneur (another title Andros had bestowed upon himself), with the habit of wearing almost unbuttoned black silk shirts, over a caramel tan from Aspen, come along? She'd never questioned Andros's wealth or hinted-at royal pedigree (he'd referenced "my cousin Milo, the Archduke"), as both were simmering ingredients of his Euro-spell. After her early years of deprivation and using brown paper shopping bags from the supermarket as luggage, Linda had surrendered, to marble bathrooms the size of all the places she'd ever lived in, combined.

When Andros was exposed as Andy Schlatt of Oklahoma City, with warrants out for coke dealing and embezzlement, and he'd hightailed it with the earrings, Cartier tennis bracelet, and sapphire-studded Piaget timepiece he'd lavished on Linda, the shock, subsequent FBI investigation, and, even worse, the public embarrassment at having been so naïve confirmed all of Linda's most conservative inclinations: men were lying dogs, every designer item was a grenade, sex was a dangerous distraction, and she had only herself to blame. Training as a flight attendant promised escape, from Aileen's random, alternately sobbing and screeching calls, and her own horrendous choices, plus she might spot Andros/Andy on the shuttle to Boston, maybe concealed behind plastic surgery. Rather than confronting him, she'd quietly alert federal agents on the ground, and chuckle as they boarded the plane with shackles and their pistols drawn.

Linda's in-flight career had been a respite, a handy blur before choosing a more viable future. She hadn't quite lived anywhere, and her friends were other flight attendants who'd head off for weeks at a time and then rendezvous for a wine-bar Friday night in Omaha or a Disney World–spa weekend in Orlando. Linda was great at her job, because she could be gracious and helpful and temporary, her smile both warm and professional. Aside from turbulence, an unlikely midair collision, or a soused, readily deflected passenger, nothing could touch or harm her, and her detour with Andros/Andy was left behind and below, as a rookie mistake. She was, often literally, in a decently compensated holding pattern.

But when she came across Sean, in an aisle seat in Business Class, her face froze. Because much like Sean, Linda had a type, a weakness for cleft-chinned, clear-eyed, almost cartoonishly handsome guys. As Rob later educated Sean, "Linda thinks like a gay man." Linda was helplessly aroused by fictional Prince Charmings, soap opera hunks with towels knotted around their narrow waists, and bomber-jacketed big-screen fighter pilots (not so much the actual middle-aged, golf-addicted dads she dealt with in the cockpits).

Sean had of course noticed Linda while boarding, but shunned eye contact. He'd allotted time to think, to hash out a foolproof game plan. He saw a wolfish businessman "accidentally" brushing his loutish hand against Linda's ass, until whatever she told him caused the blood to drain from his blotchy face, followed by a dad shushing his squabbling toddlers while gaping at Linda as she chatted with a grandmother telling her how pretty she was, "like a movie star."

Sean felt physically wounded, as if Linda had hurled an unopened can of soda at his chest. He'd never fallen in love before, so he couldn't comprehend the sensation, attributing his weakness and difficulty breathing to cabin pressure. But he had to do something. He couldn't exit the plane without not just Linda's cell number but an honest connection, convincing Linda he wasn't another of the thousand airborne douchebags she'd already pertly greeted and secretly loathed.

He waited, leafing through his fitness magazine. He requested nothing. Linda approached, checking her passenger manifest.

"Mr. Manginaro?" she said.

Sean smiled, and Linda stifled a gasp. Sean's smile was generous and winning, not some dopey frat boy come-on. She hadn't watched his TV show, but his comfortably masculine self-reliance thawed her most vulnerable and therefore to-be-resisted longings. She almost opted for asking Carol, her coworker, to cover this aisle. Except she'd rather die. She smiled back at Sean, at first briskly, but then a more lifelike and gleeful grin broke through. "What can I get you?"

"I'm good," said Sean. "But thank you."

They didn't speak for the remainder of the flight, but after they'd touched down at JFK, as Linda stood by the hatch, Sean told her, "I'll totally understand if you say no, but I'd love to see you again." This sounded, as Sean's brain was telling him, "super gay," but Sean couldn't toss off "Would you like to grab coffee" or "How about dinner." He couldn't go generic, like a leering jerk-on-the-prowl.

Linda had already jotted her number on a paper cocktail napkin, which she shoved into the breast pocket of Sean's shirt, a move she'd sworn she'd never get anywhere near, not after Andros/Andy.

"Thank you for flying Delta," she told Sean, which, as he recounted to Rob years later, "made me shoot fucking squigglies in my pants."

8

TREMBLE WOODSPILL

W hen Tremble opened her eyes, she stayed very still, because she wasn't clear on her location. She'd learned that before climbing out of a stranger's bed, off their couch, or from beneath their kitchen table, she should get her bearings and excavate her clothing, her hunting knife, and the Dora the Explorer backpack she'd pounced on at a thrift store. Dora was also her muse, as an audacious and inquisitive, well, seven-year-old Latina explorer, whose adventures had her freeing a captured mermaid and foiling a wily fox.

The room was dark, with sunlight leaking in beneath a pillowcase duct-taped to cover a square window-like opening with ragged metal edges. Okay, Tremble surmised, I think I just got wasted and had a threeway with one of my exes and either his brother or his cousin. If she had in fact slept with Howey Breenaster, both were possible. But she was definitely at Howey's place, because it was a shipping container, which had been loaded onto a flatbed truck and then deposited in the woods near a clearing where a satanic ritual had taken place years earlier and bodies had been found. No one had ever solved why the bodies had been missing thumbs and wearing conical birthday party hats. Howey had settled on this spot for his recycled home because, as he'd told Tremble, "Like, what are the chances of another satanic ritual slaughter in the same place, right? So I figure I'm good."

As Tremble recalled why she'd gotten drunk and had sex with Howey and his extended family, her rage came thundering back. Yesterday someone named Arjun had texted her, relaying that her New York editor, Rob Barnett, had left Welstrom & Stratters and would no longer be in contact. Tremble adored Rob, because he'd read her blog posts and called her directly, announcing, "You are my new favorite writer in the entire world. Who are you and why aren't you famous already?"

Tremble was twenty-three, but she'd been dreaming of becoming a writer since pretty much forever. But in Jacksburg, Arkansas, this was despairingly unlikely, and she'd never told anyone of her ambition, except her best friend Randall, because everyone else would either zone out or say something belittling, like "Who the fuck do you think you are?" Even in school, before she'd dropped out of tenth grade, thanks to extended absences and flicking cigarette butts at more than one teacher, she'd known better than to even hint at passing along one of the poems or short stories scribbled on her yellow legal pads. These pads were housed in her backpack, which never left her sight. She'd kept her insatiable reading, of everyone from Toni Morrison to Elmore Leonard to Alison Bechdel, under wraps as well. She wasn't scared of being scoffed at, as an egghead or a snooty-ass white-girl wannabe, but talking about her work and her favorite writers might diminish everything, and even Randall knew enough not to ask nosey questions. Writing was sacred to Tremble, and until that first contact with Rob, she'd prayed alone in her church. Her blog, also titled *Life as We Fucking Know It*, with a few hundred hits, had been a tentative bid at going public, and risking a fearful exposure.

But now—what the fuck was happening? Would her book deal be canceled? Would she have to work with a different editor, someone stupid or with a telephone pole up their ass or just not Rob? The prospect of getting published had floored and terrified Tremble, because it might be a mirage, or she'd do something to annoy Rob and her contract would be revoked, and she'd regret ever becoming so hopeful and spending hours in a far corner of the public library, memorizing Rob's editorial notes on her ten-year-old TroneTek laptop, a relic held together with thick rubber bands. Tremble loved writing because of its privacy and daring, and because after a childhood in foster care, the pages were hers alone.

Rob expressed his edits as suggestions, never absolute commands. Rob wasn't just Tremble's editor but her first reader, so he occupied a berth somewhere between Santa and the Wizard of Oz. Tremble hadn't met Rob in person so far, which seemed right. They could speak more directly online and occasionally via Zoom. Tremble wasn't quite ready for Rob in three dimensions. His standing-right-there-in-front-of-her reality might make her burst into tiny scraps of lined yellow pages, fluttering into the sky from joy and doubt.

But yesterday afternoon, upon scanning that unwelcome text, Tremble, rather than calling Rob (she had his cell number), had done what she tended to do under stress: she'd shoplifted a bottle of hard lemonade (a daytime favorite), smoked the rest of the weed stored in a Pringles can (at Randall's house, where she was currently crashing, while he finished rehab), and walked two miles to Wally's Pork Pit, a truck stop and roadhouse near the highway, and hooked up with Howey and whatever buddy or relative was serving as a lookout on a drug deal.

Which was boneheaded, Tremble admitted to herself, sitting up on
the mattress shoved against a rusted wall of the shipping container. She
needed to find Rob Barnett and fucking shake the truth out of him,
only she'd never been within five states of New York City, so she wasn't
sure how to go about this, but she vowed: if I can't get ahold of Rob, I'm
gonna kill someone at random. No, she scolded herself, don't do that,
because then you sure as shit won't get your book published. But she
wasn't ruling out killing anyone who got between her and Rob Barnett.

9

LINDA AND SEAN

Linda's last bridal shower, held at an airport lounge a week before her marriage to Sean, had been haphazard and jolly, with a guest list of fellow flight attendants, college roommates, and Aileen, her mother, who'd somehow managed to show up quasi-sober and given Linda a six-pack of Budweiser, nestled in heavily Scotch-taped, reused Christmas wrapping paper. The gift table was stacked with edible crotchless panties, a cardboard cylinder containing a poster of Linda's high school crush (a boy band "rebel" wearing a leather motorcycle jacket over his shirtless, waxed chest), a waggling neon-blue dildo (intended to be the ceremony's traditional "something blue"), a magenta feather boa, and rhinestoned plastic tiaras for everyone.

The party had been lighthearted and allayed Linda's foreboding about Sean. She loved him dearly. He was undeniably gorgeous, he made her laugh (often by being deliberately idiotic), he'd charmed her friends (by taking an interest in their lives and workout routines), and unlike so many guys she'd met, he was fanatically motivated. She'd watched reruns of *WarForce*, and he'd mockingly sent her photos of his bodybuilding competitions (in which he'd been grotesquely stained orange and clad in postage stamp–sized "posing straps," while flexing, pointing dramatically skyward, and body-oiling fellow competitors). Sean was, above all, gregarious. He wanted the whole world to have a great time, and his devout optimism was an ideal foil for Linda's militant caution. He'd taken her whitewater rafting, skydiving, and Jet Skiing, securing her lifejackets and body harnesses, and making ferocious love afterward. Linda had never met anyone so entirely physical as Sean, and his bear-hugs, massages, and fifty-mile countryside bike rides had taken some getting used to, but could be exhilarating and wonderfully goofy—Sean often demonstrated that he could bench-press Linda.

Sean was unswervingly dedicated to starting his own business, opening Defiance as an early contender in the nascent boutique fitness industry. The gym had already transferred from a dank, narrow, windowless basement to half an upper floor. Sean was fascinated by how money could be raised and invested, he did his fiscal homework, and unlike with Andros/ Andy, his backers were real and aboveboard. He had told Linda, "I want to be a millionaire, at least on paper, by thirty and then keep going." After six months of dating, Linda had moved into Sean's studio apartment a few blocks from the gym, but they yearned for more square footage and even some outdoor space, maybe somewhere beyond the city.

Sean's solidity soothed Linda and led her toward safety, far from the vending-machine-breakfast, five-schools-in-three-years havoc of her childhood. But her qualms were hardwired: Did Sean, or any guy on Earth, really pine for becoming a husband, or was this a choke chain and a capitulation, a pussy-whipped descent from raucous bachelor freedom? But when Sean had proposed, after midnight sex and champagne at his deserted gym, he said, "I'll tell you the truth, I've never thought about getting married, I mean, that was like something our parents did. And everybody I'm related to is divorced like, a lot. But when I think about seeing you with any other dude, or about you just walking around with every guy hitting on you, it kills me, it fucking rips my guts out. I mean, I don't just love you, although I sure as fuck do, I LOVE YOU. I love everything about you, even when you smack me for talking about your perfect ass. I love when you tuck your hair behind your ears and how you can get babies on cross-country flights to stop crying and how sometimes I catch you looking at me and I can tell you're thinking, He's such a moron, but then you smile and I fall apart, but you know, in a guy way. I want to make you so happy that you actually start to believe in happiness, and when I see all those dickheads sending you drinks and telling you about their expense accounts, I'm gonna tell 'em sorry, asswipes, she's taken. She's fucking *mine*. And yeah, I know that kinda makes me a caveman or a stalker or whatever, but I'm so damn cute. And I also love that you put up with my bullshit and you get that some of it's real and that I'm trying to be better, and that Defiance is for you, and for us, because, oh shit, now I'm gonna start crying like a chick, but when I look at you I fucking tell myself, Be worthy of her. Make her smile every day. Don't fuck this up . . ."

Then he dropped the wiseass chatter and, shockingly, had tears in his eyes. Linda was a sucker for a great-looking guy being overcome by emotion, and not being able to handle it. Sean in tears meant he cherished Linda, because he didn't just want to fuck her. She had more power than that. She could transform him into a blubbering wreck, and if that wasn't love, love didn't exist. Most of all, more than anyone she'd ever known, Sean almost convinced Linda that love was every bit as amazing as it was supposed to be, that love could quiet her childhood disarray, her adult blunders, and her not-unfounded suspicion that the overall

concept of love was primarily a sighing female fantasy, of being appreciated and becoming a family with someone and not having to keep dieting so strenuously, and that love was also a last-ditch ploy men resorted
to, as a final Hail Mary, most often in exchange for the sex that would
ultimately bore them. Sean opened a small velvet box with a not-half-
bad diamond ring, like the one Linda had casually circled in a fashion
magazine ad, pretending to want Sean's opinion (they'd both applauded
her shamelessness).

"Will you marry me?" Sean had asked, naked and down on one knee
(his own breed of shamelessness—Sean always felt better naked). Linda
had been hopelessly embarrassed and wildly elated, first answering, "I
guess so," then looking into Sean's eyes, an intimacy which frightened
her, for a sincere "Yes," and finishing with a heartfelt "Did my saying yes
just give you a hard-on?"

But now, three years since their extremely combative divorce, Linda
was amid a very different bridal shower, on the spacious top floor of a San
Francisco Victorian whose windows had been expanded at great cost for a
panoramic view of the Presidio, the Golden Gate Bridge, and the Pacific
Ocean. The guests included Jennifer Aniston, the vice president's wife,
the female CEO of a booming shapewear firm, and Oprah Winfrey, all
in deference to Trone Meston, whom Linda had met while earning extra
cash by subbing as a member of the flight crew on Trone's private jet.

Trone was the third-richest person in America, a ranking that he
never bothered contesting, telling Linda, "Once you're in the Top Ten,
does it really matter how big your dick is?" Linda loved Trone, which
surprised her. She hadn't been looking, but Trone was as far from Sean as
she could get. Although she couldn't fathom why, with only three days
to go, she'd sent Sean that evite to the wedding.

10

LOVE AND LITERATURE

Rob often pondered why romantic happiness was a limited topic in literature. In the most critically hosannaed, Booker Prize–awarded novels, adult characters rarely fell in love, but engaged in drunken, unsatisfying sex to self-medicate amid gazing-out-on-the-Welsh-marshlands loneliness or Easthampton writer's block. Marriages were the refuge of embittered enemies, chortling over the children they'd ruined. "Romance" was a niche domain, a flourishing and far more lucrative aisle of the publishing supermarket. Lovers scampering rosy-cheeked through a flower-bedecked chapel were for chamomile-engorged cat owners and substitute teachers paging furiously through bodice-ripper-of-the-month paperbacks, or the latest Jane Austen redo, in which the flinty heroine is now a fiercely unmarried executive assistant resisting her tousled, divorced soccer dad of a boss. Unlike many editors, especially Rob's mentor Susannah, who'd dismissed them as "suckers," Rob devoutly respected romance readers: they were braver. If insane. Because maybe an everyday penchant for the more Technicolor regions of true love was a mental illness to be treated with clanking metaphors and book jackets with bare-chested, flowing-locked hunks, their paramours draped in their rugged arms like off-season overcoats.

After seven months of sinfully rewarding, often weekend-long dates, swathed in the cotton candy cloud and good manners of infatuation, Rob and Jake had dared a nightmarish test of their ardor: they would travel together. Rob had an upcoming book fair in London, where he'd promote W&S titles and look for new acquisitions, while Jake could source antiques at the London shops.

"Are you truly ready?" Beatrice, Jake's work-wife, asked Jake, over lunch at their desks at Crawbell & Company. Mr. Crawbell allocated an exact thirty-five minutes for this meal, with "no odors, crumbs, or plastic debris." Which was fine with Beatrice, who was Jake's age but with the frostiness and aplomb of a dowager dryly outraged by horseless carriages.

Beatrice had been raised in Parsippany, New Jersey, and attended public schools, but had reinvented herself as a perpetually disappointed distant-royal-relation making do in a Kensington bedsit. Beatrice, born Tiffaneigh-Carla, never disowned her tristate history, but since childhood she had swooned over silk scarves printed with horse bits and stirrups, fine leather goods, teabags in Wedgwood canisters, any BBC show with liveried footmen, arcane spellings of colour and honour, and the needless use of a Malacca cane.

"I visited Los Angeles for an overnight with my first serious entanglement," Beatrice confided, in not a full-on Mayfair accent but something decidedly not Parsippany. "I adored him, but he wore—what are those woeful garments? Sweatpants. Just so. He wore sweatpants on the plane. I asked him if he'd broken his ankle or if thieves had stolen his trousers, but he replied no, he merely desired comfort. Comfort—can you imagine?

"Then, at our hotel, he commandeered my side of the bed, and arrayed his toiletries across the entire countertop in the loo. He monopolized the mini-bar and every hanger. He placed muffins from the complimentary breakfast in his pockets and towels in his valise. When a chambermaid came upon him with his throat cut, I was never charged."

Some of this was accurate, but Jake had one request: "Say it again. Say 'loo.'"

"Loo," Beatrice repeated, with a verbal caress. "If I have children I shall christen them Loo, Lorry, and Flat."

Beatrice half-smiled at her own genteel lunacy and then, with Parsippany candor, told Jake, "Don't do it. You're still in that honeymoon, everything-he-does-is-incredible phase, you don't need to see what he leaves in the shower drain."

"You've met Rob," Jake countered. "You thought he was wonderful, or as you put it, 'I appreciate your affection.' We can't stay in New York forever. And you love London, don't you?"

"More than my own existence. Although I've never been."

Jake wasn't surprised by this admission, as Beatrice's Britishness was wholly concocted, as a collage of Regency footstools and sensible dresses in Liberty of London prints. Beatrice slavered over England to such a degree that any real-life contact would only be a crushing comedown. Still, Jake, who'd only spent brief amounts of time in London as a student, jotted down all of Beatrice's recommendations for hotels off Piccadilly, the annual Chelsea garden show, and shops that sold "the Continent's most durable brollies." When asked what she'd like as a souvenir, Beatrice had grown misty and requested that "A commemorative Jubilee cup and saucer would be lovely."

Jake was decisive about his and Rob's compatibility. He dominated Rob's willing, shuddering body, and admired Rob's reverence for books and his gift for cultivating new and even controversial talent. Jake wasn't taking Rob for granted, but he'd meet him in a lobby or on the street and think, Of course. Jake could glance at an ottoman, a Velázquez, a peony, or a human being, and unhesitatingly absorb their value and significance. Done.

Jake favored airports for their cinematic impersonality, so he traveled as an elegant spy, in a black turtleneck, black jeans, and a tan raincoat. His luggage was leather and silver and never wheeled. Wheeled luggage, Jake knew, foretold the collapse of civilization. A person's luggage was an expression of practical style, not a pet on a leash.

As he waited in the terminal, with his carry-on at his feet, Jake saw Rob heading toward him, in his publishing drag of a fitted tweed blazer, jeans, and a crisp white shirt. Rob had a leather duffel on a strap over his shoulder, a choice which gave Jake a spasm of almost sexual bliss. Jake stood and kissed him. For gay couples, a public smooch is a choice and a political statement. Jake hoped they'd outraged any nearby evangelicals.

Once they were in the air, Rob scrolled through manuscripts on his laptop while Jake perused *Architectural Digest*, his trade publication, like *Modern Thresher* or *Gastrointestinal Digest* for people who care deeply about side tables, although, as he'd told Rob, "No one reads shelter magazines. You visit them." Rob glanced up, and then Jake. They smiled. They were like astronauts on board a space capsule, hurtling through the early stages of love.

Things got dicey in the hotel lobby, when the desk clerk couldn't bring up their reservation on his screen. Jake went chilly ("Check again, please") while Rob was overly solicitous ("It's fine, take your time, I probably fucked up"). Matters were remedied, but in the elevator Jake commented, "Everyone doesn't have to like you," to which Rob responded, with a grin, "Yes they do."

In the suite, both men were fiendishly well behaved, each exhorting the other to choose bureau drawers and any adjustment of the thermostat. They jostled in the bathroom, Jake hanging his mesh grooming tote on the door while Rob unpacked his shaving kit. Then they flopped on the bed, where Jake noted, "You have your shoes on the bed. On. The. Bed." Rob replied, "I should be deported," as he shucked his loafers.

Over the following days they became less deferential. Jake had no interest in seeing *Troilus and Cressida*, no matter what up-and-coming English firebrand was naked in it. Rob went numb after thirty minutes of museum-going, especially with grayish Regency engravings. Jake had given Rob explicit directions to a restaurant, but Rob lingered somewhere else, at a pub with a similar name, and it took an hour on their phones to reconnoiter. Rob described every foreign rights rep he met at his book fair, while Jake became irrationally incensed after not buying an overpriced onyx bust of Apollo for a client.

Finally, Rob spent over an hour on a business call, causing the couple to miss the first three trains to the garden at Wisley, a horticultural landmark an hour outside the city, even though Jake had emphasized, more than once, that the wisteria might only be blooming for a few more hours. "It happens once a year!" he exclaimed, not hiding his ire. "It's fucking *wisteria*!" said Rob, more out of exasperation with the German publisher haranguing him.

Jake glared at Rob, rethinking everything: Who was this slovenly business geek, who still hadn't shaved? Rob fumed, loathing Germans, all languages he didn't speak, gay men, and Jake. Then they both burst out laughing, as Jake gasped, "I don't think I can ever love you! Not after what you just said about wisteria!"

They paused, both giddy and chastened, because they'd just had their first fight and this was also the first time either of them had used the word "love," except in reference to Daniel Day-Lewis.

11

A DECISION

I'm going," Sean announced, at Defiance and with defiance.

"Going where?" asked Rob.

"I'm going to Linda's wedding. She invited me. Because you know what that means—she wants me to stop her. She still loves me and she knows she's doing the wrong thing. It's like she just ordered me to save her."

Rob's head was fogged in, from getting fired so abruptly, the absence of Jake, and the certifiable craziness of everything Sean had just said. Rob had lost his bearings; if he tried to stand, he'd topple over. "What are you talking about? Sean, how many times has Linda told you—she hates you, she's moved on, she thinks you're pathetic, and if you ever come near her again she's going to call the police."

"Which to me says, 'Sean, I love you and divorcing you was the biggest mistake of my life and I'm about to make another. So that's why I'm inviting you to my disaster wedding because you have to fix this.'"

"That's not what she's saying."

"Then why did she fucking invite me?"

Rob didn't have an answer. For the past three years Sean had pursued Linda relentlessly, with daily "Have an awesome morning!" texts,
and proposals of just-friends lunches, with Linda shooting back lengthy
emails beginning "You destroyed my life and our family through your
unbelievable selfishness and being a pile of pigshit and what part of
'I never want to see you ever again' don't you understand" and then
getting vindictive. Still, Rob had to admit that Linda never went what
Sean called "radio silent." Sean was addicted to renewing their love and
Linda couldn't stop adamantly refusing to. There was definitely a vola-
tile, ongoing reverberation between them, but Rob dubbed it a pathol-
ogy, a post-divorce doom spiral. Rob couldn't let go of Jake, but that was
different, both because it was a death, not a divorce, and because Rob
hadn't done anything wrong. Except for one enormous action that was
clawing at him and shrieking for resolution.

"And you're coming with me."

Sean was staring at Rob and past him. When Sean started planning something, whether it was competing in an Ironman triathlon on
Kona or bribing his daughter into being in the same room with him,
he wouldn't be deterred. Sean bullied his own life, believing that people
could be forced into happiness, with a crowbar if necessary. This was
both demented and endearing; Sean never abandoned anyone, or any
undone task. He was incapable of letting anything slide or recede. And
he didn't just hold grudges—he enshrined them and shook them awake
every morning and hissed in their ear, "I'm right here, motherfucker."

"Where is this wedding happening?"

Sean reread the evite, with its attached, detailed map and travel tips.
"It's on a private island off the coast of Maine. The guests are staying at
some estate for the whole weekend."

"I'm sure Linda doesn't think you'll actually show up. It's a formality. Or maybe the guest list coordinator found your address in Linda's emails and accidentally invited you. Maybe Linda doesn't even know you got invited. Or maybe she's trying to show you she's happy, so you'll finally move on with your life. Or maybe the evite is her ultimate revenge and you should take the hint. And why would I ever go with you?"

"Because you can stop me from stabbing or strangling that billionaire Trone Meston cumstain, unless we figure out how I could get away with it. I mean, you're smart like that. And you can tell me what you think, of the whole setup and whether I should bring a crossbow or go all in on a bazooka. And Linda likes you, so you can be like, my spokesperson. You can talk to her and tell her how great I am. You can tell her it's okay for her to ditch that fuckwad and admit that she's still obsessed with me."

"Sean, I can't, it's too nuts, they didn't invite me and the whole thing is a terrible idea and you'll just end up feeling even worse and I . . . I . . ."

"You were fucking fired. And your husband is dead. And you're getting like, seriously old. What else have you got going on, bitch?"

"Bitch" was one of Sean's greatest endearments, and it meant he was serious. His frankness had sliced through Rob's bullshit. Rob was flailing on every level, in equally futile and suicidal directions. Maybe this trip was the worst possible notion, or it might serve as a form of electroshock, zapping both men back to life, or at least acceptance. Rob hadn't traveled since Jake's death, because every destination would be either a meaningless void, or a hideous reminder of some earlier happiness. Rob's and Sean's lives had both stalled, amid the rubble of loving another human being too desperately, and they were both perilously close to losing hope altogether.

"Holy mother of fucking shit," said Sean.

"What?"

Sean was holding up his phone, explaining, "It's a fucking Trone-Phone. I'm paying this turdbucket to fuck my wife."

"Only technically. Although—it gets worse."

"How?"

"Trone Meston bought Welstrom & Stratters. So in a way—he fired me."

Sean was hefting Rob's weights back onto the rack. "You're doing this," he said. "Get dressed, go home, and pack all of your fancy gay-ass clothes. We're going to that fucking wedding, and we're gonna fix you, too."

PART II

12

TRONE MESTON

Trone Meston was born fifty-one years ago in Derrington, Nebraska, a town of under eight hundred residents, as Timothy Mrank, a name that didn't do him justice. He'd come up with "Trone" at age five and "Meston" a few years later. Timmy Mrank would go nowhere, but Trone Meston sounded memorably historic and like an imperial title from some hallowed Middle Earth realm: "All bow before the Grand Trone of Meston!" It was a name that not only prophesized universe-rattling supremacy but required it. A failure named Trone Meston would be irreducibly sad. Timmy/Trone's parents, depleted from barely sustaining the family farm, had given birth to eleven children, mostly as unpaid help, so they hardly noticed the eccentricities of Trone, their eighth offspring, until they had no choice.

Trone was a genial, aloof child, fascinated by everything, but from a scientific distance, like a Venusian emperor hovering in a spaceship above Earth's atmosphere, arbitrating whether the planet's inhabitants would become friends or a midday snack. He was an indifferent student, skimming through English and Geography, which didn't interest him, but diligently plowing through college-grade volumes on statistics and psychology. At eight, he designed experiments that tracked his siblings and the farm's chickens, researching whether the animals reacted more affectionately to, say, George or Ethan, who ultimately wrung their necks, or might gravitate to the company of Brianna, who fed them. Trone wasn't unfeeling, but he'd deliberately mislead the chickens with grain and then shoo them toward various family members. When his mother witnessed these disruptions, Trone explained, "I'm finding out if chickens can form meaningful friendships." The results were inconclusive, which spurred Trone toward a more coherent study of humans.

He would stand silently, almost invisibly, in the corner of the schoolyard, observing the formation of cliques and budding romances. He was equally drawn to the personal lives of his teachers. He'd loiter by the faculty parking lot to discern who was retrieved by an argumentative spouse, who primped for a date in a rearview mirror, and who was driving home fatigued and alone, nibbling the remnants of yesterday's takeout and sucking the soy sauce off their fingers. He began interviewing schoolmates (without a notepad or recording device—Trone's memory was his first and most efficient device): "Why do you like Christine? Is it because she's blond and pretty or because she's good at soccer?" "Why did you kiss Jason near the swing set? Did someone dare you to?" "Are you and Kevin just trading comic books and cinnamon graham crackers or are you also having sex?"

When Trone would ask these questions, his fellow students would pause, with alarm or even violence, but then, in almost all cases, they'd talk to Trone, sometimes for hours, about their irritations ("I know everyone still calls me Bucky Beaver, even though I got my braces off a year ago"), their gnawing family issues ("My sister is the smart one and my brother's the jock so I'm like, nothing"), and their troubled aspirations ("I kissed Jason because I love his thick eyebrows and because my cousin's getting married and she's seventeen so I need to start thinking about stuff like that").

Trone wouldn't judge or sympathize. It was his consuming, affectless interest that drew people in. He wasn't a gossip or a snitch, but was compiling data. His engrossment was flattering; the popular kids imagined they were being pedestaled as stars, while the more overlooked students preened from the unfamiliar scrutiny. Trone was rumored to be writing an insider's book on adolescence, or recruiting cast members for a teen sitcom, or winnowing the overall group for someone to become his best friend on the basis of a quiz. None of these was true. Trone wasn't even sure what he was up to, but he was driven. He wasn't after smarm, but telling details, for some future project or invention that would inevitably lead to his ruling the world.

This craving for authority was both pure ego and philanthropy: the world, he could foresee, would be duly and slavishly grateful for his insights and assistance. His heroes were innovators like Thomas Edison, Henry Ford, Alexander Graham Bell, and eventually, Steve Jobs—people who created or developed something astonishingly new that changed everything. Trone never wavered. He'd been impeccably anointed. He wasn't after revenge against kids who ignored him or adults who underestimated him; he couldn't be bothered. Although his large family was a spur, prompting him to become not merely the most outstanding offspring among many, but the one his siblings and parents would brag about, and borrow money from, and, inevitably, idolize and fear.

In high school, Trone required a relationship, for firsthand documentation, and to convince another person that he could be a person, too. He opted for Martha, who was savvy, on time with her schoolwork, and well liked because she was good-natured and worked after school at the Dairy Whirl, a burgers-and-ice-cream hangout. Trone marched over to Martha in the cafeteria, where she was sitting with a friend, whom Trone drew into the conversation to make a decent first impression. "Hi," he said to both girls, and then to Martha, "I liked what you said in English class about how Juliet was a rich girl who probably just wanted to piss off her parents, and that she barely knew Romeo." "It makes sense," Martha replied. "Back then, she wouldn't be going to college or getting a job, so Romeo looked like an okay deal. If he hadn't died, it would've been over in two weeks. I watched the movie with Leonardo DiCaprio and I wanted to yell at Claire Danes, 'You only like him because he's Leonardo DiCaprio!'"

Trone and Martha began hanging out, and Trone would maintain a conversation just by seeking Martha's opinion on anything from an MTV video ("All those guys have their mom's mall hair") to the President ("He's sleazy but he's doing an okay job") to her plans for pharmacy school ("I'll be helping people, along with job security"). Trone would listen with an alacrity that struck Martha as unsettling and supportive. He'd ask questions to prove he hadn't spaced out, and he helped her pick a financially workable college.

Trone was comfortable around Martha, because he could study her family's worn but well-cared-for ranch house, her shampoo choices, and the sci-fi novels on her bookshelf, especially the Astral Academy series, where androids in a utopian future were programmed to educate human teenagers. Trone was positioning himself as Martha's boyfriend, a soulmate who'd love and respect her, qualities that would earn her devotion.

When Martha dropped him after three months, Trone was stunned. Hadn't he done everything correctly? He'd never berated or neglected her, he'd complimented her essay on the community impact of her dad's hardware store, and the two times they'd had sex, he'd let her take the initiative, and he'd held her afterward, which was something he'd read that females desired and males forgot to do.

"You're great," Martha had told him, after summoning him to the Dairy Whirl during one of her breaks. "I mean, there's nothing wrong with you. It's just—you treat me like a lab rat. Like you're either going to very gently and sweetly kill me or follow me to pharmacy school and wait outside the classroom door like a golden retriever who's always happy to see me."

"And that's bad?" Trone puzzled, not offended but bewildered.

"It's . . . weird. I mean, my mom says you're the nicest boy she's ever met, but you never talk about yourself. I mean, we graduate next year. Trone, what are you going to do? Who are you going to be?"

Trone thought about this, chewing his lip. It was a good question. It didn't bother or frighten him, because he'd established his destiny: world domination. But he didn't want to brag or deal with niggling aspects of how he'd conquer the universe. He was under way, and the particulars of his all-encompassing victory would be unveiled to him soon enough.

"I don't know the exact parameters, or whether it's going to be a product or a service, probably both. But I'm going to catalyze something that will impact everyone on Earth and alter their lives for the better. And I know the field I'll be concentrating on. The arena."

"The arena? Like, which arena? Like a football stadium? What are you gonna change forever?"

All the while he'd been courting Martha, Trone's mind had been whittling his future, with an eye to the extraordinary. If he was being honest, he wasn't surprised by Martha's rejection. She'd been a trial run, a primitive demographic attempt. Which had led to utter clarity.

"Love. My arena is love."

"Okey-dokey," said Martha, edging away. "Gotta get back to those hot fudge sundaes and frozen yogurt Pogo-Pops."

13

PAOLO AND DAX

As Rob was ransacking his apartment, pulling his supplies and wardrobe together for the wedding trip, Tria warbled, "Happy anniversary, Rob and Jake!" Jake had programmed this yearly greeting, which Rob had intended to delete but couldn't. Now the words were ominous, as if Jake were mocking Rob from the grave and pointing an accusatory, perhaps skeletal forefinger. As Rob moved to silence Tria, she declared, "Urgent call from Paolo Baumgarner!"

"How fast can you get over here?" Paolo begged.

"Are you okay? Do I need to take you to the emergency room?"

"I don't know. Maybe. I can't even talk about it. But can you please come here right now?"

Rob was in careening flux, from his job loss and climbing aboard Sean's kamikaze mission, so rather than grill Paolo about the fine points of his dilemma, he raced the two blocks to Paolo's building, just in case this was a true medical crisis. Paolo had a history of breakdowns (over being ghosted by one-night stands and leather jackets left in coat checks), panic attacks following any conversation with his mother in

Texas (who'd say things like "Tell me again, Paolo, why can't you live
in Dallas half the year and organize my shoe racks?"), and a threatened
suicide attempt upon turning forty-five, ten years ago ("I should've expected this, but it's not just that I'm alone, my gums are receding. When
I smile, I look like one of those reservoirs in Utah where the water's
almost gone and you can see ancient rowboats").

Rob didn't bother ringing the bell. He had a key, and the door to
Paolo's transcendently spotless apartment was open. Paolo, like his
mom, was an acolyte of sparkling surfaces, bottles of spray cleaner emp-
tied weekly, and white walls repainted yearly. Rob heard sobbing from
the bedroom, certain he'd see Paolo undone by a smudge on the white
satin duvet.

But the truth was more upsetting. Paolo was lying fully clothed
on the duvet, wearing sunglasses and a striped dish towel, knotted
babushka-style, on his head. As Rob entered the room Paolo leapt up
and shoved himself into a corner, as if melting into the wall itself. "Oh
sweet Jesus!" he cried. "It's you! Did you see anyone in the lobby? Or
lurking outside the building?"

"What's going on? Why are you dressed like an elderly Slovakian
movie star?"

"Okay. Okay."

Paolo was pacing, his breathing uneven. He almost spoke, but
couldn't. He perched on the edge of the bed. He removed his sunglasses.

"I'm sorry for getting you involved in this, but I didn't know who
else to call. And you're going to tell me to contact the police, but I'm
too embarrassed and I don't have any real evidence, but if I stay here
I'm going to end up as one of the bodies in the first few minutes of
any *Law & Order* episode where gay men are being killed by either a

psychotic hustler or a closeted parish priest who's on a mission from the Lord."

"Paolo?"

"I'm not making this up and I'm not being paranoid. I just . . . I've been very lonely, and I didn't want to burden you because I know you're still dealing with Jake, but I went on this new dating app, it's called Hunkr. I got an email about it as a special promotion, which said I was a member of New York's elite professional class and that I deserved to meet someone, and I'm quoting, 'buff, totally fun and re-latable, with a graduate degree.' I know it sounds like a scam, but I've been on all the other sites for ages and I've either fucked everybody or had coffee with them or been rejected by them because I'm too old or because I look like a dentist. But that's why Dax was such a real possibility."

"Dax? Paolo, come on. You're smarter than this. Because no one named Dax is ever a real possibility, because no one is ever really named Dax."

"Please just listen. I assumed Dax wasn't his real name, because sometimes online I call myself Pietro or Doc Dickstuff or Lord Bram-well DeLoache. Shut up. But here's the thing about Dax: he's a dentist, too. In dental school I always refused to date other dentists because it felt inbred and because I was self-loathing and because they all looked like dentists. But Dax's photo was incredibly hot and age appropriate, and when we chatted on the app I could tell, he's really a dentist, well, an oral surgeon, because he knew about this new titanium post being used for dental implants, it's twice as durable as stainless steel."

"But you've actually met him? I mean, not just online or over the phone or in a dream?"

"I met him two weeks ago, at Starbucks—we were both being care-ful, so if we didn't click there'd be no huge investment. But he looked even better than in his photos, with just the right amount of silver at the temples, this Cary Grant chin, taller than me, and these incredible Siberian-husky blue eyes. He looked like either a guy who drives his Jeep off-road in an erectile dysfunction ad or everybody's fantasy of the divorced dad who moves in next door while exploring his sexuality and who was once an Olympic swimmer but is really modest about it and keeps his gold medals in a drawer. And I'm not being superficial, because he was also a seriously nice guy, he looked me in the eye, he had a sense of humor, he drank a mocha latte but he'd brought breath mints, and we talked about our practices—he's part of a group on the Upper East Side, once a year he flies to Guatemala to volunteer at a free dental clinic to remove infected wisdom teeth, but more than that, and this is going to sound so juvenile, but we talked about love."

"Paolo . . ."

"It was—amazing. I told him stuff I haven't even told you. About how I'm not sure love even exists or if it's just a marketing tool to sell en-gagement rings and color-coded roses or if it's a storyline that first-world countries came up with after everyone stopped having to wake up with the sun, till the fields, and die at thirty-four, so they needed a new sense of purpose and love seemed like this unreachable, extraordinary concept, and an alternative religion. And I told him about the guys I'd dated, and how I thought I'd loved at least two of them, and it wasn't that anything went so horribly wrong, it was just that neither of them checked every box, like flawless forever husbands, and I know that insisting on perfec-tion is self-sabotaging but I couldn't help myself, I'd hear my mother's voice in my head saying, 'He's very nice but why is he still just a loan officer at an off-brand bank?' or 'His tube socks have permanently worn away the hair on his shins,' so things would end. And I told him about you and Jake and how your relationship convinced me that love was tangible but that after what happened it seemed like the pain wasn't worth the effort, that your loving Jake only made losing him so much worse, and how ever since he died you've been pushing yourself to recover, but I can tell when you're fixating because your eyes get clouded over, and I keep trying to think of a way to help you, but grief isn't just a phase, like when I went platinum blond even though I knew it was a turning-fifty cliché and then the L'Oreal came off on my pillowcases."

Rob didn't say anything because Paolo was right about Rob obsessing, over whether he was being held accountable for having loved Jake so fiercely, and beyond that, if what Rob had done, what he'd participated in during Jake's last days, could be termed a crime, especially in the eyes of God, if God existed, something Jake had always vehemently denied, mostly, Rob had always assumed, to spite his parents. Rob was drowning in his life and he couldn't begin to counsel Paolo on his.

"And Dax told me about how he'd felt the same way I did, and about how people in New York are so picky and snobby and how no one wants to settle, or revise their expectations, so they end up alone, watching old Julia Roberts movies on basic cable as if they're documentaries from a parallel universe. So I asked Dax if he wanted to be in love and he got really quiet but then he reached out his hand across the table and he said, 'Yes. Because I am in love.'"

Paolo's story was making Rob uncomfortable, while also causing him to root for someone to appreciate Paolo and quell his eternal self-image morass and tell him his sideburns had finally grown in symmetrically, regardless of the truth.

"So I was staggered and scared and trying not to overthink, so I figured, let's see where this goes. And Dax didn't seem to be fishing for a reply, you know, for me to say 'I love you' back. Which was good because I was soaring, because this great-looking, smart, funny guy had said he loved me and I was trying to decide if I was in an M. Night Shyamalan movie, where I was actually seated alone and hallucinating my dream guy, and I wanted you to meet Dax to find out if you could see him, too, or if you'd humor me and laugh at whatever the empty chair was saying and then you'd stage an intervention with all our friends, maybe with daiquiris and microwave popcorn so I'd think it was a Tony Awards party."

"I don't think that would work a second time."

"Probably not, but I didn't want to squash everything, or have you gently tuck me into a straitjacket, swearing it was a Comme de Garçons peacoat, I just—I wanted to go with it, for a little more time. To float on that absurdly fluffy love-at-first-sight-in a-musical-where-the-lights-dim-on-everyone-but-Tony-and-Maria cloud. And Dax was so incredibly patient and attentive and he even loved to spoon in bed, which is my number-two orgasm, right after sex with an Australian lifeguard. So it was all very Prince-Charming-with-blowjobs and midlife ambrosia until he asked, really sweetly and offhand, as if it was our shared joke, when we were having butter pecan cones from this food truck in Central Park, he said, 'Which do you love more? This ice cream cone or me?'"

Rob was apprehensive, as Paolo's soft-focus, romping-in-the-meadow-with-animated-bluebirds affair began its descent, into a lurking maniac drama starring Jennifer Lopez or Jennifer Garner or anyone named Jennifer who wanted at least a Golden Globe nomination.

"One night we went to that off-Broadway, English schoolboy, all-male version of *Romeo and Juliet*, with everyone in blazers with leather satchels, and afterwards he turned to me and said, 'I would die for you. I'd take poison.' Which made me think, that's incredibly sweet, and also, he's an oral surgeon. He has access to poison."

"You should have called me from the theater, or sent me a photo with 'HELP ME' written on your forehead."

"I know, although I would've had to write it in reverse letters which would be time-consuming and I would've ended up writing 'EM PLEH.' And I kept telling myself, maybe this is what love is all about, maybe it's supposed to be overwhelming and a touch scary, until we were in bed and he started to choke me, and fine, I'd asked him to do it but only a little bit, but then he got this demonic look in his eye and he said, 'Say it. Even if you're not sure, even if it's just to see how it sounds, please say it.' And I didn't know what to do, so I thought what the fuck, give it a try, maybe I should stop being so uptight, and I said, or I moaned, since he was still pretend-but-not-really choking me, I told him, 'I love you.'"

"I'm shocked you're still here."

"Me too. Because the second I said it, he looked not just happy but—enraptured. Blessed. As if I'd granted him a magical wish or promised to take him as my plus-one to the Met Ball. And I didn't know if I'd meant it, I couldn't even begin to decide, but I knew I'd made a huge mistake, because Dax basically took it as a marriage proposal. Although he kept swearing that he wasn't holding me to any sacred vow and that we were still learning about each other, and then he got me to agree, okay fine, the idea turned me on, but I said I'd have sex with him in his office, after hours."

"ARE YOU OUT OF YOUR MIND?"

"Stop interrupting, because he could be here any minute or he might be listening if he planted a microchip in my ass, that's really a thing, that's how chess champions receive secret signals during a match. But we were in his office and the lights were off and fine, it was sexy, as if we'd broken in, and running around an oral surgeon's office naked is kind of a porn thing . . ."

"Only if you don't have insurance and you really need a root canal . . ."

"And I'm in the chair, with my legs wrapped around him and we're making out and before I know it my wrists are tied to the arms of the chair with rubber tubing and he's licking my shoulders and saying, 'If you ever leave me I'll kill myself.'"

"Oh my God."

"And then he untied me and laughed it off, but I knew he was serious so I made up some excuse about getting up early for a YouTube tutorial on the risks of embedding diamonds in the front teeth of rap artists, especially if they don't have a Waterpik, and I got the hell out of there. And the next day I spent three hours composing this totally thoughtful email, about why we needed to take a break, because I had to do more work on myself before I could be open to anyone else, and how because we were both dentists there might be an ethical issue, and how I should be there for my best friend Rob because he was still grieving, which is true and I apologize for using it as an excuse, but I thought you would understand."

Rob did rely on Paolo, as a witness to his love for Jake, and to entertain him and keep his gloom from festering. For Rob, Paolo's self-narrated travails were like some gay Dickensian epic, with fresh chapters every week or sometimes hourly. Susannah, Rob's beloved former boss, had told Rob that the most commercial novels, the transporting page-turners, felt like feverish gossip. After a loss, friends become more in-dispensable than ever, not because they can replace a loved one, but because they remember, and explanations are rarely necessary, and late-night sobbing isn't met by get-over-it-already eye-rolling. Rob had al-ready loved Paolo, but now they were bound by both heartbreak and an imminent dentist-on-dentist conflagration.

"So you sent the email?"

"Yes, and after two minutes he replied, with total sanity, saying he got it and he hoped we could stay friends and colleagues. But since then, this whole week: on Monday I got a manila envelope in the mail, with a paper dental bib inside, neatly folded, but with my name on it, in what I'm pretty sure is blood. And I got so freaked out that I did something stupid: I burned it, because I didn't want it in my apartment."

"Meaning you don't have the evidence."

"Meaning I'm an idiot. And then two days ago I got this antique valentine, of a huge smiling molar holding a bouquet of flowers with the caption, 'You're the love of my life—and that's the tooth.'"

"Was it signed?"

"No, but it was scented—with the smell of mint floss. And then today at work the receptionist told me I had a new patient, named I. M. Yours. When she said it out loud, we both got scared, and so we canceled the rest of the day and I ran back here, which was probably the worst thing I could do, because he knows where I live and he's going to kill me or kidnap me and yank all my teeth out so no man will ever want me, and I have to get out of here, but I can't go to my parents' place because of course he'd try there, and I don't want to max out my credit cards and check into a hotel and sit under the covers and shiver, plus have you ever seen those infrared videos of what's left behind on hotel sheets, even after they launder them, it's like a petri dish, so I was wondering if I could stay with you, except that doesn't work either because I talked about you and he Googled you and was impressed so he could track you down at home or at work."

"Except if he goes to W&S he'll find out I've been fired, which I'll fill you in on, and you're right about not staying at my place, even though I won't be there, because here's what you're doing: you're driving with me and Sean to his ex-wife's wedding in Maine, where Dax will never find you and we can work on getting you an order of protection."

Paolo's eyes got wide as he sorted through every aspect of what Rob had just said. Then his gayest nerve endings, heightened by his Nice Jewish Boy credentials, kicked in, and he said, "A Maine wedding. Give me ten minutes to pack. I'm thinking sporty/casual rehearsal dinner with a collarless ecru linen shirt, my good espadrilles, and a knotted bandana with a just-for-fun print of tiny hearts in honor of the bride and groom, and, at the very least, a dark suit for the ceremony with a deep cobalt raw silk tie, formal but not funereal, and a complementary pocket square in a subtle houndstooth."

Rob had no idea if he could smuggle Paolo into these scheduled events, but at least Paolo had become clearheaded and goal-oriented, so Rob advised, "And a pastel-but-not-Palm-Beach cotton crewneck to toss over your shoulders for any possibly chilly clambakes on the beach."

"Canary yellow? Powder blue? Heathered lime? No, I'll bring an assortment, just in case."

"Go! Ten minutes!"

14

THE TUDOR

For the first two years of her marriage, Linda tamped down her expectations and thought of herself and Sean as still dating, so their life together was youthfully breezy, a matter of "Hey babe, how about trying that new Greek place?" and pre-brunch weekend softball games with friends in Central Park. Some couples fumble, gaining weight, not bathing and leaving takeout containers near the garbage but not in the garbage, as if since closing the deal and that week in Aruba, they can relax. Often the bride continues in fully glossed, French lingeried huntress mode, wary of unmasking any defects, in case an annulment is still on the table, while the groom reverts to bachelor squalor. The subsequent sniping and buyer's remorse, Linda had witnessed, were more than common, so she stayed observant and reasonable, alert to whatever acceptable-or-not form her wedlock with Sean might take.

But Sean blindsided her, by becoming even more exultant, more forgiving of her quirks, and as always, a sexual powerhouse. Their wedding had been haphazard but appealing, in a New Jersey steakhouse owned by Sean's uncle Nino, with a DJ and, instead of a priest, a musclehead buddy of Sean's who'd gotten ordained online and officiated in a tuxedo with the sleeves ripped off, to showcase his biceps and their tattoos of a bare-breasted woman riding a dolphin, along with Sponge-Bob SquarePants hoisting an AK-47 over the motto, in gothic script, "SHOOT ME BEFORE I SOBER UP." Among the ragtag guests were many of Sean's employees and most of his costars from *WarForce*, who wore their costumes from the show as a raucous tribute. Mistress Karin-ska had cut the wedding cake with her mighty Sword of Destiny.

Linda had joined in the occasion's why-the-hell-not vibe, as it was wackier and more authentic than the day she'd been married to Andros/ Andy, in a high roller's suite at an Atlantic City hotel with a gold toilet, both of them in custom-made Prada, with a Greek Orthodox priest in full clerical regalia. While the proceedings had had a flashy and cer-tainly pricey glamor, Linda's wedding to Sean was more improvised, with a neighborhood glad-you-could-make-it friendliness and a lack of pretension.

Sean's business surged, sprouting two more branches in other parts of town. Linda never had to nag Sean about applying himself. His en-thusiasm for the workouts he devised, the top-of-the-line equipment he invested in, and his varied clientele was infectious. Linda heard about, and often met, Sean's favorites, such as a celebrity dermatologist (who could spot the use of Botox and fillers from across the street), an art gal-lery owner (who snuck Linda and Sean into shows with lines around the block), and a Wall Street guy who'd made billions, retired at thirty-two, and then dedicated himself to competitive skateboarding.

"Everybody loves you," Sean would tell Linda in bed. "They think you're so hot." As she stared at him, he'd add, "And really smart. Really, really smart."

"You are disgusting," Linda would reply as Sean laughed uproariously. Sean loved his own jokes so unashamedly that Linda would punch him in the stomach and start laughing as well.

Sean successfully tempted Linda to quit her airline job and work at Defiance, enrolling new members. Sean would stick his head into her office and confidentially inform the customers Linda had already persuaded, "And if you get the platinum elite package, I marry you. Ask her."

Linda would sigh, because these newcomers would invariably be captivated to learn about her life with Sean, as either a porn scenario or a brochure-ready Manhattan love story. "You're married to him?" a female advertising exec asked. "But isn't that weird, with him having his hands all over other people's bodies every day?"

This was true: Sean was intimate with some militantly athletic, often younger women, the sort who ran on treadmills in full makeup, thongs, and flesh-colored, midriff-baring tops, who all harbored crushes on Sean, as did most of the men, gay and straight. Sean wasn't big on boundaries, without being leering or inappropriate. If an employee made anyone uncomfortable, Sean would take that staff member aside and they'd be gone. But as he'd clarified to Linda, more than once, "I need to touch people, to correct their form, and hug them when they finally get something right, and just joke around with everybody. If I got nervous and watched myself every second, people would hate it. I'm hands-on."

During her days at the gym, Linda could keep an eye on Sean, but she never became a paranoid harpy, and took a secret pride in being married to such a lusted-after man. As she told that exec, "There are only two things you need to know about Sean. He's great at what he does, and he's a five-year-old. No, I take that back. He's a five-year-old who's just eaten all his Halloween candy and his sister's and decided to jump off a roof into a swimming pool."

After two years of ramshackle good times, on a Saturday morning in April, Sean commanded Linda to put on "real clothes" and get in the car he'd rented. Linda was dubious, as she wasn't fond of surprises. Aileen, not to mention Andros/Andy, had cured her of ever welcoming a stranger's knock on the door or an envelope from a government agency stamped "THIRD NOTICE." She especially hated surprise parties, which struck her as sadistic, like humiliating ambushes. "Today is a good thing, babe," Sean pledged. "You're gonna love it."

Sean drove to East Amberly, a Connecticut suburb an hour and a half outside the city. From the car window, Linda took in a quaintly restored Main Street, with the awninged brick storefronts hosting a ballet-as-exercise studio, a shop that sold hundreds of varieties of vinegar, a boutique limited to costly French clothing for children, three coffee shops (two of them also performance spaces), and an ice cream parlor with outdoor seating and a chalkboard listing the Flavors of the Day: Pistachio/Marigold Fusion, Bruised Walnut Gelato, and Vanilla Without Borders. Linda steeled herself, because late at night, after she'd thought Sean was asleep, she'd spend hours taking an online video tour of exactly this town, produced by the East Amberly Visitors Bureau. Sometimes, as the camera doted on the windows of a converted 1875 bank that displayed drippingly glazed platters and hand-thrown vases from a local pottery, she had to shut everything down, because she'd get too aroused.

Next came a decently landscaped Stop & Shop, a stretch of pasture with gamboling horses and a split-rail fence, and an outlet barn stocked with high-end patio and deck furniture (the brands that cost more than most people's living room stuff). Linda thought Sean was cruelly teasing her so she kept silent, as if being kidnapped. They passed through the ironwork gates of a charmingly wooded neighborhood of 1920s houses on lots of an acre or more, interspersed with modern places, split-levels and Cape Cods set among old-growth oaks, Japanese maples, and not-too-tidy clumps of azaleas. Then Sean made the meanest conceivable move. He tried, without much success, to not grin maliciously as he pulled into the driveway of a Tudor home.

As a kid, when her dad was arrested again, or Aileen disappeared leaving behind some frozen dinners, a bag of bridge mix, and a carton of expired almond milk, Linda had sequestered herself with a library book called *American Tudor*, with page after page of both mansions and cozier homes in the prewar Tudor style, with half-timbered stucco façades, mullioned windows, and meandering gardens. Linda had never yearned for life in a castle, which came off as dank and forbidding, but every horror, from parental neglect to isolation to an absence of hot water, or any water, or electricity, because six months of unopened bills had been shoved under the litter box left behind by a previous tenant, would be obliterated by a Tudor.

Sean had walked in on Linda scrolling through Pinterest boards of Tudor details, and pages from Tudor home ownership associations, and countless tristate-area real estate listings, from Tuxedo Park estates (where the yearly taxes began in the hundreds of thousands) to New Hampshire fixer-uppers with peaked rooftops, stone wishing wells, and, inevitably, the arched oak front doors that Linda was especially fond of, as thresholds to safety and the storybook allure of cushioned window seats, carved newel posts, and enchanted bedrooms under the eaves. Especially as a teenager, being granted her own bedroom had seemed both inconceivable and voraciously desirable, instead of a cot in a living room that smelled of a recent fire.

Linda had never come across this exact house—Sean prided himself on vaulting a step ahead of her Googling. Maybe, Linda thought, they were dropping by one of Sean's out-of-town clients, but there was a "For Sale" sign on the lawn, beside the boxwood hedge. Ordering herself not to cry, and stopping herself from rolling down her window for a more direct inspection of the property, Linda said, in an even, noncommittal voice, "Fuck you."

"At least take a look," said Sean. "I have the key."

Linda didn't budge, thanks to the unthinkable peril. Up until this second, her marriage had been provisional, an ostensibly good idea but still subject to revision or even cancellation. Sean had applied himself to pleasing Linda into an irrevocable commitment. He'd plotted to make her so happy she'd ditch her caution and irony. He would jettison her thrift-store-winter-coat and overnights-at-the-laundromat history and indisputably prove that love didn't just exist but could redefine her life. He understood that words alone, or even soul-shaking sex, frequent compliments on her abs, dinners at her favorite sushi place, and house seats, courtesy of a Broadway producer trying to lose his gut, would barely dent Linda's prideful intransigence. Only a Tudor could breach the Long Island damsel's ancestral defenses.

Linda fought mercilessly. If she left the car, if she took even the mildest sniff of the shockingly clean-scented air, with a top note of pine, if she, God forbid, toured the premises, this would be tantamount to surrender. She'd be Sean's forever. Fuck Sean, she told herself. I can still leave, he can drive me to the train station or I can hitchhike. I can protect myself. But she was bone weary from her struggles, as both a child and an adult, and her subsequent armoring, from keeping love not just at arm's length, but stashed in a storage locker at the bus station with her yearbooks, graduation robes, flight attendant uniforms, and diary entries wistfully scribbled with the pernicious words "someday," "in-ground pool," "lawn," "greenhouse," "jonquils," "kissing," and "joy."

She stepped out of the car, her lips tightly pursed, as Sean brought her gently up the flagstone pathway. He was brimming with resolve, to please his implacably dark-natured bride and be justly congratulated. Sean wished there was a cheering throng and a marching band to commemorate his victory, and he'd checked on the availability of at least a trumpet player, but a skittish Linda might flee. But he could tell, from the helpless tears at the corners of her eyes, and the sob she was choking back, that he was nearing the finish line, in first place.

Sean unlocked the front door, and Linda crossed that unholy threshold into, damn that fucking Sean—an honest-to-God foyer. That extraneous, introductory space which spoke of a homecoming. The floors were an original if glowingly refinished oak, to complement the built-in bench nestled in a nook of the sturdy staircase. Linda was shamefully devoted to *House Hunters*, that HGTV perennial where couples, the wife often pregnant, would inspect the blandest tract homes in Atlanta or Akron or Boise, fetishizing granite countertops, vague "bonus" rooms, and outdoor firepits. Linda was an admitted architectural snob, and she'd pity these hapless first-time buyers, referring to foam-core moldings as "charm and character" and coveting the most obscenely prominent three-car garages, garages grossly larger than the houses themselves, garages that hooted, "Just picture all the ugly recreational vehicles inside, not to mention the stacked plastic bins of more crap we bought and don't need!"

Linda thought differently, which was why Sean took her through an expansive living room with oak beams and a limestone fireplace chiseled with a coat of arms. The house was unfurnished, but sunlight filled every corner via the French doors to the backyard. Sean had an intuition that while Linda was a Tudor freak, she wouldn't care for the sawdust, cost, and intrusion of remodeling. The bathrooms were new, with the gleaming white tile and nickel hardware attuned to the house's origins. And then: say hello to the kitchen. "Try to resist, give it your best shot," the Tudor demons hissed. "We dare you."

Linda wasn't a zealous cook (Aileen had shopped for, or shoplifted, packaged foods at gas station mini-marts), but a kitchen spoke of a permanence and gravity that had long eluded her. She remembered only peeling linoleum, greasy, empty, battered metal cabinets with fossilized ant traps, and a refrigerator with one rotting jar of olives. This kitchen was her redemption: white woodwork, with a soapstone sink and, yes, an island, where guests would gather picturesquely, toasting each other with white wine and garnished Triscuits, and this island, rather than the expected, tired marble, had a lustrous mahogany surface.

Linda had seen enough, although she'd gladly have wandered from room to room for hours, predicting furniture placement. But she still hadn't succumbed entirely. She hadn't gifted Sean with a speck of gratitude or acquiescence. He doubted himself, panicking that he'd mistaken Linda's taste, and underwhelmed her. Maybe this house wasn't big enough or on some historical registry, or maybe there'd never be a house that could equal Linda's lifelong Tudor reveries.

Linda strode out to the backyard, with its fruit trees, hydrangeas, and pergola. It was almost a gooey manufactured canvas by Thomas Kinkade, the so-called "Painter of Light," who hawked his garishly idealized takes on ye olde inns and chimneyed, thatch-roofed, Seven Dwarf-ready cottages on the home shopping networks. Linda was occasionally waylaid by the Kinkade dreck on porcelain trivets and mugs, but she'd rebuke herself, "I'm not a Disney whore."

She stood with her back to Sean, asking, "Can we afford this?"

"The three Defiance locations are doing great, I've got my eye on a waterfront space in Brooklyn, and I've had feelers from LA and Seattle. We're good."

"But do you like it? You'd have to live here, too."

"I love it. I've been looking for months, and the broker hasn't shown this to anyone else, and the second I saw it, I said, this place will make Linda give me a hand job."

Linda stared at him. What if she bought Sean an electrified collar, so she could use the remote to deliver a punishing shock when he said things like this? But he was right.

"And you're good with moving out of the city? And commuting?"

"We can keep our place in town or grab a studio, for when we want to stay over. But yeah, I can't wait. It's a real house. It's you and me being grown-ups."

They'd talked about this leap, but was Sean prepared to forgo the bar crawls with his buddies, and Manhattan's instant access to everything? Would he miss the city and blame her for taming his rowdier habits? Would he be lessened by quiet nights at home, seasonal yardwork, and runs to big-box stores for rakes and septic tank pellets and watering cans? Was she taking the wrenching wrong turn of many young wives, who overhaul their rambunctious, ball cap–wearing, club-going dudes into sexless and obedient husbands?

Sean had brought up having kids, something else that Linda longed for but hedged on. Would she repeat Aileen's misdeeds, like ignoring holidays and pawning the microwave? Late one night, in bed, with the two of them dozing off, Linda had allowed that "a kid might be nice, or at least something to think about." This was a hardcore "absolutely," in tentative Linda-speak. Sean loved puzzling her out, interpreting her bylaws and hesitance, in hopes of coaxing her across a swaying tight-rope to happiness. Linda was the toughest cookie he'd ever met, and therefore his greatest challenge. Leaving Jersey for LA, dealing with the *WarForce* fallout, and founding a business had been nothing com-pared to wooing Linda and decoding her broken upbringing, or non-upbringing, and her terror and mistrust of not just permanence, but marriage itself. There was something heartbreaking in her hard-won superstitions and rejection of too-obvious pleasure. This was the key to their devotion: rather than snuggling and cuddling, they dueled. Linda's smile was Sean's ultimate trophy.

"So—do we put in an offer?" Linda asked, clinging to an inevitable derailment.

"I already did. Full ask. If we want it, the owners take it off the mar-ket today. It's ours."

Linda had no idea what was happening to her, or maybe she did. Everything was starting to quake. Her legs went weak, as if the Earth were shuddering, and her breathing intensified. She might be having a seizure, or maybe Sean had drugged her. The warring armies in her brain were shouting insults and raising their weapons, but she was helpless to intervene. She was stunned because, instead of her changing Sean, he was infiltrating her every defense, disarming every security device, and flooding her nervous system with—what? Adrenaline? Some possibly fatal new street drug? Those repulsive protein shakes he swore by? Love?

Then she was in Sean's arms, kissing him with an abandon she'd never indulged in. Was he getting his way, by bribing her with a Tudor? If she continued her slide, what was she courting? More gullible disgrace? Legal repercussions if Sean's finances were fictional, as with Andros/Andy? Was this love or idiocy, or had she ceased to worry about the difference, which reversed every promise she'd made to herself?

Sean stopped kissing her, and spun her back toward the house. "Go on," he instructed. "Take your time. You know you want to."

He couldn't see her face but Sean knew: Linda was smiling.

15

TREMBLE'S DECISION

Dear Tremble,

I should call you, and I will, except right now life has become challenging. But please be certain that I adore your book and ardently believe you're an extraordinary writer with a terrific future. I never gush like this unless not gushing would be reprehensible. I've had the best time working with you, and I'd love nothing more than to continue our relationship, but I'm not sure this will be possible.

I've been coping with a situation at Welstrom & Stratters, which I won't bore you with. But I've been ousted, and a return is extremely unlikely. My dilemma is this: I don't want you to change a sentence or a syllable that you don't agree with. You may be assigned another editor. Most of the W&S staff are fine people, but there are exceptions. I know how hard you've worked, and switching publishers would be an additional and unnecessary hardship. At least until recently, W&S has had a proud tradition of publishing gifted, fearless, and even outrageous authors to the widest possible readership, and you deserve nothing less.

I'm on my way out of town, to a wedding in Maine of all things, but I should be back within a few days, when I'll try to secure your future. I'm sorry I've got no greater timeline just yet, but your work must remain your own. Thank you so much for your patience, your genius, and for those photos you've been sending me of people who marry inanimate objects. The lady who's engaged to her blow-dryer was unsettling and touching, especially when she threw a bachelorette party for the blow-dryer and invited her hot rollers and teasing combs.

Always your fan and friend,

Rob

Tremble read this email at least fifteen times. It had clearly been written under duress or even in captivity, and it might contain hidden clues or warnings, but it hadn't been forged, because only someone as old as Rob would send an email. Rob had enemies at work. He'd designated such people, during phone calls, as "difficulties," "opposing opinions," and once, "God willing, surmountable obstacles." When Tremble hated someone, she'd break into their apartment and leave mannequin parts in the sink and shower, or stand a few feet away from them at a fast-food place licking a plastic fork. She was seldom violent, but had cultivated a reputation. She'd once filled a town councilman's Honda Civic with expired meat, after he'd voted to ban LGBTQ-themed books from the high school library. The books remained imprisoned on eighteen-and-up shelves, with proof-of-age ID required, but over a year later, the councilman still smelled like rancid pork.

Rob Barnett's being treated like shit, Tremble deciphered, and if I don't save him, I'm lower than fucking sirloin covered with green mold.

First off, she'd have to pull together enough cash for travel to not just

New York but Maine. Why the fuck would anyone live in Maine? Why not just grow a pair and get your ass to Canada? Maine, to Tremble, was an outpost of nasty old white men in one-room cabins, with fishing equipment in their laps and their wives' rotting corpses beside them in narrow wooden beds. There'd most likely be snow and a rocky coast-line dotted with lighthouses. Tremble put the population of Maine as, at most, twenty-two people, all with snowmobiles, corncob pipes, and those yellow oilcloth slickers with matching floppy, wide-brimmed hats. Her vision of Maine was dependent on logos for cough drops and mov-ies where a young couple's car breaks down during a nor'easter and some murderous, snaggledtoothed local taps on their window with a pitchfork. Tremble could handle these people. Maine was probably like Arkansas only with thinner criminals.

But where could she scrape up the money to get there? She was down to the last few dollars of her minimal publishing advance (Rob had apologized for the amount, wailing, like all editors since the begin-ning of time, that the publishing business was dying). She could scour Howey Breenaster's shipping container for drug money, which wouldn't be stealing if she donated a portion to the free clinic, which treated locals for everything from racoon rabies to a fractured leg suffered while dirt biking naked. But as a rule, Tremble only stole from people she didn't like. And she hated Dr. Churn LeBloitte.

Churn wasn't even a doctor. As Jacksburg's mayor, he'd strong-armed the local high school into awarding him an Honorary Doctorate of Ac-complishment (he'd dictated this title to the student hand-lettering the diplomas). Churn had been elected on the following platform:

A special license plate authorizing him to park anywhere, including on strangers' lawns, "so I may respond to crisis situations."

Making even illegal handguns legal, "in matters of property disputes, driveway confrontations with estranged second wives and trees, which may be capable of attack."

The denial of voting rights to people who "hold unChristian views as to America and who sit in the booths at Wally's Pork Pit reserved exclusively for properly elected officials."

The removal of books from public libraries if they contain "profanity, insults to the white race, discussions of gender identity which confuse normal people, and suspiciously spelled longer words."

The banning of books especially infuriated Tremble, because her greatest wish was for local teenagers to someday read *Life as We Fucking Know It* for free. She'd had run-ins with Churn. He'd had her arrested for public insolence (she'd called him a cracker butt plug at a town meeting), suspicious behavior (she'd sat on his front porch ostentatiously reading the Wonder Woman comic that illustrated the superheroine's bisexuality), and befoulment of private beverages (during a brief stint bartending at Wally's, she'd floated a dog turd in Churn's beer, labeling it a "gourmet ice cube"). In each instance, a defiant Tremble had spent up to a week in a holding cell, until the town's sole police officer released her (after Tremble wouldn't stop yowling unruly songs with titles like "Dr. Churn Little-Dick's Tiny-Balled Blues" at the top of her lungs).

Churn paid for his at-least-five-daily meals, beleaguered wives and mistresses, twelve Cadillacs, and three homes (one of them a replica of the Taj Mahal, only smaller and with aluminum siding) through a range of businesses, most prominently a five-second car wash, a website shilling "a no-physical-exertion weight loss revolution" called Dr. Le-Bloitte's Vitamin-Enriched 10-Pounds-Off-Today Demulsifier, and, in a brick building attached to his law office on Main Street, Our Lord-4-

Less, a budget boutique stocked with "artistic artifacts of human faith." While Tremble respected truly religious people, as long as they didn't shove pamphlets with sketches of unborn fetuses wearing hats in her face, Our Lord-4-Less was where Churn laundered the profits from his criminal activities, such as the sale of bogus hunting and fishing licenses, and basement "nonsurgical but almost" butt lifts utilizing procedures that Churn's nephew Tugger had borrowed from a TikTok video. Tugger would reassure his patients, "You're in good hands because my uncle is a doctor."

Tremble crept toward Our Lord-4-Less from the back, so as not to rile anyone in Churn's office, mostly the site of lazy daylong poker games and consultations with clients seeking quickie divorces ("I just can't stand her yammerin' at me to stop clippin' my toenails at the table") and falsified birth certificates ("Make it say I'm blond"). Tremble handily picked the shop's locked rear door using a mini-screwdriver. No one was in the boutique, since the lights only came on after 11 p.m., when Churn's associates left their wads of bills for Churn to deposit as untaxed "religious-oriented revenue."

The shelves and glass cases housed Jesus in the most contemporary settings. For example, in a 1950s-inspired resin sculpture where he was steering a Ford Fairlane convertible with three leather-jacketed apostles in the back seat and Mary Magdalene riding shotgun in a cashmere sweater and a poodle skirt. There was a tropically themed poster of Jesus surfing in Hawaii, with his robes and tresses wafting, guided by angels wearing Ray-Bans. Mugs were decaled with the mottos "Pray for Decaf" and "Jesus Christ, This Is Good Coffee." A porcelain nativity depicted Mary, Joseph, and the Baby Jesus in matching Arkansas Razorbacks team jerseys, and the Wise Men toted golf bags and contributed a keg, a bucket of chicken, and a blender. A modest collection of paperbacks had such titles as *Living a Godful Life Without Cholesterol*, *How Prayer Can Triple Your 401K Overnight*, and *True Bible Stories from America's Greatest Civil War Heroes*.

None of these dust-shrouded items would ever be sold, and Tremble acquired a bottle opener employing Moses's mouth, but where was the money? She bumped against a life-sized bust of the most Caucasian Virgin Mary imaginable, with blindingly white skin, come-hither scarlet lips, and platinum hair extensions cascading from beneath a veil fashioned from a Confederate flag.

Could Churn be so thick-skulled as to squirrel ill-gotten cash anywhere near such an obvious hiding place? Of course. When Tremble tilted the trampy Virgin forward, and reached into her hollow innards, she fingered three stacks of twenties held in place with twine.

As Tremble counted out almost $2,000, she heard a bovine bleat from the office next door, most likely emitted by Churn while either rubbing himself against a wall or finishing a herd's worth of ribs. Or maybe Churn's having a heart attack, Tremble hypothesized, as she planned to divide the money between travel expenses and paying Howey Breenaster to spray-paint a campaign billboard of Churn with the tagline "ASK ME ABOUT THE STAINS ON MY PANTS."

Later that night, as Tremble watched Arkansas recede from the window of a Trailways bus, she was purposeful and, although she'd never admit to it, scared shitless. She'd never before left Jacksburg, where she could map every hideout and unlocked motel ice machine. She was testing herself, as an extension of her writing. Did she have what it takes to maneuver in the larger world? Her parents had died when Tremble was seven years old, in an especially grisly crash while they were making love in their secondhand pickup truck, which because of the town's lack of streetlights and warning signals, they'd unknowingly parked on a railroad crossing. Tremble hated this horrific memory, because it had left her an orphan, but she cherished her mom and dad for leaving this Earth in each other's arms.

Tremble knew she'd write about her parents, but not just yet. Rob had understood, telling her that while these deaths were monumental and worth exploring, the event belonged to her, and she shouldn't feel pressured to share her response until she was equipped, both emotionally and as a writer. She'd been grateful for this advice, because she liked to remember her parents' lives as a great love story and not simply tragic. She'd told Rob, "I have to know more about love before I can get into it. I want to do them justice."

A week before the accident, after Tremble had been teased mercilessly at school because of her name, her Mom had told her, "When you were born I had a message from the Almighty or the cosmos or whoever's in charge of making babies special. It was a voice saying, 'This little girl is on her way. She's going to do things, big things, crazy things, and sing her own song. And that song will make folks tremble.'" This story had been a salve, and a touchstone, when other kids had mocked her as Trombone or Trample. It took guts to introduce yourself with, "I'm Tremble Woodspill," and as she thought about it on that Trailways bus, Tremble anticipated meeting so many new people across state lines. And best of all, if she could be watchful and Churn's subsidy didn't run out, she'd be meeting Rob Barnett face-to-face.

16

ISABELLE MCNALLY

Isabelle McNally was verging on hugging herself, consensually. It wasn't just that she'd weeded out Rob Barnett, even though he'd been irritating her for months. She hated his well-mannered defense of his authors and his understatedly expensive wardrobe. Cisgender white gay men, Isabelle verified, no longer counted as a minority. They were the lapdogs of an obsolete cultural hegemony, and Isabelle loved saying the word "hegemony" so much she'd tucked it within her critique of the vegan brownies at the Ethical Foods café near her apartment in Bushwick. These brownies, Isabelle had told her two scrupulously curated friends, a diversity officer for a prep school and a nonbinary filmmaker, were baked with refined sugar and were therefore "exemplars of the defunct hegemony of the dessert mono-sphere."

Isabelle had been raised in Culbert, Ohio, a perfectly acceptable small town, neither hideously conservative nor militantly left-wing, but this bland, contented averageness had not only chafed—it had caused Isabelle the most mortifying and ongoing embarrassment. Her parents, an affectionate and puzzled algebra teacher and an insurance broker, had backed Isabelle in every way, lavishing her with TroneTek products that exposed her to the injustices of a larger world and guided her to blame, for example, sex trafficking and blood diamonds on her hometown of Culbert and her parents.

Isabelle, to her credit, had formidable reserves of concern for the chronically homeless, exploited immigrant laborers, and the victims of microaggressions targeted at male preschoolers wearing nail polish, even though none of these outrages had been detected in Culbert. Isabelle's schoolwork had been dull and politically offensive. By third grade she was imploring her teacher, "But why do we celebrate the Fourth of July when the Founding Fathers were white men, slaveowners, and prob-ably smelled?" Isabelle lived online, where she bonded with like-minded activists all over the world, although she fumed impatiently when some of them also burbled about boys and skincare. Isabelle was interested in these topics as well, but with caveats. She'd pore over the Kardashian sisters' posts, but would condemn their moral torpor, toxic femininity, and, as she wrote in a college application essay, "their willingness to profit from a capitalism which deforms them."

Isabelle was fundamentally lonely. She was smarter and more in-quisitive than everyone around her, and ached for the intoxicating fury of a dorm room back-and-forth about unionizing the cafeteria staff. College was her grail: not the elitist echo chambers of the Ivy League, but her arcadia, her Olympus, her Bloomsbury, the notoriously radical and mindfully underwritten (no drug companies or alumni with ties to fracking) Cadmonton College.

Cadmonton, founded by crusading utopians in 1961, was nestled in a Vermont glade, with twisting, single-story, solar-paneled build-ings for the lowest environmental footprint. It was as if the college were apologizing to the local elms and hillocks, and squeezing itself into a guilt-ridden crouch. Isabelle had watched the school's promotional video on YouTube hundreds of times, freeze-framing at the shot of undergraduates seated on logs beside a stream, wearing loose, ungendered clothing, with hairstyles hovering between bedhead and electrocution, passing a conversation flag among themselves. Whoever held this flag would speak, at length, without interruption, especially from male students, who even at Cadmonton would claim to hold acute and superior knowledge of say, the failure of privileged white feminism. The flag itself was an adaptation of the LGBTQ+ rainbow, with newly banded stripes in mauve, burnt sienna, and plaid, identities Isabelle could only, thrillingly, guess at.

Isabelle memorized the list of "alternative and non-canonical" fields of study (which weren't termed majors, as "major" denoted an abhorrent military bureaucracy). Her favorites were Beyond Queer Allyship; Reliving Trauma Through Musical Theater; Thwarted Careerism Among Female Cave Artists; Fascism and Badminton; Eleanor Roosevelt and the Tyranny of Hats; and Emerging Voices in Your Room. Isabelle coveted the vehemently questioning spirit and appreciation of plant-based sandals beaming from every student's face. Cadmonton represented the opposite of her high school's pep-rally and popularity bias. No one at Cadmonton would be popular, only respected and complimented on whatever fragrance they'd blended from the fifteen essential oils shipped to every incoming student (anyone daubed with a store-bought, chemically enhanced, brand-name perfume was hosed down in a cinder-block chamber as if they'd been exposed to radiation rather than Calvin Klein's Eternity.)

Attached to Isabelle's application was a novella in which she roomed at Cadmonton with Emma Goldman and Sojourner Truth, who marched beside her to end the conservatorship of Britney Spears by her authoritarian father. She was accepted on early enrollment, and Cadmonton didn't disappoint. Isabelle's college years were so ideal they crippled her. She'd been not merely heard but ideologically embraced, by people who'd inhaled intersectionality and who never made dumb jokes about waiting for a green light at the intersection of dream journaling and underclass empowerment.

Isabelle sexually experimented with a Filipina who identified as a warrior goddess, a queer man who taught her about weaving wildflower penis wreaths, and a three-person collective dedicated to having sex with food to vanquish the patriarchal miasma long associated with eclairs and body shaming. Isabelle was cognizant that every topic she held most dear could be maligned as a fancy hobby or the subject of satire; what she revered about Cadmonton was that she could ignore or deconstruct these hectoring critics, and have the best possible time pulling every thread of heteronormativity, race, and economic reform to probe how the world functioned and how it might be dismantled and corrected, preferably by her.

Cadmonton was an oasis of ecstatically tormented, competitive midnight confessions and nonspecific backrubs. The outside world (which Isabelle had named the Media-Supported False Reality) would present far more odious challenges. Luckily, Isabelle had swung her vintageponchoed self into New York just as private schools, publishers, and museums were headhunting young people to oversee departments of representation, workplace misbehavior, and hurtful language (Isabelle's Semantics Study Group had analyzed the tribal slur of the term "headhunter"). The director of personnel at W&S had been taken by Isabelle's codifying how master bedrooms, a designation that reeked of empire, shouldn't be labeled as primary bedrooms either, which still implied caste, but as activity-optional spaces. "Rooms should be self-identified," Isabelle had more than suggested. "I would obligate our authors to speak with their rooms rather than imposing archaic cultural norms."

Isabelle's natural assurance, her Cadmonton degree (not called a bachelor's but a certified celebration of self), and her undeniable knack for investigation had made her an instantaneous hire. She was making her presence felt at W&S, and ejecting, or rather "dehiring," Rob was her first important policy statement. She wasn't thoughtless, and she'd sympathized with Rob's unemployment, but she'd disbursed ample warnings and opportunities for not just grudging change or mindless obedience, but evolution. She'd done what had to be done, to usher W&S into a new era of sensitivity and openness.

That night, she ate meatless tacos at her apartment with her life's sole asterisk, with the one shrouded corner where she wavered: her boyfriend Lance. Although she never spoke the word "boyfriend," except once by soul-curdling accident when Marfa, the nonbinary filmmaker, had been bragging about meeting Sandra Bullock to explore a short film about food banks, and Isabelle, desperate to compete, had said, "My boyfriend Lance says I remind him of Sandra Bullock."

Once she'd accepted the job at W&S, but a day before starting work, Isabelle had attended a Young Literary Professionals event in the lobby of JobHub, a building that rented cubicles with Wi-Fi, beanbag chairs, and a choice of framed posters reading "YOU ARE NOT YOUR JOB," "BELIEVE IN BELIEF," and "LOOK INSIDE AND PULL SOMETHING OUT." She hadn't known anyone there, and since the evening was sponsored by a Peruvian vodka, she'd sampled one of their botanical blends. So when someone of medium height, wearing a hoodie that shadowed their face, showed her a video of a panda careening down a waterslide, she'd thought the person was a lesbian, until the hood was shoved back to disclose a young stockbroker trainee named Lance Barrelman, who hailed from Rhode Island and liked to watch soccer, compose rap songs about his favorite soccer players, which he'd post with the tag SOCCERBRO, and make his own craft beer from a kit he'd ordered on Amazon. He'd tagged along with a friend to the event, where he'd hoped to meet "chicks into books or at least podcasts about books."

Ordinarily Isabelle would have scoffed at such a benighted creature, but she was tipsy and he'd asked if he could touch her recycled twill jumpsuit, which he nicknamed "kibbutz ninja." Isabelle, months out of college, had been unattached and cowed by the noise and outfits of the event (so many thickly knitted yet midriff-baring Etsy sweaters!). So when Lance had shared his Uber and then politely invited Isabelle up to his aunt Debbie's condo in Flushing, where he was housesitting while Aunt Debbie was in Arizona for the winter, she'd consented. And when Lance had asked if he could kiss her "gently and briefly," she'd said yes, and then she'd ripped off his hoodie and weirdly sincere *Friends* T-shirt and shouted "Yes, shut up, yes!" as Lance continued to carefully request permission for each subsequent physical contact, until finally, a satisfying hour later, as they lay, sweat-drenched, atop Aunt Debbie's lilac-patterned sheets, which matched the bedskirt and canopy, Lance worried, "I know you said penetrative intercourse was okay, but I just wanted to double-check."

This was the problem. Not only was Lance honorable and aware, the sex was mind-blowing, and if Isabelle was being honest with herself, far more multiorgasmic than anything she'd undergone at Cadmonton, where her nurturing and stroking sessions had been soundtracked by

acoustic ballads about banning fossil fuels and were almost indistinguishable from naps beside stuffed animals. Lance was sweet-natured
and furrowed his brow while Isabelle enumerated, say, issues in marketing Pacific Islander poetry collections, but mostly he gazed at her
lustfully, inhaled her locally sourced, paraben-free detangler and downloaded golf tournaments on his phone, which Isabelle found strangely
erotic. She was, of course, titanically stricken at having attracted such
an inappropriate source of ravishment, and she'd never even alluded to
him with any of her friends or coworkers (until the Sandra Bullock slip).
She classified him as an outreach project, or as someone so unacceptable
he counted as an unheard-of gender-preference category, but mostly she
dodged thinking about him at all until they were in bed together.

Lance is not who I am, she'd told herself the morning she'd gotten
Rob fired. She wouldn't be grouped with cisgender heterosexual Caucasian women, but characterized only by her essence, as a progressive force
for equality, as Isabelle McNally, smashing the paradigms and making
a difference. And even better, later that same day, Arjun passed along
the windfall of her young lifetime, something so precious she at first
forbade herself from telling her friends, because they'd feel less-than. But
her fingertips were already group-texting the development, because she
would be a guest at the wedding of Trone Meston. Arjun had been invited
because Trone had purchased the conglomerate that owned W&S and
was multitasking the wedding as a meet-and-greet-and-intimidate opportunity, for what he'd trademarked as "members of the Meston-verse."

For Isabelle, Trone Meston was beyond judgment. He was an intra-
venous fluid, someone who'd shaped her being. Isabelle's first computer
had been a TroneTek Lapster. She'd had her own Troneville page at
twelve, without her parents' permission, because everyone at her school

had already posted a profile, photos, and hourly musings. Troneville had usurped Facebook as a younger and more far-reaching town square, because there were over 578 gender options, a daily name-changing function, and the relationship status descriptions included Married But Not Like You Think, Pan-Curious When I'm Out Of State, and Alone Because I Have Standards. Troneville's global dominion rested on a simple truth: at heart, everyone is a tween with twinkle lights draped over their bed.

Two years earlier, TroneTek had premiered Trondle, which the marketing materials trumpeted as "Not a hookup app or a dating site, but an unprecedented means of meeting your truest love." As with even TroneTek's most aggressive fans, Isabelle had been confounded: Was this overreach? Was Trondle (a queasy mashup of "Trone" and "fondle") a cheeseball gesture toward exploiting the foolhardy and the unwanted, especially women? Was the word "love" too fraught and clichéd for serious discourse?

Trondle users submitted not porn-influenced, heavily improved selfies and a smattering of Interests and Turn-Offs, but answered only three questions:

1. How necessary is love to your personal well-being?
2. Would you be willing to rent/purchase a home and/or vehicle with a romantic partner?
3. Have you ever said "I love you"? To whom?

Users responded in two sentences per query, many in less. An algorithm, keyed to code words and phrasing, sent an alert to each suitably aligned couple's TronePhones (the service wasn't available on any other brands; the necessary purchase of TroneTek goods accounted for Trondle's revenue). Shockingly, Trondle achieved almost 12 million committed pairings and 5.8 million marriages, besting every other matchmaking service in history.

Trondle was reviled online and jeered at by late-night talk show hosts, but its membership surpassed 50 million and counting (if a match soured, sequential strangers were selected, and while most people sought love, others thrived on being pursued, and on snootily spurning each opportunity, gloating over their continued desirability—they'd often not even meet their potential partners, but store them like baseball cards in a shoebox). Privately, Trone considered the venture an only partial success, a baby step toward his ultimate mastery of human interactions. Linda had ignored Trondle, as chilly and unlikely. Isabelle hadn't dared sign on, because her truest love was already known to her: Trone Meston himself. Trone's age and gender were immaterial, as love dissolved such barriers, even if Isabelle had written an op-ed on these topics for the *Cadmonton Quarterly* entitled "Age and Gender: Instruments of Oppression." Isabelle's love for Trone was both vague and all-devouring. She knew it was impossible, but it felt inevitable. Isabelle had spent her life seeking an equal, someone who wouldn't merely be attracted to her, like Lance, but would understand and challenge her. Someone almost beyond love.

And now, via fate or networking or secular prayer, Isabelle and Trone would unite. While Isabelle hadn't been invited by name, Arjun had been encouraged to bring staffers. Hours earlier Trone had dropped two announcements, in the manner of a Beyoncé or Taylor Swift releasing an album with little fanfare, knowing this was the highest, most effective route to global obsession, like a nonchalant, oh-by-the-way declaration of nuclear war.

First, Trone was getting married to someone named Linda, who no one seemed to know anything about, and while Trone hadn't supplied additional biographical information, the instantaneous Sherlock-caliber searches by people like Isabelle had exposed Linda Kleinschmidt as a flight attendant, the mother of two, and the ex-wife of an obscure TV actor and gym owner named Sean Manginaro, all information that Isabelle rated as ordinary and unworthy of Trone Meston, unless this Linda person was some breed of savant.

The wedding was to take place in two days' time on a private island off the coast of Maine, a property that Trone had been developing at unthinkable expense over the past four years. Trone kept his personal life zealously concealed, so Isabelle was still processing the presence of Linda, who Isabelle conceived of as primarily Someone Not Isabelle.

As if Isabelle's mind weren't sufficiently vaporized, Trone had added a far more shattering and molten announcement. At his wedding, Trone would be presenting not just a new TroneTek commodity, but "a concept which will replace thought" and "redefine love forever." Would this be an outgrowth of Trondle? A separate and costly TroneTek device? A lotion or a patch? Whatever it might prove to be, word of Trone's next-level offering had already enthralled the planet, and Trone's wedding was its nexus. And Isabelle would be there.

Isabelle was twenty-three years old. She lived in Bushwick, among immigrants and white people her own age who congratulated themselves on learning the immigrants' first and last names and waving to them. She had a down-low, discardable lover. She was adeptly cleaning house at W&S, and as a reward, she was going to meet Trone Meston, and not on a Zoom or a mass email, but as an IRL colleague. The only thing left to tweak was, when she mentioned the invitation offhandedly to her

friends, if she should call him Trone, which might come off fangirly, or a
more swaggering Meston, as if they hung out at an exclusive after-hours,
highest-of-stakes, international-waters cryptocurrency casino.

Isabelle was right about herself, in terms of prizes and trajectory.
Her life was careening forward at warp speed, as she'd intended. And
she was in love. Not some plastic-daisies-and-drugstore-candy-box love,
or the rote, nice-try love of her coupled friends, for whom buying a
cheap couch together was the height of communion. Isabelle's love was
destined, a union of enlightened individuals, of two people who'd speak
in an immediate shorthand of worldview, futurism, and systems (the
words tattooed on Isabelle's right calf, a gesture that had constituted
her senior thesis at Cadmonton). Isabelle could barely contain herself as
she packed her favorite oversize, off-the-shoulder crocheted top, which
was sensual yet not basic and tawdry (words she associated with Linda,
who'd been, let's be frank, a flight attendant—not that Isabelle would
condemn flight attendants per se, but certainly the predatory ones like
Linda, who'd undoubtedly deployed her tight-bodied sexuality to be-
witch an innocent Trone, and Linda was, what, forty-seven? Isabelle
wouldn't just be meeting Trone, she'd be rescuing him). This is happening, Isabelle told herself, as planned. No, not just as planned—as fated.

17

EAST AMBERLY

During those first years in their Tudor, Linda had sunk deeply into—no, she still couldn't even think the word, let alone speak it aloud, not yet, so let's call it something like happiness. Something similar to happiness but less hokey. Something next door to happiness but peering over the fence. She was shocked by the discarding of any self-preservation. Her life was, if pressed, she'd at least say good. Good-ish. Good, you know, for what it was. It was as if she'd removed the batteries from every emotional smoke alarm and told herself, fuck everything, I'm going to, okay, she'd at least let herself toy with the idea—she was gingerly dipping a toe into, or almost diving headfirst into, or, fine, she'd tempt the gods and every variety of incipient disaster—she was a somewhat happier version of Linda Kleinschmidt.

Being Linda, she progressed step by step, as her schedule at Defiance shrank to three mornings a week, because the lure of the Tudor and East Amberly was too potent. To people raised in a suburb, the atmosphere can come across as suffocatingly dull, a loop of snowblowing the driveway in January, low-fat blueberry muffins at the outdoor café near the train station, Hot Yoga Flow workouts at the mom gym, visits from plumbers and furnace repair teams, sitting in traffic behind mammoth SUVs, and stultifying weekends as your spouse coaches Little League baseball, watches NFL football in the finished basement, chars burgers, and nods off after a fifth beer in the recliner.

But to Linda, who'd only known lying to impatient landlords on Aileen's behalf, mismatched dining table chairs found on the street and patched with duct tape, and the all-night glare of headlights from the turnpike just outside her window, East Amberly was not merely exotic and wondrous but downright interstellar. She passed her first year as a newbie, or possibly a Russian mole undercover as a busy American gal. She haunted the big box stores, nabbing budget-savvy, twenty-five-roll bundles of paper towels, and then she'd buy a countertop paper towel holder, and a quilted cover for the toaster, and a blender in the same aquamarine enamel as the toaster, and at the Pottery Barn outlet, which was practically giving them away, she'd stockpile throw pillows and questionable accent pieces, like wooden bowls that held spheres bent from reeds, and wall art utilizing Arizona license plates and iron gears that had never been used in machinery but manufactured in China as "collectibles." One afternoon Linda canvassed three home goods stores to compare the microscopically differing sets of bamboo wind chimes she'd checkmarked online, and she'd called Aileen for the first time in a year to report, "Guess what, I bought wind chimes."

Sean followed Linda's Connecticut expeditions with love and amusement. She wasn't a hoarder or a spendthrift; each purchase was minutely assessed and often returned. Linda was tiptoeing toward a new life, a life he was delighted to abet. Sean wasn't especially acquisitive himself, with a limited wardrobe of Defiance-trademarked workout gear and few other needs. He bought a handful of Dude Dad must-haves: a mid-range "chronometer" wristwatch, a Harley, and a small fiberglass boat for a nearby lake. He'd come home to find Linda wandering amid half-opened boxes, taking a break with a glass of wine, and she'd demonstrate her latest stepladder or rotating spice rack or "whatever the hell this thing is." They were playing house, because that was what couples their age did, and because it was fun to imitate those couples, while pretending you weren't becoming them.

The second year, Linda asked Sean, over a lazy Sunday brunch of bagels, croissants, and lox, in a gingham-napkin-lined basket, "So—a baby. What are you thinking?"

Sean had anticipated this conversation. Early in their dating era, he had agreed to having kids, on an abstract level. There was something sad about guys in their thirties without wives or offspring. Something enviable as well, but mostly depressing, like, bro, get with the program.

Linda was serious. She wasn't someone to suggestively leave parenting magazines atop the hamper in the bathroom or coo over a TV show where an exquisitely groomed actress gives birth to a pristine, obviously five-month-old infant. Linda hadn't been sure she wanted kids: What if she forgot to pick them up after school, for hours? What if she ignored them in favor of late-afternoon talk shows and weed? What if she was Aileen only even more addled and absent? She'd also vacillated about Sean as a dad. He'd be great at tossing a toddler on board his motorcycle, and refereeing backyard push-up contests. He'd be a rowdy, active father, swinging a five-year-old laughing through the breeze. But what about the hard stuff: Could Sean be a disciplinarian, could he be relied on during a colic or measles outbreak, would he get enraged with a kid obstinately bored by whiffle ball?

"We won't have a kid if you don't want one," Linda decreed, spreading cream cheese on a cinnamon-and-raisin bagel, because this was America.

Sean looked out the window at the yard he mowed every other week, and pictured a kid or more doing cartwheels or leaving a bike out in the rain. He accepted that these moments were sitcom nuggets. He had no idea what actually having a kid would be like. But this was a challenge, something Sean lived for. Tell Sean he couldn't accomplish an objective, or that he'd come in, at best, twelfth in a competition, and he was yours. I can have kids, he thought, watch me.

"We're not just gonna have a kid," Sean told Linda, downing his whey protein shake. "We're gonna have an amazing fucking kid. We're gonna have the best kid ever. I mean, look at us, is this a super-charged gene pool or what?"

"Yeah, but what if the kid is weird or hates us or ends up with the worst parts of both of us?"

"Then we'll put it on eBay. Babe, what are the worst parts of us? You've got trust issues and mom issues and you're like, five-two on a good day. You're a nasty little munchkin. And my problem is that I'm too fucking perfect. So the kid might be jealous or intimidated. But none of that matters because our kid is still gonna be better-looking than every other kid in the fucking neighborhood."

"What is wrong with you?"

Linda was staring at him, as she so often did, dazzled by his robust ego and ebullient idiocy.

"That's the fucking problem, and believe me, because I've thought about this. I've worked on it. I've been like, totally honest with myself. I've asked myself, Dude, what is wrong with me? And you know what the answer is?"

Linda wondered if Sean's brain could be removed from his admittedly well-shaped skull and dissected and studied, say, later that weekend.

"There's only one thing that's wrong with me. I need a kid!"

Linda laughed, because there were no guarantees. She'd taken a dare in marrying Sean, and another in moving to East Amberly. Having a baby was, of course, a far greater unknown, with the most worrisome downside. But one of the reasons, probably the main reason, she loved Sean was that he helped her take risks, the wildest possible swings. Once again, she was believing in Sean, and in the hazy-but-possible presence of goodness in the universe, and later that afternoon, as they made love with an increased sense of purpose, Sean whispered in her ear, "Can you feel that? I just gave you totally incredible baby jizz. I mean, we could sell that."

Three months later, during an ultrasound, Linda's ob-gyn congratulated the couple on having twins. This wasn't what they'd signed on for. This was too real. This was God laughing at them, for conceiving so readily.

"Twins? Like, two babies?" Sean asked.

"Yes," said the ob-gyn, a young woman who'd often been asked to define "twins," by other expectant dads.

"Twins," said Linda, rocked by the savage effect on her body, the opportunity to ruin two innocent lives (four if she included herself and Sean), and the sheer effort: two sets of everything, twice the crying and comforting, two tiny mouths, four tiny arms, the exhaustion, the expense, the inevitable comparisons between the matched set.

Sean keyed into Linda's totally understandable shock, which solved his own. Sean obeyed an unshakable roster of masculine imperatives, a bible of manhood: A man doesn't flee the scene of an accident, especially if he was at fault. A man doesn't pee in a stranger's shower, only his own. A man is patient with people who whimper and clutch the side of the pool while he's teaching them to swim. A man helps his friends move. A man raises money for the sick child of a drinking buddy. A man calls his dog "buddy." And above all else, a man supports his wife in every way. Once he's taken a vow, a man is obliged to ride his wife's mood swings. A man makes his wife feel better about everything. A man consciously lowers the emotional temperature during arguments, even if his stoic placidity only makes his wife more livid. A man physically threatens a guy who's ogling his wife at a bar, even if his wife insists she's disgusted by both men's asshole macho bluster. A man makes his wife feel safe.

"Okay," said Sean. "I know what this is. It's like one baby isn't enough. It's too easy. Anybody can have one baby, that's like baby practice. But what's like, a trillion times better than one baby? Two fuckin' babies. It's like the big dick of having babies. So when we're taking 'em out of the car, and people are going, 'Dude, what a cute baby,' we can say, 'Yo, you think this baby is cute,' and we haul out the other one. *Boom!*"

Linda smiled, barely processing the news. She had Sean, which, on a certain level, would mean three kids. But Sean was one of the world's great optimists, and more than ever, Linda clung to that. And she estimated that, thanks to Sean's strength and agility, he could juggle the physical demands of twins, lifting two chortling babies high over his head and corralling them on a playground as they speed-crawled in opposite directions.

Jesus, she thought. I'm married, I live in Connecticut, in a Tudor, and now I'm having twins. I'm all in. I guess I mean this. She suppressed a desire to scream at the top of her lungs with everything from mind-bending what-the-fuck-are-these-babies-doing-inside-me panic to helium-strength I-already-love-them-beyond-life-and-death euphoria.

————

As her belly swelled, Linda was set on reinventing herself as a cool mom-to-be and even, although she'd never even hint at this to anyone, a sexy mom-to-be. She worked out, adjusting her kettlebell and running routines, and abstaining from any stretch-paneled, voluminous specialty garb, save for a pair of white jeans with an elasticized waistband. She browsed for tank tops in larger sizes and a few gauzy skirts, but otherwise she stuck to leggings, Defiance T-shirts, and men's dress shirts with the sleeves rolled up and enough buttons undone to reveal a camisole.

"Babe, you look amazing," Sean told her, watching her get dressed. "You're like mommy porn. Have you ever seen that stuff, there's all these websites with pregnant chicks having sex. But you're like, what those chicks can only dream about. Get over here."

Linda was torn, between smacking Sean for visiting such sites, applauding the depraved feminism of promoting pregnant women as sexual beings, and wishing she'd never heard of mommy porn.

At the gym, Sean confided to Rob: "Linda's six months in and I still can't get enough. At first I wondered, Hold on, am I like all of a sudden into fat chicks? But that's not it, and sometimes she says she's too tired, so I respect that. But here's what I'm worried about: What if my dick hurts the babies? What if it slams into one of their little heads and leaves a dent? Or what if they fight over it?"

Rob became Linda, contemplating this muscular lout. "You should worry. Because I've read that if you have sex with a pregnant woman, sometimes the baby can actually bite the guy's dick off, because the baby's hungry."

"Is that true? Where did you see that?"

"Online. And you're having two babies, so they might start a tug-of-war. Or one baby might say, 'Why isn't it bigger?' and the other baby would answer, 'Maybe tomorrow she'll have sex with somebody who's hung.'"

"Okay, now I don't believe you."

"Google it."

Rob would report to Jake as Sean grappled with his daddy-to-be turmoil. Sean was, as always, energized and diligent, hammering together two cribs, installing two baby seats in his truck, and painting two bureaus to which he'd ultimately add the babies' names, once they were selected. A subsequent ultrasound indicated a boy and a girl, or as Sean liked to tell Linda, "a real baby and another one," just so she would kick him in bed. In truth, the genders were a gift, as they'd make further offspring either unnecessary or a far-in-the-future decision. Linda downloaded lists of names, despite Sean's rooting for Blaster and Blasterette. In the trend of the day, they went for the not-too-quirky yet not-too-traditional Bridger and Morrow. Jake told Rob that these names sounded like a wine cooler, a law firm on a soap opera, or animated bunnies in a Disney film. Rob and Jake made a point of taking Linda out to lunch during her pregnancy, so she could vent about Sean. "He's being great," she admitted. "He takes me to my appointments, he's doing the carpentry in the nursery, he's making sure I eat right, and he keeps saying he's stoked. But every once in a while I want to ask him, 'You know these babies are real, right? Real human babies?'"

"He's going to be a great dad," said Rob. "As long as he doesn't start training them for the shot put."

"And you do look terrific," said Jake.

"I'm a fucking house. I'm a barn."

"Oh, please," said Rob. "You're the only pregnant woman I've ever seen who still has a great haircut."

"And every woman in this restaurant is checking you out," said Jake. "And thinking, maybe having a baby isn't so bad. Unless they're thinking you're a model with a pillow under your shirt."

Linda consequently advised every mom-to-be she encountered, "Talk to gay men. They know what their job is."

———————

Two days after Linda gave birth, Sean recounted the ordeal to Rob, during their workout: "Man, it was intense. I mean, I thought I was prepared, but *I was not prepared.* We'd gone to those classes, and I'd tried really hard to pay attention, but after a while I'd started thinking, come on, basically it's the mom's job to have the babies and it's the dad's job to, I don't know, stand a few feet away and go, 'Yay, Mom! Way to have babies!'

"So it's three in the morning and Linda wakes me up and says, 'It's time.' And I go, 'But it's not supposed to be for two more weeks,' and she says, 'Get the car started.' So I'm driving to the hospital and we're timing the contractions and I guess I'm a monster because I kept thinking, Please don't have the babies in the car, the upholstery is almost brand-new. But she makes it to the hospital over in New Canaan, and they get her into a wheelchair and her doctor shows up and she's amazing, she says she figured this might happen, and I'm thinking, *So why didn't you tell me?* And they give Linda some drugs but not enough, because she's still moaning and cursing me, she's saying, why doesn't she have one of the babies and I can squeeze the other one out of my dick, which of course makes me picture it and I'm like, *No way!*

"And we're in the delivery room and they give me a gown and the hat thing, and I'm thinking that Linda's the quarterback and she'll shoot those babies out of her cooch and I'll go long and catch them, but that's not how it goes. I'm holding her hand and telling her to breathe and push, and she's screaming, 'YOU DID THIS,' and I'm trying not to laugh, but I tell her, 'Okay, just push these suckers out and I'll redo our master bathroom,' and she screams, 'AND THE KITCHEN!' And there's nurses and everyone's doing their thing and I'm picturing the babies shoving each other, like 'Me first!,' 'No, me, motherfucker!' and then I see one of the baby's heads and it's covered with glop but it's like, whoa, that is a baby, and then I see that it's the boy baby and his dick is not bad at all and I want to tell everyone, 'Yup, I'm the dad,' but I figure maybe not yet, and then the girl baby comes out, and I'm thinking, Of course she's late because she's a chick so she was still getting ready, but I don't say that out loud either, and they're cleaning the babies off, and I'm still holding Linda's hand and she's all sweaty and wiped out, but she kinda looks amazing and they hand the babies to her and she's holding them, it's like there was a sale on babies, and she looks up at me, like she still can't believe it, and I say, 'Babe, you're a champ,' and I go to take one of the babies, but she's not ready to let go of both of 'em, not yet, and I'm thinking, Okay, now I'm a dad. Like all of a sudden I'm wearing khakis and a windbreaker."

"So did it feel like a miracle?" Rob asked.

"Sort of, but I mean, that's how the whole having-babies deal works. It was more like, So now does everything change? Linda and me? The whole world? Or am I just, me with babies? I don't know, man. I'm working on it. But yo, let's do chest and legs, because you gotta get stronger, for when you start babysitting."

Linda was sent home from the hospital after an overnight stay, and Sean had made sure a nanny would be on-site for the next two weeks. Bridger and Morrow were, so far, exceedingly well behaved, napping for hours at a time and blowing spit bubbles and greedily drinking the breast milk Linda diligently pumped. The most definitive revelation was their continued presence: these babies were here for at least the next eighteen years. They were permanent fixtures. When Linda's mind drifted for a few seconds, to a TV commercial or a meal of her own, her thoughts would lurch: Where are the babies, what are they doing, do they know who I am yet, and what am I doing wrong?

Linda forced Sean to return to work, to pay for the babies' toys, healthcare, and eventual therapy, but even more so he wouldn't start squirming from their new circumstance. Sean deserved independence and a social scene, to deter him from being buried beneath a daycare center's worth of multicolored pacifiers, instantly outgrown onesies, and quilted duffels jammed with blankies and bottles.

Linda sat on the living room couch, with the twins asleep in matching nearby bassinets, and the nanny in the kitchen unwrapping a tinfoiled sandwich while chatting on the phone with her sister in Queens. Linda almost called Aileen, who'd of course promised to drop by the hospital to view "What are their names? Bridget and Martin?" but had never shown up. Linda hadn't expected her to. Someday, years from now, Linda would introduce the twins to Aileen by saying, "This is Mommy's mommy. Or so she claims."

Linda would be fiercely attentive, even smothering, anything to forestall neglecting her kids. Everything was in order: Sean, the Tudor, the baby-proofing on the sharp edges of the coffee table and all the lower cabinet doors, the list of emergency phone numbers stuck on the fridge with a stork magnet (with additional copies throughout the house), not to mention two spots being held on the pre-K waiting list at a well-thought-of local public school. But I'm a hopeless fraud, Linda thought obsessively, as if she'd bought this life from a home goods store and was still trying to read the directions, most of which were printed upside down in the tiniest font, in an unknown and possibly nonexistent language.

This is what I want, she told herself. This is the right idea. Sean and I will figure this out. But of course, capable child-rearing, let alone a coherent marriage, depended on something Linda was barely familiar with, and would innately dispute: trust. But I'm doing this, she averred. It's not even a choice. I will fucking make this work, even if it's just to fend off Aileen's triumphant, you-thought-you-were-so-much-better-than-me sneer.

And then—it happened. Some cosmic wheel of rapture turned skyward and doves were released, as Linda made the most treacherous move of all. She beheld her sleeping babies and her artfully rough-hewn teal ceramic lamps and her cream-colored wool Berber carpeting (which she'd already Scotchgarded, twice). She reached out her arms, as if she could enfold her mirage of a home and these two slumbering new lives, along with the man she loved, despite the fact that he'd wanted to write M and B on the babies' foreheads with Magic Marker.

I think I may be . . . Say it, Linda. Say the goddamn word. You're ready. If not now, when? Fine. Yes. It's time. I'm . . . happy. Fuck me. No. People can be happy. It's not just a rumor. There's an herb garden on glass shelves in my kitchen's bay window. Maybe all this isn't happiness itself, but it's a start, it's equipment for this inconceivable task, it's what other people have—the people whose homes and lives Aileen would drive us past, in her latest boyfriend's corroded, twenty-year-old Range Rover, on her way to a court appearance, which had been scheduled for the day before, but she'd lost the subpoena. And I'm so fucking tired. But—I'm happy. No, not just that. I'm . . . someone else. Someone new. Love, for Sean and our kids, has changed everything, and I'm not going to qualify that, even as my eyes sweep the room for wood to knock on.

When the nanny entered, bringing Linda an oversize chocolate chip cookie on a paper napkin, she encountered a sight familiar from her long career (eighteen years, at least twenty-five babies and counting). Everyone in the living room was smiling and lightly snoring and asleep.

On Friday of that week, Sean's last two clients of the day canceled. It was July, so they were helicoptering out to Southhampton and flying up to Provincetown, respectively. Rob had left with Jake to visit friends on Fire Island the day before, after gifting the babies with two exquisitely hand-stitched stuffed animals, a giraffe and a penguin, in a pale blue damask and a hunter-green corduroy, from a Soho company founded by one of Jake's clients. A certain strata of gay men give only museum-gift-shop baby gifts, because someone has to resist the battery-operated hot-pink plastic crap that will accumulate grime during its first use (and which the infants will prefer). "So you want both of my kids to be gay," Sean had commented, to which Rob had replied, "No, then we would've given them books."

Rather than battling rush-hour traffic to Connecticut, Sean waited out the highway gridlock at the bar of an Irish-themed pub on Eighth Avenue, one of those pleasingly dim, grubby hangouts owned by a single family for over sixty years. Sean usually retreated to a gay-centric restaurant because he liked the company, and where he'd be admired yet not enticed. But this afternoon, for some reason, he revisited O'Malley's for the first time since his college days.

The place was fairly empty, like much of Manhattan in the summer heat, but a very pretty girl named Stacie was tending bar, to fund her tuition at the nearby Fashion Institute, where she studied Business Administration. Stacie wasn't half as beautiful as Linda, but she was twenty-two and wearing a T-shirt with the bar's shamrock-and-harp logo knotted under her breasts, and a denim micro-skirt, a look that drew generous tips from the construction workers and post office employees who frequented the pub.

Sean chatted with Stacie. While he flirted with everyone at Defiance, he hadn't gone bar-crawling in years. He asked where Stacie had grown up (Wisconsin), how many siblings she had (two older sisters), and where her boyfriend was right now (Stacie had no idea, since she'd dumped him six months earlier because he wouldn't shut up about the Knicks). Sean kept his banter blameless but targeted, based in time-tested strategies he'd retired long ago. Young women liked to talk about themselves, and once Sean let it drop that he worked in fitness, Stacie avidly catalogued her flaws ("My butt is so flat") and wheedled for tips on upgrading her cardio routines ("I hate spin classes") and diet ("Do you do that keto thing?"). Sean took this seriously, recommending flexibility warm-ups and interval training ("Do the bike for fifteen minutes, then sprints, then the stair climber, then do the whole circuit three more times. You'll be dead but your legs will look phenomenal").

In between waiting on a handful of other customers, Stacie would head back to Sean. Having Googled him, she called him Blaster and interrogated him about the show. Stacie was ten years younger than Sean, but her dad had taped every episode of *WarForce*. This made Sean feel prehistoric, but older guys, especially older guys who filled out their Defiance T-shirts as impressively as Sean did, were very much Stacie's go-to fantasy material. Sean was still too youthful to reconceive of himself as a daddy figure, but this category awaited.

He didn't bring up Linda or his newborn twins, and Stacie didn't ask, and he'd slipped off his wedding ring at the gym, where it hampered workouts. He'd ordinarily retrieve it from his wallet before hitting the street, but he hadn't.

Stacie said, in passing, that her shift was ending shortly, and she was starving. There was a pause, as Sean compelled his mind to go blank and not compute traffic patterns and plausible excuses and the costly gourmet mini-cupcakes he'd pick up later as a surprise treat for Linda. I'm not doing this, he told himself. I was only checking to see if I still could, if my bulging pecs and blue eyes were still functioning, or had been mothballed. To find out if I was still in the game, without actually playing. I love Linda, and those babies are the best thing that's ever happened to me—this was true but also a tether, a blinking warning light, an extremely pleasurable cage which he'd willingly locked himself into, while being able to peer through the bars at the other animals, one of whom had tugged her streaked blonde ponytail through the opening at the back of her ball cap, a habit that Sean and his crotch thoroughly approved of.

Sean excused himself, after tucking the receipt scrawled with Stacie's cell number into his gym bag, just to be polite. That was enough, at least for right now, to give him a testosterone boost, an on-the-hunt sizzle. No harm, no foul, he told himself, making a grateful escape, as Stacie bit her lip over his rock-hard ass in that brand of athletic-fit jeans he'd happened on, for men with over-developed thighs, or in bodybuilding parlance, "wheels."

I'm good, Sean told himself, steering his Jeep up his East Amberly driveway, to his now seriously overpopulated house. Am I growing up, he deliberated, or getting old? What's the difference? Richer, more lasting satisfactions or gaining ten pounds (something he'd read happened with each passing decade, despite vigilant exercise)? Am I turning into my dad or am I some lucky hybrid of happily married father of twins and stud-on-the-town? What are the rules for this shit and how do I know if I'm breaking them?

18

UNDERWAY

Rob, as a pack mule, lugged two of Paolo's bloated Gucci garment bags, while Paolo followed with a wheeled, molded carbon suitcase the size and luster of a Volvo. Paolo had donned an even larger Jackie O–scale pair of sunglasses and a wide-brimmed raffia beach hat, to disguise himself. "Do you think Dax would recognize me?" he asked Rob, who replied, "Only if your dating profile picture is of your mom playing canasta by the pool." When they stopped off at his apartment, Rob finished his own packing. Most of his nicer shirts were at the dry cleaner's, so he opened the louvered door to Jake's side of the bedroom closet. Rob had trained himself to never do this, because the fastidious elegance of Jake's wardrobe was a powerful expression of the man himself. The expertly folded sweaters, the baskets of socks and underwear, all rolled like gourmet hors d'oeuvres, the rack of linen jackets—Jake had prided himself on attaining the optimal metric for linen garments, between too-stiffly starched and accordion creased. "Wearing linen," he had decreed, "requires that rarest of attributes—grace."

Jake's clothing was still infused with the light, lemony scent he some-times favored, from a pharmacy in Naples. He'd tuck a bar of similarly fragrant soap beside his Marine Corps–ready stack of white T-shirts ("colored T-shirts are trying too hard"). Jake's closet was rigorously art-directed, and Rob had once switched two of Jake's belts on a hanging rack to find out if Jake would intuit the crime and restore order. He had, along with leaving a Post-it adhered to Rob's far more arbitrary clump of Levi's, reading "I forgive you. Once."

Jake's closet made Rob smile and then, as he started to sob, there was Paolo's hand on his shoulder: "I always imagined that Jake could iron handkerchieves with his mind."

Rob faced Paolo: "I know I should donate all of Jake's things, but I can't. I just . . . I'm not kidding myself, I don't think he's coming back, it's just every time I almost borrow something, I can feel his hand slap-ping mine, like he's saying, 'Don't touch my things.' He was so strict."

Jake's wristwatch glinted from a porcelain tray. The watch had been his grandfather's. It wasn't an inherently valuable item, just a chunky Timex with a leather wristband. But Jake had adored his grandfather, who'd died when Jake was twelve. "He was probably gay," Jake had speculated, "be-cause he'd sneak me out of my father's church and take me to the movies. And he'd listen to my problems with my parents until one day he gave me this watch and smiled and said, 'The first chance you get—run.'"

Jake had kept wearing the watch, even after he wasn't able to move more than his eyes, let alone raise his arm to check the time. For that last year, Jake had asked Rob to dress him, for a semblance of his previ-ous life and personality. Only in the final months did he succumb to the practicality of sweatpants and slippers. But he'd died with the watch in place, and now Rob reached for it, then jerked his arm back.

"Take it," Paolo advised. "Wear it. You don't need to obliterate him. And it's a beautiful watch. From the first time I met Jake I thought that watch was so sexy. Very shop-teacher-I-had-a-crush-on."

Rob was sitting on the bed, heaving, unable to move. Going to Maine, to a stranger's wedding, would be ludicrous. But Sean was right. With his job and Jake gone, there was nothing keeping him in the city. Paolo had retrieved the watch and was buckling the band onto Rob's wrist. Maybe, Rob thought, the watch will bestow superpowers, so I can point it at, say, Isabelle McNally and her head will burst into flames. Rob never wore a watch, let alone Jake's. He rotated his forearm, with its unaccustomed weight, asking himself why it hadn't stopped at the exact second of Jake's death. This made Rob recall the evening surrounding that death, so he shut his eyes, something he'd been doing more frequently, to blot out horrific or simply unbearably personal memories. As Rob and Paolo passed through the kitchen, Tria offered, "It's fifty-eight degrees outside with partial sun. Have a great day!"

"Come on," said Paolo, "we have to meet Sean. And if we run into Dax, I'm going to use you as a human shield, is that okay? I mean, I once gave you a free cleaning."

––––––––

Sean was behind the wheel of the Defiance van, parked on a street near the gym. The van ordinarily transported equipment and team members competing in tristate area events. There was a racing bike in the rear, which still left room for everyone's luggage, and Rob climbed in beside Sean, with Paolo in the back seat. The van was painted with an outsize version of the Defiance logo, which made Paolo comment, "This is giving me PTSD about summer camp, when a van would take us to the lake for swimming lessons and archery. I totally identified with convicts on a chain gang being bussed to a work farm upstate. I would keep my earbuds in and play my entire Barbara Cook library. But no one came to rescue me."

"Are you gonna be okay?" Sean asked Paolo. "Are you gonna barf? Because you can hang your head out the window like a beagle."

"I'm good. I'm just going to lay down on the seat until we leave the city, in case Dax is following me."

"Is Dax a real person?" Sean asked. "Or is this like gay Dungeons & Dragons?"

"I think he's real," Rob ventured. "Paolo only hallucinates boyfriends while he's watching movies about male strippers."

"I wasn't hallucinating! Channing Tatum spoke to me from the screen, but we both accepted that there'd be career issues keeping us apart, the dentist vs. stripper thing. But you wait, in the next sequel he swore he'd wear a dental smock and then rip it off, while thinking of me. He said the movie would be called *Open Wide*."

"But explain to me again," Rob asked Sean, "why are we driving to Maine instead of flying like human beings?"

Sean sighed, easing the van into traffic: "Because we have two days to get there, and if I stay here I'll sit around and get drunk and go crazy, and if I get up there too early it'll be even worse, because I'll grab that Trone motherfucker and beat the shit out of him and get arrested, so we need to come up with like, a vision quest. So by the time we hit Maine, we have a one billion percent foolproof, killer plan and we'll just methodically execute it, like a Jason Bourne movie, or one of those Jason Statham things where he massacres thousands of drug cartel bodyguards without taking off his jacket and tie."

"But, and no offense," said Paolo, or Paolo's voice, since he was lying huddled along the back seat, "isn't this whole thing a little Cro-Magnon? Like, are you going to chloroform Linda and kidnap her? Or will you just watch her get married and torture yourself? Sean, wouldn't it be easier to just turn gay? That way you could act incredibly gracious, which would make Linda insane."

Certain gay men, Paolo included, honestly believed that the power of millions of homosexuals, masturbating as one, could laser their desires directly at a chosen straight guy and rearrange his gender preference DNA (as a form of gay prayer). So far this thesis had failed with the male model in a Giorgio Armani cologne campaign, several Olympic water polo champions, and such universal lust objects as Chris Evans, Chris Hemsworth, and almost anyone named Chris or Brad. This is related to another American syndrome, in which any even mildly handsome male actor is designated as gay by two groups: gay men, deluded enough to think they'd have a shot, and straight men, who strive to eliminate rivals. Straight women, conversely, will often refuse to accept the homosexuality of even out gay heartthrobs, because "he might not be totally gay." All of this results in, for example, half the country alleging over Thanksgiving turkey that Tom Cruise is gay ("Everybody knows that"), the other half assigning him cowboy-booted, mirrored-aviator heterosexuality, and stragglers extrapolating that "He's like some whole other thing, 'cause he's a Scientologist." Tom's multiple marriages, and his tabloid-reported interviewing of prospective girlfriends, will be entered into evidence by all factions.

When Rob and Jake had lectured Paolo on the uselessness and even self-loathing of panting for straight guys, Paolo had replied, "Excuse me, do you think any scientific breakthrough happens overnight? The effectiveness of a mass gay ray is still being tested, but I'm telling you, the last time I saw Jake Gyllenhaal on a talk show, I could tell he was starting to question everything."

"Dude," said Sean, "I'd go gay in a heartbeat, I'm so jealous of you guys, it makes everything so much easier. I mean, Rob, I know that you and Jake had fights, but you'd get over them in five minutes. And you'd never accuse each other of being a man. And you wouldn't get all bent out of shape if one of you just accidentally glanced at some other dude's ass, right? But my problem is, when I think about fucking a dude, it just isn't happening."

"Have you even tried?" asked Paolo.

"No. I mean, have you tried having sex with a woman?"

"Don't be ridiculous. A man having sex with a woman? When has that ever happened? It's an urban legend, like alligators in the sewers. And it's insulting to lesbians. You are so insensitive. Which means you are straight."

"Would you have sex with Chris Hemsworth dressed as Thor?" Rob inquired. Sean idolized Thor, as an extension of, or heir to, Blaster. Chris Hemsworth was also one of the few stars Sean deemed in decent shape, "although he needs to work on his calves." Sean thought seriously about the sexual aspect, tilting his head to each side, as if Chris Hemsworth might proposition him later that day.

"Maybe. But I'd be the top. And I'd get Thor's magic hammer. Because baby, you know what the ladies say? They say, 'Sean, you do have a magic hammer.'"

While Sean was howling with laughter at this, Rob and Paolo were rueful. "You see?" Rob told Paolo. "Only a straight guy would say that."

"Will your kids be at the wedding?" Paolo asked.

"I think so. Bridger isn't speaking to me at the moment, and Morrow warned me not to come. He says I'll ruin everything by yelling or by shooting myself in the middle of the ceremony. Which is not the worst tactic. I mean, what if I stand up and say how much I love Linda and then shoot myself, but maybe just graze my ear? And she'd rush to my side to hold me and she'd look into my eyes and remember how much she loves me and maybe I could pretend to die."

"And only her kiss can bring you back to life," Paolo added.

"Or anal," Sean considered. "So maybe the shooting myself thing could work, you think?"

"No," said Rob, "because you could accidentally shoot one of the bridesmaids or the minister. And Linda would just roll her eyes and ask, 'What is wrong with you?' You need a much better angle, or maybe we should just go to the wedding, sit there quietly, and you can use the experience to, once and for all, get over this whole thing. To accept that Linda isn't coming back and stop stalking her."

"What's the difference," asked Paolo, "between a hopeless romantic and a stalker?"

"Weapons and free time," Rob ventured.

"I'm not a stalker," said Sean, "because she invited me. So if I don't do something, something major, I'll regret it forever. And Rob, you can't really talk about accepting shit. Because you are not dealing with Jake, not at all. I watch you, and I know you, and you're completely stuck. Like, two weeks ago, when I said, 'Let's try those new balance exercises with the physio-ball,' you looked at me and said, 'Why?' And I said, 'Because you're not getting any younger and you don't want to break a hip.' And you said, 'No, I mean, why do anything?'"

19

PARADISE

If there was a moment when Linda's antennae had quivered over a substantial menace to her sometimes-ragged-but-unexpectedly-real homespun happiness, it occurred during the twins' twelfth birthday party, which took place at the Tudor with a high-decibel batch of other kids and a handful of parents, stepparents, and newly acquired parental love interests called things like "Dad's friend" and "Mom's tennis guy."

Sean was running late, at a Chicago conference that headlined one of his go-to motivational speakers, a Black ex-marine named Hoyt Malveaux, who was also an ex–drug addict, an ex-alcoholic, and a multiple ex-husband. He'd spent a few unspecified years in jail following a pitbull-sperm-smuggling deal gone bad, and hit "every sort of rock bottom" before refashioning himself as "the guru of get-off-your-ass." Sean had followed Hoyt on YouTube, taking inspiration from Hoyt's many "Never Enough" speeches. Sean was especially galvanized because Hoyt was six feet, five inches of pure muscle, showcased in trim-fitting slacks and custom-made dress shirts, which clung to Hoyt's massive shoulder caps and jutting chest. Sean was all about hard, concentrated work of all kinds, and Hoyt was pushing him even farther.

Sean had sat in a hotel ballroom with a range of Hoyt devotees, including small-business owners; lifelong fuck-ups foraging for an abracadabra answer; lower-middle-class immigrants who were already holding down three jobs and sending almost their entire paycheck back home to Honduras, Syria, or Guatemala; older, recently downsized execs; kids still in business school; and anyone else who wanted a way out and up, a means of becoming their own boss or a homeowner.

"You probably think you work pretty damn hard," said Hoyt, roaming the stage, part commander in chief, part diesel-fueled stand-up. "You put in the time, you feed your family, you're always on the lookout for the next opportunity. Well, let me tell you something—you don't do shit. You're barely trying. You're working at maybe, at most . . ."

He snorted dramatically, as if doing the math in his head, as if he hadn't repeated this equation thousands of times.

"Twenty fucking percent, and for most of you, it's more like half that. You get home at 10 p.m., you wake up at 5, you only take Saturdays off, your kids barely see you. Well, fuck you, loser. Wake up at 4, get home after midnight, stop sleeping in on Saturdays, because you know what? Your kids don't need to see you—they need to see what you can do. They need to be proud of you. Your kids need an example, of a mom or a dad who's putting out 90 percent, 98 percent, and even that's not enough, why aren't you fucking cranking out 110 percent, 500 percent, you lazy fucking snowflakes?"

For some reason, being accused of such inexcusable sloth made the crowd leap to its collective feet and not just cheer but fist-pump and howl. Sean, without meaning to, stood and yelled, "FUCK, YEAH!" As everyone sat, Hoyt continued, at full volume into his hand mic, for the next hour, bellowing such catchphrases as "Your mama was wrong—being your best self means JACK SHIT," "You can always do more and you fucking KNOW IT," "If you're not pushing yourself too hard, if your doctor isn't worried about you dying on your feet, if your brain isn't fucking exploding with fifty new ideas a minute, you're doing it wrong," and his watch cry, "There is no enough! There's only fucking NEVER ENOUGH!"

Since his kids had been born, Sean had known a relentless thrum of anxiety, an insistent harkening to never let up, to exterminate even a second's complacency or ease. Some of this was physical: he was running fifteen miles a day, then biking fifty miles and swimming at least thirty laps. He'd reached 190 pounds of etched sinew at 4.5 percent bodyfat. He loved his wife and twins more than ever, but they might be a trap, a lulling nest, something anchoring him in place. Hoyt tapped into Sean's greatest virtue—his unstoppable zeal to improve—and his most hazardous tendency: a bottomless terror of peaking and slipping downward, of never measuring up to his own unreachable expectations. Sean had also just turned forty and spent each morning shaving away the white hairs sprouting along his chin. This was both vanity and a foreboding, not of death but of a death without sufficient accomplishment, without going full, balls-out, I-will-wipe-up-the-floor-with-my-competitors Sean Manginaro.

After the speech Sean had bought Hoyt's latest book, titled *You're Fooling Yourself and You Know It*, at a card table in the hotel lobby, and he'd posed for a selfie beside Hoyt, who dwarfed him and who, after clamping a beefy arm around Sean's shoulders for the photo, asked, "What are you doing in the next thirty seconds to super-charge your pathetic fucking excuse for a life?"

This had rattled Sean, as his next hour was spent in traffic, in a rental car on the way to the airport, the antithesis of any enriched-plutonium thrust upward. With his flight delayed, Sean sat in a nameless airport bar, nursing a beer served to him by Erinn, a twenty-five-year-old off-season snowboarding instructor. Erinn had recognized Sean, not from *WarForce* but an in-flight magazine article on "12 Entrepreneurs Under 40 to Watch." When Erinn guessed Sean's age at twenty-eight, he didn't correct her. He was drawn to her goofy smile, her ponytail, and her trim ass, but mostly he liked that since she was working at an out-of-town airport bar, any encounter became weightless, off the clock, something occurring in a phantom zone without guilt or reality.

They had sex at Erinn's nearby apartment, with her two roommates due back any minute. Sean couldn't acknowledge what he was doing, only that he hadn't had sex with Linda in a month, he'd only been able to run three miles that day, he was in Chicago, and Hoyt Malveaux had stud-shamed him. Afterward Sean convinced himself that nothing had happened, and he bought too much junk at the O'Hare gift shop for his kids. To expunge his slipup, in its weakness and self-disgust, Sean would never tell Rob about it, not even as some vague, abbreviated afterthought. He told Rob pretty much everything, more than he told Linda. Rob's gayness was a buffer, a foreignness, a permission, but not this time. If he didn't tell Rob, everything was fine. Plus, since he hadn't cheated on Linda before, despite constant, completely workable offers, he'd earned a fortieth-birthday bonus coupon, a wild-card free-bie. Cheating was like a spa day for a dude, a rare indulgence amid over a decade of sacrifice and top-of-the-line nice-boy behavior. Sean knew this was a rationale and a perilous invitation to further misdeeds, but his more feral, in-the-moment instincts had reasserted themselves—his inner Hoyt Malveaux had throttled him by his still-not-thick-enough neck and hurled him at Erinn.

When Sean strode into the twins' party, as it was winding down, Bridger and Morrow were almost too sated on buttercream frosting and root beer floats to mark his arrival. They were splayed on the couch, their eyes heavy-lidded, like lushes on a bender, but the sight of Sean, bearing multiple shopping bags, roused them as they tottered into his arms.

"Dad, it was so much fun," said Bridger. "Mom made cupcakes and regular cakes, so everyone could choose, and we had that kind of ice cream with stripes."

"I got a Patriots jersey and cargo shorts and two books on spiders," Morrow added. "The pictures are so cool, there's this one Brazilian spider with like, fifty-eight legs."

"And I want to see it, dude," Sean assured his son, "and both of you, I'm so sorry I'm late, I'm such a dick, but they canceled half the flights because of a weather system in fucking Michigan. But I brought you calendars and titanium water bottles and these Toblerones that are like, twelve feet long."

"I'm glad you made it," said Linda, kissing him. "The kids know it wasn't your fault."

"I hate that fucking airport," said Sean, and as he grabbed Linda into a modified bear hug, which was Sean's version of a handshake, he glanced away, toward the picture window overlooking the backyard, for less than a second. Linda didn't deliberately notice this, but it was recorded in an ever-observant lobe of her brain, a surreptitious sentry post that she'd developed as a child, as she lay in her makeshift bed and heard a rising police or ambulance siren, and listened for how close it was getting, and then the crunch of gravel a few feet outside.

Linda had meant to retire this early-warning system, but it had been merely rejiggered to a neutral setting, awaiting instructions. Now a pilot light flickered, and later that night, in bed beside a snoring Sean, she wrestled with any unwarranted suspicions. Sean had been delayed for an explainable cause and was deeply apologetic. Was his sincerity somehow disquieting, his omission of any jokey self-defense? Had he even gone to a conference?

NO, Linda reproached herself, I'm not doing this. I need to stop poking around, just because my life is at least temporarily on track. If I become skittish or clingy, that's on me. Sean's a good man, as he's proved time and again. Shut up. Go to sleep. Don't be this person, this prickly amateur detective, this previous iteration of Linda, the one for whom happiness wasn't only a hoax, but a snickering liability. Yes, most of my friends are separated or multiply divorced or on whatever pill has replaced Prozac, but none of that is mandatory. I'm not Aileen and I'm not a frazzled suburban Nancy Drew on cheating patrol, ending with a 2 a.m. online search for legal representation and ordering a copy of *Divorce for Dummies* from Amazon.

Linda finally drifted off, after burying Sean's inopportune glance in the farthest, dustiest filing cabinet of her roiling brain. Sean and Linda were now engaged in that sometimes necessary and more often toxic stage of any marriage: denial.

20

OPEN ROAD

As the van rolled through Yonkers, Paolo dozed in the back seat while Sean concentrated on the road and his destination, which wasn't so much Maine as Linda. Rob could read on trains and airplanes, but not in a motor vehicle; he'd get carsick. Gazing out the window caused his mind to open, as if the van and the highway were a safe space, a time out from his ordinary compulsions. His thoughts drifted to the task at hand: his life, or lack thereof.

Jake's illness had begun after he'd broken his arm, following an inexplicable fall in a parking lot. The bones had never healed properly and his strength hadn't returned. The doctor had said it might just take time, but then a numbness and atrophy had reached his shoulder. Jake had checked into Columbia Presbyterian for two days of extensive tests, and the next week the doctor had sat Jake and Rob down and explained that Jake had ALS, also known as Lou Gehrig's disease.

That moment had been pivotal, the split second halving Jake's life into a before and after, and Rob's as well. Rob had reached for Jake's hand, his nearest hand, which wasn't able to mimic Rob's grasp.

Jake and Rob had both latched onto a helplessly gay reference, as both of their *Entertainment Weekly*–subscribing brains crackled with a movie title: *The Postman Always Rings Twice*, a melodrama in which an adulterous couple outwit an arrest for killing the wife's husband, but the wife dies in a car crash for which her lover is imprisoned. Jake and Rob had both thought: they'd swerved around AIDS, but had been blindsided by an even more implacably fatal illness. They might've howled, "It's not fair!," but the random horror of AIDS had taught them: nothing's fair.

Jake had asked about the disease's progression, and the doctor had spoken very carefully, saying there was no treatment let alone a cure, and very little ongoing research, and that the average life expectancy was two to five years, although a handful of patients lived longer. He'd cited Stephen Hawking, the celebrity physicist who'd survived for decades, eventually speaking through a computer, with his emaciated body draped over a wheelchair. Which was a life Jake had no interest in; as he'd later remark, "I won't be anyone's Best Terminal Illness Oscar."

That first night, back at their apartment, Rob and Jake had sat across from each other. Rob almost said something, about how Jake would be an anomaly, some unique case without further symptoms, but he knew Jake would hate that, any clutching at phony relief. Jake had finally said, as a statement of fact, "I'm going to die." He added, "And yes, I know that everyone's going to die. I'll just be heading out sooner than expected, and horribly."

Rob waited and then, at a loss, said, "That's more than likely true." Jake replied, "Thank you," and then started crying, with raw choking sobs, which was the first and only time Rob had ever seen him do that. Jake had prided himself on a certain majordomo crispness, even at funerals of people they'd both loved. Jake would be dry-eyed and tell Rob, "If we start wailing now, when will we stop?"

Rob held Jake, both of them weeping, until Jake's body had gone completely limp and slumped to the floor. Jake looked up at Rob and said, "Just practicing. And you *dropped* me." They both started laughing, that demented end-of-the-world kind of cackling, when there's nothing else to do. Then Jake had sat back in his chair and asked, "So where should we have dinner?"

———

Jake had joined an ALS support group online, but stopped after a few sessions, because as he'd told Rob, "The people are amazing but it's too depressing, since every week someone, or sometimes more than one person, disappears."

Jake kept swimming and running, which the doctor had recommended. And for a few months his condition stabilized, or at least didn't decline. Until one day, while he was bicycling home after work, he'd fallen. He hadn't broken anything, although there'd been a nasty bruise on the side of his face, and he'd walked his bike the rest of the way home. And he'd told Rob, "My left leg is going. It didn't hurt, it just—it wasn't there."

They'd had takeout and talked about other ways of Jake getting to work. Jake had faced obstacles one at a time, rather than as part of a tsunami. Rob asked if he could tell Paolo and Sean about what was going on. Jake thought about it, touched his bruise, and asked, "What if I just tell them you've been punching me?" But then he said, "Fine. But just Sean and Paolo. Because they won't be assholes."

Sean designed a workout program, to emphasize whichever of Jake's body parts was still usable. He continually modified Jake's routine, refusing to let Jake give up, until one day, when Jake was lying on a mat, and he and Sean had been passing a medicine ball back and forth, gently, Jake had tried to hold the ball and couldn't. It rolled away. So Sean said, "I'll get the ball and we'll go again," but Jake said no. He wasn't complaining or even frustrated; he thanked Sean for mapping out the exercises, but said, no more. Or just one day a week. He said he wasn't going to get better and should decide how to spend his time. Which had frustrated Sean, who hated anyone giving up, and he was furious at not being able to fix Jake. Sean hadn't wanted to start bawling, so he'd just said, "What? Do you want to get fat?"

Jake had loved Sean's beach-season attitude, but after fourteen months Jake was fading, faster and faster, and soon couldn't feed himself. He could walk, and sit if Rob helped him, but he'd lost the use of both arms. Rob would bring the spoon or fork to Jake's mouth, and sometimes Jake would dribble or cough things up, but he insisted on using linen napkins because "I want to be like a three-hundred-year-old English viscount in his twilight years." And sometimes he'd still want to head out to the guys' favorite restaurant, a little Italian place a block away.

Paolo had arranged to meet up at Del Giorgio's one night. Rob and Jake arrived early and were sitting near the window; Rob had begun to factor in extended travel times for Jake's mobility. Rob waved, and Paolo discerned, from Jake's face, that Jake was trying to wave, too, which was impossible, so Jake had been picturing himself waving, something Paolo could see on Jake's face. And while the group had enjoyed themselves, Paolo was worried about Rob, and what the situation was doing to him, and he brought this up later, over the phone.

"You're being superb," Paolo said, "but you have to take care of your-self." Rob replied, "I just don't want to make things worse. I want Jake to be as happy as he can be, and as active, for as long as he can." Rob and Jake had been a team. Rob hadn't wanted to act like Jake's nurse, but he had no choice. He hadn't wanted to behave as if Jake were already gone, but Jake's death was always right there. Toward the end they had a healthcare aide, but Rob had still done everything, getting Jake to the doctor, dressing him, feeding him, and wiping his ass. Paolo had told Rob, "You need a break, it's too much," and Rob had answered, "Not now. Not while he's still here. I love him."

After just under two years Jake had been placed in hospice care, so he could die at home, which was what he'd wanted. During his last month, he lost everything. He couldn't move or speak, so he'd communicate by blinking his eyes. Jake's brain had been untouched. He'd known every-thing that was happening to him, but he hadn't been equipped to stop it. A nurse came by once a day, to take his temperature and blood pressure, and see if Jake needed anything. He hadn't been technically in pain, and was in bed most of the day, but the nurse and Rob would lift him, and turn his body, to avoid bed sores.

And then, during a final night, Jake had died. If he forced himself to, Rob could remember every detail, but this was forbidden. Even now, in the van's limbo, with his closest friends, Rob couldn't get anywhere near that evening. This was how Rob had been living, his mind spas-ming from one memory to the next, like a passenger alone on a sinking sailboat, hurling ballast into the sea, as the waves overtook him. Not yet submerged, which would be a release, which he hadn't earned. Rob re-membered Hastings, whose suffering and vile death Jake had witnessed; Jake had stood by Hastings, seeing him through. But had Rob been as devoted to Jake, or chosen a shortcut? He touched Jake's watch, wondering if he should toss it out the window, as a gesture of repentance or futile anarchy.

"You okay?" Sean asked. "Were you asleep? You look a million miles away."

Oh Jesus, Rob thought, I'm trapped in my least favorite kind of story, an illness memoir, books that so often read like either move-toward-the-light crap or unrelenting dirges. The only thing Rob hated more were tales of recovery, from drugs and/or alcohol and/or gambling and/or an eating disorder and/or loving too much. While Rob sympathized, as he paged through such manuscripts, he'd always think to himself, If I have to read one more chapter, I'm going to vomit, fall for a guy with a facial tattoo, lose the apartment at a blackjack table, and take heroin. Or even better, just start skimming.

21

BLASTED

As Trone Meston sat in an enveloping, honey-colored kidskin seat, aboard his private jet, somewhere over Michigan on a flight path to Maine, he was an exceedingly happy man. He couldn't pick which achievement he was more satisfied with: his upcoming marriage to Linda or the invention, no, the global astonishment, no, the flat-out parting-of-the-Red-Sea apotheosis he'd be revealing just before the ceremony. But selecting a favorite was unnecessary, because the Galileo-scale advancement and the blessed occasion complemented each other, as a triumphant joining of romantic fulfillment and international cross-promotion.

Linda was across the aisle, absorbed in her phone. They weren't sitting side by side because they were adults whose love was secure, and wasn't for show. This was one of the many things that had drawn Trone to Linda: She got it. She got him. She didn't plead for hourly smooches or gushing testimonials. When Trone had told her he loved her, months earlier, she'd been surprised, then thoughtful, then tickled, and finally pleased. Like Trone, she'd assessed every parameter of a life-changing opportunity and made an informed decision.

Linda looked up from texting Aileen, who might be appearing at the wedding or might end up in some other city or country entirely, zonked and lured by a man, a Ponzi scheme, or a discount coupon for a fast-food burger and fries. When Linda returned Trone's smile, her first thought was, as always: He's not my mother. He was the person most unlike her parents she'd ever met. He was eccentric—no, that was too generic—he was odd on a colossal scale. But he was fiendishly intelligent, curious in his own alpha-nerd manner, and loving in the strangest ways. He'd once longed to buy Linda a Portuguese soccer team.

Only now, seated in the extravagant caress of Trone's jet, Linda was irked, almost to distraction, at having invited Sean to her wedding. She still couldn't fathom it. How had her fingertips and her Limited Edition TroneBook XVI (one of the few gifts she'd accepted from Trone) acted so independently of her brain? Before she could marry Trone, she'd lay this wayward miscalculation to rest. She'd analyze her error and move on. To accomplish this, Linda revisited a centrally painful yet often re-wound memory: the devastation and scudding implosion of her marriage to Sean.

After that earliest suspicion, when Sean had made his last-minute, overly effusive entrance into the twins' twelfth birthday party, Linda had detected hints, some minor and others less so, of Sean's possible cheating. On a rare weekend brunch in the city, they'd run into a nubile twenty-three-year-old on the street, a recent hire at Defiance whom Sean had neglected to mention. Linda was interested, because while Sean hugged everyone, he didn't get anywhere near the frisky, so-blond-it-hurt Avery, with her Defiance T-shirt artfully sliced above her toned, flat stomach. Why was Sean being physically reticent?

There was a recently divorced young mom in East Amberly who'd opened an upscale candy store just off Main Street, with glass canisters brimming with foil-wrapped treats, an on-site chocolatier, and a mail-order sideline. Sean would bring the twins pecan caramel turtles in the shop's signature daisy-patterned paper sacks. The shop owner was stunning, in certain ways a younger Linda, and she was overly friendly, causing Linda's sensors to beep. Sean didn't like candy, and Melyssa was air-kissy and almost too fascinated by Linda's workout routine, asking, "Does Sean give you special off-the-record tips? It must be so great to have a live-in coach."

In both these instances, Linda had chastised herself: Don't be this person. Don't start interrogating Sean, or keeping tabs on his appointments, don't turn every other woman into a rival, or Sean's next wife. Linda hated this creeping trepidation, and used it against Sean. Why was he refusing to age? Was he so overbooked because his business was doing well? Why had their sex life become intermittent then suddenly passionate, as if Sean were remembering to care? And again she'd flagellate herself, driving past that candy shop even though it was out of her way, and calling herself a terminal bitch and a soap opera character, staking out her husband's morsels, as if the car's trunk held a flashlight, rope, and shovel.

But this time bomb of insecurity had been disrupted by the prospect of Sean taking part in a *WarForce* reboot titled *WarForce Reunion: More War II*. The streaming services were starved for content, so every even meagerly successful vintage show was being hauled out of drydock, clumsily rethought, and served up to remind an aging audience of their elementary school viewing habits. When a junior development exec at the cable network's weekly pitch session had said "*WarForce*" and then played the show's pounding theme music on her phone, half the room had yelled "Blaster!" while the other, younger half looked puzzled and asked, "Um, what's *WarFace*?"

The script was tinkered with to highlight next-generation additions to the *WarForce* squadron, because only Sean was still in good enough shape to stir his fan base's memories and libidos. He wasn't as steroid-humongous as in that earlier incarnation, but he actually looked better, more seasoned and manly. As Paolo informed him, "You're the ultimate DILF. Not just a Dad I'd Like to Fuck, but a dad who doesn't look like anyone's real dad."

When Sean's long-dismissed agent had called him with the offer, Sean had been flummoxed. He'd stopped thinking of himself as an actor, if he ever had, decades ago. He was on a rising career path, as the face and founder of the Defiance brand: Would a reappearance as Blaster be a time-wasting detour or a cross-marketing plus? The money wasn't great, but Sean wasn't saying no. The rekindling of his twenty-something self was a kind of time travel. He consulted with his family over a Thursday night dinner.

"Blaster?" said Linda. "Again? Would you wear the spandex suit and kill people?"

"I read the script," said Sean, "and it's sort of like the first one, but everyone except me is younger, like Professor Headspace is a seventeen-year-old tech wizard, and Krazy Karl is just called Karl because you're not supposed to call people crazy anymore, and he only turns invisible when he's having extreme social anxiety. And Pretty Boy is some new guy they found on TikTok doing dance videos, and Mistress Karinska is called Ms. Karinska, but she's still a female bodybuilder with a Sword of Destiny, only she uses it to defend battered women and homeless families. And Blaster is doing anger management, but once the country gets attacked by an intergalactic drone army, the government brass let him go off his meds and get mad and pulverize the half Martians/half robots who are building a secret headquarters underneath Salt Lake City, where everyone thinks they're Mormons because they carry briefcases."

Bridger and Morrow, who were now sixteen, swore they'd never watched the original series, out of cringing humiliation. They loved their dad, but after pulling up photos online, of the hugely buff Sean with a star-studded headband and a codpiece with a stylized eagle, they'd covered their eyes, and would run from the room when Linda brought up syndicated reruns. Linda had found *WarForce* handy, as a parenting tool: "Listen, if you keep dumping your gym clothes under your beds, I'm going to ask Dad to Blasterize you."

Bridger and Morrow were gaping at Sean in horror. "Dad," said Bridger, "you're not actually gonna do that again, are you? I mean, I would have to like, change my name and move to Australia."

"There's still a *WarForce* game," said Morrow, more reasonably. "It's free and nobody plays it, but I downloaded it just to see. And Dad, the animated you blows up jeeps filled with South American drug lords, which is really racist."

"I think that's why the reboot is going with a drone army," said Sean.

"How long would it take?" Linda asked. "And where would they shoot it?"

"Maybe six weeks, on soundstages in LA. You guys could fly out and watch the filming, although it'll be really boring."

"Dad," said Bridger, going for a reality check, "you're incredibly old. You're like, forty-four. When you're Blasterizing someone, you could throw your back out."

"Would there be a new game?" wondered Morrow, with a hint of interest.

"Probably," said Sean. "And okay, I know it's going to be a shit-show, but the script is kind of funny, and it could be good for Defiance. I still get business from people who remember the show from the first time around, and last year I did Comic-Con and the *War-Force* booth had a line all around the convention center. I made a ton of money just from signing stuff and doing selfies and selling some of the old action figures I had in the basement. And that money is why we have a pool."

Linda and the twins were softening.

"Could we landscape the pool?" asked Linda. "It's still bare bones and doesn't really go with the house. And could we redo the garage, which is falling apart?"

"Could I go to Paris with my friend Mackenzie, whose parents invited me?" wheedled Bridger. "So I'd be out of the country while you were filming, and then I could go skiing with them in Switzerland, too?"

"Could we rewire the whole house, so we stop having those WiFi outages?" Morrow chimed in. "And now that I have my learner's permit, could I get a party van? It could be reconditioned, or an ice cream truck or whatever, but I would fix it up."

Sean smiled. He'd been counting on his family's glinting-eyed greed to sway the voting. He made a magnanimous why-not gesture, using both hands. He'd already begun amping up his diet and leg routine. He wouldn't juice again, but he had designed a program to produce lean muscle and peak veinage, which, coupled with diligent tanning and a minimizing of the silvery strands at his temples, would, if not turn back the clock, at least stop the younger employees at Defiance from calling him Sir and Mr. Manginaro, as if he were a doddering, three-thousand-year-old mutant form of his father.

"Well, I think it's heavenly," said Paolo, after hearing about the reboot. Rob had told Jake as well, who wasn't yet sick.

"It's either too sad for words," Jake determined, "with Sean painfully trying to recapture the most Where Are They Now parts of his youth, or Sean will become a masturbation fantasy for a whole new generation."

"He showed me the costume sketches on his phone," Rob confided. "And I congratulated him, I said he looked like my favorite Cher album cover," which was when the three men began harmonizing on "If I Could Turn Back Time," flipping their imaginary yards of dark, flat-ironed hair and waggling their tongues.

22

SEAN IN WONDERLAND

Sean was housed in a rental apartment only slightly more upscale than the anonymous hideout he'd been stashed in decades earlier. The atmosphere was eerie, as if he were in one of those movies where the main character gets to relive some crucial moment from his formative years, over and over again, until he absorbs a moral lesson and corrects his hapless current self. Only Sean couldn't settle on why he was here, aside from the paycheck. Everyone was gushing at him, about how he hadn't aged a day, and the younger cast members, all under thirty, were deferential and beseeched him for career tips: "Do I need an agent and a manager?" "Should I appear in costume at press events?" "This is for streaming—will that hurt my chances at a movie career, or is it all the same now?"

Sean hadn't been near LA for years, and he'd forgotten how unnatural and inviting the days could be. Someone was always fussing with him, with his hair and makeup, or fetching him the egg whites and skinless chicken breasts he'd ordered from a recommended health food spot, or driving him to be interviewed at a hotel cocktail lounge, or running lines with him in his trailer. Sean was becoming unmoored, not so much from revisiting his past, but in getting primped and pumped into a cartoon superhero/needy actor combo. He'd always been vain, but with a fifty-eight-more-reps, trouncing-people-half-his-age-in-the-backstroke gusto. He'd been after self-improvement, not self-love. But this was LA, where therapists advised their bipolar patients to get liposuction and inject the removed fat into their frown lines.

The filming was trudging along, as dull and enervating as he'd remembered, with minute-by-minute adjustments in lighting and camera angles, and hours of downtime, in his underwear, being cooled by an assistant with a hand-held fan when the air-conditioning wasn't enough. He called Linda, telling her, "It sucks, just starting and stopping all day long, with everyone on their phones looking for their next job. Everybody's really nice and the Professor Headspace kid is funny as hell, but I miss you and the twins. Tell them it's incredibly hard being a TV star with superpowers."

What Sean didn't say was that being engulfed by ambitious, casually scheming people so much younger was demoralizing. He didn't envy these cast members, or the twenty-four-year-old director, in her overalls, pigtails, and baseball cap, placating and hassling with a crew of seen-it-all-twice Teamsters. Sean prodded himself to be cheery and grateful, so no one would think he was a diva or, far worse, some crochety old fart with memory issues and hackneyed tales of the first show. He emailed Rob, and called him a few times, but he couldn't express his mood, because it was ill-defined and might get whiny. Rob asked, "Are you okay? You sound bummed out, or sort of off. Are things falling apart?" "No, it's all good, lots of fun and hotties and there's a gym right down the block from where I'm staying. It's just . . . nah, I'm just not used to waving my arms and yelling 'We've got company!' at some assistant holding a tennis ball on a stick, which is where the special effects drone army will eventually go. I'm fine."

He wasn't, but the shoot would be over soon enough, and he'd ask if he could keep his golden wristbands and winged helmet to give to his kids, who'd taunt him but might privately be thrilled by a Hollywood souvenir. After a Friday lasting from 6 a.m. until close to midnight, he was kicking back in his trailer, in a robe with a beer. He'd been making some friends at the gym, but people in LA planned their downtime months in advance, as they had canyon hikes and classes on auditioning techniques and consultations for laser resurfacing of both their cheeks and the Brazilian teak doors to their guesthouse.

There was a tapping on the trailer door, and Nara Charlton, the twenty-two-year-old actress playing Ms. Karinska, stood outside, in a Malibu uniform of shredded denim micro-shorts, a ribbed white tank top, some sort of barely existent vest, and wristloads of bracelets made from brass wire, glass beads, braided rawhide, and tarnished flea market rhinestones. Her waist-length, chemically sun-streaked hair, with an expensively encouraged waft of waves and tendrils, looked camera-ready, even though, when in character, Nara wore a thick scarlet topknot, for a Slavic samurai effect. Seeing Nara in the doorway, posed against a surprisingly clear night sky, was like a drop-in by LA itself, or by one of the city's many gorgeous, frighteningly in-shape, gleamingly smooth-skinned ambassadors.

"Hey," said Nara, her voice lighter and friendlier than Ms. Karinska's forbidding growl. "Long day, huh?"

"Not bad," said Sean, quickly hiding the icepack he'd been applying. He'd done something, most likely more than a sprain, to his ankle during a combat sequence earlier in the day, but he hadn't wanted to bring it up or consult the company nurse, for fear of seeming frail.

"You were amazing," said Nara. "Got any more beer?"

She was flirting, which energized Sean; flirting was his go-to antidepressant. He dug into a nearby cooler and tossed Nara a beer, which she expertly caught in one hand. Sean reveled in being around physically adept people, even opponents. He understood them, in their quest for unflappable cool, as if starring in a trailer for the movie of their lives (the trailer, with its hyperactive cuts and jaggedly propulsive music, was always more viscerally exciting than the full-length film; the trailer was the movie's dream of itself).

"Everybody's gone home," said Nara, curling into a swiveling armchair facing Sean. "Or to that bar on Doheny. We're the only ones left."

Sean had been working opposite Nara for weeks, but always in costume, and often while marking elaborate fight choreography. They were companionable but not yet friends. It wasn't easy to hang out while encased in molded polyurethane body armor and, in Nara's case, mountainous wigs and glowing red contact lenses.

"How did they find you?" Sean asked, as an opening feint. Sean's flirtation technique depended on power plays, on keeping a woman attracted but off-balance, with a mix of compliments and swagger, until she yearned for his approval but wasn't sure why.

"All-natural bodybuilding. I was Ms. Real Olympia and I've been getting into MMA," by which she meant mixed martial arts. Nara was solidly muscled but slender. She disdained bulk, preferring the coiled edginess of kickboxing and karate. She'd also appeared on *The Ninja Next Door*, a reality competition for, supposedly, farm-fresh elite athletes who'd joust with padded lances, swoop along zip lines the length of a soundstage, and hop across huge, fiendishly constructed rolling cylinders, accompanied by videotaped and edited, heart-tugging backstories, in Nara's case a hard luck saga of a dad with pancreatic cancer, a family-owned ranch in foreclosure, and a tireless mom working five jobs to make ends meet (some of this was true). Nara had placed second, still netting $50,000 and, more importantly, the notice of execs in the fitness econo-sphere, the same pasty, comb-overed con artists who'd cajoled Sean years ago and today.

"You look great," said Sean.

"I need to work on my quads."

"I wasn't gonna say that, but sure. I can give you a program."

"So are you from here?"

"Back East. Jersey originally. You?"

"Spokane, Washington. Kind of a pit. You know, last night I watched the original *WarForce* show, which was great, I mean, it's old-school, but you were the best thing in it. And even now, you're in awesome shape, what are you, like thirty-eight?"

Sean was forty-four. He might've weighed whether Nara was flattering or even needling him (his actual age was available online), but he chose not to. She was so pretty, and her abs, framed in her more revealing costumes, were off the charts, even if, as with him, the makeup artists outlined and shaded the actors' bodies to accentuate every striation and hollow.

"Do you mind?" asked Nara, already slipping off her handkerchief-sized vest. "Don't you hate wearing clothes?"

Sean grinned. Nara's cards were being flung across the table. He had no intention of having sex with her. Since he'd been in LA, he'd backed away from, or firmly rejected, numerous seductions, but he fed on the enticements, especially with his body creaking and aching. Nineteen-year-olds squeezing Sean's biceps were verification that he was still a contender.

"You know what they say," Nara murmured, discarding her flip-flops to more fully model her flawless pedicure; Sean hated grimy or uncared-for body parts. "What happens in the star's double-wide, stays in the star's double-wide."

"Jesus."

"We're the two hottest people on this project. You know that."

Sean was turned on by aggression, and his robe had opened, flaunting his chest and maybe more. He wasn't wearing underwear.

"But you know what?" said Nara. "Maybe you're tired, which you have every right to be. I'm coming on a little strong, which I don't usually do. It's just, fuck, you're Blaster. My mom wanted to fuck you so bad."

Sean practically levitated with fury. Was she baiting him? Messing with him, so he'd flounder during the next day's shooting and they'd give her his stunts? Was her mom as hot as Nara? Sean had a buzz, from his prescription painkillers, which had become a necessity, the three beers, and—from Nara, standing up, grabbing her flip-flops, and heading for the door, a move intended to highlight her workout-elevated ass, which probably had its own agent and manager. If Sean had been in New York, her coming on to him would've been sufficient, a luscious fan's thong-tossing tribute. Since that Chicago waitress, he'd fucked maybe two other women, both out of town, both readily dismissed blips of weakness, time-outs after long hours on the phone and his laptop, with Linda, with his accountant, with the Defiance branch managers, with that zillionaire art dealer who was after Sean to train his five-year-old nephew, with the company in Malaysia that exported $12,000 racing bikes, with the IRS agent who was auditing those exports, with everyone he relied on, everyone he kept at bay, everyone who made him feel not exactly trapped but constrained, dependent on videoconferencing and invoices and overnights to Florida to check out that possible, overpriced Miami location. Sean loved his life but despised it. He was being choked, buried alive, by paperwork and a two-hour commute each way from Connecticut, and Linda's completely justified but repeated texts about a dead tree in the backyard that might, during a storm, fall onto the house, and that outpatient surgery on his rotator cuff he'd been postponing, and the twins' troubles at school (Bridger was shining academically but getting into fights, while Morrow was lagging in English, in anything that distracted him from gaming).

Sean made a bet with himself. If Nara turned back, without Sean having to raise even a fingertip or say a word, he would fuck her. But if she made it out the door, he wouldn't chase after her, and he'd be grateful for the passing danger, the appreciated but superfluous offer, the man-that-was-close window to remain blameless.

Nara turned, slipping her tank top off over her head, with a practiced dexterity. Her flawless breasts had most likely been purchased. Female bodybuilders, fleeing any ounce of body fat, were almost always silicone upgraded. But Sean loved even surgical perfection, and now Nara was in his lap, kissing him, and because they were in LA, and in a studio-supplied mobile home, appropriately called a honeywagon, with an espresso machine and a mini-fridge stocked with Evian and limes, and because they were so far from the rest of Sean's life, his real life, and because he wasn't thirty-eight and Nara was opening his robe with both hands, and gasping, which meant he could still make a woman gasp, in Sean's mind they were rehearsing a scene, so nothing counted. Sean was back on the high wire, risking his entire life, maybe even blowing it to smithereens, but mostly he wasn't thinking at all, about anything but fucking Nara so she'd remember him, not just as Blaster, as a sexual autograph, but as the hottest fuck of her life, as the one she'd try not to think about with her boyfriend or husband, especially if they were younger than Sean—Sean was going to win.

23

CROSS-COUNTRY

Movie and TV shoots are compacted versions of summer camp, in which a limited time span intensifies every connection. Feuds erupt hourly, eternal friendships are sworn, and romances simmer, flare, and immolate, because everyone's internal clock is sped up, and after the final wrap, no one will ever make contact again until the premiere, if then. Nara kept stopping by Sean's trailer. He was insulated by his distance from home and the surreal quality of two superheroes having unquenchable sex. Sean and Nara were using each other, and yes, he was getting off on not just the rabid lovemaking, but at being so brazenly pursued by a fitness freak half his age. Turning Nara away would have been an insult to all other middle-aged straight men who dreamt that Sean was doing exactly what he was doing. Sean was a couch potato's sexual saint, the MVP quarterback they were cheering from the stands and toasting with oversized plastic cups of beer.

When Sean called or texted Linda, he repeated his usual, true enough account of drudgery and boredom. He was fully compartmentalized, with his wife and lover on opposite coasts, as if air travel and, more significantly, the internet didn't exist. Nara was Sean's first and only high-profile dalliance, and he barely resisted when Nara began posting selfies to her over 12 million followers, of Nara and Sean back-to-back in full costume, their arms fiercely folded. She went further, with images of Sean slumped in his canvas-backed director's chair, shirtless in his Blaster tights, with Nara on his lap, wielding her Sword of Destiny. There were shots of the full cast raising brews at a Santa Monica beachfront hangout, panoramas that Nara cropped to include only Sean and her, side by side.

The tabloids and gossip websites began to repost these steamy, provocative insider's candids of a *WarForce Reunion* hookup. Longtime fans went berserk, having inhaled so much fan fiction of just such a torrid coupling, of Blaster and Ms. Karinska naked, on board an international space station, cavorting in wolfish, antigravity hyper-sex. The *WarForce* media team denied nothing and issued corollary photos, drawing millions of likes and heart emojis and eyeballs. The scummier websites called Sean "the Blaster-Stud," and asked "Is Cheating on His Wife and Kids One of the Blaster Disaster's Superpowers?" Pictures of Linda and the twins, lifted from their social media accounts, were everywhere, and Nara was indicted as a "SuperSlut," "Ms. Homewrecker," and "the Blaster Bitch."

It was the first time Linda had heard from Aileen in almost two years. Aileen had somehow retrieved her daughter's cell number, probably from a scrap of envelope buried in the grime-encrusted nether regions of a fold-out couch. Aileen barely said hello, opening with "Jesus, Lindy, he's fucking rubbing your nose in it! And have you seen that Mrs. Katinka—you could bounce a quarter off her ass! What is she, fifteen? You must feel like crap on toast!"

Linda ended the conversation, saying, "I can't talk, I've got to pick up Bridger at soccer." Which was true, and Linda prided herself on punctuality, as an example to her kids, but right now she could barely remember where or when the match was happening.

Linda had been skimming the *WarForce* press releases, and she'd watched a YouTube video of the cast being interviewed about how psyched, stoked, and thankful they were to be "part of this classic American story the whole family can enjoy." She'd giggled as Sean dropped his voice to a gruffer, more solemn and macho octave, because he was "Blaster's guardian" and "a link between the *WarForce* legacy and its bold reimagining." She'd texted him, "You sound like an anchorman on a local channel," which Rob had done as well.

· But now Linda was unable to concentrate, tossed into the whirring, blinding center of a cyclone, an assault, a reassertion of every dark, self-punishing accusation she'd been dodging for so long. She struggled to clear her mind, to operate from a clean, practical set of priorities, but this was impossible. She kept repeating, sometimes under her breath, then forthrightly, then screaming, "Fuck. Fuck. Fuck. FUCK."

No, Linda reconsidered, don't do this. Don't assume Sean's guilt and too instantly convict him. She loved Sean and that had to temper any volcanic rage or desire to—what? Bash in his manly skull with a pickaxe? Book the next flight to California, with the aid of her airline buddies, and confront him, after scraping "WHORE" with her car keys across the enameled exterior of Nara's Jaguar? Never speak to him again except through lawyers who would financially decimate him?

Be methodical, she told herself. Do your homework. Don't let Aileen be so sneeringly and boastfully right. She grabbed her laptop and rather than heading directly to the official *WarForce Reunion* website, with its promises of previews and win-a-signed-Blaster-phone-case trinkets, she searched Sean Manginaro, Nara Charlton, and Sean Manginaro And Nara Charlton Fucking, and this third attempt blossomed, with everything from Nara's Instagram, to on-set cellphone video posted eighteen hours earlier by members of the catering crew, to just-added "investigative reports," with "substantiated rumors" of an explicit sex tape from Inside Hollywood, Smut Glut, Celebrity Smackdown, and brief paragraphs in the more traditional Entertainment sections of mainstream news sites.

She studied the solo photos of Nara, spray-tanned in a white one-piece with cutouts, swiveled beside a multitiered bodybuilding trophy as tall as she was, in even less clothing on that ninja reality competition, and in her countless selfies, where she'd simper, shove her admittedly world-class butt at the camera, and act as if she'd just happened to be captured, wearing only a completely unbuttoned denim shirt, white panties, and a baseball cap, her legs angled for maximum sleekness, her chin implant tilted down, her suspiciously green eyes Photoshopped to dinner-plate dimensions, her nose little more than a comma, and her billowy collagened lips at fully glossed inflation, like twin air mattresses.

Nara was pretty, Linda recognized, under the heading Look at Me I'm a Man-Stealing Slut. No, that wasn't fair, maybe Nara had somehow been innocent in all this. Except everything about her was merchandised and, if necessary, voluptuously exaggerated, to embody a fourteen-year-old boy's notion of an unreachably hot babe, a CGI fantasy available only in California, or through a virtual reality headset. Linda was far more beautiful than Nara and indisputably classier, but also indisputably two decades older. So that's what Sean wants, Linda determined, a blow-up doll without a gag reflex— No, Linda told herself, shutting the laptop, Nara—and was that really a person's name, it sounded more like a dolphin—Nara was beside the point. Of course Linda hated Nara, but Nara could've been anyone, or any suitably toned assembly of body parts. What stung so terribly was that Sean, who she'd have thought would at least have better taste, had chosen Nara over Linda.

Linda looked up, unsure of how much time she'd just spent online while her phone, which she'd silenced, was vibrating uncontrollably, from call after call. Linda had to climb into her Prius and retrieve the twins—Morrow was at the mall—but she couldn't move. She took in the living room and the Tudor encasing it, and the furniture and rugs and lamps and the pointless-but-coveted 25 percent cashmere throw tossed across a chaise, and she hated all of it. She hated what it represented, and how much thought and effort she'd spent in browsing for these items and arranging and rearranging these rooms, but what she really hated was how much she'd loved all of it, every painting by a local artist and color-coordinated switch-plate cover and the dented copper tub that held logs beside the fireplace. Linda had foolishly believed in these purchases, in buying and burnishing her dream like one of those computer games where people created villages and farmhouses and lakes to build some digital environment, some serenely pleasing home and landscape where they'd be infinitely if fictionally content.

Linda hated herself for being not just a fool but a human being. She'd known this would happen. She hadn't been needlessly cynical— she'd been right. Everything was over. Nuked. Leveled. And her calamity was so mercilessly public: she was the haggard, spurned older wife, the junked jalopy, the bewildered hausfrau shielding her face in the Costco parking lot. Everywhere she went she'd be recognized and pitied, at best. Strangers would be commenting, "Yeah, that Sean guy traded up, good for him," and bros at sports bars would be yelling, "Way to go, Blaster!" And she'd have to explain herself, and answer to so many forcefully concerned renditions of "How are you? No, I mean it, really, how are you?"

She checked her phone, which listed calls and texts from so many unfamiliar numbers, undoubtedly reporters, and over and over again, and right now—Sean. Against any wailing shards of self-preservation, she picked up.

"Hey."

Linda didn't say anything. She had no idea how to begin, but then she did—fuck him. This is all on him. Make him do the work.

"Linda, you know it's not true. None of it."

This struck Linda harder than the initial blow, from the photos and the online chatter, because Sean was lying and, so much worse, he thought she'd believe him, or worse than that, choose to believe him.

She hung up, already piecing together what she'd tell the twins, and debating whether she'd use the phrase "Your fucking loser dickhead father who couldn't keep his dick in his pants." She almost smiled, something she wouldn't do again for almost a full year.

24

GETTING OVER IT

Sean and Linda had split up three years ago, just about to the day before her flight to Maine. That first year Linda had hunkered down in the Tudor, devouring a stack of post-breakup *You Can Be Happy Again*, *Life Without Him*, *Alone Isn't Lonely* self-help bestsellers. She'd highlighted insightful passages with a marker, skimmed the various authors' follow-up works (*Alone Still Isn't Lonely*), and then ignored every word of advice. These books were divorce porn, packed with aphorisms suitable for only the quickest fixes (lasting approximately as long as it took to read them) and written to reassure bereft women that there were millions of other equally bereft women out there scarfing even greater quantities of ice cream embedded with chopped-up Oreos, while in fragrant sweatpants and a fetal position atop the unwashed bedding they'd dragged onto their sectional sofas, fuming at the Hallmark channel small-town cuddlefests they couldn't stop bingeing, set during either a pumpkin-spiced, leaf-strewn autumn or a cinnamon-eggnogged Christmas week at a snowbound inn.

After reviewing every now-dashed milestone of how her life might have proceeded with Sean—the twins' college graduations, their weddings, the nest egg, Sean's well-earned retirement, the travel—Linda had gradually recovered some version of herself. The Tudor was sold, fully furnished, and Linda and Sean split the proceeds, with 70 percent for her, along with child support and alimony, something Linda was mildly ashamed of but had held out for to hurt Sean as deeply as possible. He'd acquiesced without argument, to every codicil, while pleading that their marriage wasn't over.

But it was long over. After that rocky first year, the twins had finished high school and were doing decently in separate colleges, although while Linda and Sean had sworn never to exploit their kids as pawns in the split, this wasn't always successful (Bridger was Team Linda—"Dad is such a total pig"—while Morrow kept his head down).

Linda had rented a budget-conscious studio in midtown and gone back to work, as a gesture toward sanity. She'd renewed friendships with fellow flight attendants, bought a stationary bike, and had run into Rob at a Starbucks on Madison Avenue, a few months after Jake's death (she'd attended the memorial, keeping her distance from Sean).

"Hey," she'd said, bringing her lemon square over to the small table where Rob was toiling at his laptop. "Are you editing a great murder mystery about a woman who hires a trained assassin to kill her ex-husband with a poisoned protein shake?"

"Yes." Rob smiled. "He dies while he's jogging and his body gets chewed up by the treadmill. It's called *The Corpse Wore Nikes*."

"I'd buy it. How are you? Shit, I promised myself I'd never ask anyone that, because I hate it when people use their concerned-human-being voices."

"I'm okay. As I just said in my chipper, but-still-feel-sorry-for-me widower voice."

They chatted, being careful with each other, but pleased by the reconnection. Finally Linda asked, "So I'll say it, because I'm an asshole—do you miss Jake?"

"A lot. Too much. It's gross. You know, the whole sitting at Starbucks by myself thing. Do you miss Sean?"

Rob was genuinely curious, on his own behalf and Sean's.

"No. Sometimes. But whenever I think about him, about something fun we did together, maybe something with our kids, I can't help myself, I start wondering if he was lying, or if he fucked someone else afterwards, or what was going on in his head. So I try not to think about him."

Linda had also Photoshopped Sean's face out of previously celebratory family photos, which hit him especially hard, because he'd had the earlier versions printed out and framed. "I don't get it," he told Rob. "She's trying to act like I never existed."

Photos, Rob knew, were highly charged—any images of Jake, or the two of them together, had become radioactive and could cause entire days of disconnected sorrow.

Then Linda had improbably met Trone, surpassing any Hallmark trope—*The Billionaire and the Flight Attendant, Love in the Clouds, Can I Get You a Brighter Future?*

After that first, all-business encounter on Trone's jet, Linda shunned his campaign. She turned down every opportunity for coffee, dinner, or just a stroll along the tarmac. The notion of dating the world's third-richest man was too absurd, and would paint Linda as an especially obvious gold digger, although as a friend pointed out, any snapshots of Linda with Trone would go viral within seconds and drive Sean berserk, a thought Linda could live with. But she was set on moving past petty vengeance, alluring as it might be, and having Sean exist as, of course, the father of her kids, but little else. A footnote, a barely remembered wrong turn. That was why she'd ultimately capitulated to an initial salad with Trone: he wasn't Sean. He was cerebral and, while not overweight, almost bodiless, and while bizarrely witty, not an exhausting cheerleader for life itself. He was unlikely enough to justify at least a conversation, which had lasted almost three hours. The diner near the airport had stayed empty of customers, and it had only occurred to Linda afterward that Trone had paid for this shutdown.

Trone had been placidly avid for every detail of Linda's childhood, career, and marriages. Because any future with Trone was laughable, Linda had been honest. Trone disarmed and fascinated her, especially because he wasn't obviously sexual. He was the first heterosexual man she'd ever met who seemed sincerely, if clinically, interested in what she had to say. It was, as she'd told a friend later, "Weird. Like, majorly weird. But good weird."

That whatever-it-was with Trone had been followed, the next week, by a dinner at his Tribeca penthouse, a full floor so glisteningly white and almost unfurnished it resembled a lab, and Linda was convinced she'd become a consumer test subject, who'd be handed three Trone-Phone prototypes and asked to compare them. Instead, Trone's personal chef made the most mouthwatering sushi of Linda's life, polished off with a selection of McDonald's fruit pies, Trone's childhood fetish.

This not-unpleasant evening had led to films in a hushed private screening room, a Philharmonic concert, a Broadway musical with theater hangout drinks afterward with Hugh Jackman, and a leisurely yacht excursion around Manhattan—this had been the couple's first night of lovemaking, which had been remarkably fun if not all-consuming, again thanks to Trone's unwavering attentiveness and skill. As Linda told a friend, "It was like sex with the friendliest robot, that only wanted to make me come and then fill out a response card. It was great because it wasn't really like sex, it was like—eating one of those astronaut meals from a sealed foil pouch and realizing it really did taste just like filet mignon."

Linda hadn't been coerced but courted. This was new. She was accustomed to men working every tired come-on and straight-guy entitlement, but Trone was something practically unique: a gentleman. Yes, he lacked Sean's vigor, off-the-charts sexuality, and bouncing high spirits, but this was, if not a relief, an entirely different phenomenon. Trone was both enigmatic and completely transparent, and of course his billions, his good-natured, highly trained staff, and his countless vehicles made life scarily seamless. But for the first time in so long, and maybe in forever, Linda was also undergoing—the absence of upheaval. An unforced—tranquility? An almost abstract subset of happiness?

When Trone had proposed, six months later, Linda's first words were "Shut the fuck up." Trone had smiled and replied, "I knew you would say that." Linda rebuffed any call for marriage, but Trone had diabolically pertinent, United Nations–caliber arguments at the ready: "First of all, I love you. You're smart and prickly and you really don't give a damn, all of which turns me on like crazy. And while you've shown only the mildest interest in my work, you're intrinsic to it, as I'll soon demonstrate, to you and to the planet. You've helped me rethink love and reach a radically new methodology."

Linda had no idea what he was blathering about, but she didn't have to. With Trone, she wasn't "falling in love"; they hadn't been mapping a future together. They'd been, as far as she was concerned, hanging out.

"Also," Trone continued, "I think you love me, in perhaps an untried sense of the word. Because if you didn't, you'd never have stayed the course. Of course I'm rich—my wealth has quadrupled within the past three weeks, and probably the past three hours—and I'd like to see what you'd do with it. You couldn't bankrupt me, even if you tried. You'd wear yourself out. But I amuse you, I'm the man you never expected. You most likely don't trust me, because you no longer trust anyone, but you can rely on me. I'll never hurt you and you know it. And we share an independent loneliness—we enjoy seeing each other, but not every day. We're grown-ups. Which sounds crushingly sad, but it doesn't have to be. And of course if things don't work out, you'll be fully provided for, along with your children, whom I'm truly fond of. Here's my thinking: Give me one good reason why we shouldn't attempt this. Why we shouldn't make each other unconventionally happy."

Linda hadn't answered, or participated in any further discussions, for another month. She'd sat with Trone's proposal, sometimes forgetting about it entirely, although she eventually ran it past the twins. Bridger squinched up her face at the thought of her Mom having sex with anyone, but she'd researched Trone's charitable foundation and approved of his massive contributions to the arts and climate change awareness, along with his distribution of free TroneTek devices to underprivileged schools around the globe (she suspected this was also an astute, long-game indoctrination of future TroneTek customers).

When Morrow asked, "Does Dad know?" Linda replied, "It's not your dad's decision. I'll tell him, if I say yes, but I'm not consulting him. I'm asking you and your sister." Morrow, on spring break, had been sprawled atop a sleeping bag in Linda's apartment, vaping, as he asked, "So, this Trone dude is working on something big, right? Like he keeps posting all these teasers, with just a box and that electronic music, and you keep saying he won't tell you what it is. But if you marry him, we can probably get whatever it is for free, right, or at least at a discount?"

"Morrow, are you saying I should marry Trone just so you can get the latest tech product?"

"That's not the only reason. I mean, I've seen the two of you together, and I can tell that he like, loves you and he's nice to you. So once you factor in the device, which might be awesome—like, maybe it can change your fingerprints or let you watch movies on the inside of your eyelids—then it sounds like a decent deal, right?"

Linda hugged him and said, "I raised such wonderful children, with the values of low-level drug dealers nodding off in the back of a squad car and trying to scratch their noses while they're handcuffed."

"You did good," said Morrow, grinning. "So when do we get the new TroneTek thing? Like, at the wedding?"

That seemed to be what Trone was promising, although Linda knew better than to pressure him or lean on his employees, who rarely told even family members where they worked, for just this reason. She never worried about the state of Trone's business interests, which was an advantage of dating a billionaire.

So here she was, the flight an hour or so from Maine, where the day after tomorrow she'd be getting married. But why was she preoccupied with whether Sean was going to show up? He'd returned his digital response card, indicating he'd be accompanied by a plus-one, but who? Nara had evaporated within weeks of the public scandal, after auctioning her "intimate story" as a prime-time special, a ghostwritten quickie paperback, and a short-lived talk show in which she'd lumbered through interviews with "models and actresses" who'd had sex with minor-league celebrities, leading to paternity suits and STDs, and who'd been moved to "help other women in the same position."

So who was Sean bringing and why did Linda care? And why had she invited him? To parade her newfound status as a marital and financial lottery winner? To impress upon Sean that they were finally, irreparably, leave-me-the-fuck-alone-forever done? To turn a corner, not toward healing, which would never happen, but a lessening of her seething hatred for Sean, which could still be ignited by the Defiance logo on any passing van or T-shirt? She hadn't been near him in over a year, since the twin's high school graduation, where he'd looked inarguably older, especially around the eyes, which she'd pointed out. What was she expecting this weekend? Some down-to-the-wire melodrama with a thundering soundtrack and a rope-swinging retrieval? Would Sean stab Trone and then himself, for an if-I-can't-have-you-nobody-can finale? Would the twins be retraumatized at seeing their parents together, or would this further normalize their wayward family? What did Linda want? And why, for the first time in her life, was she craving the unknown?

25

TREMBLE AND
ISABELLE EN ROUTE

Tremble had an hour to kill before her bus to Logport, Maine, so she left the Port Authority terminal in Manhattan and headed to a place she'd heard about and seen onscreen, mostly beneath the opening credits of a rom-com or in a climactic scene where Godzilla spits fireballs at hordes of stampeding, shrieking tourists: Times Square. At first Tremble couldn't locate this area. She walked along 42nd Street, cradling her backpack like a nervous white lady tourist with her church group from Omaha, taking a breath but still wearing the backpack in front, crammed with Mayor LeBloitte's dwindling cash, a batch of legal pads, and an almost-empty bag of honey mustard pretzels.

Tremble's parents had promised her a trip to New York but died before keeping their word. Back then, Tremble had refused to accept their deaths and assumed they'd return to find her. In her early teens, Tremble had begun to hate her parents for selfishly abandoning her. That's why she hadn't written about them yet: she couldn't, without settling on some definitive point of view.

Tremble still wasn't sure if she was in Times Square, until she turned a corner and Jesus fucking Christ on a biscuit, there it was: an open, blocks-long trapezoid with hundreds, no, thousands of people craning their necks at the multiple-stories-high LED screens hanging off the buildings and advertising Korean pop stars, the stern-yet-glamorous hosts of morning shows, and any number of lusciously photographed TroneTek products. There were panhandlers dressed as Minnie Mouse, a princess from *Frozen*, and so many versions of Spider-Man, although Tremble's instant favorite was a topless woman, her breasts painted taxi-cab yellow but fully exposed, wearing a matching yellow Minions mask, which she'd shoved back onto her forehead so she could smoke.

Times Square, Tremble told herself, is exactly what the inside of my head looks like. She was dying to share this revelation with Rob, but her messages kept going to his voice mail. She'd hoped Rob would introduce her to the city, because he loved it so lastingly. He'd talked about spon-soring a visit as her book was being released, for media opportunities. Tremble had barely believed she was verging on becoming a published author, but now that prospect, like Rob himself, was in grave danger. His email had mentioned Maine, and a friendly Welstrom & Stratters receptionist had divulged, over the phone, that staffers were on their way to Trone Meston's wedding, an exact destination quickly Googled.

As Tremble made her way back toward the bus station, someone yelled her name. Unlike with Bobs or Marys, she'd never think, Oh, they're looking for a different Tremble Woodspill. But she didn't know anyone in New York except Rob, and when her eyes darted, she could've sworn she saw—Mayor LeBloitte, his eyes fiery, pointing right at her from half a block away. Had he followed her, was there surveillance foot-age of her grabbing his money? Fuck him, Tremble told herself, here's another great thing about New York City: you can lose yourself in the mob, and no one, especially not some sweating, bloated Jacksburg turd-master, can track you.

When her bus pulled out of the station, Tremble relaxed. Times Square is so fucking great, she knew, but it's not why I'm here. And I don't have time for a screaming buttwad like Churn LeBloitte. I have to rescue Rob, and my book, from whatever the fuck is about to go down in Maine.

———

Isabelle checked the highway sign from behind the wheel of her rented, hybrid Honda Insight, a vehicle named, Isabelle was convinced, with her in mind. She'd just crossed the border into New Hampshire and would reach the Logport ferry sometime tomorrow. She'd almost taken a bus, given that multiple passengers might conceivably reduce the vehicle's emissions, but Isabelle had packed two suitcases, a shoulder bag made from recycled jugs of detergent, and her Mom's hard-sided makeup case (which could be considered vintage, and was arranged with Isabelle's aloe-based, cruelty-free cosmetics in reusable glass containers, except for the salmonberry lip tint, which Isabelle loved so much she considered it a medical expense).

Isabelle was conforming to the most abusive societal norms around female appearance, but she was going to meet Trone Meston.

She'd told Lance she'd be attending a W&S sales conference, which in a way she was, but the idea of inviting him to come along was socially excruciating. How would she even introduce him? As "my boyfriend"? "My friend"? Or with a more bluntly cavalier "that's my fuckboy"? All of these were equally problematic, and besides, Isabelle wanted Trone to view her as single, available, and worthy.

As Isabelle drove, the Tremble Woodspill manuscript nagged at her. She liked the book, but it troubled her, especially its humor. Isabelle kept humor at a remove, as a lesser pursuit, a bourgeois sidebar diluting the impact of trauma and despair. She was the person at a party who could recognize when a joke had been made, because people were laughing, but to her the laughter was demeaning, or common, and possibly at the expense of an endangered ocelot or someone, like herself, who suffered from a diagnosed allergy to jewelry that hadn't been bought at a street fair.

Trone will understand everything, she reminded herself, especially why she'd eliminated Rob Barnett, but how would she actually go about meeting Trone, and more critically, would she able to prevent his marriage? Could she get to him in time, so he'd recognize his grisly error while there were still a few seconds to correct it? Stop it, Isabelle warned herself, you sound deranged. On a practical level, Isabelle knew she was at best an insect at Trone Meston's gala picnic. She had little chance of being introduced to her idol, and absolutely no shot at romance. She was certain of all this, but she was young and in love and had spent her early years (in between annotating Kafka and any book with the words "democracy," "turmoil," and "neglect" in the title) bingeing on long-running TV shows where attractive white people shared expansively bohemian apartments and formed couples. She'd been indoctrinated with glamorous Caucasian desire.

Don't fantasize, she scolded herself, you're not some flouncing network single. Trone Meston isn't going to squint at you from a distance, or maybe as he approaches the altar, stand stock still as if struck by the most politically informed lightning, and then cancel his wedding. That's just not going to happen. "But it might," whispered the personal shopper or fashion magazine intern of so many hit programs, wearing so many pairs of skinny jeans with so many sleeveless turtleneck tops.

You are not named Rachel or Andrea or Mallory, Isabelle vigorously admonished herself, while waiting at a traffic light in some small town that undoubtedly underpaid its female employees. She wrangled a truce with her winsome sitcom urges. Here's what this weekend is going to be about, she told herself: I will definitely not run off with Trone Meston. That's ridiculous. Instead, I'll be presented to Trone, I'll appear on his radar, and even our briefest greeting will embed itself in his moral cortex. On his honeymoon, as he makes love to whoever that Linda person is, my face will be all he sees, and that face will be appreciating Trone's latest, momentous advance, with some lyrically worded tribute that mesmerizes him. And while he'll work tremendously hard, because he's a caring human being, to sustain the fraud of his marriage to that scheming flight attendant, I'll fill his consciousness, and he'll ask an associate, or hire a private detective, to uncover my whereabouts, and then Trone will show up at the W&S offices, clutching a bouquet of wildflowers purchased from a community garden, and maybe a copy of the garden's composting guidelines. It's a Cinderella narrative, fine, but between equals, a mindful Cinderella story that will captivate the world with its rightful justice. Not boy meets girl but visionary meets activist.

Stop it, Isabelle yowled inwardly, all but slapping herself, don't be depraved. She pulled into the parking area of the Airbnb she'd booked for the night, which was a spare room over a lesbian couple's tax preparation offices.

"Hello there," said one of the lesbian accountants, wearing a "King Charles Spaniels Lives Matter" sweatshirt. She was joined by her partner, in deductibles and love, who was Asian but Isabelle couldn't immediately pinpoint a clear-cut heritage. Isabelle condemned herself for this lapse, and then bowed slightly in a respectful manner with a hint of Zen ritual.

"Come on in," said the second woman. "I'm Ha-Joon and this is Shira."

Korean, Isabelle all but sang, and Jewish-American!

That night, as Isabelle drowsed beneath the quilt on the upper half of a bunk bed (a spaniel, one of the couple's five adored pups, was occupying the lower bunk), she dared to recap the film that she'd write, direct, and star in, and in which Trone would invest. She did this every night, as a lullaby crossed with a visualized and therefore concrete outcome. Isabelle had been conceptualizing this movie since childhood, and while she still hadn't written a word of the screenplay, her filmmaker friends had certified that once her idea was fully laid out in her mind, the actual script would be practically an afterthought, a formality, more a blueprint than some tired grid of dialogue and description. The subject of the film would be, inevitably, a young woman making her way in the world, toward a hard-won but fulsome destination, and would include an Oscar-winning supporting role for Tilda Swinton.

Rather than becoming bogged down in production design and sound mixing, Isabelle summoned the movie's opening night, at either Cannes or the New York Film Festival, as Tilda embraced Isabelle during a tumultuous ovation, and Trone stood a few feet to one side, gesturing to Isabelle, and taking no credit for her artistry. "It's all Isabelle," he'd tell the press.

This glorious ascendance was interrupted, at the Airbnb, by the spaniel's snuffling and a series of texts from Lance: "Wassup?," "You good?," and accompanied by a photo of his penis, "Missin ya!!!" Oh please, Isabelle all but shrieked, we are so breaking up, although she did save the photo in a file marked "Outsider Art Monograph, etc."

Lance would never get anywhere near her onrushing quasi-reality. This weekend's wedding, however misguided, was an invaluable step, toward that tearful hug with Tilda. Maybe Ha-Joon and Shira could have insights into Trone's speedy annulment. With every day, every hour, I'm getting closer, Isabelle vouched to herself, closer to having my obituaries read "Isabelle McNally-Meston dies at 108, Winner of 12 Academy Awards and Also the Nobel Peace Prize." Trone's wedding is where I begin.

PART III

26

ARTEMIS ISLAND

Trone had purchased Artemis Island from the last surviving member of the Darworth clan, a Maine dynasty whose lumber fortune had dissipated over two centuries, until its sole asset, fifty acres of untouched offshore real estate, was held by the octogenarian Millicent Darworth, who steadfastly identified with the island's namesake goddess, renowned as a huntress and virgin who'd declined all suitors. After protracted negotiations, as Ms. Darworth was set on never selling and being buried beside her ancestors in the island cemetery, Trone's representatives had paid twice the property's assessed value. Millicent died a year later, leaving her multimillions to an Estonian bird sanctuary.

Over the past four years, some two thousand or so employees had been brought over to thin the island's dense foliage and build Alchemy, an estate and conference center, designed and constructed at some unimaginable cost. Alchemy, the fruitless science of transforming lead into gold, had attracted Trone, who'd tell interviewers, "I'm turning gold into architecture." The wedding guests boarding a fleet of rented ferries were the first human beings, aside from Trone's staff (who'd all signed ironclad nondisclosure agreements, and who'd been frisked and metal-detected upon arrival and departure) to see the island up close and, for the weekend of Trone and Linda's wedding, inhabit it.

"Oh my sweet fucking Jesus," said Paolo, who'd been standing at the prow of a ferry, imitating Barbra Streisand's bouquet-brandishing trip to catch Nicky Arnstein's ship via tugboat in *Funny Girl*. (Sean, who despite his friendship with Rob, was clueless about gay signifiers, thought Paolo was re-creating a landmark moment from *Titanic*. The difference between *Funny Girl* and *Titanic*, Jake had once opined, should be the centerpiece of any Queer Studies curriculum.)

"How did they get all of this over here?" Rob asked.

"Cash," said Paolo. "I heard it was over eighteen billion," and then, to Sean, "but you bought Linda a nice house, too."

Sean was glaring at the island, searching for flaws. This wasn't difficult, as Trone's New England paradise was both staggeringly beautiful and monstrously vulgar. As many others had done with corporate campuses, Trone had taken a quaintly vintage style and inflated it to the size of an urban airport. There was the soaring, sprawling Alchemy Hall, with its multiple wings, and a countless array of outbuildings and guest cottages, all in a shingle style bastardized with Craftsman details and Federal accents. It was as if an English country home, a robber baron's rustic Adirondacks camp, and a Frank Lloyd Wright parking garage had been forced to marry at gunpoint.

The island's original old-growth oaks and birches had been retained and befriended by even more mammoth trees airlifted into place by military helicopters. There were copious wharves and boathouses, a fabricated white sand beach (the opposite of Maine's naturally rocky coastline), an underground state-of-the-art hospital, and assorted gazebos, cupolas, porticos, and cobblestone pathways, as if fifteen pastoral small towns had conducted going-out-of-existence sales.

"It's like a new section of Disney World," said Paolo, and Rob replied, "called Moneyland."

"So this Trone jackoff lives here?" Sean asked, as the ferry pulled into a marina.

"From what I've read," said Rob, "it's one of his fifteen homes and he can write the whole place off as a business deduction."

"It's like . . . an ultimate white-collar penal colony," Paolo decided, "where all the wardens wear matching monogrammed polo shirts and get stock tips from the inmates."

———

As Isabelle's ferry docked an hour later, she was conflicted. On one hand, Artemis Island encapsulated the mega-excesses and vile encroachment of capitalism on a bender. On the other hand, once she and Trone had become a couple, she could rethink the island as an artists' retreat and add a museum of Micmac and Penobscot tribal basketry, along with the Isabelle McNally-Meston Film Institute (Isabelle intended not only to pioneer her own oeuvre, but to motivate young female directors to make films about her as well). Under her guidance, the island could embody a great American future, and she would check if there was a day spa on the premises, for a discreet blowout and a manicure, although she'd already had two manicures in the past week, always handing the Vietnamese salon workers unsold copies of W&S books, from the firm's stockroom (this was Isabelle's elevated version of a tip).

Next time I come here, Isabelle told herself, as staff members greeted her on the dock, hefted her luggage, and directed her toward Alchemy

Hall for a cottage assignment, all these people will say, "Hey, Isabelle,"
and hug me, because they'll get my egalitarian vibe. Some might even
call me Izzy, which I'll graciously discourage, unless they're disabled or
undocumented, in which case I'll put up with it.

———

Tremble was nearing the opposite side of the island in a fishing boat that
stocked the hangar-like kitchens with fresh lobster, clams, and mussels.
As an extremely uninvited guest, she'd scoped out the harbor in Logport
and slipped a teenage deckhand weed and a Hulu password. Her backpack was her only luggage, and she nabbed an Alchemy T-shirt from a
boathouse storage closet. She'd been sure that for such a grand occasion,
mainland help would he hired in droves, and if she was in uniform, she'd
be undetected.

Look the fuck at all this, she thought, blending in as she devised a
temporary living situation. It's like a city made from Legos, or it's one of
those golf resorts where world leaders meet to discuss income inequality
and how to ignore it the rest of the year. Tremble wasn't over-awed by
rich people's gaudiest playthings. Such gross opulence interested her, as
material, but she didn't yearn for it. There'd be too much upkeep and
people hissing at her to keep her feet, her backpack, and her personality off the furniture. Being rich is so much work, she decided, but I bet
there's okay food.

———

The Alchemy Hall lobby had a vast cathedral ceiling composed of math-
ematically quarter-sawn and joined local timber. Despite at least ten
seating areas, with Stickley-style couches and armchairs upholstered in

rugged leather and Navajo blankets (thus exploiting slaughtered animals and an indigenous culture in each piece of furniture), this central zone couldn't help coming off as the atrium of a business hotel in any Midwestern city. As Paolo remarked, "It's Ralph Lauren Prairie meets Embassy Suites in Akron." Beneath copper chandeliers that mixed wagon-wheel forebears with modernist sleekness, the guys stood before a round central desk the size of a carousel, with eager, scrubbed young people wearing TroneTek warm-up jackets as they consulted TroneTek screens and handed out bottled water, also with the TroneTek logo on the labels.

Sean explained that Rob was his plus-one and Paolo was an emergency dental technician, requested by Ms. Kleinschmidt. Using Linda's maiden name was grindingly painful for Sean, but she'd reverted to it. At least she wasn't Linda Meston, not yet. Come to think of it, he didn't know if she'd be taking Trone's last name, but if she wasn't, this would be yet another hopeful sign of her ambivalence.

"All good," said the bright-smiled young woman behind the desk, and Rob recalled how Jake's most scorned expressions were "all good," "no worries," and "not a problem," because "Whenever people say those things they really mean, 'Go fuck yourself.'" But this Trone clone, as the staffers had nicknamed themselves in private, was a model of efficiency, informing the guys, "Ms. Kleinschmidt said we should accommodate you in every way." Sean jumped on this—was it a coded symbol of longing? Maybe Linda had even thought Sean would be bringing a girlfriend and wanted to seem generous-minded, even as she surged with jealousy.

A young man brought Rob and Paolo to a guest cottage and Sean to another. While these cottages were close to each other, the privacy-conscious greenery made each structure on the island invisible to its neighbors.

"This is lovely," said Paolo, appreciating the king-size beds, the brand-new lodge-style furniture, and the soaps embossed with the TroneTek signature T topped with a circle, which resembled a crucified stick figure. "The sheets are twelve-hundred-dollar Italian, the duvet is hand-loomed, and have you seen the bathroom? It's the size of my apartment if I lived in a much nicer apartment. Jake would've hated every inch of this place."

Rob laughed. Jake had disdained what he called "boutique hotel wet dreams." After Jake was diagnosed, they'd splurged on a trip to London with business class air travel, a suite at the Savoy, and orchestra seats for West End shows. London had been one of their touchstones, and while they wallowed in top-tier extras, there'd been an undercurrent of fear: Would this be their last trip together? How soon before Jake was immobilized? Was he already unduly fatigued? When would he die?

Linda's wedding was in fact the first trip Rob had taken since Jake's death. Paolo was performing beautifully, but he couldn't replace Jake's ecstatically scorching assessment of any overdecorated space. Rob could hear Jake eschewing the "matchy-matchy" aspect of the fabrics, the cowboy revival desk cunningly manufactured to seem antique ("I love the fake wormholes"), and the too-central placement of the flat-screen (featuring a channel of TroneTek products, with a sweeping buildup to whatever Trone would be rolling out at the wedding).

"I'm going to take a walk, to see if there are mechanical deer and bunnies hopping around," Rob decided. "Can I get you anything?"

"Nope," said Paolo, sinking into his $10,000 mattress. "If you see Dax, tell him there's only room for one gay dentist on this island."

Paolo was joking, but he'd received several ominous texts from Dax, with uncaptioned photos of dental equipment, including saliva ejectors, extracting forceps, and scaling periotomes, all innocently helpful devices that also resembled instruments of torture and murder weapons.

Sean's cottage was, if anything, even more lavish than his friends', and the imperial presence of Trone Meston loomed, from the TroneTek logo on the bedside notepads to the complimentary bottle of Tronelle Vineyards chablis. Sean was in enemy territory and his nearness to Linda was inflaming him: Where exactly was she? Was she watching him via some hidden video feed? Had his check-in been reported?

Restless for fresh air and physical exertion, Sean stripped down to black Defiance compression shorts and, shirtless, left for a run. It was dusk, but the trails were well lit, and he hoped, if there were cameras in the trees, that both Linda and Trone would have access to footage of what great shape he was in. Sean had been dieting and adding extra miles, so his abs and pecs had peaked. As he ran, he couldn't tell if the sounds of birdcalls and rustling branches were natural or prerecorded and piped in through speakers disguised as pine cones or unblinking owls.

Sean pushed harder. He loved running, for the sheer physical punishment, the ramming against boundaries, and the no-equipment-needed freedom. While he ran, Sean's love for Linda entwined with the pain in his thighs and the pounding in his chest. He barely noticed a well-tended poplar grove or the night sky, until he rounded a curve leading to a substantial pond, no, it was a swimming pool, landscaped with jutting rocks and a waterfall. The heating mechanism was causing clouds of mist. And there, standing on a slate ledge, in a bikini, was Linda. Her hair was wet and she was about to dive. She was poised, thinking about— How Trone's godlike billions had paid for so much fake splendor? Whether this weekend was a fresh start or a dead end? Sean and how their love was drawing them back together, right this second?

————

Rob had wandered toward Alchemy Hall. There were other people around, but it was past dinnertime, so most of the guests were heading to their cottages. He climbed the wide granite steps and entered the almost-deserted grand chamber, the chandeliers now dimmed. There were at least three atmospherically roaring gas fireplaces because, as Jake would remark, of course there were.

Rob noticed a self-service bar, of fieldstone and mahogany, carved with a deliberately crude frontier version of the TroneTek logo and set with a row of glassware and beverages. As he chose between the crystal pitcher of freshly squeezed orange juice and whatever kiwi/mango/merryberry tasted like, someone rose slowly from behind the bar. First Rob saw a topknot of hot-pink and neon-blue-tinted dreads, and then an open, if also apprehensive, face. Rob realized this person was now fully standing up. This wasn't a tall person.

"Tremble?" Rob stuttered, recognizing her from their video chats and a blurry author photo, submitted from her phone.

"Yeah?" said Tremble.

"It's Rob Barnett."

Tremble's face broke into the most gratifying, almost tearful grin as she catapulted from behind the bar, enveloping Rob in a gut-busting hug.

————

Sean stepped back into a shadowed area. This was a thrilling opportunity to—do what exactly? Speak with Linda casually? Swear his enduring love, as he had so many other times, to so little effect? Congratulate her on marrying someone else? He'd cooked up so many vague, operatic schemes, but nothing had clicked. Right now was the dream. They both looked great and, being practically naked, undefended. The area was secluded. Sean told himself, This is why I'm here, this is the moment, maybe Linda had even engineered this, it's so preordained, so Romeo and Juliet only older and divorced, so Sean and Linda at our damp, tight-abdominaled, vitamin-supplement-ad best. They could run away together, tonight.

"Sweetheart?" said Trone, appearing a few yards from Linda, in khaki shorts and a madras shirt.

"I just needed a swim," Linda told him. "I'd forgotten how long flights can still affect me. I get a little foggy. But the night air is heavenly, and the water is exactly the right temperature—are you coming in?"

"Not just now, I've got a Zoom thing, but I saw you leave, in your bathing suit, and you look fantastic by the way, but I just wanted to make sure you were okay. I know the boat ride was a bit choppy and it's a big weekend—you're good?"

"I'm great. I'll go back with you."

"Not getting cold feet? Pre-ceremony jitters?"

"Not at all. This place—I'm still exploring. But it's spectacular."

"The island's debut. I didn't want you to see it until things were ready. We've been working on it for so long."

"It's fabulous. Help me down."

Trone reached out his hand, Linda retrieved her robe from a boulder, and they walked off. Had Sean botched his chance? And why wasn't

Linda nervous, or was she lying to Trone, because she hadn't seen Sean yet? And Trone was obviously out of shape, he'd never take his shirt off in public, but he was—not hideous. Most guys that rich are either too tan or have hair plugs or they've worked out with someone like Sean so they have minor muscles they're way too pleased with. But Trone looked like—a nice-enough doctor or lawyer on a soap, or some dude in a lab coat on a commercial recommending an antihistamine. And his voice was—not nasal but maybe a little too modulated, like his sound engineers should make an adjustment. Sean couldn't dismiss him as a dweeb or a brat with his pasty arm around Linda's shoulders on the cover of his corporate brochure. And Trone had acted believably concerned about her. But was that enough for her to marry him? Once you layer in those billions of dollars?

Sean didn't move until he was sure they were gone. Greeting the happy couple would've been humiliatingly awkward and counterproductive. He had to see Linda alone. He ran five more miles and finally back to his cottage, to stop himself from replaying that moment by the pond on an endless loop of near-victory and sudden loss and retrenchment. Fuck me, he thought. Fuck everything. I'm doing this.

———

"Rob!" Tremble yelled, then lowered her voice, because she was trespassing, after all. But she'd found him!

"Tremble, it's . . . it's so great to see you, to meet you in person, but what are you doing here?"

"Because you're in trouble, even if you don't want to talk about it, but I had to find you, and help you."

"How did you get here?"

"Two buses and a boat. I'm seeing America. New York was awesome, especially Times Square, and I think we drove through New Hampshire, but this place—Jesus fucking the Virgin's ass. It's like that HBO show where everybody's a robot in a theme park—shit, wait, are you a robot?"

"Not so far, although we are talking about Trone Meston."

"The tech bitch? Is this all his?"

"Pretty much. And have you heard about the wedding? He's getting married."

"So you know him? From where? Are you a guest?"

"I've never met him, although I think he bought W&S. I'm the guest of a guest. I'm not really sure what I'm doing."

"Come on," said Tremble, grabbing Rob's hand and guiding him to a secluded nook, where they could occupy enormous leather armchairs facing each other. Tremble was a third Rob's age, but she'd taken charge and he was both distressed for her safety and grateful for her presence. She was wearing a staff polo and had a copious ring of keys clipped to the belt of her khakis. "Tell me," she said. "Because you look, not like shit, not exactly, but like you just fell off a pickup truck onto a dirt road and hit your head on a rock and maybe you've got a concussion."

This was oddly specific, and Tremble was also correct. Rob's grooming habits were intact, but in the cottage mirror he'd been blurry and shell-shocked, a ghost from a Japanese horror movie.

"Oh, Tremble," Rob said, weirdly certain he could confide everything to her. "First of all, I'm still working to protect your book, but the office is closed on the weekends. I got fired, by a sensitivity associate named Isabelle McNally. I sent you her suggestions, but I wasn't sure I agreed with any of them. But I didn't want to sway you one way or the other."

"That cooze bullshit? And how I'm not supposed to call myself a mutt? And that nobody's a cocksucker anymore, which is gonna be big news to all those cocks out there going, hey, suck me right now. And what else was on that list? I wasn't supposed to say pussy fever, even though I can tell you from experience that is a diagnosed condition, like when I saw this UPS delivery chick, with her sleeves rolled up and those tight brown shorts and the boots, I came down with a raging case of pussy fever. I had to be hospitalized."

"I told Isabelle that, at one of our sessions. She called it problematic."

"Pussy fever? Problematic? Does she have a pussy, I mean, is it functioning, can she dial it up? Man, the only effective treatments for pussy fever are molly and Fanta and grabbing that UPS bitch and telling her, it's time for your delivery, and me and her jumping into the back of her truck!"

"Which I love," said Rob, smiling. "That essay, comparing sex with people from different delivery services, it was wonderful, and made me look at the DHL guy in a whole new light. But Isabelle is just—she's very convinced she's right, about everything. And I tried to keep the discussion open, but she said that it's generational and that I had to go, or that's what she told my boss. So here I am. Nowhere."

"Okay, we're gonna fix that. But there's something else. I can tell. You can't even breathe. What's going on? Don't be a bitch and say you're fine and don't make me drop you on the ground and pound your head until you spill everything. Tell me. Now."

Rob stood, took Tremble's hand, and brought her out of the building, to a gazebo he'd noticed earlier, yards down a nearby trail. There were no lights, or anyone eavesdropping, which would help Rob feel marginally less terrified. He sat Tremble down on the octagonal built-in bench, while he paced and chided himself to not think about being in a gazebo, as if they were having a 4th of July hoedown in a brass-band family-oriented musical, or to edit himself, the way he so often did, but to just start talking, wherever it went.

"Okay. Okay. I was in a relationship for twenty-eight years with Jake, the most incredible man. And we were so happy, we were gay happy, which means insanely happy in a doorman building. I wish you could've met Jake, you might've thought he was a tight-ass and he might've called you a pansexual demon child, but then he would've made you ravioli and you'd have realized that his hair really was that color and you would've been crazy for each other. Before he died, I read him some of your stuff, and he blinked five times, which meant he loved it. He only blinked five times when we watched *Singin' in the Rain* and I entertained him by doing my ridiculous version of Gene Kelly's umbrella dance."

"He blinked?"

"He had ALS. That's what he died of."

"That's when everything stops working, right? My cousin has MS, which is shitty, and she's in a chair now, but it's not ALS. I mean, that's like being buried alive, right?"

This was why Rob could talk to Tremble: she wasn't being careful about Jake's getting sick. She wasn't placing it in some gentle, bogus all-things-have-meaning context, like in one of those "What Illness Can Teach Us" TED Talks.

"Right. It's as bad as it gets. But since Jake died, I've been a mess, of course, but there's something else going on, and I know it's crazy except it's not, or maybe I'm totally losing it. And I haven't talked to anybody about it, because . . . because if I do . . ."

"Keep going. I've got you. I won't tell anyone. Unless I write about it and then you'll have to accept it as my editor, but we can deal with that later."

Rob glared at Tremble for a heartbeat. She was a badass and a real writer, which meant she'd spare no one. But fair enough.

"Jake wasn't an angel and neither was I. And the sicker he got the angrier he got. And how could I blame him? He wasn't asking 'why me?' but he was coping with the fact that he'd always been frustrated with people who asked 'why me?' especially during AIDS, when he said the question was, 'why anyone?' But now it was happening to him, and he was the most fastidious man, except more and more he was dependent on me, to button his shirt and put on his socks and brush his teeth. We tried to have fun with it, because what else are you going to do, but when he couldn't manage almost anything he turned into this powder keg, he hated being helpless and he hated me trying to be nice and he hated everything and when he could still talk, or wheeze, he would scream, or do his version of screaming, 'LET ME DIE! WHY ARE YOU DOING THIS TO ME?'"

"But . . ."

"I know, and he knew, that I hadn't given him ALS, but I was the person who was there, I was witnessing his decline, I was cutting up his food in restaurants and trying not to tell the people who were staring to go fuck themselves, so I was Jake's target. Which I completely understood and I'd remind myself about what Jake was going through and I'd forgive myself for being grateful that I wasn't sick. But there were moments, after he couldn't speak and we were trying to figure out a blinking code, when he'd just sit there, propped up on the couch, with tears running down his cheeks, which every cell in his body was aching to wipe away but I had to take a Kleenex and do it, which made me cry, which only made Jake more pissed off, and with these tiny bits of air he'd push himself as hard as he could and I could hear him, in these tiny garbled words, saying, 'Fuck you.'"

"Yeah. Not easy. The worst."

"No, that's what came next. Because at the beginning, of course we'd talked about suicide. Jake said he wasn't sure he'd do it, but that he wanted the option. And at first I was shocked, but come on, we weren't talking about someone who was depressed, although nobody had any more right to be depressed than Jake, but back then, he wasn't. He said that having a fatal illness came with only one perk; when someone else started whining, about their Uber being late or CVS being out of Rice Chex or their mother telling them to lose weight, Jake could tell them, 'I hear you and I love you and I have ALS. I win.'"

"Damn right. Good on him."

"So as Jake got worse we did more research, because New York doesn't allow assisted suicide, almost no states do, except Oregon, and we'd have had to move there and establish residency for at least six months, and it was already too late for that. And we could've flown to Sweden, but even there we'd have to consult with two separate doctors and apply for permission, and Jake didn't want to spend his last days in a foreign country with, as he put it, 'too much blond furniture that belongs in a Montessori school.' And so we went to the Hemlock Society website to get information about the drug cocktail, which has prescription elements, and there's the version where the person puts a plastic bag over their head but Jake said, 'I'm not going to be dry-cleaned to death.'"

"I'm loving Jake."

"I knew you would. But then he got really bad, he wasn't just miserable, he was—despairing. We got him into an experimental drug trial, but as I was hoisting him and his wheelchair into a cab to go to the clinic, we got swiped by some idiot on an e-bike and Jake fell and I got tangled in his chair and eventually people passing by helped us, but Jake said fuck the trial, which was only promising minimal results, like maybe he'd be able to move his pinkie for three extra days. He just wanted to get back to the apartment, so we went back and sat there, staring at each other. And you know how even in the most dire situations, there's some tiny spark, some faint but undeniable relief, but we both knew this was different. This wasn't a long goodbye, this was either proof that God didn't exist or that God was a sadistic pig. This was hell's waiting room. And Jake could move his head the tiniest bit and he nodded toward a shelf, and there was this little carved wooden box that he'd bought in Bali, and I opened it and there was a note inside, and it said 'Now. Ask Paolo.'"

"Whoa. What did Paolo say?"

"He said that he'd talked to Jake months earlier, when Jake wanted to know about drugs that Paolo might have access to. And Paolo had agreed to tell me about them. He said he couldn't administer them, which would be illegal, but that if Jake said it was time, Paolo would give me the drugs and Jake and I could do the rest. And that night I had a conversation with Jake, or our version of a conversation. Me talking and Jake blinking. And I said, 'Does this mean you've considered every other route, including the possibility of a miracle remission, but this is what you want?' One blink, which meant yes. Because there are no remissions with ALS. Some people live a few years longer, and accept their physical limitations, but ALS is a death sentence, for everyone. So I said, 'I completely understand your wanting to die, to stop this nightmare, but you won't be able to grind up the pills and mix them with juice. I'll have to do that and I'll have to feed them to you.' One blink."

"He was asking you to kill him."

"Yes. And he wasn't just asking. Once Jake had made a decision, it was absolute, whether it was about refusing to use the same tired Home Depot white subway tile for a kitchen backsplash, no matter what the client said, or never talking about his family, or ending his life. And if I didn't help him, Jake would consider it a betrayal. Jake trusted me. But still, I went through what every still-healthy person goes through, meaning every adolescent debate team argument, such as, under what circumstances is murder justified, what do we owe to the people we love, what lines was I willing to cross. I went over it with Paolo, and he said that among healthcare workers it's an open secret that there are end-of-life patients who don't want to be resuscitated, who hate every second that prolongs their horrifically painful existence, which can't really be called an existence, let alone a life. And that doctors and nurses don't deliberately kill these patients, but they respect their wishes, and make them as comfortable as possible, and either allow them to die or do something more aggressive."

"Please don't tell me you talked to a priest."

"No, because if I did that Jake would come back from the afterlife and spray paint 'PIG' or 'MIDDLEBROW' on our bedroom wall, and I'm not especially religious, except, as Jake would say, about Ryan Gosling. And I knew that if this was some hack short story, the priest or the rabbi character would be brimming with wisdom and would teach Jake to savor every second of life, no matter how agonized."

"There's this priest in Jacksburg, Father Clanter, he's tight with Mayor LeBloitte, who's the world's biggest asshole. Every time he sees me, like on the street or at Wally's Pork Pit, he says, 'You're headed for Hell, young lady.' And I always ask, 'Can I get a lift?' Mostly he laughs, because he's drunk. But asking him for advice would be so fucked."

"Exactly. Paolo said he'd completely understand, whichever way I went. And I couldn't ask anyone else about it, like Sean or my own doctor, because it was so private and I didn't want to implicate them. And basically, I didn't have a choice, or that's how I saw it. It was about Jake and what he wanted, what would bring him peace."

"Right. Of course. Duh."

"So that last night, I got him into bed, wearing his favorite pajamas, white with navy blue piping from Harrods in London, he said they made him feel like Prince Philip on his wedding night. And we watched some of *Singin' in the Rain*, and a YouTube thing about Jake's favorite villa in Tuscany, and some stuff which Paolo had shot on his phone when we'd all rented a place on Fire Island, the year after Jake and I met. And there we were looking young and carefree and getting ready to go out dancing, and I asked Jake, 'Do you have any idea how much I love you' and I swear, he somehow managed to roll his eyes, which was his version of yes. Then he blinked, so I knew it was time. First I gave him this liquid sedative, through a straw, which made him woozy, but not so out of it that he couldn't swallow. And I mashed up the pills in orange juice and I could see on his face what he wanted me to do, so I used the straw, and he could only take these tiny sips, but he finally got it all down."

"And Paolo had said that I needed to watch Jake, to make sure he didn't barf the pills back up and choke on his own vomit, which can happen. So I sat there, and at first I held Jake's hand, but that seemed to give him a tremor, so I tucked his arm under the blanket. And he was more and more out of it, but he kept his eyes on mine, until they began fluttering shut, and then they closed. And I couldn't tell if he'd died, Paolo had said it might take three hours, so I waited. And he coughed once, but that was it. And after four hours I talked to Paolo and said that Jake didn't have a pulse and Paolo said it was time to call 911.

"So I did, and when the EMTs got there, they were great, there were three of them, and Jake would be pleased that they were hunky guys with their sleeves rolled up over their biceps like on one of those network medical shows. They angled a gurney into our bedroom and lifted Jake onto it. Once I'd told them Jake had ALS, the EMTs looked at each other, and one of them nodded at me. They checked Jake's vital signs and told me how sorry they were. I went with Jake's body to the hospital, where his doctor signed the death certificate. I had the feeling that everyone knew what was going on but understood and they weren't about to call in the police or a medical examiner.

"And that night Paolo took me back to the apartment, and he sat with me, but I thanked him and told him to go home, and he gave me an Ambien and I actually slept, or lost consciousness, I was so beat and overwhelmed. But I woke up around 5 a.m., completely lucid, because I'd done it. I'd killed Jake. And I didn't question any of it, I knew it was what Jake wanted, what he'd demanded, and I'd ended his suffering.

"But at the same time: Was I congratulating myself for being so gallant and honorable? And was I not-so-secretly glad, or at least relieved, that Jake was gone? Because I didn't have to keep taking care of him? Was I happy that I could stop being a full-time nurse and stop waking up every hour to make sure he was breathing, and pureeing his food and worrying about him for those few moments when I wasn't around, when we had a healthcare aide or I was in the shower? Was I really just being repulsively selfish, and had I done everything I could to convince

Jake to stay with me? And is all of this knotted up with how much I adored him and how angry I still am at the universe and even at Jake for getting sick and ruining our life together? Am I disgusting if I ask 'why me?' when I'm physically fine, when I have the luxury of however many years I've got left? And do I even want those years if Jake isn't here, and am I being the worst spoiled brat and the person everyone will avoid at a cocktail party if I keep spilling my guts and feeling sorry for myself and claiming some good-citizen blue-ribbon status because I took care of a dying man, which is just the way I'm behaving right now? It's been over a year and shouldn't I at least be starting to get over all this, because I feel like I'm wallowing and whimpering and lost and a total piece of shit?

"And I've been dealing with all this, or not dealing with it, which Paolo and Sean have been graciously tolerating, but I can't rely on them forever. Luckily, I love editing, especially your book, so I can lose myself in word changes and passages I want more of, and that's a gift. But it's not the same thing as being at peace. And I came on this trip to give Sean a hand, to help him either convince his ex-wife to run off with him, or to be okay with her getting married, like I'm a person to ask for advice on emotional stability. And yes, of course I wanted to see Artemis Island and get a look at Trone Meston and I'm stealing the TroneTek body oil and bee pollen facial masque from the bathroom. But yeah, that's where I am. And I'm so sorry to dump all of this on you, when we should be talking about your extraordinary book."

Tremble sighed and squinted and scratched her neck. "We'll talk about my extraordinary book later, *in fucking detail*, and I may have to grab a hunting knife and head back to New York and gut, what's her name, Isabelle McFuckface?"

Rob was about to caution Tremble not to gut Isabelle, but he was undone, so he'd save common sense and legal issues for later.

"McNally. She's Isabelle McNally."

"Right. Isabelle Cuntwad Douchenozzle McNally. But first let's do you. Tell me if I've got this right: Jake was gonna die one way or the other. And he wanted like, some control over that. He wanted to be in charge. Only he couldn't be, so he asked you to help him. And because you loved Jake beyond everything, you did. Only now you're driving yourself wacko because you're guilty and missing him and it's turning you into a Christian martyr grief zombie head case. Is that it?"

Rob nodded, which was when Tremble stood up, hauled off, and smacked him, hard, right across the face, sending him staggering backwards.

"Tremble?"

"Okay, I'm really sorry, that wasn't right, I need to rephrase that."

Then she smacked Rob again, even harder.

"Stop that!"

"Dude. Rob. Remember when you sent me my manuscript, with all those edits and questions, and when I opened it I went, whoa, so he really read my book and he thinks it's not 100 percent perfect exactly the way it is, and he's telling me to do more work on it? And you highlighted all the bad stuff in red . . ."

"It wasn't bad stuff, it was the transitions and paragraphs I had questions about . . ."

"No, don't back off, it was bad stuff, and you were basically slapping me, and after I got over myself and really looked at what you were saying, almost every single time, you were right. And I was so grateful. That you were calling me on my shit."

"It wasn't shit . . ."

"Yeah, a lot of it was. And you helped me. Because you love my book. And you believe in me. So I'm returning the favor."

As Tremble got closer and Rob anticipated her next slap, he hunched over to deflect it, but Tremble was faster and she used both hands to slap him on both sides of his face.

"Tremble! Stop it! I'm old and I'm gay and I'm fired and I'm very delicate! I'm an editor, or I was! I live in Chelsea! And even when Sean gave me some boxing drills for upper body strength, the only thing I hit was a punching bag, which I named after a Republican senator! I don't do hitting or slapping!"

Tremble grabbed Rob by his right hand, swung him around the gazebo repeatedly until he was dizzy and off-balance, and then shoved him onto his back on the floor and straddled him, pinning his arms to his sides.

"Dude. Bro. Here it is. You loved Jake. He loved you. Which is major, it's as major as it gets. And then you both got a raw deal, because he got sick and you had to watch. Which is as sucky as it gets. But it is what it fucking is. You stepped up. You did the hard thing. Like I did, when one of my foster Dads was coming into my room so I got a shovel and the next time he tried it I took a chunk out of his head and sent him to the emergency room."

"Really? You should write about that . . ."

"The next book. But I did what I had to do. Which got me shipped back to the Jacksburg Juvenile Detention Facility, which sucked almost as bad, but I started writing and then I aged out of the system and then I sent all that stuff to you and you said it was a book. So I owe you."

"Don't hit me again!"

"I won't. On one condition. Don't be such a fucking cooze."

The beam of a flashlight illuminated both their faces, because Tremble was leaning over Rob's immobilized body.

"Everything all right here?" asked the security guard, one of the many ex-FBI agents Trone had hired away by promising doubled salaries and pensions.

"CPR," said Tremble, letting Rob up. "I'm a trained paramedic."

"All good," said Rob, cringing at the phrase. "No, we're fine."

"We don't have a curfew here on the island, but most of our guests have turned in. It's a busy weekend. So you might want to get some rest. And can I have your names?"

"I'm Rob Barnett, and I'm a guest of Sean Manginaro. And this is . . ."

"I'm his daughter. Isabelle Coozeface McButtslut Barnett."

"Coozeface?"

"It's a family name," Rob explained. "And we're heading back to our cottages. But thank you for being . . . so diligent."

27

REHEARSAL DINNER

Rob and Tremble walked back to Rob's cottage in silence as Rob absorbed Tremble's counsel and kept an eye out for any further slapping or spinning. He had Tremble spend the night in his cottage, where she met Paolo, taking one look at him and blurting, "Gay dentist." Before Paolo could mount a defense, Tremble told him, "I'm kidding! Rob told me about you and I'm in awe. I'd much rather be a dentist than a doctor, because you don't have to memorize as many organs. And being a gay dentist is great because I bet you make your patients look fabulous, like if I were you I'd open a chain of budget gay dental clinics called Superteeth."

This appeased Paolo, who was equally dazzled by Tremble's journey to Artemis Island. Over Tremble's protests Rob gave her his bed, since she'd been napping on buses, while he took the voluminous couch, and everyone passed out from long-distance travel and gazebo wrestling. As Rob drifted off, he questioned whether Faulkner had ever hurled his editor to the floor and sat on him, but Tremble was a godsend.

Saturday was all about the rehearsal dinner. The trio kept to themselves, ordering in breakfast and lunch so Tremble wouldn't be conspicuous. Sean went for another run, troubled by the *WarForce Re-union* movie being streamed on Showtime. The movie might remind Linda of his misdeeds, although he'd been lovingly photographed, buff, and had saved America. "So when you're being Blaster," Tremble asked him, "are there wires attached to you so you can fly, and did they pad out your costumes to make you look even bigger?"

"First of all," Sean sniffed, "Blaster flies by using hyper-propulsion."

"As one does," said Paolo.

"And I didn't need any padding because there was a gym on the set so I could get pumped before each take."

"Much like Meryl Streep," said Rob, "in that Margaret Thatcher movie."

They were all pigging out in Rob and Paolo's cottage. The allure of a leather-bound, hand-inscribed, twelve-page room service menu was irresistible. "I should publish this," said Rob, studying the desserts.

"So, Tremble," said Paolo, once the coconut cake and apple tarts had been delivered in a wicker hamper, "how do you think Sean should handle the Linda situation? Do you think he has a prayer?"

Rob was curious about Tremble smacking Sean or getting him in a headlock. She was compact but formidable, with reflexes sharpened in custody, and despite Sean's hyper-propulsion abilities, Rob's money was on Tremble.

"Okay," Tremble told Sean, "so you were married, you have two kids, and the reason we're all here is because she's marrying the Ultra-Lord of the Known Mestonverse, who's gonna launch his own space station into orbit next year, that's the general fucking idea, right?"

"A space station," Sean scoffed. "Rookie disaster move. Think about the upkeep, getting replacement parts, not to mention Blaster has his own space lair on the moon, where he does these zero-gravity workouts by lifting his space cruiser. With one arm. My idea."

"Cool," said Tremble. "But here's what's going down. She invited you. And you're not gonna beg or start crying or calling Trone out or doing any of that I'm-a-straight-dude-so-I'm-gonna-act-like-a-big-fucking-baby shit. Don't be a dick. Nobody wants that. You're gonna show her what she's missing. You're gonna show everyone. You're Blaster. You're Sean fucking Manginaro. Prove it, bitch."

———

Linda, meanwhile, was having brunch with her kids in Trone's private wing. Bridger and Morrow were suitably gobsmacked by the scale and amenities of the island, but both having just turned twenty, they didn't evidence the slightest appreciation or get caught rotating their heads a quarter of an inch to inspect the fifteen-foot ceilings. They'd both ordered enough food to last for weeks. Their awareness of Trone's fortune had brought out stockpiling tendencies, like cave people transported to an all-you-can-eat buffet.

"So did you sleep all right?" Linda asked. "Do you like your suites?"

"They're okay," said Bridger, tearing a still-warm croissant in half and setting aside another, for placement in her complimentary TroneTek carryall, which had arrived pre-packed with a sweatshirt silkscreened with Linda's and Trone's faces, specially treated cloths for cleaning TroneTek devices, shortbread cookies frosted with the TroneTek logo, and hardcover copies of Trone's self-published memoir, titled *Best Meston: Troning My Life.*

"At first I couldn't find any ports for recharging stuff," groused Morrow, "but then some guy at the front desk said the suites had ambient recharging, so if you just leave your phone or tablet or whatever on any hard surface, they'll be fully powered within thirty seconds."

"So it's fun being here, right?" Linda asked hopefully, as if her kids had previously been stashed in a hollow tree.

"So Mom," said Bridger, "you're doing it? The marriage thing?"

"Yes," said Linda, "and it's not a thing. You've spent time with Trone, he thinks you're great, and God knows he's been generous, although Morrow, I had to stop him from building an enclosed gaming amphitheater out here, just for you."

Morrow's deliberately vacant expression didn't vary, while he inwardly screamed, MOM, CALL HIM BACK AND SAY DO THE AMPHITHEATER!!!

"Do we have to go up there with you, at the ceremony?" asked Bridger.

"No, of course not, you should do whatever you're comfortable with. But I want both of you to feel included, because we're expanding our family."

"Is Dad coming?" asked Morrow, keeping his tone unreadable.

"I invited him, but who knows." Linda was lying. She was almost positive that Sean had been lurking the night before, near what the island's architect called the Sylvan Lagoon Feature. She'd heard someone running close by, but as she'd turned, Trone had found her. She'd been too flustered to call out, to see if the runner was in fact Sean, although his rhythmic tread and controlled breathing were familiar.

"If he's here, are you gonna talk to him?" asked Bridger.

"Of course I'll talk to him. It would be perfectly fine to see him, and I hope, if he shows up, that you'll talk to him, too. He's still your father."

After that first year, when Bridger had implacably cut Sean out of her life, as a demonstration of both maternal and political loyalty, there'd been a thawing, a tentative rekindling of communication. Morrow had never stopped speaking to Sean, but their lunches in the city had consisted of Morrow mumbling that everything was fine but he wasn't going to spy on his mom and tattle back to Sean. Sean had plied him with tickets to sporting events and concerts, neither of which interested Morrow. It wasn't easy bribing a kid whose greatest pleasures could be achieved by racing his fingers across a keyboard or console, to slaughter half-werewolves/half-alien-vampires (the two species had mated).

"Mom, if Dad asked you to break it off with Trone and get back together with him, would you do it?" asked Morrow.

"That is ridiculous," Linda replied, rapidly switching the subject to appropriate wardrobe for the rehearsal dinner ("Anything you'd like to wear as long as it's not embarrassing or slutty or unwashed"). The twins didn't push, but they both noticed that Linda hadn't answered the question.

———

The wedding's most celebrated guests, the movie stars, media magnates, and heads of state, would be flying in aboard private jets on Sunday for the ceremony and reception alone (a few were even sharing jets, which they considered a gesture toward saving the rain forests). The island's landing strip was set a camouflaged distance from Alchemy Hall, with ground transportation in souped-up golf carts. The rehearsal dinner was at 5 p.m. and limited to the wedding party and closer friends of the bride and groom, and Sean was surprised to find a table number texted to his phone. Rob and Paolo would accompany him, while Tremble kept a lower profile, so her presence wouldn't cause her, or all of them, to get escorted off the island or worse—with the wedding itself imminent, security was everywhere.

The dinner was being held in one of the island's more restrained dining rooms, but with the architect's signature rough-hewn oak beams, whitewashed shiplap along the walls, and large inset LED screens, framed in braided twigs, that morphed through images of TroneTek products, from the first, now classic TronePhones to the ever-slimmer TroneTome eReaders, to evocatively shadowed, silvery-gray boxes, shot from below to seem like ancient monoliths, containing whatever precedent-shattering widget Trone would unleash the next day. Branding his own wedding might be construed as mercenary and demeaning to his fiancée, but this was Trone Meston, so everyone felt exponentially more aquiver at attending not merely an epic celebration of romantic love but a historic occasion potentially surpassing a moon landing or the first foil-wrapped TV dinner.

"What do you think it's going to be?" Paolo asked the table, situated toward the rear of the room and consisting of himself, Sean, and Rob. "You know, Trone's new baby?"

"Wouldn't it be great if it was a pair of safety scissors?" Rob proposed. "And Trone thought he'd invented them?"

"Does he really invent anything?" asked Sean. "Or does he just pay other people to come up with stuff and he takes the credit?"

Another guest was checking the table numbers and then the faces. It was Isabelle McNally.

"Rob?" Isabelle exclaimed, as if she'd smelled a spewing skunk perched on one of the chairs and nibbling a dinner roll.

"Isabelle?"

"What are you doing here?" Isabelle asked this without bothering to conceal her condescending shock.

"I'm a plus-one. And you?"

"I'm . . . I'm a guest of Trone's."

Rob hadn't expected to see Isabelle ever again. But he'd waved to Arjun and a scattering of other W&S staff members in Alchemy Hall, so Isabelle must be part of that group. His mind pinwheeled: Should he snub her, or with Tremble as his mentor, slap the shit out of her? But Rob heard his mother's voice in his head, admonishing "You weren't raised by wolves. We say please and thank you, even to those beneath our contempt."

"Everyone," said Rob, his voice clenched, "this is Isabelle McNally."

"The chick who fired you?" said Sean, and Rob was secretly grateful for his choice of the word "chick," because Isabelle was bristling.

"Well, isn't this awkward?" said Paolo, loving every syllable.

"Maybe I should sit somewhere else," said Isabelle.

"No," said Rob, beginning to savor the confrontation as well. "The room looks full and you'd inconvenience everyone. Join us."

As Isabelle gingerly took a seat amid Rob's allies, the ambush escalated. Tremble, dressed in a waiter's uniform consisting of a white high-necked jacket and sleek black trousers, stood over Rob's shoulder. "Good evening," she said, "I'll be taking your drink and dinner orders. We have a choice of chicken, lobster, a vegan option, or the farm-fresh cooze, in a light cocksucker sauce with a side dish of braised pussy fever."

———

Linda was seated at the front of the room, beside Trone and the twins. Even Bridger admitted that her mom shone, in an expensively simple cream-colored silk blouse, exposing just enough collarbone, and a cobalt-blue velvet skirt; she had the offhand elegance of a movie star presenting an Oscar and upstaging the actresses in chiffon prom night effusions. Bridger was starting to resemble her mom, in both her epic bone structure and surly, mistrustful nature. She was wearing a jeans jacket over a white tank top and a black leather miniskirt, but she was definitely going to borrow everything Linda had on at a later date, without asking.

Trone had no family at the dinner. He'd been generous toward his parents and ten siblings, bailing them out of jail, paying for their medical needs and the homes and vehicles they'd requested. But his largesse had been bartered. His family would abstain from all interview requests, produce no childhood photos (there weren't many) for unauthorized books or articles, and never be seen near, let alone within, any of Trone's legion of homes and offices. Trone liked his relatives well enough, but he'd outgrown them early on, so his guests at the dinner were his legal team, his top two executive assistants (who were required to record Trone's random thoughts, for a future museum archive), his dermatologist (who treated suspicious moles and provided the custom under-eye night cream that Trone denied using), and a senator Trone was leaning on for a tax break on an incipient TroneTek campus in lower Manhattan. Trone's peers, meaning a cadre of almost-as-wealthy titans, who one-upped each other with Lake Como villas and of-the-moment restaurant ownerships, would descend in the morning. Trone couldn't quite call these bigwigs his friends, because no one in that financial stratosphere has time for, or any interest in, chummy, non-business-related chatter. These tycoons functioned as a jury, barely masking their ruthless competition with shiv-like compliments along the lines of "I like your new chopper—the old one was getting shabby."

"Are you having a good time?" Trone asked the twins.

"Sure," said Bridger, "this island is awesome. Did you do an environmental impact survey prior to construction?"

"Bridger . . . ," Linda began, menacingly.

"Of course we did," said Trone. "Half the island is a wildlife preserve, we use a geothermal heating and cooling system, and our sewage treatment facility is the most efficient in the country. Morrow?"

"I like this place. It's like if a Bond villain was trying to help people."

Trone laughed. The twins were their own breed of petulant fun, and Trone attributed their intelligence and wariness to their age and Linda's example. Twenty-year-olds were far less annoying than wailing or chirpy toddlers, or any age group expecting hugs. Adult stepkids were a pleasing concept, as if Trone had fabricated and focus-grouped them.

Linda was relieved that everyone was getting along, and she wasn't consciously searching the tables for Sean, but there he was, in a blazer and an open-collared shirt, which was Sean's equivalent of a tuxedo. A decently dressed Sean was heart-meltingly attractive. He looked like an effortlessly magnetic Hollywood legend illuminated by flashbulbs in a courtroom, or testifying earnestly before Congress about funding for the arts. He was talking to Rob and some younger, rigidly upset woman, but then his eyes met Linda's.

———————

"Isabelle," said Rob, "this is Tremble Woodspill."

"But why . . . why are you dressed like a waiter?"

"I'm working undercover."

"What?"

"As a paid assassin."

"What?"

"Tremble came a very long way to find me," Rob told Isabelle. "She's understandably worried about her book's future at W&S."

Rob was getting more forthright, thanks to Tremble's gazebo assault and a memory of Jake describing him as "not even passive-aggressive, you make up polite excuses to get off the phone with robocalls."

"Why the fuck did you fire Rob?" Tremble demanded, blocking Isabelle from standing and escaping. "He's a great editor."

"I don't really think this is the time or place to get into that," Isabelle objected, "but it was a thoroughly justified and vetted dismissal."

"Fuck that. He made my book better. And he found it. And you keep trying to make it into something else. Fuck you."

Rob almost interrupted to mediate the fracas, because Tremble's hands were now on Isabelle's shoulders, firmly keeping her in place, but Paolo touched Rob's knee under the table, because the impending brawl was so entertaining.

"Tremble, you're a gifted author, but Rob has misled you. I'll be happy to discuss my notes at any other time, but—oh my God, is that Trone up there? Rob, do you know him?"

Dear Lord, Rob thought, is Isabelle asking me for an introduction?

"I think I'm gonna speak to Trone myself," said Tremble. "About what's going on with Rob."

"No!" Isabelle exclaimed, because Trone was her property, her vision-mate and her soul's executive producer, and hers alone.

"I think somebody has a crush," said Tremble, "I think somebody wants to lady-bone the big boss."

"Excuse me," said Sean, leaving the table, "I'll be right back," and then, to Rob, "Get into this, pal. Get in the ring."

Shit, thought Linda, he's coming over. No, it's fine, I invited him, although I still have no idea why, but these are his kids, so this is perfectly normal, it's even helpful, he had to meet Trone at some point or other. But why was Sean born to wear snug blue jeans, and why is he moving with such sexy, animal-like stealth, and why is he smiling?

"Hey guys," said Sean, with a hand on each twin's head.

"Dad!" said Morrow. "You made it!"

"And you're almost dressed up," said Bridger.

"All of you look great," said Sean, extending his arm to Trone. "Sean Manginaro. I'm the evil ex."

"So you are," said Trone, with a speculative grin, shaking Sean's hand. Sean's grip was steady but not crushing, and his skin was rougher than Trone's; Trone exercised by closing his eyes and picturing spreadsheets, or occasionally having his driver stop the limo so Trone could get out on a grassy highway divider, perform two deep-knee bends, then return to the back seat and his phone. Linda had incrementally related her history with Sean, straining to stay equitable and long-past-it, and Trone had seen photos of Sean and asked his assistant to prepare a file, but this was more visceral, with muted, portentous drums on an imagined soundtrack. Sean was amiable and relaxed, unlike many heterosexual men, who most often grew either tiresomely obsequious or irritatingly cocky around Trone, longing to become his new best friend, business partner, and golf buddy, or spoiling to belittle him in public, for barroom bragging rights. Tremble had reminded Sean that he possessed a rare, invaluable, practically unheard-of superpower: the ability to intimidate even the most powerful men, just by being Sean Manginaro.

"Nice to see you," Linda told Sean, smiling a bit too forcibly.

"Thanks for inviting me, and congratulations, both of you. And I'm loving this island. Great job."

"Thank you," said Trone, unexpectedly dwindling into a scrawny twelve-year-old stammering beside the toweringly rugged high school quarterback. Trone was far from gay, but straight guys developed instant man crushes on Sean. His potent physical presence transformed everyone into a woozy-eyed, diary-keeping ("I think he looked at me!") besotted teenage fan, except of course for Bridger, who asked Sean, "Who're you with? Who's that woman?"

"She works with Rob. Except she fired him. Mr. Meston, Rob Barnett works at one of your companies, or he did, and he's a fantastic editor and a seriously good guy. I don't think you want to lose him. But hey, this is your weekend. So have a blast, and don't let my kids act like jackals, and I'll see everybody tomorrow."

Then he was gone, not quite sauntering back to his table, but cleaving the crowd and leaving his ex-wife, their kids, and Trone Meston with their mouths open, their napkins fluttering to the floor unnoticed. When a star is warm, friendly, and self-deprecating, everyone's yearning increases a thousandfold, and they're left in his or her wake with so much left to say.

"He's . . . he's a good-looking man," said Trone.

"Eeewww," said Bridger. "Did you ever see his TV show? Where he looks like he's wearing an aerobics outfit from the eighties? At least tonight he had on clothes."

A locker-room peek at a naked Sean sprang unbidden into Trone's normally non-sensual brain. He wasn't breathless, not exactly. It was more like the sensation when an idea struck him. Pleased and electrified.

"That's enough, Bridger," said Linda. "He looked nice, but we're all getting older. And that's one of the problems with athletes, even if they stay in shape, they end up with chronic arthritis and bone spurs. Sean lives on Advil." Linda wasn't sure why she was being so snarky, or was she claiming Sean, by trading insider tidbits?

"Dad's a stud," said Morrow, and then to Trone, "He told me to say that."

After a second, everyone laughed, grateful to dissipate the undeniable heat Sean exuded, the masculine aura of Sean-ness, not like a pungent frat-boy cologne, or a post-workout sweat, but something that was magnified by the formality of the occasion, as if a lion had paced agreeably through the dining room, not roaring, not yet, but unmistakably carnivorous. What the fuck was that about, Linda asked herself, and why was everyone at the nearby tables still swooning toward Sean and dropping their utensils?

28

A MIDSUMMER NIGHT

Later that evening, nearing midnight, as a fog began to infiltrate the island, Sean sat in an armchair in his cottage, analyzing his progress. He'd almost slugged Trone, but Tremble's wisdom, about the persuasive effect of nonchalance and a cannier seduction, had kicked in. Sean was fully recharged. This was now a fair fight.

Sean left the cottage. The fog was everywhere, so he didn't run, but, in just a white T-shirt and jeans, he moved deliberately, obeying his instincts, in both his memory of the island's topography, and the clues about Linda's availability.

He reached the pond, or the fake lagoon, whatever it was. The haze was blurring everything, although the full moon's reflection was a luminous arrow, striking a shimmering path across the water. Linda, who'd changed into a simple white linen dress, was seated on the rock outcropping above the pond, dangling her bare legs and sandaled feet. Sean's arrival didn't surprise her, but she refused to come off as a tremulous schoolgirl or a lovesick fan.

"Hey," said Sean, from a few yards away.

"Hey."

"Nervous? About tomorrow?"

"Not at all."

"Can I talk to you?"

"We are talking. Although we probably shouldn't be."

"Why not?"

"I can't fucking imagine."

This was the Linda Sean remembered: cranky and challenging, forever needling him. He held out a hand, to help her clamber down from her perch, a gesture intended to rile her. She brushed this attempt aside, then teetered, and Sean steadied her.

"Happy now?" she asked. "Have you rescued the fair maiden?"

"I'm working on it."

They began to walk, with the fog insulating their conversation, as if whatever occurred could be later dismissed as a moonlit dream or a weather-driven accident.

Before their divorce had been finalized, they'd met with a couples counselor, because that was what people did. Linda left midway through the first session, claiming, "I can't listen to him justifying himself." Sean hung on alone for two more sessions, being brutally honest about everything he'd done and why, with a succinct "I love her and I'm garbage." The female therapist, like every woman in Sean's life, had stared at him, appreciatively and with a this-is-beyond-my-skillset appalled wonder. Linda was too hurt and Sean too stoic. Neither had any interest in jabbering endlessly about circumstances they were both already familiar with: after returning from California, Sean had admitted to everything. Linda's resolve, to never permit further humiliation, was absolute. Some sappy, tentative, psychobabble-encouraged "breakthrough" wasn't just unlikely but impossible. The facts defeated therapy.

"So you're happy?" said Sean, as they strolled through Trone's deluxe forest, both looking straight ahead.

"Very."

"I'm glad. Trone seems like a decent guy."

"He is. It's shocking, because he doesn't need to be. Are you seeing anyone?"

"Nope. Not since us."

"You're lying. Bridger saw you on one of those dating apps so I checked it out. There's a photo of you leaning against your truck, wearing a plaid flannel shirt over thermal underwear, so we'd see the pecs. Very Connecticut cowpoke. And what did the profile say? 'Not interested in a relationship. No pressure or commitments. No feelings.' You should've told me that before I married you."

"I put that in the profile because I did marry you."

"So how many hotties? Age-appropriate or anything over twenty-one?"

"Age-appropriate. Mostly. But only for sex. And not much of that."

"Poor baby."

Sean had rehearsed so many speeches, but improvised instead. "I know you still hate me and I know the reasons. And I'm glad, truly, that you've finally moved on. But I'm not sure I ever will. I know I can't complain, because I smashed up everything, but—I'm not doing that again. A relationship. Too dangerous."

"What about with me?"

Sean staggered, clutching his heart: "Did you just say that? Did you fucking open that door? Are you that evil?"

"Just asking a question. Would you? If I asked?"

"No."

"Because it would happen all over again? The cheating and the lying and tearing everything apart?"

"No. Because aside from everything else, it would be too much work. Since you'd never trust me, and I couldn't blame you."

There was a wooden bench outside Sean's cottage. They sat. Sean stretched his legs out, asking, "Do you ever think about me?"

"Of course. When you're late with the checks for the kids' colleges."

"You are such a bitch."

"Yes I am. That's what you taught me. When we were together, that was the only time I let my guard down. The only time I said, toss the dice, load the dishwasher, add a half bath to the basement, go for it."

"And I fucked it up. All of it."

"Not all of it."

"Name me one thing I did right, one thing you don't regret, one thing I was good at."

Linda was watching Sean, as he strummed every wistful note, aggressively fishing for absolution, attributing every mistake to himself, his blue eyes searching the darkness, because he was such a heartbroken piece of crap. It was adorable. This was the Sean she remembered: sly, controlling, ignorant that his major-player riffs were transparent, that he was, at most, twelve years old at all times, smelling faintly of liniment, basic soap, and whatever shampoo was on sale. She straddled him.

"You didn't send a wedding gift," she said, leaning down to kiss him, which lasted until she pulled away.

Sean thought about hoisting Linda manfully in his arms and carrying her across the threshold into the cottage, just so she could make an outraged noise and undoubtedly say, "Jesus Christ, put me down, you asshole," and take off, shaking her head. Instead, he picked her up and deposited her, standing, on the ground. None of this would be happening without the fog and the island and the sheer unlikeliness of the evening.

Sean took a few steps toward the cottage. He pulled his T-shirt off over his head. Linda wanted to laugh or applaud or ask if he was posing for the cover of a romance novel, maybe something about a lonely lumberjack or a widowed pediatrician with a cabin in the Rockies. But when Sean climbed the steps, she followed him.

———

Rob was alone and spiraling. Tremble had been summoned by a service captain to wait on other tables and had disappeared, either to do as she'd been asked or, more likely, to get the hell out of the dining room. Isabelle had excused herself, telling Rob, "You shouldn't be here and you should accept your own deficiencies. I'm not trying to offend you, but this is a tool for growth." Rob had barely stifled his schoolyard urge to yell, "You're a tool for growth," and empty a carafe of ice water on her. Paolo had gone in search of the men's room and hadn't been seen since, most likely because he'd met a man. Dax's unlikely but still possible appearance wasn't interfering with Paolo's horniness, and he'd passed a handsome security guard earlier and wondered, "Do you think this island is like one of those huge cruise ships, where half the staff members are fucking the guests?"

Sean could talk Rob down, but he'd left for his cottage. The rehearsal dinner was breaking up, so Rob headed out by himself, oblivious to Tremble having dissolved a tab of blotter acid in his mug of tea fifteen minutes earlier. Tremble had slapped Rob to improve his outlook, but this hadn't been entirely successful. Isabelle's presence at the wedding was undermining Rob, so Tremble had implemented further assistance. She almost never drugged people without being asked to, but Rob was so woebegone and solitary, and his ordering a mug of tea, "Earl Grey, oolong, whatever they've got, it doesn't really matter, it's tea," had verged on spinster-touring-*Downton-Abbey*-filming-locations tragic. So Tremble had dug her tiny Dora the Explorer change purse from the larger backpack and plucked out her last hit of LSD, which she'd been saving for the bus ride home. But this was an emergency. Secretly dosing Rob was just what Dora would do, if her show aired later at night on a more sophisticated streaming service. Even Boots the monkey, Dora's BFF, would approve.

Rob lacked any aptitude for geographical direction. For their trips, Jake had bought maps and travel paperbacks months in advance, then handily navigated Milan or Buenos Aires. Jake had been Rob's guide in so many ways, and he'd also nimbly exchanged currencies, ending each sojourn with none of those now untenable pesos or euros or yen that Rob would tuck inside his underwear drawer.

The fog was impenetrable and Rob almost reversed course toward Alchemy Hall, but there weren't any visible signposts. His head had begun to spin, pleasurably, and he was no longer disturbed at losing his way. Maybe I'm edging toward a cliff, he thought, without a hint of anxiety, and I'll topple into the Atlantic. Or maybe I'm about to be clawed by a bear or squeezed by an anaconda, both of which might be interesting. He'd been hiking for some time when a voice murmured, "You're lost and you need to pee." Rob had no idea who was speaking, maybe it was an impertinent pine tree or Jesus Christ, who was inevitably on Trone's guest list, flying in unassisted. Then the voice said, more loudly, "Go left, ten steps. Just do it."

Maybe this was an automated TroneTek system, some hyper-upgraded version of Rob's kitchen-counter Tria, or a GPS that had assumed ultimate control. The voice continued: "Here."

Rob couldn't discern anything but an open glade or meadow, ringed by fog. It was incandescently lovely, like a three-dimensional panorama of some storybook illustration, or a Maxfield Parrish mural blending an unnaturally purple-and-yellow sunset with exquisitely rendered, Easter bunny–pink clouds and fragrant, night-blooming jasmine. Jake emerged from a floating orb, and Rob wasn't surprised in the least. Jake was walking, fully healed, and wearing jeans and a beloved gray cashmere crewneck, his red hair especially lustrous in the starshine. Rob smiled, so glad to see him.

"Murderer," Jake said.

"Excuse me?" Rob replied, because Jake had hijacked the lyrical, artwork-reproduced-on-a-placemat mood.

"I'm joking," said Jake. "And didn't you love the way I stepped out of the radiance, like a cross between the Virgin Mary appearing to Bernadette and a gay *Field of Dreams*?"

Rob couldn't speak. Some sliver of reality had crept in, frightening him. What was happening? Was he having a stroke? Had grief fractured his brain? Had he fallen asleep, or was he nearing death itself, with Jake as his acerbically angelic welcoming committee?

"You have to stop," Jake said. "You didn't kill me. Well you did, or you certainly lent a hand, but only because I asked you to. And because the alternative was unthinkable."

"Was it . . ." Rob couldn't help himself. Whatever this was, he was inside of it, and reeling from Jake's ghostly materialization, this celestial moment of contact. "Your dying—was it painful?"

"Excruciating. Inexpressible torment. Like a drug overdose in a club bathroom, or a child singing 'Send in the Clowns' in a kindergarten talent show. Please. It was nothing, except pure release. As if after being trapped in a box the exact dimensions of my body, I could move my limbs. As if that wretched curse had been lifted. And by the way, you weren't proving your love or your nobility. It wasn't some award-winningly turgid movie of the week starring washed-up TV stars from thirty years ago called *Journey to Heaven* or *On the Wings of Barbiturates*. You helped me. I already loved you. You know that."

"But . . . but . . . it let me off the hook."

"From what? Disinfecting my bedpan? Being an audience member to an exceptionally repulsive disease? ALS wasn't a test, or the culmination of our marriage. But 'in sickness and in health' did come into play. The whole thing, it was exactly why I stopped talking to my family. Because they lived for punishingly useless drama like this, for divine retribution. Oh, Rob."

Jake's eyes had gone cloudy, as if he was as muddled and inconsolable as Rob.

"What?"

"I don't know what this is either. I don't know where I've traveled from or how this is happening. But I'm not questioning it. You look terrible. Maybe I should blame Sean."

"I got fired."

"I'm aware. Maybe I'll be granted some supernatural hall pass, to shave Isabelle's head, or force her to read a book without making a minority representation chart. But you can do this. You can fight for yourself and for Tremble. You love what you do, and you're going to need that. The only thing worse than my dying would be you reliving it endlessly, as if that was the only part of our relationship that mattered. Our love isn't a manuscript you can keep rereading, juggling chapters and struggling to fix the ending. Shit."

"Jake?"

"I have to go. I'm being, I'm not sure what, summoned or whatever it's called under these circumstances. Just believe that I'm grateful and I adore you and don't move the Eames chair closer to the window, which you've been itching to do, because the leather will fade and crack. Don't use my death as an excuse to disobey me."

This last sentence convinced Rob that whatever was going on, it was real. The apparition was lofty and annoying.

"But, but . . . oh my Lord," said Rob. "I still have so many things to ask. And this feels like a CGI special effect where Luke Skywalker receives eternal life lessons from Obi-Wan Kenobi, in some astral medi- tation zone. But getting pointers from my dead gay husband is next level. Or like an updated version of *A Christmas Carol* that would get a GLAAD Award. Or like you should give me an invaluable clue to solv- ing some fiendish mystery."

"It's Lady Fairfield in the library with an ice pick."

"Jake . . ."

Rob reached out to touch him. That was what he'd missed, a spon- taneous hug or a make-out session or just knowing Jake was in the next room. Jake's illness had stolen so much, everything, but most especially a normalcy, the daily nudges and neck rubs, the weekend lounging in bed, the Netflix choices, all the casual proofs of love in their life as a couple. Jake's hand almost met Rob's, in an LSD-encouraged echo of the Sistine Chapel ceiling, which had made both men so happy, as they'd craned their necks at the original, together on a trip to Rome, when Jake referred to the surprisingly vivid, recently restored colors as "Barbie's Vatican."

Jake was gone. The fog was lifting. Rob was only a few feet from his cottage. And still a million miles from mental health. There was some passionate question left unanswered, some signal or token that Jake, or his exceedingly well-lit avatar, hadn't had time to pass along.

————

As Isabelle was striding back to her cottage, which she loathed sharing with two other faceless W&S junior deputy whatevers, who kept wanting to play Pictionary and compare celebrity sightings, someone grabbed her from behind and shoved her to the ground.

"Yeah, that's right, whorefuck," said Tremble. "We're gonna talk, for real."

Tremble was kneeling on Isabelle's shoulders, as Isabelle fruitlessly waved her clenched fists, condemning violence while heaving to upend a tiny powerhouse.

"Tremble, why are you doing this? I'm advocating on your behalf! I'm honoring your work!"

"Bitch, you fired the dude who bought my work and showed it to you and defended it! Rob told me I was a fucking writer and you told me I'm not!"

"That's not what's happening here! W&S has standards which I'm revising and upholding! This isn't just about you!"

"It's MY BOOK, you fucking pisshead! I don't mind being edited, because Rob made my book better! You just want to make it sound like you! Are you a writer?"

"I'm exploring intersectional creative outlets . . ."

"You're doing what the fuckety fuck? Exploring intersectional creative outlets? Is that like some discount mall?"

"Please let me up! I'm a proponent of monitored, equitable discourse!"

"You're a proponent of being a fucking pussy. Okay, you know what let's do? W&S is owned by Trone Meston, right? He makes the real decisions. So let's fucking go and see him."

Isabelle had meant to connect with Trone at the rehearsal dinner, or at least catch his eye, but he'd been preoccupied with that blond woman, fine, with his fiancée. There were only a few hours before tomorrow's ceremony, so why not direct Tremble's rampaging toward a finer end, specifically Isabelle meeting Trone one-on-one?

"Let's do that. Let's go see Trone," Isabelle told Tremble, who was looking at Isabelle's neck and mentally tattooing it, maybe with an ad for *Life as We Fucking Know It*, or just the words "I SUCK."

From her encounters with Churn LeBloitte and at least two of her foster fathers, Tremble had an inkling of how egocentric and self-promoting men behave, so she anticipated where Trone would be on the eve of his wedding—he'd be doing business, like Churn gathering his deadbeat henchmen at his office in Jacksburg. While touring the island, Tremble had taken note of its marina, where Trone's yacht was anchored. Trone would be too restless for even the island's presidential suite or finance center, and he'd want to be reachable only on his own terms. Tremble let Isabelle get to her feet, so they could make their way to the water.

Tremble had never been on any boat larger than a rusty fishing trawler, but she was adjusting to so many firsts: Times Square, Artemis Island, meeting Rob in person, and now the SS *Mestonia IV*—Trone's previous, three smaller yachts had been sold to lesser rich people, as an oligarch's equivalent of hand-me-downs.

"You think we can just walk onto his boat and they'll let us meet with him?" Isabelle dithered, trailing behind Tremble, and straightening the medallion on her necklace, an agate heart wrapped in copper wire, hand-hammered by a Bushwick artisan to symbolize the human condition and leave green marks on Isabelle's skin.

The marina had been measured to accommodate the mammoth vessel, which housed two helicopters, a hovercraft, a flotilla of Jet Skis, five decks, and enough staterooms for twelve guests, which is the legal limit in the United States for even the largest private yacht, although there was a crew of forty. The yachts of Trone's mogul cronies would be marooned farther out to sea, so they'd have to gaze upon the supremacy of Trone's step beyond a mega-yacht, called a giga-yacht (Trone was having something twice the size blueprinted, which might achieve statehood). Tremble, with Isabelle in tow, chatted up the security guard standing beside a pair of chained stanchions on the dock.

"So hi," said Tremble, "we really need to see Trone Meston. Like, immediately."

"And you are . . . ?"

"Welstrom & Stratters personnel Tremble Woodspill and Asswad McFartknocker."

"Isabelle McNally," corrected Isabelle, who was regretting this entire adventure.

"Hold on," said the guard, repeating the women's names into a walkie-talkie. A minute later, he told them, "Welcome aboard."

Tremble charged up the gangplank followed by a mystified Isabelle. Or maybe, Isabelle thought, Trone had received word of her inroads at W&S, and was eager to praise her face-to-face. Maybe he approved of her having Rob fired.

The yacht was hushed and so tastefully appointed that it shrieked we-could-have-used-garish-brass-and-rosewood-and-animal-prints-like-some-Miami-Beach-gangster-but-we-chose-not-to. There was a spotlit Van Gogh of a shadowy potato field hanging on a brushed steel wall, and behind this Tremble and Isabelle were ushered into the main salon, a room running the length of the yacht, with more fine art, built-in seating mixed with the occasional French antique bergère, for contrast, and navy-blue carpeting patterned with the TroneTek logo and tiny life preservers, for a nautical touch. And there, seated on a central, curving banquette, was Trone Meston, in jeans and a raw silk saffron tunic he'd purchased in Singapore and had copied in twelve jewel-toned colors, with a side closure at the neck and finely braided gold trim. This tunic was unusual, comfortable, and suggested a matron from Great Neck hosting a dinner party while preening in everything she'd bought on vacation. Trone held up a forefinger as he finished a call on his TronePhone. He'd often brag about transacting deals in every world capital, using a single device.

"Welcome," said Trone. "I was told you wished to see me. And I couldn't resist an audience with anyone named Tremble Woodspill. What are you?"

"I'm a writer, or I'm trying to be. You own W&S, right? The publishing house?"

Trone glanced at an executive assistant tucked in a corner, who nodded assent.

"Yes, I believe I do. It was acquired, if I recall, for its back catalogue, as a content resource."

"Exactly," said Isabelle, who'd been starved for an opening in the conversation. "I'm Isabelle McNally, the sensitivity associate, and I've begun combing through everything W&S has ever published, for material that can be adapted for episodic streaming, as well as gaming, songwriting, and merchandise potential. I envision taking a text we already own, using in-house talent for a fiscally responsible overhaul, and exploiting the result on multiple platforms. All within parameters of inclusion, diversity, and social responsibility."

"And Ms. Woodspill?"

"I made this bitch spit up her lunch. My book is called *Life as We Fucking Know It* and it's about these incredibly messed-up people in Jacksburg, Arkansas. I love a lot of them and I wanted to tell people why, and I also wanted to show how hard it is to sleep in the back seat of a Toyota Camry with a dog and a baby, and figure out which one farted. And the people in my book talk about cooze and cocksucking and being mutts, and I guess Isabelle doesn't talk like that, or she doesn't approve of people who do. And she told that bullshit to my editor, Rob Barnett, who's the best dude ever, and who thinks I should write the way I want to write. So Isabelle dumped his ass. She got him fired."

"Isabelle?"

"That's technically accurate but it's far from the full story. I had directives, for improving Tremble's prose, and eliminating passages and word choices which might alienate or cause discomfort to queer people, people of color, and women."

"Fuck you! I am a queer woman of color! And you're not! I'm just gonna motherfucking say it! You are . . ."

Isabelle's eyes widened and she held up her hands to halt what was coming, as if it were a speeding, out-of-control freight train with a madwoman at the throttle.

"You are a white cisgender heterosexual with a college degree and your parents love you. You are a fucking *NICE GIRL*, bitch!"

Isabelle quaked, feeling naked and humiliated, as if she'd been accused of war crimes or stealing tribal lands or not showing a homeless person the TikTok of her speaking out at a City Hall forum on homelessness. She longed to deny every word, but she couldn't, because Tremble had a final weapon of mass destruction to detonate.

"And I bet you have a fucking *BOYFRIEND!*"

"*NO I DON'T!*" Isabelle yowled, at a choked top volume. "*I DON'T HAVE A BOYFRIEND!* I've experienced pansexual relationships at college and I'm open to every ethnicity, sexuality, and gender avenue! Ask anyone in Bushwick! *I DO NOT HAVE A BOYFRIEND!*"

"Yo, Izzy?" said Lance Barrelman, standing a few feet away, wearing hopelessly out-of-date high-waisted, acid-washed jeans, an oversize New England Patriots jersey, and a terry-cloth tennis headband.

"Oh my God . . . ," Isabelle sputtered. "Oh my God!"

"Young man?" asked Trone.

"Yeah, I'm Lance, Izzy's boyfriend. She hasn't been answering her cell and I knew she was doing some kind of business trip, so I thought, she works so damn hard, and I had miles, so I flew up to surprise her. I'm being a good boyfriend, right? That's what I explained to the dude on the dock, back in Logport, and the guy outside your boat, which is pretty damn sick, by the way. Oh, and Mr. Meston, just so you don't think your security guys are high, I work for Waltburg Bramm, the brokerage house, which you own? And I've got my employee ID, with the chip, so the guards were cool. And congratulations on getting married. Izzy, you should've told me it was a wedding, hint, hint. I like weddings. You and me, we could like, do a wedding."

Which was when Isabelle collapsed in a dead faint into Tremble's arms. Grousing with resistance, Tremble performed moderate CPR on

Isabelle, doing chest compressions accessorized with a few not-so-light slaps, Tremble's specialty. The executive assistant handed Lance a bottle of vitamin-infused TroneWater, which Lance tipped into Isabelle's mouth as she spumingly regained consciousness.

Trone had grasped the conflict between Tremble and Isabelle instantly. He didn't oversee an empire without parsing human nature in all its frailty and infighting. The device he would premiere at his wedding would be his finest apparatus for diagnosing truthful human emotion. Tremble and Isabelle's ruckus was merely a warm-up, an opening act, Trone thought, cracking his knuckles.

"Tremble," said Trone, "I've heard good things about this editor, from my fiancée's ex-husband, of all people. So if Rob Barnett values your work, and if you heed his guidance, that's all I ask. On your word, I'll reinstate Mr. Barnett, and let you continue your collaboration. But if your book proves an abject failure, artistically or commercially, we'll part ways."

"So I can tell Rob, that he's been rehired? That he's back?"

"At once or whenever you choose. And Isabelle, you musn't regard my decision as a slur or a criticism. It's much worse. It's a vote of little or no confidence in your judgment."

Isabelle almost passed out a second time, as her vision of herself and her unparalleled rise disintegrated. She wasn't who she thought she was, and that left her exposed and vacant, scrambling for someone to blame: Lance, for testifying to her heterosexuality? Rob, for using Tremble as a pawn in his plot to regain power? Her parents, for never understanding why she'd stuck Post-its on every piece of living room furniture, labeling the manufacturer's ties to Saudi Arabia?

"But fear not," Trone continued. "Isabelle, you're far from unique. You're self-centered and cerebral and you've never heard the word no.

But I appreciate your placard-bearing insistence on your own opinions, your ability to charge ahead, brandishing your diploma from a school without grades, final exams, or an English major. I'm confident you've been keeping a file, of notes for a film which you'd write, direct, and star in. Playing a brilliant, misunderstood, uncompromising but still sensual young person, buoyed aloft by friends with globally sourced vintage wardrobes. Could you send me that file?"

"I . . . I . . . of course. As soon as I'm near my TroneBook."

"Well played. Isabelle, strivers like you can be irritating, smug, and a waste of everyone's time. But your snobbery and antagonism might be symptoms of something bold. Or not. I'll share with you my simplest secret: I listen. I pay attention. And only then do I proceed. That's real genius: giving people what they've told you they want, even if they don't realize they've done so. For right now, Isabelle, you'll remain employed at W&S, because your sensitivity suggestions can stave off online eruptions and onrushing lawsuits. But you'll report directly to this Barnett person, who may be overdue for retirement or could be a golden resource, or both. And as for your boyfriend . . ."

"Lance!" said Lance, stoked that Trone hadn't forgotten him.

"Lance, you're a fine influence. You remind Isabelle that she's far from politically irreproachable. And I like seeing the two of you together, with Isabelle fuming and you, how would you classify yourself?"

"Chill."

"Indeed. Now all of you, get off my boat. I've got fifty-eight more calls to make, a sheaf of contracts to delay signing, and I'm getting married. And, as I'm sure you've been apprised, thanks to an inescapable bombardment by our media armada, I'll be presenting something which will change your lives forever."

"Okay, so what the fuck is it?" demanded Tremble. "Stop this teasing shit."

"Is it like, a next generation golf simulator, for practicing?" guessed Lance. "'Cause if it is, I am so down for it."

"No, and Ms. Woodspill, I'm not teasing. I'm framing the future. I'm contrasting the world as it is, with how I'll remake it."

Trone's obviously prepared remarks, and the fact that his pronouncement had just reached the resonant pitch of a *Star Wars* opening-credits voice-over, brought Isabelle close to orgasm, even closer than her evenings with Lance.

"So you're not gonna tell us, are you, you dick-licking smegma-lizard?" said Tremble, with amusement.

"In the words of the Almighty," Trone replied, "when all the suffering people since time immemorial begged, 'When will you help us?' My answer is, 'Tomorrow.'"

Linda gently lifted the covers, slipped out of bed, and retrieved her clothing, at Sean's cottage just after 5 a.m. She glanced back at his snoring, muscular body, which seemed to be doing push-ups even at rest. When some people sleep, they recall infants or angels; Sean made Linda think of a Labrador retriever or a Saint Bernard, sprawled on some warming hearth or forbidden couch. She could've kissed him or rubbed his ears, but instead left silently, as she might still be getting married in a few scant hours. She'd never been this unsure, or this free. She'd let the day decide.

Rob awoke at 7 a.m. to Tremble's text: his job was safe and she'd return to the cottage shortly, with breakfast, to celebrate and continue
going through her manuscript. She'd added, "Cumlicker McCheesejizz
is sticking around, but you're her boss."

Rob scarcely believed these developments, but Tremble was an astonishment and he blessed her. A nagging thought: Did he want his job
back? Had the universe been nudging him to explore something new?
But was some tumultuous shift even advisable at his age? And hadn't he
been undergoing enough seismic activity?

For now, his place was with Tremble, and maybe in representing
a sliver of the W&S legacy, of his beloved forebear Susannah and
the old-schoolers, the Olivetti outlaws who'd loved books more than
their families, the people who'd spent an odd vacation week on Cape
Cod or along the coast of France, where they'd had to be reminded
to lower the current draft of whatever novel they were obsessed with,
in favor of some postcard-ready vista. It wasn't necessarily a whole-
some or productive tradition, but like a surviving inhabitant of some
remote Siberian village, Rob was one of the few people who still spoke
the dialect.

More alarmingly, he was reviewing everything Jake, or the Jake-like
phantom, had told him. Jake, or the Jake of Rob's delirium, had fully
absolved him. Which left Rob more at odds than ever. What was he
still searching for? What omen or talisman? There were all those famed
stages of grief, such as anger, arguing, and upending many family-size
bags of peanut M&Ms directly into one's mouth (Rob may have invented this last response), but then everything wrapped up tidily with
acceptance. But accept what? That Rob would be alone forever? That
nothing meant anything? If my life is a book, Rob concluded, I'm at the

epilogue. I'd return these latest pages to the author with "Jake's dead. And?" scribbled after the final paragraph.

Rob would escort Sean, who was equally fragmented, to Linda's wedding. Rob and Sean had both lost spouses, but Linda's remarriage could be taken as a direct repudiation of Sean. Would he be destroyed, would he disembowel himself with a samurai sword and crawl toward the altar? What would Sean have to "accept," especially given that Sean never accepted defeat?

———

Paolo woke up in the far-less-posh quarters of a sous chef from Alchemy Hall. As he had been hunting down a restroom, he'd opened a steel door and observed the kitchen's frantically efficient staff, especially Arthur, or was his name Andre or Daniel? Whoever he was, he was forty-ish, French, and after mutually decrying those American supermarket brioche hot dog buns, Paolo and his companion had kissed furiously behind a dumpster and run to the companion's cell-like bedroom in barracks-style housing.

The sex had been fevered and clandestine and neither Paolo nor Arthur/Andre/Daniel had noticed the figure passing by the window whose teeth were glinting especially white and conceivably causing an ignored Dax Alert on Paolo's phone, a ping that indicated either an incoming text or physical proximity.

———

Once Sean saw that Linda had gone, he spent the early morning alone, with a new certainty. He downed his customary, motor-oil-and-gravel protein shake, then showered, shaved, and dressed for the wedding in his Blaster outfit, complete with full-body silver-and-magenta spandex, a gold fiberglass breastplate and codpiece, gilded leather boots, and his winged helmet. He'd held on to his Blaster suit as a memento and to wear at the conventions where he sold his signature on *WarForce* collectibles. The suit fit perfectly, if as uncomfortably as ever, because the synthetic fibers didn't breathe. But that didn't matter: as the mirror told him, Sean looked sensational. From his gym bag he pulled another souvenir: Blaster's phaser, a cartoon space-age implement, which had passed through the island's metal detectors. The phaser was enameled with silver paint and while it didn't shoot bullets, it wasn't a harmless toy. Like a *Star Wars* light saber, even a replica purchased from Amazon for an eleven-year-old's birthday, it possessed a power all its own.

29

THE WEDDING

By 10 a.m. the air was crisp, the sun as vivid as if Trone had commissioned it, and the celebrities were being convoyed from their yachts via skiff, and from their jets by golf cart or, in a very few cases, on foot, as the stars in question undertook the quarter-mile walk on the advice of the nutritionists, flexologists, and chiropractors they'd brought along. Isabelle sat in Alchemy Hall, opposite Lance. She'd let him spend the night in her cottage, but not in her bed, and they'd barely spoken. Isabelle hadn't recovered from her conversation with Trone, and her degradation by Tremble. Each time Lance had begun assuaging her, Isabelle had held up a hand. Lance was waiting her out, having brought both of them coffee.

"Um," Lance ventured, "so are you glad I'm here?"

"Do you . . . do you think I'm full of myself and overopinionated and wrong about everything?"

This was, of course, a trick question. Lance had been tutored by earlier girlfriends on how to answer. His dad had also tipped him off: "Nobody, man, woman, or child, ever wants to hear the truth. It's not your friend."

"Of course not, Izzy. I think you're awesome."

"Really? So you disagree with Trone?"

"I think he really likes you. He wants you to keep working at W&S. And he thinks you're like, of value. Like, big value. Super value."

"Would you . . . would you like to come to the wedding?" she asked, although she directed the question to the empty chair next to Lance. "I'm not saying we should sit together."

"That'd be cool. No worries. I can sit like, a few feet away."

Isabelle took another sip, her eyes shut. She couldn't look at Lance, which would entail integrating him into her dented reality.

"Let's go," she said, rising, with Lance counting off a respectful few seconds before trotting after her, as he posted photos of the Alchemy Hall ceiling and seating areas on his Instagram, captioned "I'm going to Trone Meston's big wedding shit! Your boy Lance! The Barrelman rocks!"

———

The ceremony itself would take place at noon, in the Artemis Island nondenominational Spirit Space, a cathedral-like structure embraced by the forest. Raw timbers alternated with copper panels, and streams of water cascaded from pipes cunningly tucked beneath the eaves. The building appeared to be growing, or a remnant of some long-ago civilization being reclaimed by nature.

"Look at this place," Paolo told Rob as they followed the pathway, in their navy-blue suits (Rob wore one of Jake's ties, while Paolo accented his open collar with a knotted silk bandana and a lapel pin of a dancing bicuspid in rhinestones). Sean was beside them, in his *WarForce* finery. When Sean had first shown up at Rob's cottage in this glitteringly heroic regalia, Rob and Paolo had guessed that he was having a full-on stress-related episode.

"What are you doing?" Rob had asked gently.

"I'm going to the wedding."

"Where will you park your starcruiser?" Paolo quizzed him.

"Sean," said Rob. "I don't know if you want to do this."

"I'm doing it."

"As your friend, who only wants whatever you want, can I ask why?"

"Because I'm making my case. This is who I am. And I don't want to be polite. It's my only chance. I want to make sure that when Linda does whatever she's gonna do, that when she makes her choice, she really sees me."

"And then," said Paolo, "will you fly around the Spirit Space?"

"Maybe."

"Sean . . . ," Rob began.

"No. Guys, you can't stop me and you shouldn't bother trying. I know this seems nuts and maybe it is. Last night I was Sean Manginaro, the coolest dude ever, all restrained and smiley and nothing-gets-to-me. Which worked, to a certain extent, actually, if I told you everything that happened, it worked to a major extent. But today's the main event. All the fucking marbles. Balls out. Dick swinging. Hello, Sean Manginaro. Hello, Blaster. You've seen the king, now enjoy the crazy. Take a good fucking look."

Rob and Paolo glanced at each other with a why-the-hell-not esprit, since Sean was in charge, and this trip had already been a once-in-a-lifetime loony undertaking. They both loved Sean, so why not love all of him? And why not look forward to a billionaire's wedding with a special-guest-star superhero? Rob and Paolo would be Blaster's mortal wingmen, or the federal task force auditing his destruction of Earth's enemies.

———

In a small room behind the main chapel Linda was scrutinizing her hair, makeup, and simple, cream-colored satin slip dress in a full-length mirror, except she wasn't. Her mind was ricocheting among the day's array of outcomes: Should she cancel or postpone the wedding, and risk hurting Trone and rejecting his billions? Corral Sean and head for, if not the hills, Oprah's jet, because Oprah would understand and in return negotiate an exclusive prime-time interview with the renegade lovebirds? See if Trone and Sean would be interested in a throuple? Each time she almost settled on a sensible plan of action, she'd argue herself out of it, and as she was about to flee, so she wouldn't have to choose anything, the door opened—no one had knocked—and there was Aileen.

Aileen retained vestiges of Linda's beauty, weathered by at least three thousand years of rough living, covering jail time (for dancing naked in front of the White House, to protest offshore oil rigs), an anarchist commune in Taos, and driving a getaway Jeep for an ex-con who'd chained the Jeep to an ATM, so that they dragged it half a block before the Jeep's battery died. Today Aileen had selected a rainbow tie-dyed terry-cloth beach cover-up over almost-clean white leggings, with a sprawling necklace of what were most likely white Styrofoam Christmas tree ornaments held together by paper clips. Her intermittently blond mane was haphazardly and mountainously teased and scattered with plastic daisies, and her peach-colored lipstick had been generously applied. The splintering, hot-pink patent leather of her open-toed platform shoes had been touched up with an almost matching shade of nail polish, although her toenails themselves were zebra-striped. But Linda was awed by a dumbfounding fact: Aileen had made an effort.

"Mom?"

"Hey, baby. Sorry I didn't get here sooner. They almost didn't let me on that goddamn ferry thing, 'cause I was carrying an open bottle of whiskey. Which I told them, first of all, it was in a paper bag, and second, it was a wedding present for you, but it got confiscated, so—yay! I'm your present!"

Linda remained standing, because she was stunned and to resist wrinkling her dress.

"Look at you, so pretty—wait, is that the whole dress or just the part that goes under the real dress?"

"It's the whole dress."

"But isn't your guy rich?"

"This was custom-made."

"Well, you look good, what do I know? Baby. Your big day."

As Aileen said this, she grabbed a folding chair, lit a cigarette, crossed her legs, and exhaled a stream of smoke.

"That's right. My big day."

Linda's attitude toward her mother was conflicted, to say the least, and she hadn't seen her in over three years, since Aileen had followed up her phone call gloating over Sean's adultery by giving interviews to at least five tabloids, crowing, "A blind man coulda seen that shit coming," "I told my little girl, that man would fuck a gas tank," and "My heart is goddamn breaking, and not just 'cause of my grandbabies, little Badger and Marco."

"So you're doin' it? You're marrying that Tony Marston, who makes the phones and shit?"

"Trone Meston."

"Right. Okay, I'm gonna cut to the chase. You probably didn't expect to see me. And yeah, I'm supposed to be in court tomorrow, for like some parking violation or shoplifting a ham or whatever, but, and I swear I'm not lying, and I'm not gonna hit you up for anything, even though I came all the way from Syosset, on some dude's moped, for cryin' out loud, but it was like I heard a voice or something. Sayin' my baby needs me."

Linda gasped. She didn't hate Aileen; Aileen was too helpless. Aileen hadn't been equipped to be a mother. She'd made a few half-hearted feints at, say, filling a lunch box with expired canned goods, or leaving a birth control pamphlet from Planned Parenthood (with a ring stain from a coffee cup on it) on an eight-year-old Linda's pillow, but Linda couldn't blame her for being so quickly misled, by heavily inked men with greasy ponytails who promised to buy her a VCR, decades after VCRs were obsolete (Aileen had a cardboard box of VHS cassettes stored, or left behind, in a friend's attic, along with some counterfeit money orders and a porcelain ballerina lamp). Linda's grandmother had been married eight times, so at a measly four go-rounds, Aileen was an amateur. And Linda herself was coming up on a third ceremony, so she couldn't really talk.

"I maybe shouldn't be here, this is way too fancy for me. Which is how you like it. But, shit, you're abso-tively right on the money, you got out. You got away. You did good. Jackpot! But baby, 'fess up—you happy?"

"Um, I don't think you have the right to ask me that."

"Of course not, but that's why I'm here. Somebody's gotta do it. Most other people, they're scared of you, since you're so shiny and clean and you put it out there, right up front, that personal shit is way off-limits. No dice-arooni for little Miss Prissy Panties Linda. But this Train guy, he's number three up at bat, right? And I visited you that time, no, two times, with Sean, there's a pretty-boy name, in Connecticut, can you believe it, I actually went to wherever the fuck Connecticut is, and I gotta say it, since you got divorced I've been askin' myself, should I make a run at your ex? 'Cause holey moley, Sean is one steamin' chunk of man-muscle. I mean, wow-ee kazow-ee, cut me off a slice of that big juicy . . ."

"Mom . . ."

"But I'm not gonna do it, see, I'm gettin' better like, boundaries. But I saw you with him, in that frilly little take-off-your-shoes-because-we-got-fucking-nice-shit house, I checked it out, and you were like, big-time happy, I mean, up the wazoo and comin' out the other side. Not just the trees and the swimming pool and the three kids . . ."

"Two . . ."

"Really? Did one of 'em die? No, you're right, two. But you loved him, didn't ya?"

"I'm not talking to you about this . . ."

"Fine, whatever, so just listen up. Maybe now you love this other guy, Tram, maybe Sean ran you over with a Mack truck, maybe you did what you had to do. But baby, I'm just gonna tell you, whatever is goin' on here—don't do anything just so you won't be me. You know what I'm sayin'? And I get it, I'm not anyone's goal model . . ."

"Role model . . ."

"Yeah, so what the hell do I know, but you're my baby, and I know you better than you think I do, and I don't blame you, for wanting everything that's gazillions of miles away from your dear old mommy.

But that's not a good enough reason to do whatever. So here's all I'm sayin'—ask yourself, what in the good Lord's goddamn name do you really mother-effin' want? Way down, in your lady-gut. When he walks through the door, which guy is gonna make you jump his bones? And I'm not just talkin' about s-e-x, although there's nothing wrong with gettin' laid from here till next Tuesday, till you're screamin' like a banshee with her finger in a socket, but I'm talkin' about the whole enchilada, although just between you and me and his Levi's, I always kinda thought that Sean was pretty hubba-hubba in the enchilada department, if you know what I mean, but which guy, Troll or Sean, which one makes you act like an idiot who's been knocked on the head with a skillet, in a good way, with a love-skillet, which sweet-smellin' motherfucker makes you forget any other guys are even out there? Which guy makes you think he's worth it, whatever shit he's gonna put you through? 'Cause, lemme tell ya, no guy is fuckin' perfect, sooner or later they're all gonna steal your kidney after you pass out from NyQuil and rum, did I tell ya about that? I was datin' this hockey player, stud city, only three fingers on his right hand but they got the job done, I woke up in the ER with a fuck-load of stitches and one goddamn kidney, 'cause he needed the other one for his ex-wife, this fuckin' school bus driver, I mean, good for her, but do ya really need my kidney for that? But it made the guy kinda like a hero in my book, I mean, he came through, not for me but for what was her name—Tabitha? Tarantula? See?"

Aileen lifted her top, revealing a prominent, barely healed scar—her most outlandish tales were often the most accurate.

"So that's what you're lookin' for—the guy who really cares. Who goes the fuckin' distance. Oooh, can I take one of those bottles of gourmet supermarket water? Are they free?"

As Rob, Paolo, and Sean joined the crowd filling the Spirit Space, the other guests either gaped at Sean or gave him the side-eye and wouldn't be rattled. Some people surmised that Sean was a prime minister from a country they'd never heard of, in ceremonial garb, while others hazarded that Sean was a preview of Trone's product launch, its gleaming mascot from Tomorrowville. The vice president of the United States, a normally sedate white-haired Mormon, became eye-poppingly exhilarated, because *WarForce* was his favorite show of all time. "Blaster!" he called out, waving his arms over his head. "Big fan!"

The chapel itself was enchanting. The high whitewashed plaster walls were inset with differing shapes and sizes of glowing, abstract stained glass, like a child's jubilant crayon drawing, or curling up inside a Miró. There was an airiness to the room that Alchemy Hall sorely lacked; the chapel was hope itself. There was a chunky altar-like object, fashioned from copper, down front, and the pews on either side were angled toward each other, for a hey-there friendliness. Everyone had an excellent sight line on the proceedings along with an unimpeded view of whoever was sitting across from them. This arrangement also made celebrity-spotting a breeze, as no one had to yank their head around.

Without any need for consultation, Rob, Paolo, and Sean took seats in a rear pew, waving to Bridger and Morrow in the first row. When his kids saw what Sean was wearing, they didn't just die of embarrassment, they plummeted into another sinkhole of shame entirely, inwardly changing their last name and maybe wearing eyeglasses with fake mustaches attached to become unrecognizable. Isabelle roosted in a middle pew, three guests away from Lance, who was wearing khakis and a prep school blazer over a knockoff Ralph Lauren rugby shirt, with the little embroidered polo pony replaced by a flaming skull. Tremble snuck in just as the double doors were closing, slipping into the pew beside Rob, having acquired a navy-blue suit of her own, with a polka-dot necktie worn over a Zora Neale Hurston T-shirt. She'd threaded a small Artemis Island banner, nicked from Trone's yacht, in her hair, which was now tinted in shades of purple and lime green. Everything about her was joyous and reflected the room's painterly vibe.

"What'd I miss?" Tremble asked her pew-mates.

"Nothing so far," said Rob. "You look fantastic."

"This is the strangest wedding I've ever been to," said Paolo, "and I'm counting the lesbian wedding in New Orleans with stripper poles and a Make-Your-Own-Vibrator crafting booth."

"This will be interesting," said Sean.

"Yeah," Tremble told Sean, inspecting his getup. "I'm digging it."

As he got used to it, the more Rob endorsed Sean's outfit as well. Sean wasn't hiding. He was proclaiming to Linda and everyone else that he'd made life-torching mistakes and he'd prevailed at other times and he was owning all of it. He wasn't fooling or sweet-talking Linda, he was daring her to make the most all-encompassing assessment of their life together, weighing the out-of-body highs against the annihilating depths. He was telling her, *I love you and this is who I am. This is who you invited to your wedding. This is who you loved, and might love again.*

The chapel was packed, with Supreme Court justices and chartbusting recording artists and legendary designers, ranking each other, as to who was closest friends with Trone (meaning who'd been most useful to him).

"Is that . . . ," Paolo whispered to Rob, indicating a deeply respected newscaster.

"Yes, and he's had his eyes done again. You can always tell when the crow's-feet are pointing upwards."

Music began, composed for the occasion by a Juilliard-trained Pulitzer winner and performed by an internationally sought-after soprano, backed by a piano, a viola, and shivering timpani. The work was lilting yet suspenseful and, not coincidentally, the soundtrack on the internet spots for Trone's mystery product.

As the lighting shifted, glimmering molecules floated through the air above the crowd's heads, coalescing into the figures of Trone and Linda, standing at opposite sides of the altar. This effect was astonishing and had been achieved by a Vegas illusionist in coordination with the Trone-Tek engineers. Linda's fluid, body-skimming dress would be copied all over the world for its elegant restraint. The style highlighted Linda's toned arms and shoulders, and her freshly blonded hair was worn in a becoming pageboy tucked behind her ears. Linda hadn't been overly fussed with. As always, she carried herself like a woman who just happened to be extraordinarily beautiful, as if she were chastising her admirers to "oh please, get over yourselves."

Sean watched her with tears in his eyes. Linda persisted as the woman who answered his physical checklist, while exciting and confounding him, and today she was glorious, a lustrously understated goddess. Sean, Rob, and Paolo were all thinking, That's such a great dress, because on a certain level, they were all the same gay man. Bridger and Morrow momentarily emerged from their frozen pods of disgrace to appreciate their mother, especially because she wasn't decked out like a middle-aged comic book character. "That's my mom," Bridger told the man sitting next to him, who happened to be the CEO of the company that manufactured Bridger's favorite sneakers and board shorts.

Isabelle estimated that Linda was attractive in a mildly elevated, professionally "cute," mom-on-a-sitcom manner, lacking Isabelle's own more quirkily intelligent, French poetess/Bushwick-indie-bookstore-owner originality, but she was irked that everyone was all but moaning over Linda, except for Lance, who only had eyes for Isabelle and was subtly indicating that the label at the rear neckline of her thrift store forties dress had flipped up.

When Linda saw Sean, at first she rolled her eyes, as if she couldn't believe the stunt he'd pulled, but then, as he kept his gaze on her and raised his fist in the Blaster salute, she almost giggled but didn't, because she was unexpectedly choked up. Sean was the world's most aggressively outrageous moron, but he was her aggressively outrageous moron.

Trone had on one of his signature tunics, in a lushly golden brocade, with a burgundy crushed velvet sash stretched diagonally across his torso, along with drawstring linen pants in a filmy white voile. He resembled either the exalted high sultan from some far-off planet teleporting onto the flight deck of the *Starship Enterprise*, or a second-tier royal advisor in a Broadway revival of *The King and I*. This ensemble, which he wore with the self-pleasure of a billionaire duck in a Saturday morning cartoon, entertained Linda. She loved that Trone wore what he liked, risking the internet's jibes. He fearlessly knew himself, which Linda found kinkily sexy. Which today was also true of Sean. Linda was being fought over by video-game characters who'd crossed into each other's phantasmagorical realms, as if Morrow were at the helm, mainlining Mountain Dew and pizza as he supplied each hero with advanced weaponry, like unthinkable cash reserves or triathlon stamina. Was this about who loved Linda the most, or who she'd succumb to? Was she Guinevere, torn between the stalwart Lancelot and the worldly King Arthur, or had she become the most hapless teenager ever, pursued by both Beavis and Butthead?

The official bride and groom met at the altar and faced the crowd. Trone widened his eyes and the music ceased. The lighting slightly de-emphasized Linda and poured artificial sunshine upon Trone, as if he were about to be drawn into the heavens, because God craved his perceptions.

As Rob took in this spectacle, of the far-from-helpless lady caught between suitors, both of whom proved why straight men should never dress themselves, he was remembering his own wedding. Gay marriage had been legalized, but he and Jake had come of age earlier, so it hadn't been a priority. They'd talked about getting married but without any pressing need. Marriage was a bit assimilationist and deadening, a we're-just-like-you bid for heterosexual acceptance. But once Jake had been diagnosed, marriage became a necessity, so that Rob could participate in his medical care, and oversee bank accounts, the mortgage, and, although this was unspoken, what would become of Jake's estate.

Jake was still able to walk haltingly and use his left arm when, one night in bed, he'd turned to Rob and asked, "Will you marry me? Because we need to do that."

"Of course."

"Shit."

"What?"

"I know that, before, we weren't sure that we wanted to get married, but now it's so clinical. Especially the way I just said it. I should've gotten down on one knee, but, well . . ."

"Okay. All of this sucks and we both know it. But even if you weren't sick, you're the only person I'd ever marry. And somehow that sounded even more backhanded."

"We can either go to city hall, or we can have a wedding-ish sort of whatever here at the apartment."

They went with the second option, and invited Paolo, Jake's boss Mr. Crawbell, Jake's colleague Beatrice (in a Bridgerton-inspired bonnet), Rob's family, and a handful of other friends and coworkers. Sean and Linda were on the list; they'd been divorced for a year and both had offered not to come, if a joint appearance would be awkward, but Rob and Jake had insisted. Quill, Rob's trans sister who taught third grade in Boston, had been ordained years before, through the online Church of the Helpful Non-Sectarian Friend, so she could preside over vows that took place in queer synagogues, migrant encampments, and jail cells. "I love marrying people," she'd told Rob, "I feel like I should have a wand."

While the ceremony was set for a gloomy Saturday in October, Jake had decreed hydrangeas and lilacs, because lilies or any arrangement of white flowers would be funereal. They hired an out-of-work actor as bartender and ordered finger food from a nearby deli. Beatrice had overseen the cake; "I'm doing something traditional," she'd divulged, "but with just the right amount of manly excess."

Jake had been seated in the Eames chair, with Rob standing beside him. As everyone gathered, Quill said, "Today is about Jake and Rob and why they belong together. Because as Jake once told me, he made Rob get a better haircut and Rob made him relax about plastic hangers. The moment I saw them together they made perfect sense and in so many ways, in all the most important ways, they were already married."

Sean and Linda were on opposite sides of the room but glanced at each other. Linda quickly looked away, but Sean kept staring, trying to will Linda to look back. She wouldn't.

Rob took Jake's hand. They were both crying but refusing to admit it. Jake's illness made their wedding both fraught and more deeply committed, because their love was already under siege. Rob had a fleeting, preposterous thought, that the wedding might cure Jake, that the power of their love would sweep all obstacles and medical truth aside. He'd instantly admonished himself, for such *TV Guide*-horoscope-and-burning-incense denial. But as they exchanged their vows, Rob and Jake could barely manage the words, and in fact, Jake's speech began to slur. Thankfully, Paolo stepped in, announcing, "Okay, if I don't meet someone soon I'm going to slaughter a busload of schoolchildren," and everyone laughed, as Rob knelt beside Jake and kissed him and they both traveled the entire emotional spectrum of human life in ten seconds.

———

"Good afternoon, everyone," Trone began, with an evangelical gesture, half papal encyclical and half drum major. "I'm sure many, if not all of you, are condemning me, for leveraging this blessed occasion as what appears, on the surface, to be the crassest marketing opportunity. But in fact, as you'll perceive within a very few seconds, the TroneTek Anteros encapsulates the magnificence of this day and all similar days. Because Anteros was the Greek god of requited love. I'd like everyone to reach beneath their pew."

The room was spellbound, as the guests searched to find the small, violently tasteful, pewter-toned box worshipfully photographed in the TroneTek teaser ads and now being held in their hands.

"You may open the boxes with this caveat: your Anteros will not be activated, by a TroneTek remote surge, until after the ceremony today, should there be a ceremony."

Rob, like everyone else, was soon inspecting what looked like an oversize digital watch, with a pewter-toned mesh band and a glossy, round, dark screen, slightly wider than a poker chip.

"It looks like a large-print watch for old people," Paolo whispered.

"Or a fitness tracker from five years ago," Sean speculated.

Rob was still wearing Jake's heirloom watch, which he reluctantly replaced with the Anteros. Jake would hate this device; as he'd stated, "Smartwatches are just ugly bracelets for the sort of people who wear their earbuds everywhere, rather than have thoughts."

Isabelle divined that Trone would be sending her personal messages on her Anteros, so they'd be able to communicate without Linda eavesdropping. Tremble was admiring her Anteros but planning on stenciling the band in a purple and hot pink stripe. Lance was hoping his Anteros would post real-time soccer scores.

Everyone in the chapel was turning their Anteros-clad wrists this way and that. The wealthiest guests were especially pleased that the devices were free.

Sean's Anteros matched his already sci-fi attire. He was fixating on Trone's exact wording: "should there be a ceremony." Had Linda raised an objection? Had she and Trone been feuding? Would his phaser become unnecessary?

"Maybe we're all going to be electrocuted," Tremble suggested to the guys.

"I was thinking that," Paolo concurred. "It'll be like Jonestown or that suicide cult where everyone was wearing matching orange T-shirts and white sneakers. I remember thinking that if I had to wear that outfit I'd kill myself, too."

Trone had handed Linda an Anteros, the only version in a more old-world rose gold, but she had no idea of its function. Trone chivalrously adjusted the clasp around her wrist.

"All of my life I've been intensely curious about this emotional transaction we classify as love," Trone continued. He wasn't raising his voice, but every word had a crystalline clarity, thanks to the almost imperceptible microphones dangling from equally invisible filaments lowered from the ceiling. The chapel's acoustics were eerily pristine.

"As I child I would argue: Were my feelings for my parents or my siblings love, or proximity? How could I establish definitively if those feelings were returned and to what degree? How did my devotion to a pet, for example, differ from my interest in a fellow human being?"

"He is so weird," said Paolo.

"He's the Joker's creepier cousin," Sean claimed, "or a replicant."

"He's just wired differently," said Tremble. "Like with a litter of puppies, it's not always the runt, but there's one puppy that's only barely interested in food or the mom. It just wanders around."

"I have devoted my life to the study of love," said Trone. "My products have exponentially increased human interactions, but I wanted to go farther. So ten years ago I set up a secluded, unmarked lab, to scientifically investigate the existence of love. We began with the most primitive cellular communication, between, for example, atoms of yeast, fungi, and slime mold. Why did reproduction occur between certain cells and not others? We progressed to the beloved farm animals of my youth and the effect of pheromones, which are chemical factors facilitating sexual attraction and mate choice. But I pushed my team relentlessly, to apply our findings to humans."

"I once dated a fungi," Paolo confided. "But it left me for a damp rock."

"The presence of pheromones in human beings has been extravagantly debated, especially when boosted with axillary steroids produced by the testes, ovaries, and adrenal glands. These substances, we found, could be measured, but still, did they indicate infatuation, lust, commonality, or something stronger? Is love the collective result of these primal indicators, or something more, something magnified, something unto itself? Does love, in fact, exist?"

"Well, I do love testes," said Paolo, making Tremble giggle and Rob shush them: "A rich person is speaking."

"Two years ago a breakthrough occurred. We invited couples at every stage of their relationships to participate. All ages, races, genders, gender preference groups, and more extended configurations were included. There were people on first dates, on the eve of their engagements, towards the conclusion of a first married year, couples who'd never married but had spent decades together, couples who'd once been passionately attracted but now revolted each other, triads who'd stopped speaking to each other but all had their names on the lease, and a nine-person synergy known as the Honey Bunch. We collected data linked to skin sensitivity, perspiration, increased respiration, genital response, retinal dilation, tactile enhancement, and more. Until finally, through an electronic pulse applied to the wrist, we were able to calculate a participant's precise longing and regard for someone else, and of what quality and duration. In short, we isolated love."

Everyone's facial expressions mingled interest and hesitation. They'd followed Trone's messaging, but were uncertain of its validity. What the hell was he talking about? Was it pure hype without substance? And what exactly did these Anteroses do?

"And I'm sure you're all asking, but how reliable is this device? The whole thing sounds preposterous, and what about the potential for catastrophic error, or a willed and therefore inaccurate response? What if a test subject simply wants desperately to be in love, without the actual presence of love? What if love was indicated but wavering? What if love was inspired less by physical allure than the prospect of beachfront property on Ibiza? All this was factored in through more testing with control groups. In each case, any objections or glitches subsided within seconds.

"And we refined our device, to disclose not merely the degree of love, but its variety. The readouts include filial love, maternal or paternal love, asexual contentment, annoying indecision, and the most heated and enduring desire. Of course, as with all trailblazing inventions, from the steam engine to the telegraph to the microchip, there's apprehension: How would these developments change our daily lives? Would they be exceedingly helpful or savagely treacherous? And with the Anteros, the prospect for widespread harm was seriously explored, leading to the decision: no one will be forced to use the Anteros, and its conclusions can be revealed only to the wearer or to whomever else that wearer selects.

"But I can see on your faces, that a demonstration is necessary. And so I've waited until this very moment to wear the Anteros myself. And Linda, if you have no interest in participating, I will more than comply. But throughout your life, you've conducted relationships of wildly varying distinction. So I put forth that you in particular might benefit from unequivocal knowledge and surety."

Linda was baffled. Was she being cornered by this Asteroid, or whatever Trone's gadget was called, like a rat in a maze or a squirrel solving a crossword? Last night had revealed why she'd invited Sean to the wedding: to test her resolve, to, in a sense, do just what Trone's device was promising, to unscramble who she loved, and how much. But after having sex with Sean, with sadness and pleasure, she'd arrived at the heart-spinning blindness of total freedom: she was going to head for the altar and see what happened. She was flinging aside whatever scruples she still clung to, along with her core personality, and leaving her future in the lap of the gods—and hadn't Trone just mentioned that Anteros was a Greek god?

Okay, Linda told herself, if I'm going to stop being infinitely reasonable, and wounded, and stomping the spontaneity out of every second of my life, why not go all the way? The twins were in college, Trone had proposed, she was standing up here draped in not very much clothing, with a strange piece of titanium slung around her wrist—why not consult the device, let it chime in? As a teenager, Linda had laughed at those Magic 8 Balls and folded-notebook-paper fortune-telling games, not because she thought they were nonsense but because they might not be—she liked to make up her own mind. But that was so long ago, and many of her independent decisions had tumbled into disaster. She turned to Trone and said, "What the hell, let's give it a try."

Sean was terrified. He had severe misgivings about this whole setup, mostly because it might be rigged by Trone, and he hated the lack of control. He'd had such a great time with Linda last night, they'd been at their best, only with a bonus kick from sneaking around on the eve of her wedding. Linda had rebuffed any spoken acceptance of what they were doing, in bed or afterward, but the sex had been undeniable. Sean trusted his body and Linda's, way more than this Anteros baloney—but why was Linda holding out her arm?

"My Anteros and Linda's will now be activated," said Trone, and he didn't alert some unseen facilitator—everything was already in place.

There was an underscoring from the piano and kettledrums, a crescendo somewhere between a Houdini flourish and a Wagnerian god's wrath, and then the screens on Trone and Linda's wrists were illuminated, with flickering bright white lines of code—the devices were booting up.

"The Anteros," said Trone, "has a variety of settings, which can report only a sole user's response, or that of their love object as well. I've had Linda's Anteros and mine set to a matching frequency, so our results will be displayed simultaneously, although of course they may diverge. But before entering into this marriage, we'll both be equipped with something invaluable—verified information."

There was a tingling warmth and vibration against Linda's wrist, along with an appealingly industrious, almost musical hum, as if the tiny elves within her device were whipping up a nourishing breakfast. Both her Anteros and Trone's were a restful blue, the blue of bits of sea glass in a bowl on a beach house coffee table, or a shimmering ribbon on an Easter bonnet. Then a circular dial, with a range from 0 to 100, was transposed over the cloudless blue. The dial began to climb, holding steady at 75 percent.

"Aha," said Trone, clearly pleased. "The sapphire indicates a contented and satisfying love, not an adolescent frenzy, but an earned and untroubled love between companionable adults. With an emotional intensity rating of 75 percent, which is well above average and more than is necessary for a lasting union. So Linda, may I ask: Shall we continue? Would you still like to marry me?"

The room pivoted to Linda, as during the final seconds of a nail-biting tennis match or top-tier chess summit. She and Trone were the first users to publicly test the Anteros, and certify its accuracy, and act on its findings. They would set the standard. Of course, many people in the chapel were scoffing, and treating the moment as a huckster's infomercial, as a casino lounge act only effective with the drunken and dejected, or a discounted one-time-only offer of steak knives. But Trone's heritage merchandise had revolutionized the marketplace and so many lives. Why would he resort to chicanery? Plus, everyone was tantalized: What if the Anteros worked? How would Linda, as human-kind's representative, as the lovely canary in this surpassingly swank coal mine, respond?

Staring at the calming blue of her Anteros, Linda was at peace, be-cause as her heart confirmed, the results were true. She did love Trone, quite a bit, or enough, and the promise of serenity was potent. The cushion of Trone's billions was obviously an enormous advantage, but Linda had never been rapaciously greedy. For much of her life she'd sup-ported herself, and then the Tudor and its storybook embodiment had been deceptively enthralling, even a trap. In opening herself to the pull of unalloyed happiness, she'd risked everything and been punished, not just by Sean's infidelity, but by love itself. She could instantly recall the dagger, the savage hurt, of that betrayal, that moment when everything she'd let herself believe in had turned rancid. She'd never compare her loss to Rob's, but she'd shared his howling emptiness, when his life, the most dearly held core of his life, had vanished.

The Anteros was, at last, something Linda could rely on, even more than her own soul, which had led her woefully astray. This was the ref-uge her childhood, and Sean's behavior, had denied her. She saw Aileen, at the far end of a pew, pausing in mid-bite of a cinnamon Danish, and regarding her daughter with a head-tilting skepticism, or maybe a defen-sive worry about a clanking noise from the silverware she'd dumped in a pillowcase on the floor beside her feet.

"Let's do this," said Linda, as the crowd cheered, relieved at her decision. No one had sought a demoralizing reversal, a deflated balloon, a canceled wedding at the last second on a remote island.

"Huzzah!" said Trone. "Anything's possible with the Anteros, for anyone. For everyone."

This last phrase, the wedding-goers foresaw, had been copyrighted for the Anteros's cross-media rollout, and they were right.

30

THE RECEPTION

The remainder of the ceremony, the afterthought, went off seamlessly, with brief vows and a warm if not show-offy kiss. Hologrammed white rose petals drifted from above, as Linda and Trone traipsed hand in hand down the center aisle, with Paolo telling Rob, "Digital rose petals and a product launch—it's the American dream, like the season finale of a singing competition crossed with someone giving out free samples of corn dogs at a county fair."

The reception was held at a reconfigured Alchemy Hall, with Grammy-winning entertainment, five courses, and five cakes shaped like towering replicas of an Anteros, frosted with tinted buttercream in the various color options. Everyone's Anteroses had been activated. Tremble's glowed a sunflower yellow, which the guide said connoted love for an inanimate object, and Tremble gleefully showed Rob the photo of her book jacket, which Rob had just sent her, as the dial hit 100 percent. "I love this so much," she told him. "This fucking Anteros knows its shit." Rob was so pleased for Tremble, and grateful they'd be finalizing the manuscript together.

Paolo kept alternating photos of male movie stars and porn hunks on his Anteros, causing an identical purple screen, which indicated "Love with an unattainable partner." (The color-coded results were augmented by messaging available in every conceivable language.) "How the fuck does this piece of TroneTek garbage know that Daniel Craig will never love me? I'm returning it for a toaster oven."

Isabelle, following a cleavage check in a restroom mirror, made her way to Trone's table, confident that her Anteros would interact with his for a duplicate red-and-blue tattersall, in the 99th percentile, proscribing, in the guide's listings, "a profound respect between colleagues that might blossom into an ethically debatable out-of-office affair."

"Hello again, Mr. Meston," said Isabelle, standing beside the wide round table where he sat with Linda, the twins, and Trone's most essential staffers. "Congratulations on the Anteros."

Isabelle had deliberately omitted Trone's wedding, which was why Trone replied, smiling, "Thank you so much, Annabelle."

"And all the best to you, Linda," Isabelle course-corrected, clumsily reaching out to shake Linda's hand, so her own would be in closer proximity to Trone, to prompt an Anteros response.

"Thank you so much," said Linda, as both her own Anteros and Trone's went pale gray, signaling "chronically unstable, misdirected interloper nearby."

Isabelle's Anteros flickered mauve, which she'd dreaded, as the guide had flagged this as "delusional and medication-resistant ardor." As the peril of the Anteros, in its infallible honesty, was becoming evident, Isabelle retreated, walking slowly backwards, until she slumped beside Lance at a table in the farthest reaches, the social outer Mongolia of the hall. She was so dejected that Lance shattered protocol to reach an arm lightly around her sagging shoulders, neglecting to ask consent. Without thinking—something that had never happened before—Isabelle leaned into Lance's body.

But Isabelle's and Lance's Anteroses were fully operational and humming a soft, almost Jordan Almond mint green, the symbol of "young and most likely transitory yet still memorable love."

They kissed, with crumbs and buttercream on their lips, which made their kiss even better.

"I mean, Izzo, I'm not what you were going for," said Lance. "I'm not Trone Meston or some poet who writes about what if winter were a person. I'm just a bro who's kinda turned on by a total non-bro."

"Can you not call me Izzo? Because I really hate that. It sounds like a chicken on a cartoon which scream-clucks when it's raining."

"Isabelle?"

"What?"

"You . . . you made a joke. It wasn't like, killer, but I've never heard you do that."

"Shut *UP.*"

Isabelle guaranteed this demand would be met by grabbing Lance's neck and kissing him again, as one of the other W&S employees, also seated at their table, captured the moment on their phone, as blackmail insurance in case Isabelle got too regal and started calling Trone Meston "not just my mentor, but my work-Yoda" back at the office.

———————

Sean had been sitting quietly with his friends, his legs spread, at a corner table, his winged helmet balanced on his knee. Rob asked, "Are you okay? Melting down? About to do something that will get you arrested or at least tossed off the island?"

"Better," said Sean, standing, his helmet restored to his head. The wedding had disconcerted him, because his younger, belligerent self had been shoving him to grab Linda's hand and make a run for it, or slam his Anteros on the floor, yank down his spandex, and piss on it, or slide the phaser from beneath his breastplate and aim it at Trone while howling Linda's name.

While watching Linda assert her love for Trone during the ceremony, something in Sean had shifted. He didn't envy Trone's multinational dominance; Sean's own accomplishments were more than enough. For Sean, human contact and his daily run were far more rewarding than Trone's monolithically impersonal, Everest-height hamster wheel. Sean wasn't, at the age of forty-nine, growing up, which would abolish way too much fun. He was learning to live with what he'd never call losing, but with an interim proviso, a concession to the shitstorm of things he couldn't fix or argue logically and blusteringly into compliance. Or maybe he wasn't. Maybe all that horsehit about learning and concessions was the opposite of Sean Manginaro and always would be and he could fucking make that point, right fucking now. Maybe he could stir his smoldering charm from the rehearsal dinner with Blaster's galactic intimidation. Maybe he could fucking teach everyone at the wedding a fucking thing or two, about love and technology and hyper-propulsion when applied to the human heart.

Trone and Linda were dancing, in the open space at the hall's center, amid other couples, many of them abstaining from the use of their Anteroses, until they could contact their attorneys and shrinks. The reception's singer, a perennial chart-topper whose presence had added $5 million to the wedding's bottom line, was warbling Dolly Parton's "I Will Always Love You," not the eardrum-splitting, yodeled version that causes migraines in elevators, but something more private and honest. Linda loved to dance, but Trone less so. He lived not just primarily in his head, but in only the top three inches of his head. He was manfully shuffling Linda around the floor when Sean tapped him on the shoulder. Trone stepped aside, thankful to be relieved of his duties, and smug in the affirmation of both the Anteros and his wedding. Everything had gone as he'd planned, with a sublime synchronicity of commerce and devotion; the footage was being edited for posting on the Anteros channel within hours, as an emblem of his latest and most Promethean magnificence. Linda, as Sean would be pushed to admit, had made the wisest possible choice. Trone had won, not just Linda's heart but whatever primal joust had been waged between her two swains. She'd picked the brilliantly cosmos-altering Trone over the merely physically adept, bullheaded, inappropriately costumed Sean, in front of everyone, with their Anteroses as an indisputable scoreboard. In the face-off at recess, the (DaVinci-level) egghead had bested the (purely local) brute. Thanks to another TroneTek game changer, perhaps Trone's finest to date, as he'd predicted, and as the pundits and his competitors would be forced to salute.

As Sean bowed deferentially, Trone wobbled from the walking-home-from-school-alone queasiness Sean's presence had previously caused, the twerpish jumpiness over whether Sean might deck him, or pull down Trone's pants and give him a wedgie. Rugged nods were exchanged.

Sean took Linda in his arms and they began dancing sedately. Linda wasn't sure what Sean was up to. She'd hoped her Anteros had crushed any wayward impulses, in both her and Sean, and that last night was a drunken departure, a momentary lapse. She'd forgotten that her Anteros was still activated, as was Sean's.

As they swayed, Linda wouldn't return Sean's gaze, lecturing herself, I'm a married woman, it's fine, Sean's lost whatever dwindling power he had over me. But their eyes locked and Sean smiled, not in sly victory, well, not only in sly victory, but in genuine love for Linda, a direct and pure love, without expectations. His Anteros screen burst into scarlet, with a vermilion throb at the center, and Linda's Anteros followed, identically. As anyone who'd even skimmed the guide would remember, this shade was that rarest indicator, of the most unreservedly sexual and voluptuous true love, a heedless and even mindlessly raw attraction, at a flagrant 100 percent, like the rotating, shrieking rooftop beacon of an ambulance or a squad car, or an erupting, sky-igniting volcano. Linda should deactivate the mechanism, to end this way-too-public avowal of unrestrained ecstasy, but she had no idea how to turn the damn Anteros off. The room was transfixed, as Trone flushed an only slightly less torrid shade of red. As the singer paused, knocked sideways by Sean and Linda's super-high-octane conflagration, he visualized his own first wife, the Starbucks barista he'd never gotten over. With the music halted, the memorably blaring trumpet fanfare of the *War-Force* theme was heard filling the hall, at a fully unconquered, thundering, galloping-Valkyrie volume, issuing from Sean's phone, left on his table.

Trone's team had installed a celebratory feature in every Anteros, to heighten such almost unprecedented occurrences of the most combustible, dangerously enviable love. The watches emitted laser-like beams of ruby light from Linda and Sean's wrists, crisscrossing the hall as if heralding the premiere of a studio blockbuster. The couple's seething affinity was undeniably everywhere, at rock concert or planetarium dimensions.

Aileen was standing by a column, grinning at Linda. She had three Anteroses along each arm, which she'd lifted from inattentive guests.

Bridger and Morrow vacillated between crawling under their table and a delight in their antiquated parents' open and vibrantly pulsing affection.

"It's so vomitously uber-gross," said Bridger.

"They're only doing this to punish us," agreed Morrow, but their shoulders were merrily nudging one another.

Rob and Paolo were clutching each other's forearm, thrilled by this development, by Trone's corporate jamboree becoming Sean's, and Blaster's, and Linda's grandly romantic, if fleeting, fireworks display and cacophonously hot-blooded epiphany. By the triumph of love!

Tremble was thinking about her parents, or allowing herself to. This moment, this breathtaking dazzle, was what they'd shared. Even as a kid, she'd known her parents were crazy for each other, that their touches and glances and kisses weren't ordinary. She hadn't been embarrassed by this—she'd been too young—but proud. She'd seen so many grown-up couples sniping at each other and clearly imploding, but not Harmony and Crayton Woodspill, who couldn't keep their hands off each other, and who'd be speaking in low, lustful voices, about all sorts of things, as Tremble fell asleep. But their enchantment had been their undoing, and had led to their deaths. Tremble hated to seek any moral conclusion or stern Christian admonition in this, but there was only one way she could get anywhere close to understanding her parents' lives and their impact on her own, and how such an erotically calamitous love and loss had affected her: she'd write about it.

Everyone in the hall was gazing hungrily and even tearfully at Sean and Linda, transported and aroused by their example. This was something only the most universally romantic movies, the most unexpectedly authentic porn, and the Anteroses could provide—proof not just of Cupid's handiwork but of the most surpassingly human emotion. Like gravity, the atom, and the moon, love was real.

"Thank you, babe," Sean told Linda, as the song ended, "and hey, congrats."

31

HEADING HOME

B y early evening the celebrities and magnates were aboard their yachts, with many private jets already in the air; the presence of these illustrious guests, and their massive wedding-gift donations to Trone's foundation, had been noted, and they'd already begun ignoring their Anteroses, or regifting them to stepchildren and masseurs. These tax-protected heavy hitters had little tolerance for a toy that could expose their amorous perjuries, or tinker with their prenups, or upend their careful balance of mistresses tucked away in Miami condos, spouses seated in mink-trimmed parkas by outdoor firepits in Aspen, and tennis pros who could multitask in country club saunas. Love is small change to CEOs and senior partners fending off class action lawsuits across several continents. Even movie stars and recording artists prefer the illusion of chance and self-determination in designating their next three marriages, so that the subsequent breakups can become the heartrending basis for their tell-all ghostwritten memoirs or their next three concept albums.

As Rob, Paolo, Tremble, and Sean left Alchemy Hall, like dedicated astronauts striding in slow motion, an oily, insinuatingly corrupt voice drawled, "Why, good evening, Miz Woodspill. You are hereby placed under arrest."

It was Mayor Churn LeBloitte, in cowboy boots, with his three-piece brown polyester Western-style suit barely constraining his well-fed bulk. His grimy, once-cream-colored Stetson was tipped back, to frame his swoop of drippingly greased, suspiciously jet-black hair, walrus jowls, piggishly small eyes, and unnaturally tiny mouth, set in its usual bee-stung snarl.

"What the fucksnot are you doing here?" asked Tremble.

"I'm the senior executive police chieftain of Jacksburg, Arkansas," Churn replied, holding up a gaudily fake plastic badge, glued to a Naugahyde wallet. "And you have been charged with the grand felony theft of $2,320 from the most private offices and Our Lord-4-Less boutique of the fine Mayor Churn LeBloitte, namely myself, who is also being the Jacksburg district attorney representing Our Lord Jesus Christ, one of whose commandments, as you may recall, was 'Thou Shalt Not Steal from a Highly Respected and Beloved Government Official.' I need you to hand over that cash and accompany me to my seagoing vessel, for transport to the mainland and ultimately the Jacksburg Penitentiary."

As Tremble and especially Sean were poised to intervene, Rob stepped forward, almost yelling, "You have no authority here, whoever you are, with your little Happy Meal badge. This is a private and self-governed island, and I will have you removed, if you don't leave right now, Mr. LeButt."

"That's Mayor and Sheriff and Permanent School Board President Dr. Churn Maripole Hephaestus LeBloitte! And this badge was authentic enough to permit entrance onto this godforsaken mound of Yankee dirt. And who would you be, aside from an effeminate-appearing Democratic liberal, by which I mean a servant of Satan?"

"I'm Robert Maximilian Hargreaves Barnett, and I happen to be—Ms. Woodspill's EDITOR."

Rob stated his title as if it were more illustrious than "supreme court justice" or "speaker of the house," and he was only a smidgen less imposing than the vigilante superhero standing beside him. After hearing the word "editor," Paolo, Sean, and Tremble had taken a cowed half step back, bowing their heads with respect and awe.

"And I didn't steal that money," Tremble inserted. "I liberated it. And once I get my next book payment, I'm gonna pay it back, to the people who deserve it. Because you fucking grabbed that money from the Jacksburg library fund, the Firemen's Benevolent Bake Sale, and those big glass jars you've got all over town, supposedly collecting for, what the shitwad is it, Save the Three-Toed Box Turtle?"

"Which is one of our fine nation's most under-supported charities," Churn blustered. "I have deputized my nephew Tugger to baptize every last three-toed box turtle in the state."

"You're baptizing turtles," said Rob.

"It's God's work. And why the fuck-all should I be listening to some measly little pissant editor-boy like you? Give me one solid reason why I shouldn't pick you up by your dainty loafers and send you sailing right into whichever ocean that might happen to be."

"Because . . . ," Rob began, his voice shaking, as he wasn't sure if his ability to correct Churn's sentence structure would be enough.

"Rob?"

Sean was speaking, and he'd pulled the phaser from underneath his breastplate and tossed it toward Rob, with the swashbuckling panache he'd practiced on numerous episodes of *WarForce*.

Rob, who'd never caught anything beyond a Shetland crewneck Jake had pitched at him during an especially rowdy warehouse sample sale, raised his arm, and the futuristic weapon miraculously flew securely into his palm. Maybe it was his virile insistence on his editorial credentials that had emboldened him, but Rob was pointing the phaser directly at Churn's head, with the broken veins crisscrossing Churn's cheeks, caused by decades of hard liquor, becoming Rob's guidelines.

"You've never fired a gun in your life, sissy boy. Or whatever that dang thing is."

"There's always a first time," said Rob, because he was defending not just an author, which was already a sacred responsibility, but Tremble herself. As Churn lumbered toward Tremble, brandishing the handcuffs, Rob squeezed the trigger, as he'd seen actors do in so many of the police procedural reruns he and Jake had fallen asleep to. He braced himself as a sizzle of sparks emerged from the phaser, along with a whirring noise and a minor, completely decorative inflatable lightning bolt—on *War-Force*, these effects would've been digitally enhanced in post-production, but today, thanks to the lingering magic of Artemis Island, the phaser was on Rob's side.

"Jesus, Mary, and the Holy Ghost with a bottle of hot sauce!" Churn exclaimed, as he tottered, cursed a few more times, and plummeted backwards into a rhododendron bush, imagining he'd been struck and injured, a notion that he repeated to the Artemis Island EMTs a few minutes later: "I've been incapacitated by a device not of our solar system!" The amused EMTs pretended to bandage Churn's nonexistent wound and placed him onto a police boat, staffed with actual police officers, headed back to Logport. All the witnesses testified that Churn had closed his meaty hands around Rob's windpipe and that firing a mutant water pistol in self-defense had been Rob's sole alternative to certain death. One of the police officers had also just completed an 876-page memoir titled *Logport PD: Fifty Years of Lumber-Related Crime*, which Rob had promised to read, edit, and publish.

"Okay, that was like the bad-bitch takedown of all time," said Tremble, as the four friends recovered over beers in the Alchemy Hall bar area. "But why the hell did you do it? I would've kicked Churn in the balls, just to see if my Anteros would start playing Christmas carols. Although I'm amazed his crappy little junior cowboy badge got him onto the island."

"I did it . . . ," Rob began, "I'm not sure why. Because he was after you, and because Sean was so supercharged at the wedding, so I was following his lead, and because I've been such a drag, with moping about Jake, who I think would've been shocked and pleased by what I did, and he'd say, 'You should shoot your phaser at everyone with such an obvious dye job.'"

"I was beside myself," said Paolo. "All I could think about was that Bette Davis movie where she guns down her lover in cold blood, although I think she was wearing a chiffon scarf and a fur. But Rob, you were like . . ."

"He was like Blaster," said Sean. "Or maybe Professor Headspace. But we'd be proud to have him on board the WarForce Proton Battlecraft."

"Do you think I've got better reflexes from working out?" Rob theorized.

The group, seeing that Rob was both wildly invigorated and shaking from his exploits, all backed this notion: "Totally," "You're like a tiger hunting gazelles on the veldt," "Of course, but we should start concentrating on your core, since you've been having those sciatica issues."

———

An hour later, Rob left the group, to pack for his return to Manhattan. He still couldn't believe he'd phasered Churn, and he might not recount the episode to his family, who were all staunchly opposed to violence except in assiduously researched wartime novels and PBS documentaries. But maybe I've got a special dispensation, Rob decided, given the extraordinary circumstances of the last few days. He'd hailed Sean's savvy manipulation of Trone's wedding presentation, although he wasn't sure if that brief, showboating Anteros-related coup would be enough for Sean, and whether it would impact Linda's honeymoon. Rob was still thrashing amid the soap opera contours and the commercialization of love, none of which applied to him, not anymore. If Jake had been here, he would've skewered the slick blandness of the Anteros packaging, but Rob could picture the two of them, beyond irony or cynicism, synching their devices, for the same blazing validation as Sean and Linda.

Jake had been the love of Rob's life, and Jake's premature death had made this cliché more pertinent. Before Jake's illness, the couple had roughed out a variety of retirements, years away, either in an affordable row-house flat outside London, a Provincetown shack, or maybe a converted barn in Upstate New York, a manageable home where they'd trundle slowly through the aisles at a local grocery, and huddle beneath increasing mounds of quilts. They'd never seriously investigated any of this, since their retirements had been eons ahead, but their ongoing coupledom had promised a devoted and even lighthearted old age.

But none of this would happen and Rob had to stop remembering. His largest questions would remain unanswered. Fuck me, Rob thought, I'm just a sad old gay guy, like the men whose bungalows in Fort Lauderdale are jammed ceiling-high with collections of tattered original cast albums and their mother's wedding china. Rob wasn't belittling these men; perhaps they'd adjusted to a livable routine of dear friends, online smut, and Entenmann's French crumb cake.

Rob unlatched his Anteros and shoved it back into its cardboard home. Maybe someone at W&S would like it, unless the younger folks had sailed beyond TroneTek, having been lured by an unheralded Finnish brand or something low-tech, a device stitched together with rawhide lacing from recycled hubcaps and juniper berries. Widowers had no use for an Anteros, unless they'd be posting back-in-the-saddle profiles on dating apps, a prospect that Rob found crushing and beyond his current bleakness.

He tugged Jake's watch from his pocket: Was wearing it still a helpful idea? Would it remind him too constantly of Jake, and Rob's role in his death? Oh, fuck off and stop being so operatically heartsick, Rob told himself, you've got your job back, the apartment is safe for now, and you just vanquished an Arkansas criminal and rescued Tremble, even if there were very few people less in need of a blunderingly butch rescue.

Rob confronted the most basic facts: people lose their husbands or wives or whatevers every second of every day, and Jake's grandfather's watch was beautiful and maybe haunted, and unlike the Anteros, it performed an indisputably practical function.

Rob slipped the watch back on, with its well-burnished leather band and traditional face, with roman numerals and a second hand. But there was an unusual warmth against his wrist and a humming. Was the watch breaking apart, had its fossilized gears rusted and halted, and could they be repaired? The watch face glowed, first a pale pink, then a russet, and then the billowing bonfire caused by Sean and Linda's dance. Rob jumped, waving his arm frantically as if cooling it from a vicious sunburn or stovetop scalding, but the watch only flamed brighter and more fiercely, insisting that Rob accept its spectral exuberance.

Rob had been wavering over the reality of Jake's ghost, or doppel-gänger or drug reaction, but this moment was unassailable, and so truly Jake: he was sending a message through vintage design. Their love hadn't been attested to by a TroneTek gizmo, but by the gift of Jake's most likely gay grandpa, who hadn't known Jake and Rob's out-and-about happiness and would wish them well, and who should be honored, not through grief but jubilation. Rob laughed, from a joy he'd been denying himself, a joy he'd been misguidedly convinced he no longer deserved.

Rob looked toward heaven, which was silly. He checked the room to see if anyone else had come back into the cottage and caught him doing any of this. He was alone, except he wasn't, so he did something even sillier, something directed only toward Jake, not to his memory but his essence. He kissed the crystal on Jake's watch.

Rob decided that silliness, or at least an appreciation of love's absurdity, is what's missing from the most doctrinaire romance novels. The characters are staunch and steely-eyed, as if loving another person is a form of surgery performed under battlefield conditions. Love is humanity at its best, but not necessarily its most grim. This was Jake's directive, which Rob could finally exult in. He executed a few tentative steps from his *Singin' in the Rain* routine, delighting himself on Jake's behalf.

————

Paolo ambled back toward the cottage an hour later, having taken advantage of some leftover champagne. He'd scouted for the previous night's sous chef, who alas hadn't been working the wedding itself. It was dusk and the lighting along the deserted path hadn't emerged. Paolo's own Anteros hummed and blinked the safety-cone orange that denoted an imminent romantic head-on collision, and now there were hands on his shoulders, spinning him, and his face was inches from Dax's.

"Why didn't you thank me for that valentine?" Dax asked, calmly.

"Because . . . because I was going out of town and Dax, what are you doing here? Are you . . . are you going to murder me?"

"Excuse me? I was invited—Trone Meston is one of my patients."

"But . . . but . . ."

"Did you think I was stalking you?"

"No. Well, you had been very aggressive and you showed up at my office . . ."

"Because I liked you. I thought we were having fun. Dentists can have fun."

Paolo was putting things together: He and Dax had bemoaned the frustrating media-driven image of dentists, who were so often demeaned as nerdy incels or sadistic fetishists. Dax's brash sexuality and his lustful pursuit of Paolo had been an honest effort to subvert a stereotype, to show that dentists could be hot guys. And the proximity alerts on Paolo's phone had been set off by Dax's travel to and attendance at the wedding, which were far more legitimate than Paolo's, since Paolo had been a stowaway.

"Paolo, I'm sorry that wires got crossed, and it's nice to see you, but obviously this isn't going to work out."

As Paolo angled to correct his misperceptions and maybe reestablish their relationship, there was a humming from both men's wrists, as each Anteros produced a beige and cerise stripe, which the index notated as "heavy if bumbling reconnection." Their Anteroses were either matchmaking or strong-arming the guys, which illustrated one of the device's primary glitches: the Anteros banned the unknown, that sparkle of serendipity and delectable uncertainty which is endemic to, which defines romance. The Anteros was like an SAT score for lovers: a factual report with no room for finesse, interpretation, or mystery.

"Um, so, are you headed back to New York?" Paolo asked.

"In the morning."

"Are you here alone?"

"Are you a paranoid slut in a white nylon smock?"

"Yes. According to my Anteros," Paolo admitted.

"If we grabbed another bottle of champagne and hid out in my cottage, would you promise me something?"

"That I won't hand you floss, a packet of gauze, and a sample size of toothpaste for extra-sensitive gums afterwards?"

"No, will you promise me that we can both take off these TroneTek house arrest cuffs? And just go from there?"

"But what if when we both come, our cuffs start playing 'Thus Spake Zarathustra' or 'Rose's Turn'?"

"We can do that ourselves."

They smiled at each other, and a neuron of Paolo's brain estimated how long it would take his body to decay, after being buried in a shallow grave behind Dax's cottage. Would the Anteros left on his remains be cycling through every possible color, in search of a necrophiliac? But Paolo, whose imagination mixed prescription-grade anxiety with unsolved crime–podcast fantasy, relaxed, from Dax's handsome face in the moonlight, a lighting effect that had either just been switched on by the island's overseers, or was the result of the moon, the real moon, peeking from behind an actual, Luddite cloud.

32

AN EDITOR'S SUGGESTION:
AN EPILOGUE?

A day later, Trone and Linda were aloft, en route to Madrid, one of Linda's favorite cities from her years as a flight attendant, and the capital where Trone would begin his international tour in support of the Anteros, at a TroneTek brick-and-mortar store housed in what had been an eleventh-century monastery. Trone loved the contrast between atmospheric ruins and the steel pedestals with glass cubes protecting the precious TroneTek items.

Linda was holding an unread issue of *Vogue* and painstakingly ticking through her decisions, about having sex with Sean, marrying Trone, and leaving the twins behind at Trone's new Manhattan triplex, at their request. At the wedding, Bridger and Morrow hadn't gone near an Anteros, which they'd dubbed, in Bridger's words, "a military-grade weapon of mind control." It wasn't that younger people swore by organically true love, unsullied by corporate policing; they were just more attuned to sending naked selfies and commenting, via emojis, on those of others. They preferred the instantaneous visuals of traditional hookup apps to the intricacy of the Anteros. Under-thirties also fell in and out of love more frequently, with anyone from a neighbor (because of his incredibly cute rescue beagle) to a twenty-year-old, fist-shaking, no-student-debt politico with fabulous hair.

Trone hadn't been bothered by any of this, as the Anteros market skewed older. It was best appreciated by people drained from misbegotten, sometimes decades-long matchups and overdue for a shortcut.

Before leaving on her honeymoon, Linda had spent time with her kids, even as they'd squirmed and protested they could text, scroll through TikTok, listen to music, and talk to her at the same time. Bridger and Morrow didn't have to call Trone their dad, take his name, or endorse the TroneTek catalogue, and they could see Sean as often as they liked.

"Mom, why are you so nervous?" said Bridger. "You married a billionaire who isn't a total dipshit, we know you had sex with Dad, and you look great, for your age. Chill."

"How do you know we had sex?"

"Mom," sighed Morrow, "we saw what happened when you danced with Dad. Your Anteroses had obviously hooked up. Everybody got it. Duh."

On the plane, Linda ruminated on this: both Trone and Sean had claimed her, Sean through lovemaking and Trone through wedlock. How had any of this happened? How had she gone from a raggedly unstable childhood crisscrossing five states, to getting antsy over her kids operating a private elevator in a fifty-eighth-floor penthouse? From wearing a flight attendant's uniform and taking Trone's beverage order, to sitting beside him, en route to Madrid, Paris, Cairo, Copenhagen, and Sydney?

Linda shut her eyes and tilted her head back, onto the headrest that, since this one of Trone's five private jets, didn't bear the haircare products of thousands of commercial travelers. All she'd ever wanted was a Tudor, a lawn, and an escape hatch if necessary. She'd be accompanying Trone on business excursions along with joining his official dinners, where her years of speaking with global passengers would become an asset. But mostly she was daring to enjoy the respite, not just of unspeakable wealth, a gilded safety net, but of having made an indisputably safe choice. Not a compromise, or a gold-digging scam. She loved Trone, but he didn't snivel for her slavish attention, and he wasn't provoked by the gossip, the online fury over Blaster's discarded wife seducing the planet's most unflappably off-kilter genius. Fuck the internet; Trone's money insulated her.

Did she wish she'd gone for broke and run off with Sean, maybe holding up convenience stores to reflect their second-time-around recklessness? No. As Sean had deduced, she'd never be able to trust him. She didn't especially trust Trone, but their allegiance at 75 percent covered that. No one marries a billionaire expecting honey-I'm-home fidelity and a dinner-on-the-table calendar.

Have I gotten jaggedly sophisticated, with a more advanced take on intimacy, Linda asked herself, or given up completely on all of it? Or have I stopped insistently grading people on their every moral failing, and grown up? Linda had been overtaken by fuck-everything passion, but it had unnerved her. Even before Sean had cheated, he'd made her dither, with his shameless scrutiny, remarkably agile tongue, and nonstop sexual gusto. Did she secretly believe that, at the drop of a text or a call, Sean would come racing back to her, in a pair of revealing jogging shorts, with a hungry grin? Maybe. Was this a prerogative of being, at forty-seven, a still beautiful woman who could keep a man, or more than one man, guessing? Most likely. And of course, and maybe foremost, she'd ignored her mother's advice. Aileen had been Team Sean, Team Thermos of Gin, and Team Uproar. This had its crackpot charm, but as Aileen had said, she wasn't anyone's goal model.

Everything, Linda concluded, is temporary. That was my mistake with Sean. I'd been all in. She thought about Rob, who'd had what she'd envied: a marriage of well-dressed equals, between two people who didn't need anyone else. But look what had happened. At Jake's memorial, and again on Artemis Island, Rob, despite his supremely good manners, had been devastated. Maybe he'd made her error, of believing in a perfect or at least a sustainable love. What if Sean died, or Trone? What if she was faced with one of those philosophy-quiz conundrums, where she could only save one? I'd let them battle it out, she answered herself, for that last parachute, while the twins and I were already far below, having inflated a life raft.

Maybe that's the secret, she postulated: don't overthink. She'd once been alone with Jake, following a dinner at the guys' apartment, after Rob had run out to fetch ice cream sandwiches. Jake had been diagnosed but was fairly steady. His left arm was limp, but he could walk and hold a glass of wine with his still-working right hand. Over dinner, no one had brought up Jake's illness, not deliberately, but because they'd all known each other so long and were busy gossiping. But once it was just the two of them, Linda had found the evening's lightness, its casual happiness, to be unbearable, and without thinking she said, "Oh, Jake."

"I know," he replied. Jake had already become accustomed to caretaking his caretakers, to keeping the mood brisk, and not becoming everyone's sad charity case.

"Are you okay?" Linda had asked, instantly regretting the question and lunging to withdraw it.

"I'm fine," Jake said. "Aside from the dying-in-agony thing. But no, I am fine. Because I keep thinking how much worse everything would be without Rob and our friends. And decent health insurance. How about you? And Sean?"

The divorce had been finalized two years earlier. Linda was still in its throes, but she'd never equate it with what Jake and Rob were going through. But Jake pressed her: "Don't be nice, just because I'm sick. You're allowed to be damaged. Do you wish you were still married?"

Linda had weighed this and finally said, "I wish I was still married the way things were ten years ago. When I was fooling myself. When I was a babbling idiot with a swing set in the backyard. That's the problem—happiness was my drug. I let myself get addicted. Because it felt so good, until the crash, when my supply was cut off. So still being married, to Sean? Now? No."

On the plane, she looked over at Trone, at one with his laptop. Thinking of Sean and the twins, she told herself, Don't you dare bitch or whine, even for a second. Even if everyone and everything could disappear, a possibility which, on any flight, no matter what the pilot's safety record, was a constant.

I'm sitting in a very expensive tin can, Linda knew, in midair. I'm not trusting anything, but I don't have to. For right now, I'm flying.

————

Trone, meanwhile, was watching the most updated, polished video of the wedding and his Anteros kickoff, which had reached 58 million hits on YouTube (the reception footage of Linda and Sean's dance had been omitted). This was acceptable, but not all Trone had hoped for. The Anteros was popular, but hardly a universal phenomenon. As always, Trone's personal remove from fundamental human behavior had only taken him so far. Love, it turned out, couldn't be commodified, and a majority of even the most convulsively fervent TroneTek users, the Tronies who camped out in sleeping bags and pup tents on the sidewalk for weeks before a launch, didn't want it to be. Love, unlike group chats or FaceTiming or online spin classes, couldn't be swiftly downloaded, updated, and then forgotten in light of the next hugely hyped advance.

But Trone would persevere. The middling performance of the Anteros might be a goad to a later, more significant and profitable breakthrough, that elusive ultra-creation that would become so desirable no one would recall a world without it, as with the automobile or home computer or toilet paper. People like Trone can be spoiled by repeated success and become grandiose, but Trone had been born grandiose, and for him, failure wasn't a death blow but something to be studied, like the carcass of a mastodon; it wasn't pretty but educational. Trone wasn't fazed by obstacles, and of course he'd been apprised, the night it had happened, of Linda and Sean getting together before the wedding. A quick scan of the island's security feeds had captured Linda and a shirtless Sean outside Sean's cottage and then heading within. Trone hadn't been surprised, but immersed in Linda's choice the next day. He'd wanted her to make the most informed selection, based on comprehensive facts. He'd needed Linda to be with Sean, as a variable. He was Trone Meston. If after his death his brain could be kept cogitating in a glass jar of some nutritive fluid, there wouldn't be that much difference. He'd become a next-generation,

Trone 2.0 version of himself, and perhaps more efficient and even less affected by irrational longings and bodily upsets. He'd already hired a task force to look into this.

———————

A month later, Sean and Rob had resumed their three-days-a-week workout routine. Rob wore his regulation black shorts and black T-shirt, a proper ensemble for a now sixty-year-old man who, while he was in acceptable shape, wouldn't want to strut, as a well-preserved grandpa, in something too tight or flashing too much skin. Sean had on the latest Defiance hoodie and sweatpants, with an advanced, sleeker version of the logo, a cooler-than-cool, almost abstract iteration. Sean hadn't shaved, so his silvery stubble matched the streaks at his temples. He looked great, but might add a ball cap later in the day. Ball caps were a straight guy's parasol or modest feathered fan.

"Have you heard from Linda?" Rob asked, seated on a padded bench, lifting twenty-pound dumbbells over his head, as Sean corrected his form.

"Nope. Not yet."

"Do you think you will?"

"Of course I will. She can't keep fucking that dweeb, if they're even fucking. She's gonna need a visit from Santa."

"So you're going to come down her chimney?" Rob replied, since they were both eight years old.

"*BLAM!!!*" crowed Sean, pumping his hips and swinging his arms, since they were now both five years old.

Sean had no idea if Linda would contact him for an assignation, but they'd connect as the twins' parents. He still thought about Linda constantly, but without panic, without that frantic yen to uselessly plan a lunch or an intervention or a stroll past Trone's building on West 57th Street, which had been christened Billionaire's Row. These pointlessly tall, sliver-like, wind-afflicted skyscrapers, everyone knew, were substitute penises for out-of-shape titans.

"Are you glad we went to the wedding?" Rob asked.

"Sort of. Yeah. But that island and those cottages, it was zillionaire tacky. I wanted to tell Trone, you spent all this money for fucking bark wastepaper baskets and leather barstools where the nailheads are already falling off? I mean, dude, did you get this whole place on sale at Home Depot? Did you keep the receipts?"

"You are so beyond queer."

"Excuse me, it's called taste. And I guess he forgot to buy some."

"So are you seeing anyone? Have you been swiping right?"

"Nah. I'm over it. I don't need that noise in my life. Maybe three women. But you know what's insane? Right on my profile, it says, 'I have no emotions, I'm dead inside. No possibility of a relationship.' But these chicks keep hitting on me, and I tell them, 'This is just gonna be about sex,' and they say, 'Got it,' but afterwards, they keep wanting to talk. So then I have to fake having feelings."

"More than one feeling?"

"Right? And some of them are great-looking and they're in fantastic shape, even the forty-year-olds, but they all want to get married. They all think I'll change. I catch them, hiding their toothbrushes in my bathroom, or leaving a bra behind. And then I have to put their stuff in a baggie and ask them, 'Is this yours?'"

"And do you know why they're after you?"

"Because I'm the hottest and most ripped stud they'll ever meet?"

"Because you're the only straight guy left. If they want to get laid, they have no other options. So they tell themselves, sure, he's a skeevy troglodyte mouth breather, but everyone else is gay or some dick they were already married to."

"Hold on, when you say 'skeevy troglodyte mouth breather,' is that a bad thing?"

Sean was a good enough actor to pose this question sincerely, and Rob loved playing along.

"No, no, no. It's your best feature. You should put that in your profile. 'Ladies—do you hate yourself and want to have degrading sex with a sad forty-nine-year-old man who owns a Harley that he keeps in the garage under a custom-made tarp so it won't get dusty?'"

"Can you write that down so I'll remember it?"

Sean and Rob studied themselves in the nearby mirror. Sean flexed his biceps, shouting, "YEAH, BABY," while Rob lifted his chin, to avoid shadowing the various creases in his face.

"How's the Jake situation?"

"Better. I'm getting there. I put away some of his stuff, just to piss him off."

Rob had, in fact, repainted a wall in the bedroom half-a-shade lighter than Jake would have countenanced. The place had been a sound investment, and was now worth many times what he and Jake had paid. Tremble's book had been copyedited and there were bound galleys, which Rob was eager to send out for blurbs from notable authors, because he could gush about Tremble's work without lying. Tremble's talent and her off-the-wall enthusiasm had been instrumental in restoring Rob's more agreeable personality and love of writers. After their return from Maine, he'd paid for a hotel room in midtown so Tremble could explore more of the city. Rob suspected that someday she'd move here, and ultimately spend significant time throughout the world, thanks to her devouring curiosity. At the bus station he'd said, "Tremble, I'm going to say something that people sling around every day, and you're incredibly young so I hope this isn't a burden. But you saved my life."

"Fuck yeah I did. That's why I came up here. You scratch my back, I scratch yours." She snapped a selfie with the two of them grinning into the camera: "I'm gonna send this to everybody and tell 'em, that's my old white gay editor. The fucking best!" She'd also confessed to dosing Rob with LSD on Artemis Island and he'd said, "You shouldn't do that to people, it's an unpredictable drug and I could've had a bad trip or ripped off my clothes and run into Alchemy Hall and demanded a nicer orchid for my room." "You're fucking welcome," Tremble had laughed. She was now back in Jacksburg and had texted about fiddling with a novel, "And it's totally filthy, just to give Isabelle something to complain about and jack off to."

Rob and Isabelle had called a truce and tiptoed around each other, meaning Rob would bob his head while Isabelle rattled on and Isabelle would pretend to believe Rob when he said, "These are great notes, can I have a few days to think about them?" Isabelle had received a postcard from Trone, with a photo of the Luxembourg store set inside a nineteenth-century library, all patinaed brass and sturdy oak shelves, which Trone was certain only Isabelle would appreciate. Well, actually Trone or more likely his assistant had sent this postcard to all W&S employees, with the same message, "Onwards!" Isabelle was still with Lance and had even let him meet some of her nonbinary and socialist friends, once she'd thrown Lance's accumulated hockey jerseys into a dumpster. Lance continued to provoke Isabelle, lately by watching a

Netflix show about a wide-eyed, irritatingly perky American girl, with a mysteriously unlimited wardrobe, consulting at a Paris branding agency. Isabelle professed to abhor this show as "a prime example of First World misogyny and rampant ozone layer–destroying consumerism," but she'd end up on the couch, with Lance's arm around her, as she trashed each of the gamine's outfits: "Oh please, pastel polka dots with a matching quilted purse? Again?"

"So, are you gonna start going out?" Sean asked Rob, as Rob did lat pull-downs on a chrome-plated mechanism. "I could take your picture and do your profile."

"And what would it say? Three-hundred-year-old homo seeks someone in a nursing home willing to remove his dentures?"

"No! You look good! And if you went out with like, an eight-hundred-year-old dude, you could be the twink."

Paolo had also implored Rob to consider dating, "or at least having an iced coffee with someone you'll never see again but can tell me about." Rob had replied that he wasn't lonely, not yet. He didn't fixate on memories, or pore over photos of Jake on his phone. Jake was starting to be a given, a beloved and central aspect of Rob's history, but not a hindrance. But Rob wasn't ready to affix some upbeat, fake-interested dating face. As his mother, who'd never gone out with anyone since Rob's dad had died twelve years ago, told him, "Don't concern yourself with getting back out there, or listening to anyone except me. There's a freedom to widowhood. You can stay up till 3 a.m. and eat an entire bag of cookies baked with chocolate chips, caramel, and walnuts, one after the other, as if it's your job. Just do what seems right and enjoy masturbation." Rob did.

"Look at that," said Sean, as a twenty-three-year-old female lawyer with a ponytail and a killer ass, swathed in second-skin, flesh-toned yoga pants, began doing suggestive moves with a foam rubber cylinder on a nearby mat. "Did you bring her for Daddy?"

"What're you gonna do? Adopt her?"

"That would make it even hotter."

"You are disgusting."

"I know," said Sean, beaming.

"Do you ever wear your Anteros?"

"Fuck no. I don't need some piece of junk to tell me how I feel. It's like, I know how I feel already. And I know that chick on the mat loves me."

Sean still obsessed over Linda, but he no longer dreamt of her alone in a glacial five-star hotel room, downloading photos of him in a tank top and Googling the time difference between wherever she was and New York. Linda would always be there. People you love don't evaporate. Sean was just mature enough to love Linda from a distance, and get why they were apart. Neither could sacrifice being themselves, and they were obstinate people. And secretly, neither would be as attracted to a tamed, diminished version of the other, to a less hardheaded Linda or a meekly contrite Sean.

Defiance was booming, and Sean was expanding the franchise with a canny deliberation. He wanted the business to endure. His charm and looks were intact, and the strands of silver, fine, white hair only added to his hyper-masculine aura. Paolo had praised him as "the husband of the guy on the Brawny paper towels roll."

"Jesus fucking Christ," said Sean, as Rob rested between sets. Rob was seated on a bench with an upturned backrest, with Sean's face hovering directly over his own in the mirror. "It is so fucking hard being a man."

Rob burst into laughter, because Sean nurtured his macho suffering with such tenderness, and because he was right. Except it wasn't just hard being a man; it was hard being anyone. Which was Rob's ultra-liberal, inclusive take on Sean's fortune cookie motto. It struck Rob that he'd trained with Sean for almost as long as he'd been with Jake. Maybe Rob and Sean were the sturdiest couple of all, since they didn't have sex, never tangled over finances, and were fine with seeing each other in gym shorts.

"But don't you miss sucking cock?" Sean asked.

"Of course. Don't you?"

That hot twenty-three-year-old had overheard Rob and Sean and was puzzling over their bond. Were they lovers, exes, or workout buddies? They were more than any of those. Sean and Rob held each other together, and Sean adjusted Rob's workouts as Rob got older. Sean read people's bodies, to decode how they felt about themselves and what they needed to hear, and when they needed to be encouraged. For all his studly bluster, Sean cared about everyone, even a dick like Trone, whom Sean swore he could whip into shape, "if he paid me like, half his net worth and one of his planes." Linda had left Sean and begun a new life, which didn't mean she no longer loved him. It was easy to fall in love, and no matter what happened, it was almost impossible to stop. Paolo and Dax were talking about moving in together, although as Paolo had nattered, "The only thing creepier than being a gay dentist is two gay dentists."

Tremble had forwarded Rob a new essay, sparked by meeting Rob's friends and witnessing him fire a phaser at Mayor LeBloitte, who'd been steering clear of Tremble. Only once, when they'd both been buying Slim Jims at the Jacksburg CVS, did he murmur, "I hope you're delighted with your fine new Yankee companions, and I am being sarcastic. But they better not cross the border, because Jacksburg ain't keen on sissy-boy editors."

"What about sissy-boy editors with intergalactic firearms?" Tremble remarked, as Churn defensively shielded his shoulder, which still ached in bad weather.

Tremble had written, "I'm starting to get a handle on all this love shit, and you know why? Cause there was this one guy, who had superpowers on a TV show, but in real life love was his kryptonite, it's the one thing that brought him to his knees. Straight dudes fall in love all the time but it's mostly with football teams and cars, which also betray them. Straight guys can't catch a break, which is only fair.

"And there was another guy, who was scared shitless of being rejected, because he's a dentist. Which might be the only minority people are still allowed to get weird about, maybe because dentists are a minority holding a big motherfucking needle. But dentists can also make you feel so much better, when your jaw is aching so bad you just lie on the floor and moan, praying for death. So I wish dentists only the best and guess what? That dentist met another hot dentist and maybe they can have a Dignity for Dentists march. So you know what's truly cool? Gay dentists in love.

"But the guy who really gets to me is my editor, and not just because he made me go through every sentence in my book and take out the semicolons, which he says are 'literary zits.' Rob was in love with the greatest guy, who went and died, which a lot of people think is the end of love. And that all you've got left is visiting a grave and crying your eyes out. But you know what that says to me? That Rob loved somebody, and that's as fucking good as it gets, and Jake loved him back, which is how we know that once in a while God has a decent day and stops fucking with us. I haven't been in love, not yet. But it sounds scary and horrible and awesome and just what you want, all of that at once. So that's how I'll know it's love.

"And one more thing: my parents were in love, more than anyone who's ever lived. They died when I was little, and I'm gonna tell you about them, soon, because I think maybe love is a family tradition. It's what they left me. And if I can write about them, well, I'll be saying thank you. And I can let myself fall in love with them."

————

At the gym, Rob glanced down at Jake's watch. The supernatural glow hadn't returned, which would be excessive and ultimately tiresome, as if Jake were nagging him from the afterlife. But the watch reminded Rob of love's greatest asset and enemy: time. Love shouldn't be measured in hours or years, but more was usually better. That was the root of all Rob's focus on Jake's death: a longing for even one more day together. But that's not how love works; every relationship has a clock. A hand-embroidered sampler would coo, "That's what makes love so precious," to which Rob would respond, in an editorial note, "No, that's why we don't listen to samplers."

"Stop looking at your fucking watch," said Sean. "We've still got twenty minutes of crunches and maybe some legs."

"I love you," Rob told Sean.

"Everybody fucking loves me."

"You know why?"

"'Cause of the guns," said Sean, pumping his biceps in the mirror.

"That's right. We all love you because you're the ultimate douchebag."

"Yeah, baby!"

Sean looked at Rob, and did what he had to do. "Fine," he said. "I love you, too."

The guys had never said this to each other, and now it hovered. This wasn't uncomfortable, but an acknowledgment of all they'd been through together, and of time passing.

"Stop mo-ing me," said Rob.

The woman on the mat was staring at Rob and Sean, having overheard their declarations. She'd just been blindsided by a bad breakup with a hedge fund manager, who'd told her she was six months too old for him. Love, she'd decided, was such a shitty deal, but maybe it was working for those two gay guys. Rob and Sean gave her hope, that love existed. Which just might be the meaning of life, as we fucking know it.

ACKNOWLEDGMENTS

I like the phrase "What is wrong with you?" because I use it constantly and more often it's being flung in my direction. This book began as an exploration of sorrow and loss, but love gradually demanded equal billing.

Various characters are inspired by people I cherish but aren't exact portraits: fiction always takes control as I hang on for dear life. *What Is Wrong with You?* was a pleasurable writing experience, as the narrative unfolded and often surprised me. I surrendered to a broad canvas combining elements of farce, tragedy, midnight enchantment, and the eternal value of friendship. This wasn't so much intentional as intuitive, as the many rambunctious and passionate characters insisted on being heard.

My last novel, *Farrell Covington and the Limits of Style*, represented a kind of authorial rebirth, as I rediscovered how much I adored the form. I'd published other novels but always felt a bit daunted. With *Farrell* I sought both a deeper emotional range and a structural freedom, and these goals continue in *What Is Wrong with You?* I'm thrilled that readers enjoyed *Farrell*, and I hope everyone becomes similarly attached to the yearning population of this new book.

As always, I'm indebted to my dear friends, including Scott Berlinger, Jay Holman, AJ Bernard, William Ivey Long, Todd Ruff, Dana Ivey, Dan Jinks, Albert Mellinkoff, Patrick Herold, Scott Rudin, Adrienne Halpern, Allison Silver, Barry Sonnenfeld, Kim Beaty, and Susan Morrison. I'm endlessly grateful to my superb editor, Peter Borland, and my wonderful agent, Esmond Harmworth, for their insights, enthusiasm, and unflagging good spirits. I inflict my earliest drafts on Esmond, who's supremely generous and specific, and my slightly later efforts on Peter, who's equally kind and rigorous. At Aevitas I'd like to thank Elena Steiert, Erin Files, and Mags Chmielarczyk. The staff at Atria has been invaluable, including James Iacobelli, Dana Trocker, Abby Velasco, Jane Phan, Jill Putorti, Hannah Frankel, Shelby Pumphrey, Lacee Burt, Sofia Echeverry, Paige Lytle, Dayna Johnson, Vanessa Silverio, Holly Rice, Libby McGuire, Kitt Reckord, Nicole Bond, Sara Browne, Rebecca Justiniano, Sanny Chiu, who designed and illustrated the beautiful cover, and especially production editor Elizabeth Byer, who tirelessly and joyfully wrangled the manuscript into shape.

Since this book tackles the intricacies of romance, I must mention the love of my life, John Raftis. John's a doctor, which both pleased my mother enormously and means he's extremely understanding of my writerly ailments, such as locking myself away for days at a time and requiring infusions of Snickers bars and patience. John remains not merely a saint but a saint with a driver's license and the ability to navigate airports.

My parents were both devoted readers, and while they appreciated my work in the theater and onscreen, books held the highest esteem. My mother loved bookstores, where she'd surreptitiously move my output to the front of any display. Since she's no longer with us, now I have to do this myself.

—Paul Rudnick